SECRETS
OF
ISORIA

SECRETS
OF
ISORIA

CRISTINA MACARI

Cover design by MiblArt
Interior print design and layout by Sydnee Hyer
Ebook design and layout by Sydnee Hyer
Map Illustration by Jessica Khoury

Published by Cristina Macari

979-8-9850594-0-3

To my family and friends for their endless support of my dreams and their unconditional love.

To my love, who continued to believe in me even when I didn't believe in myself.

And to me, because, well, I wrote this dang thing.

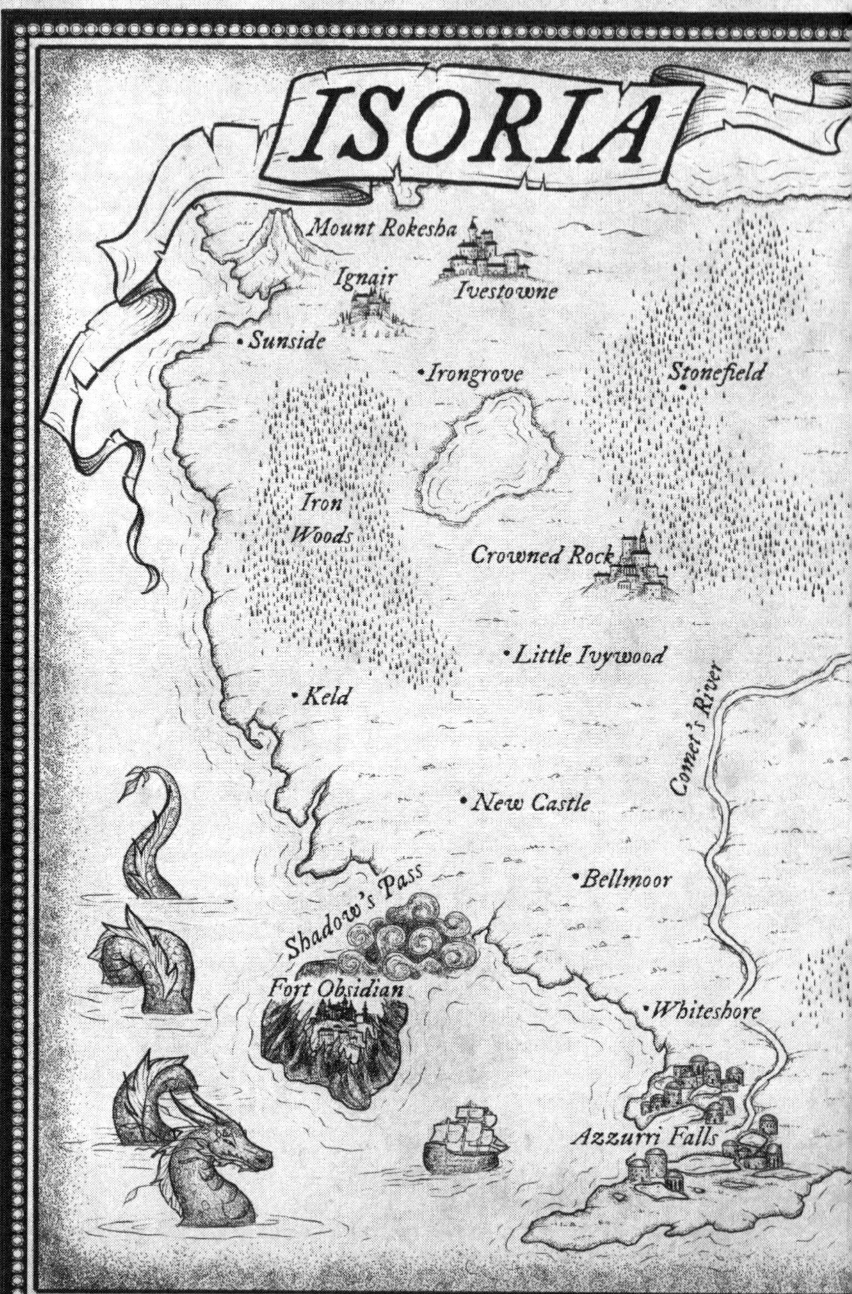

ISORIA
Mount Rokesha
Ignair
Ivestowne
Sunside
Irongrove
Stonefield
Iron Woods
Crowned Rock
Little Ivywood
Keld
Connet's River
New Castle
Bellmoor
Shadow's Pass
Fort Obsidian
Whiteshore
Azzurri Falls

Lunaris
Artus Mountains
Red Halo Island
Aria
Aerbourne
Arayis
Silverkeep
Crowned Woods
Terrona
Lightloch
Erudite Square
Avelin
King Leo's Palace &
The United Royal
Imperium of Isoria
Ozryn
Bluecrest
Aquium

Chapter 1

You're not still angry, are you?"

Mom sighed on the other end of the video call, the desperation in her voice static through my earphones. The hustling of airport travelers on her end was enough to stir my resentment. We'd said our goodbyes there not too long ago, but she didn't want us to part at odds. I couldn't help it, though. I ignored her, staring up at my grandmother's home from her front steps.

"Orion?" she tried again, her hazel eyes wide.

"Yup."

Let her decide which question I'd responded to.

"I hate how long I have to be away from you, you know that, right?" she said, her eyes sad underneath her dark bangs. "But you'll love Banden, and he'll take great care of you. It'll be over before you know it."

I sighed, coiling the earphone wire around my finger. I was used to her job calling her away for a week or so, even a month, but never a year.

She continued. "I know it's going to be a little rough in the beginning, with making friends and such. But I think a change of setting will be good for you—maybe start fresh? Especially since you were born there."

"Yeah, I'm leaving so many friends behind," I grumbled. She knew I had a solid friend count of zero. "Mom, you know that's not the problem."

I could argue with her all day, but there was no turning back. One of the clients from her small technology consulting business urgently needed her for this amazing opportunity in Eastern Europe. Now, I'd been sent to live with an apparent family friend, Banden Locus, whom I'd met only twice. He offered to rent Grandmother Corinne's house to look out for me. It was like moving in with the uncle you never saw because he lived across the country. When imagining living anywhere but South Jersey, I'd never considered Crystal Manor, the town where I'd be living with a stranger.

My parents had married young, conceived me a year later, and divorced when I was three. My father had his own life now, and we never connected. Mom didn't have any siblings either, so I had no relatives to be my guardians. Living with a stranger was the only solution.

She sighed. "Please promise me you'll at least *try* to enjoy yourself? It's a new start. You're always worried about fitting in and always hiding who you are. Be yourself. The right people will follow."

I wanted to laugh in her face. Everyone was right. I was the one who was left. The anomaly.

I changed the subject. "Considering how much you don't like Grandmother Corinne, I figured you'd hate anything that belonged to her."

Mom scoffed, her mouth wide. "Orion, please. Of course I love Corinne."

I rolled my eyes. "You call her Corinne, not 'Mom.'"

That's why I was here, because of Grandmother Corinne's stinking will. She'd just had to bequeath her house to Mom.

I eyed my new home from its tiled roofs to its stone front steps. The house could have been in the English countryside. The cookie-cutter white windows had me envisioning a woman in petticoats appearing at the chocolate-brown door. The house's tan exterior bricks were overshadowed by the redbrick walls that surrounded the property. I might have thought it was cute, but the idea of an old woman's house being abandoned for nearly a year gave me the creeps. Dead bushes hugged the walls, and the unkempt grass blanketed in dead fallen leaves was a tribute to its isolation. The late evening sky only heightened the eeriness.

"Anyway, I should go," I said, looking for the doorbell. There was none. *Seriously, how old is this house?*

She sighed and gave me a warm smile. "I love you so much, Orion. I'll try my best to stay in touch. You're the best daughter a mother could have. And happy birthday."

A surge of panic crawled up my throat, and I wanted to beg her to change her mind. Another reason I hated this move. Mom's client needed her to fly out today, October 8. My sixteenth birthday. But I forced the panic down. "I love you too." I hung up.

I knocked on the door, and without a beat, it flew open.

"Orion!" the man exclaimed, his hazel eyes shining.

I jumped back, alarmed by the sudden greeting. A familiar, cool sensation, like cold breath on a frosty day, coiled around my fingers. The "wavelengths," as I called them—resembling heat waves—shot to the door like a bullet before I could stop them, slamming the door farther open against the wall with a loud bang.

Mortified, I wished I could fade into the shadows. The winds were always invisible and did what I asked. I could imagine Mom scolding me, "No using your abilities in public. You know this!" But this was an accident.

"I'm sor—" I began but paused. How could I apologize? *I'm sorry, Banden. It was those weird abilities I was born with acting without my consent. You get it, right?* I'd always had them but never knew why, what they truly were—what *I* truly was. Mom and I had agreed it was safer if we didn't show anyone—the only straight answer I'd ever gotten from her. Despite her reluctance, though, I'd accepted myself for what I was. A freak.

But the smile in Banden's eyes warmed to sympathy. "Oh, I'm sorry for scaring you like that. I'm sure it's been an overwhelming day for you. Come on in." He gestured inside, then picked up my suitcases.

I blinked in disbelief. Did he think the wind had opened the door? But I didn't question it, thankful for his naivety. He probably wasn't as sharp anymore given his age. I knew he was around sixty because Mom had said he was the same age as Corinne, but he didn't have many wrinkles. His grayish-black, wavy hair rested above his shoulders.

I stepped into the foyer, my eyes widening at the unexpected interior. This house had an identity crisis. It was small, with a circular red rug over a polished checkered floor. A metal chandelier hung from the ceiling, and a grandfather clock ticked against a wooden wall. Double doors with small stained-glass windows led to the rest of the floor. It was like a magician lived in here, and Banden's black, ankle-length cape proved it. Underneath the cape, he wore black, and he walked around with a scepter topped with a light-green crystal ball that had white liquid floating inside it. He had been wearing the same attire when I had first met him. Absolutely strange.

Well, everything was strange about this whole situation.

"How about a quick tour, and then I'll let you settle in?" Banden said, dropping the suitcases near the wooden staircase. "How was the ride?"

"Fine, I guess," I answered to his back, following his cape as he started the tour.

In the foyer was a Victorian parlor decked in red and purple sofas and pillows, and a painting of a castle hung next to a tea table. Down the hall and through a set of double doors was a kitchen. There wasn't much to see except for the last door at the end of the hall, which led to a library.

Its small size didn't lessen its grandeur. Shelves traced its walls, and bookcases lined the center. A desk with a lion figurine sat over an enormous red rug, and across from it was a fireplace with unicorns. On the wall next to the fireplace, a mural depicted a stone archway and open wooden door that revealed rows of painted books. Quaint and cozy, this house had more personality than my old one.

But one object raised the hairs on my neck. A painted portrait of a young Corinne hung behind the desk, a gold tag engraved with her name at the bottom. Her short, dark, curly hair reminded me of a flapper haircut. Her sharp blue eyes held an air of secrecy, and she smiled cunningly, like she knew how to destroy the world. One hand held a book while the other touched the red crystal necklace around her neck. I guessed she was a vain person—and unsettling. She wasn't here, yet she still managed to have her eyes on me.

I'd never met my grandmother. She was a forbidden topic in the Candor household. Her death didn't affect me in the slightest, as awful as that might sound. Mom had a beef with her, which she never fully discussed with me. She just muttered fragments here and there about how selfish Corinne had been and how she had waited for Mom to move out after she graduated college. Despite their strange mother-daughter feud, Corinne had left the house to Mom in her will.

"I know you must be exhausted and a little homesick," he said, leading us out of the library and stopping in front of a dark room across the kitchen. "But I hope I can make this transition easier for you."

He flicked the light switch, and a vintage dining room was illuminated. A wooden table in the middle was sprinkled with colorful confetti, and two birthday balloons surrounded a small vanilla cake with unlit candles.

He shrugged. "It's not much, but I wanted to make it a little special. Happy birthday, Orion."

I took a deep breath and tried swallowing the lump forming in my throat again, grateful for the knock on the front door.

"I'll get it," I said, more than eager to be anywhere than staring at Banden's thoughtful yet depressing birthday surprise.

I headed to the front door, but as I was about to grab the knob, the door slammed open. A boy around my age, maybe older, stood in the doorway. Before I could process what was happening, he went to step inside the foyer, but I was in his way. It took him a moment to realize I was there, like he expected someone else. His green eyes glared at me.

If beauty could kill. He had thick, brown, messy hair that looked like he'd run his hands nervously through it. His tan skin complemented his bright eyes, but those eyes radiated a coolness, like sharp-edged peridots. As he stepped toward me, I had to look up unless I wanted to stare at his chest. I tried ignoring the sweet, refreshing scent of his cologne, his hollow cheeks, and his thick lashes. He wore a red T-shirt under a green jacket. His hardened jaw and rigid torso accentuated the coolness radiating from him.

"I'm—" I started to apologize and ask who he was, but he quickly dismissed me.

"In my way? Yes, you are," he snapped, flying past me, his black boots pounding against the checkered floor.

My jaw dropped as he marched for Banden, who stood in the hallway, witnessing the confrontation. Banden had scuttered into the foyer and met the jerk before I could snap a reply.

"Uh, Alec," he warned. "That's no way to treat my new housemate."

"And?" Alec's eyebrow raised. "What does that have to do with me? I don't live here."

If my jaw could, it would be on the floor. "What did you just say?"

"Okay, thank you." Banden glared at him, then grabbed his shoulders and squeezed. "Orion, this is Alec Stone, my nephew. Please excuse his inappropriate behavior. He can have a . . . strong personality. Alec, this is—"

"In his way," I suggested.

Banden sighed, giving me an apologetic smile. "This is Orion. We're here to make her feel *welcome*. She's new to Crystal Manor."

"Great." Alec feigned joy, then grabbed Banden's shoulders and lowered his voice. "Banden, I need to talk to you."

"*Uncle* Banden to you." He removed his nephew's hands. "And not until you apologize to Orion for your curt behavior."

Alec sighed, then dropped his head like a child scolded, annoyance scribbled all over his face. He put on the widest, fakest smile I'd ever seen, excess wrinkles forming around his eyes. "Orion, I apologize. Now, *Uncle* Banden, can I please talk to you?"

Banden gave him a hesitant look, but I made the decision for him. "I need some air. I'm going for a bike ride."

He paused, probably wondering if it was smart to send me out alone in a new town close to nighttime. But I didn't let him respond. I stepped into the crisp autumn air as a stream of vulgar words about this stupid move ran through my brain.

The temperature dropped, my hands freezing as they gripped the handlebars. Biking had been my mode of transportation back home, and it would continue to be so here. The wind picked up, testing my balance as it pushed against the wheels. I moved along the Hudson River, channeling my anger and sorrow into pedaling.

I hated admitting it, but my self-pity couldn't blind me to Crystal Manor's character, which was so unlike my shabby old town. The buildings had a colonial and fairy-tale, cottage-like charm to them, and the colorful leaves blanketing the ground and branches added to the cheery appeal. Most of the shops were within walking distance. And I'd thought my old town was small. Even the entrance to this town was like finding a hidden gem. My taxi driver had turned onto what looked like a driveway, a small street overshadowed by trees. The branches on either side had stretched across the road as if holding hands, their leaves creating a forest-like tunnel of oranges, reds, and yellows.

A firetruck sped past, the vibrations from the street traveling from my bike's wheels to my grip on the handlebars, and I was reminded of that fateful night when my life had been uprooted and Mom decided to move us to Crystal Manor. What I had thought was snow speckling the sky had actually been ash. I could still smell the smoke and feel the blistering heat, even in the now-chilly night. But the distant memory came and went as quickly as the passing truck.

The night grew darker, a heavy autumn mist settled in, transforming my surroundings into shadows. As I pedaled through the foggy streets, I decided the mist was a sign to head back. The last thing I needed was Banden sending a search party after me.

The fog thickened as I reached my new street, Blue Crescent Lane. The two streetlights might as well not have been there, their lighting almost nonexistent in the murkiness. My heart leaped as something moved under the streetlight, my mind inventing shapes until I was closer and halted my bike a safe distance away from it. A figure stood near the black gate, semi-hidden in the darkness.

The hairs on the back of my neck stood up. Maybe it was merely a passerby. Maybe I could ignore them. But the figure didn't leave, lurking motionless, waiting. Maybe it was a friend of Corinne's. But why show up now? She'd passed almost a year ago. Was it Banden waiting for me?

My heart pounded as every irrational thought about danger and strangers clouded my brain. I gripped my handlebars and hopped off my bike, inching toward the figure.

"Banden? Alec?" My voice shook, and I hated myself for showing fear.

I could see the figure stiffen. I expected whoever it was to pounce, but they sprinted off in the opposite direction, as if I were the fox, not the rabbit. A jolt of adrenaline coursed through me, and I dropped my bike and bolted down the sidewalk after them.

"Hey!" I called, stretching out my hand as if an invisible force could stop them. If we had a stalker, I wanted to see the creep's face.

My hand prickled with a tingly sensation, like it had fallen asleep and the blood had begun to flow again. A wavelength swirled in my palm, weighing my hand down and sending a stream of gray smoke toward the figure, who bounced forward, then crashed to the pavement with a grunt and an odd clicking sound.

I stared wildly at my hand and then the distance between me and the figure. This was the second time that the wavelengths acted without my command. And they were gray and powerful. Suppressing my bewilderment and horror, I looked back up, but the figure had disappeared. I sprinted to the corner where it had been, turning my head left and right, trying to see through the fog. But the specter was gone.

A gold glint on the pavement caught my eye. I bent down to find a coin inscribed with some sort of black animal or insect with an oval body with pointy and jagged patterns, two fierce pinchers, and a long, skinny tail. It reminded me of one of those plastic pirate coins you could buy at a party store, but this was metal and heavy. A collector's item, maybe?

A dog barked somewhere, heightening my awareness of the deserted, misty streets. The fog had swallowed the figure, or maybe it still lurked in the shadows. I shuddered, shoved the coin into my back pocket, and hastily fled through the gates of my new home.

CHAPTER 2

When I returned home and told Banden about my encounter, he wanted to run outside and beat them with his scepter. He also apologized for Alec's behavior. In an effort to spare his feelings, I assured him I was still processing everything. This whole situation must be as awkward for him as it was for me.

I didn't sleep well that night. I was restless and distinctly remembered each changing color of the sky as the sun began to rise. I slept in Mom's childhood bedroom, which contained childish fairy-tale décor—like the castle snow globe atop the dresser and the painting of a medieval village towering over hills above the bed frame. Although this room was once Mom's, I still felt like I was sleeping in a stranger's bed.

The next morning, Banden convinced me to accompany him to the Pier Fest that night. I wasn't in the mood for a carnival, but I could tell he was trying to make me feel welcome, and I had no plans. So why not?

Since it wasn't far, we biked to the pier. Back in South Jersey, Mom and I would go for weekend bike rides in the local park. It was our quality time together. I missed her regardless of my annoyance with her over this move. I had yet to hear from her. Cell service and

Wi-Fi weren't as available where she was, but she'd promised to try her best and send letters.

The ocean winds exacerbated the chilly autumn night, and I was thankful for my choice of outfit. My brown hair was frizzier than usual, so I'd thrown on a beanie to hide it. I rarely wore makeup but had put on my (definitely expired) mascara to accent my blue eyes. I also chose a thick sweater and the old, worn combat boots I wore everywhere. Mom had offered to buy me a new pair before she left, but I was as attached to them as they were to my feet; they fit perfectly.

Vehicles and pedestrians jammed the streets, and police cars blocked off Pier Avenue to passing cars. Glistening lights spread throughout the trees gave the area a mystical ambiance, and the colorful flashing lights from the carnival rides illuminated the pier, the Ferris wheel king in the darkness. The smells of popcorn and cotton candy permeated the air as the flashing of lights and dinging of bells surrounded me. Added to that was the musical laughter of teenagers rejoicing over their winnings at the game booths or spinning wildly on the various rides.

Banden purchased our tickets, then stopped to buy me a hot chocolate as we strolled through the chaos, him using his scepter as a third leg. It was still so hard to take him seriously with it. Did his walking stick have to have that much personality? And that cape. I was surprised it kept him warm enough.

"I'm sorry," he said after a few moments of silence, the condensation from his breath forming a small cloud as he spoke. "I'm sure it's not 'cool' to be hanging around with your guardian."

I took a sip of my hot chocolate. "Even if that were true, 'cool' has never been in my repertoire."

I heard Mom's words: *Please promise me you'll at least try to enjoy yourself. It's a new start.* At my old school, I had a place. Here, I could be anyone I wanted. Start over. Isolation had been my only friend in South Jersey as I'd lost myself to my strange abilities. What if someone found out? What if I was compelled to tell someone and they ran? No one would understand. I was a freak who could do strange things no one else could do. I had discovered my abilities when I was five years old, my hand hovering above my toy horse and making it move. When I was twelve, I could levitate light objects, like cotton balls or paper. I didn't know why I could do this stuff. It wasn't *physically* hurting me or anyone else. But did I use it as an excuse to isolate myself? Maybe I had been alone for so long I didn't know how to be a normal teenager. At least Mom didn't think I was a freak, even if she didn't understand. Was there anyone anywhere in the world like me? I couldn't be the only one. Could I?

"Look, Orion." Banden's cheerful mood suddenly dissipated. "I know this isn't easy for you, but don't be afraid to reach out—or if you need the space, just say the word."

He would be so kind because of Corinne and Mom. But volunteering to be responsible for a kid who wasn't even related to him was a huge favor for a friend. I'd known *of* him, but I didn't realize he and Mom were so close that she trusted him to be my guardian.

"How long did you know my grandmother?" I asked.

He smiled, a nostalgic look in his hazel eyes. "Since we were teenagers. We grew up together here."

"And you wanted to live in her house?"

I'd never heard the full story, just that he had been thinking of leaving Crystal Manor until Mom had told him she was thinking of selling it.

"Your mother's job came at the right time. She wanted to sell the house until . . ."

"The fire," I helped him. When my classmates heard about the fire, it was the first time I was acknowledged by them, but only with stares of pity and condolences. At least I had received verification of my existence.

He nodded solemnly, like he was the one who'd lived through it instead of me. "She hated that apartment you both lived in after the fire, so she decided to keep Corinne's house and return to Crystal Manor. But then, of course, her client needed her in Eastern Europe, and she didn't want to bring you across the world when you could settle in and start fresh. She needed someone to watch over you. I had already sold my house. She offered me rent for a year, and I decided it couldn't hurt to stay a little longer before I moved on. After all, I'd jumped the gun by selling my house without buying a new one." He chuckled.

Yes, Mom had been on the fence about selling the house, but I'd had faith she wouldn't keep it. Then, three months later came the fire. Mom had been working from home that night, and I thanked every star she hadn't shared the same fate as our house. I hadn't been there when it started, but I'd arrived upon a scene where red-and-blue lights surrounded my home, a victim of the furious orange fire. The investigators hadn't been able to determine a cause, calling it a freak accident. It was the uncertainty that haunted me most. But it suited me. My life was nothing but ambiguity.

I couldn't see how Banden would enjoy watching over a teenage girl, but nothing seemed to bother him. If Mom trusted him, I could learn to.

"I wonder where Alec is," he mused, scanning the crowd. "He said he was going to meet us."

"I'm not worried," I mumbled into my hot chocolate, not in the least excited to see his charming nephew again.

"Orion, I wanted to talk to you about—" he began but then paused. A kid zoomed by us, and someone slammed into me. My hot chocolate exploded all over me, burning my hand. I looked down to see a huge, dark-brown stain on my sweater and streaks of liquid trailing down my jeans.

"I'm so sorry!" the man who'd bumped into me said, then proceeded to chase after the fleeing kid.

"Oh, dear, let's clean you up," Banden said, about to head over to a food stand to grab napkins, but I stopped him.

"It's all right. I'll clean up in the bathroom," I said, gesturing toward the restroom trailers on the wooded outskirts of the pier. "I'll be right back."

The night grew darker as I neared the trailers, the small lights hidden between the orange and yellow branches all but lost to the overshadowing darkness. A shiver crawled down my arms as I approached the blackened tree line. I couldn't explain it, but the silence was strangely loud, the night too quiet for the joyous laughter on the pier.

Movement in the trees made me stop. The branches waved gently in the darkness, creaking and caging the entrance against trespassers. When I'd convinced myself I'd imagined the movement, a branch snapped, followed by a humming. Then, through the trees echoed a faint cry, like that of a wounded animal. And then it came again. Multiple voices and whispers erupted, clashing like static. It wasn't until a clear, female voice cried, "Help!" that I broke into a sprint, adrenaline pumping through my veins as I stopped in front of the trees.

"Hello?" I called into the darkness.

I thought about calling out to the police on the pier, but the cry came again—this time a familiar voice. "No, please!"

"Mom!" I bolted for the trees, my voice awakening the darkness. Her cries were my guide as my feet pounded against the dry dirt, the cold wind biting at my cheeks. I repeatedly shouted her name, hoping she'd answer me.

My foot caught on something hard, and suddenly the ground was at my face, my hands and torso scraping against spiky twigs and sticks. In front of me, a branch snapped. I looked up, and my heart stopped at the sight of a cloaked figure.

I slowly rose to my feet. "Mom?"

The figure turned. It was her. What was she doing here? Her eyes were wide as saucers and her skin white as a ghost's. Suddenly, her anxious face, dark as the shadows inside her hood, faded into smoke, her entire body following suit. A scream was ripped from my throat as the cloak dropped to the ground. It started to move like something was underneath it, and then it grew, the cloth ripping as it did so. A six-foot-tall, snarling brown beast had replaced Mom. It stood on four lion-like paws. Its body was that of a gorilla while its face resembled a mutated cat's with large, calculating eyes.

I took off running before it leaped at me. My lungs burned as I zigzagged around trees, praying to lose it. But its paw came down several inches from me, vibrating the ground beneath my feet. My body curled into a ball as I somersaulted through the air. I then slammed back-first into a boulder, hitting my head, though my back took most of the impact. Every organ and bone in my body screamed. Blood trickled down my neck, and I pushed my fingers up underneath my beanie to find an open gash. The ground shook underneath me again, a torment to my dizzying head. The beast pounced, and helpless from the throbbing pain, I awaited my fate, a deer against its hunter.

But a shadow flashed before me, and the beast was sent flying into a tree trunk. Then the shadow and the beast were in a warlike stance, ready to attack one another. A crackling sounded, and the tree roots nearby suddenly rose from the ground and seized the beast, caging it. The beast roared and thrashed about, trying to break free of the animated roots.

"Orion, run!" a familiar voice yelled, but fear and pain hindered my judgment. It wasn't until he turned his face before looking back at the beast that I recognized my rescuer. Alec?

Using the boulder for support, I wobbled to my feet, but as I regained my equilibrium, from the trees emerged seven more beasts baring their dagger-like teeth. Empowered by its pack, the one caught in the roots snapped them in half, breaking free.

"Alec!" I latched on to his arm to steady myself as the forest spun around me.

He turned around, eyeing the beasts. We moved until we were back to back as they encircled us.

"We can knock half of them out with our powers," Alec whispered, looking from one beast to another.

My eyes widened. "*What?*"

But he didn't have the chance to answer as one of the beasts lunged for him. Instead, he stuck his hand out, and dirt exploded from the ground onto two of their faces, causing them to step back.

"Cut the crap, Orion. I know you're a sorcerer. You can stop—"

"I'm a what?"

The sound of heavy pounding vibrated the ground, forcing the beasts to turn in the direction of a figure emerging from the shadows. The blood drained from my face when I saw Banden holding his scepter high.

"Alec, take Orion and shield your eyes!" Banden ordered, his face pinched in a scowl as he surveyed the beasts, which were all growling at him now.

Alec pulled me into him, his arms encircling me, as Banden struck his scepter into the ground, yelling words that sounded like a cross between Italian and French. A blinding light flashed from the tip of his scepter, forcing me to close my eyes against Alec's chest. Yelps and howls chorused as the light penetrated my closed lids.

When the blackness returned, I opened one eye at a time. The beasts were gone, leaving us as the night's predators. Banden held his scepter midair. Once he deemed the environment safe, he lowered his weapon and hobbled toward us as fast as he could.

"What's going on?" I pulled away from Alec. "What were those things?"

"Chicaneries," Banden answered, almost breathless.

"No, they had Mom. They—"

"So that's what you saw," Alec said, his dark hair matted to his forehead. "That wasn't your mom."

"A Chicanery is a creature that transforms into something or someone significant to its prey," Banden explained. "It felt the bond between you and Seraphina and grabbed her image from your mind. They're empowered by fear and hunt at night."

I wanted to drop to the dirt. Mom was okay. But creatures transforming into different beings?

Banden's eyes searched the darkness. "Orion, you need to come with us. I can't imagine what else might be lurking out here."

I stepped back. "Why don't you explain what's going on?"

"We know about your powers, Orion. It's why the Chicaneries were after you."

"What powers?"

This time, Alec spoke, taking a cautious step toward me. "Your sorcery powers. You know, 'cause you're a sorcerer."

My thoughts swirled faster than a top, intensifying the pain in my head. *Sorcerer? Powers?* Were they referring to my abilities? I must have hit my head.

Banden stepped toward me, his hands raised in surrender. "Orion, please give us a chance to explain. We'll tell you everything."

They were insane. I was definitely passed out somewhere.

Or was about to be. The pulsing in my skull hammered in time with my racing heartbeat. My vision blurred, and my body gave in, the world bleeding black.

CHAPTER 3

I woke to soft voices and darkness. I didn't remember falling asleep. My head spun as I sat up, my vision clouded with black blotches. My head pounded, and my back ached like it had been used as a punching bag. A woven blanket was wrapped around me as I sat on a red sofa.

I smelled a mixture of grass and cough syrup. In the nearby fireplace, a cauldron with a black dragon emblazoned on it boiled over a crackling green fire. A brick-red tapestry with a medieval design hung beside the fireplace. Shelves on the stone walls overflowed with jars containing unknown ingredients.

The voices started again.

I peeked over the sofa. Even with their backs to me, the two figures were familiar.

"I can't believe she doesn't know who she is." That was Alec. Banden stood next to him, tending to a cauldron that sat on a table with jars and books scattered across it.

Then I remembered. I'd been in the woods, attacked by something otherworldly. Banden and Alec had come to my rescue, and for some twisted reason, they had kidnapped me. Now I was . . . somewhere else.

There was a dark tunnel not too far away. My heartbeat pulsed in my ears as I unwrapped the blanket and slowly swung my feet to the floor, avoiding the coffee table.

"Seraphina was protecting her," Banden said.

I paused.

"How is hiding your child's identity protecting her?" Alec countered. "Suppressing who you are eventually blows up in your face."

I stood up and trudged toward them without a second thought about what I was doing. "What about my mother?"

They both jumped and turned around.

"Orion!" Banden exclaimed, a wide smile on his face. "I'm relieved you're okay. You hit your head pretty badly, but I was able to heal you before you suffered any permanent damage."

"So that's why you kidnapped me?"

"We didn't," Alec said, crossing his arms as he leaned back against the table. "Did you not hear him? You would've died. We saved you. You're welcome."

Banden eyed him. "Alec."

"What? She wouldn't have been in this mess if she hadn't decided to explore a forest *at night*. You're asking for trouble."

"The Chicaneries shouldn't have been there in the first place," Banden argued. "They're not supposed to be on nonmagus grounds." He turned to me with a gentle expression. "Please forgive us. You're in Isoria. And this is my Elixir Chamber, underneath my home."

I'd lost him after his first sentence. "Isoria?"

"It's a realm, or country, in the Atlantic Ocean, not too far off the East Coast. It's home to magical creatures and magi, or magical beings. But you're only a portal away from New Jersey, so don't worry. You can be home in minutes. You have powers, Orion, powers you received through your mother's lineage. Your father knows nothing of this and possesses no magical ability. Your mother is an enchanter, and your grandmother, Corinne, is a sorcerer, an Incendor, specifically. The enchanter gene skipped you, but not Corinne's sorcerer abilities."

"*What?*" My head hurt as I searched for a reasonable explanation. "If that's true, why didn't she tell me?"

When he hesitated, Alec gave him a sideways glance.

"You said she was protecting me," I reminded them.

"She was—*is*, I should say. I didn't agree with her about hiding your identity, but I respected her wishes."

"What are you talking about?" I pressed. They were being so vague, carefully choosing how they answered my questions. "You said you'd tell me everything before you kidnapped me."

"At least we know she doesn't have brain damage," Alec mumbled.

Banden sighed, his eyes wary as he struggled with what must be an internal battle about betraying my mother. But he admitted, "She thought she was protecting you by keeping you away from this world. She was even hiding from it herself. There was talk of an uprising that scared her, so she left Isoria."

He opened the top drawer behind him and rummaged through its contents before holding his arm out to me. A red pendant on a silver chain dangled from his fingers. My eyes widened. The necklace in Corinne's portrait.

"Corinne gave me this before she died," he explained. "A souvenir of our friendship. I took you to Pier Fest hoping I could lessen the blow about your sorcerer identity, but the Chicaneries beat me to it. Your mother trusted me to look out for you. And I'm keeping my promise."

"All because he was best friends with your grandmother," Alec grumbled. I could hear the eye roll.

If Banden was telling the truth, that meant my mother, the only person I trusted my entire life, had been lying to me my entire life. Lying about *who I was.*

"And, to be clear, you and Alec are sorcerers too?"

He tilted his head side to side. "Well, yes and no. Alec is, but I'm a Bimedeis, which means I'm part enchanter and part sorcerer. Without adding further confusion, I'll say we're like you and know what you're going through. I'm a medicinal herbal specialist as well as an elixir master. I create remedies for Isoria's injured and ill. And you should know . . . Alec isn't my nephew. He's my apprentice."

Alec's eyes shone in admiration, but his next words came out, unsurprisingly, sarcastic. "He's kind of a big shot."

"Isoria is hidden from nonmagi, or those without magic," Banden continued, ignoring his pupil. "Nonmagi can't enter Isoria without a magical being at their side and can't see it unless given Isorian Vision. Nonmagi also aren't allowed to live in Isoria."

It was like coming out of amnesia, trying to relearn who I was. My true identity. And Mom never told me. She was so lucky she was overseas. I had grown up thinking I could never fit in and be a normal teenager, that something was wrong with me, that I had a disease no one knew how to cure. But it turned out my difference was a normality and everyone was a liar.

I stepped away, wanting to run, but I didn't know where that dark tunnel led. My mind was lost in one. "Thank you for everything, Banden, but I . . . this is a lot right now."

He inched toward me. "Orion, I can't imagine what you must be feeling, but you can't continue as before. How long do you think hiding will protect you? Until you find yourself in another situation like tonight, defenseless and in danger of hurting someone or yourself?"

I wanted to hide forever, to return to the lonely life I knew. At least it was comfortable and familiar there.

"Your powers are growing stronger," Banden said. "You feel something is wrong. You know it."

He was right. Mom had kept me in the dark for so long that isolation had become my comfort zone. I couldn't live in that "comfort" for the rest of my life. I finally had answers. Even though those answers were completely bizarre.

"Okay, what do I need to do?" I said.

He grinned. "Well, now you need training. Since Seraphina isn't around, we'll train you. In the basics, that is. You'll need to understand them before we can enroll you in a sorcery academy."

My eyes widened. "Wait, I have to enroll in a school?"

He gave me a guilty smile. "Yes. At a young age, a sorcerer's powers are weak, so they're taught simple spells. A sorcerer's power grows to its full potential in their fourteenth year. At age fifteen or sixteen, they must choose an element to study at an academy. Sorcery is comprised of four elements: Air, Earth, Water, and Fire. However, you'll take the Isorian Element Performance Evaluation, or the IEPE, which evaluates your strengths and weaknesses and ranks the elements that are most compatible for you. You'll have the freedom to choose the element you'd like to pursue, regardless of your test scores. You have a choice. I know this is overwhelming, but you need training for this reason."

"But I have no experience with magic," I protested. "How can I go to magic school *and* high school?" High school was bad enough. I couldn't survive both.

"You wouldn't go back to high school. You'd take those classes at the academy you attend instead."

He pulled a green book from a shelf and handed it to me. It was like a brick—larger and heavier than any book I'd ever held. The title was etched in gold, and there was a gold outline of the earth with waves, wind, rocks, and fire surrounding it.

"*A Beginner's Guide to the Four Elements*," I read out loud.

"Do not practice any spells," he warned, a dark shadow under his eyes. "I don't know the strength of your powers, and neither do you. Now, you're probably exhausted. We'll pick up tomorrow."

Tomorrow. I still had so many questions.

"Why were those Chicaneries after me?" I asked one of the many.

He hesitated, and I noticed Alec side-eyeing him. "They're nocturnal. You were in the wrong place at the wrong time."

"But you said they're not supposed to be on . . . nonmagus grounds." It felt weird saying that.

"All will make sense soon." He smiled, but it was quick and small. "Right now, you need rest. If you don't mind, I'd prefer you stay here so you and Alec don't have to go wandering around this late at night. I have one last order to fill, so I won't be at Crystal Manor for at least another hour. But, if you aren't comfortable, I'll make other arrangements to bring you home."

I wanted to see Isoria, but I wouldn't repeat my mistake by wandering around an apparent dangerous foreign country alone with Alec at night. I also couldn't face the thought of running into any Chicaneries lurking outside Corinne's house.

"I can stay here," I said.

"Excellent. I have a guest room upstairs."

Sleep was beyond me, my mind overloaded as it was from the night's events. I shook my head. "I can stay on the couch."

He shrugged. "If you wish. I'll be right here if you need me."

Alec did whatever it was he did as Banden's apprentice while I put my sleepless energy to work in perusing the spell book. The introduction explained how sorcery was to be used for good only, to keep and restore balance, not to disrupt nature, and thought of as a tool. Magic was forbidden to be used in front of nonmagi and forbidden to interfere with and/or alter their everyday lives. The book was divided into four parts for the four elements sorcery was composed of: Air, Earth, Fire, and Water. Sorcerers who studied Air sorcery were known as Aermages; Terramancers studied Earth sorcery; Incendors practiced Fire sorcery; and Aquatists practiced Water sorcery. There were example spells for each element, instructions on how to cast them, and illustrations depicting the hand motions. There was also a technical component to these elements, which I hoped someone would eventually explain to me. The more I read, the more overwhelmed I became.

I pulled my phone out of my jeans pocket, hoping Mom had been in touch with me so I could bombard her with questions. But all I saw was the word *ERROR* across a black screen.

"Oh, I'm sorry," Banden said. "I forgot to mention that technology doesn't work in Isoria. It's been banned by the king to keep Isoria safe from being discovered and exploited by nonmagi. Cell towers, social media . . . it's all a recipe for disaster. If ships try to sail past, the magical barrier around Isoria forces them to travel around us, but to the nonmagi, it looks like they're right on course."

I sighed. Banden shouldn't have been the one to give me this book. I didn't need him. I needed Mom. I needed the reason why she had been silent about who I was and the world I came from.

But Banden's words kept crawling up my neck: *She was even hiding from it herself.*

CHAPTER 4

My eyes opened to see green flames. I bolted upright, almost knocking the spell book off my legs. I had forgotten where I was, but the events of last night slowly came back to me in flashes as I stared at Banden's fireplace.

Magic was real. I had magic, and I was in a magical world hidden within the modern world.

"Mornin', mood-killer."

I jumped, finding Alec in one of the armchairs, an open book in his hands, his boots propped on the coffee table.

"How long have you been there?" I asked, mortified.

"I like to watch people sleep." He closed his book entitled *Earth in the Art of War* and removed his boots from the table. He leaned forward, his brown hair falling short of his eyes, and snorted. "Relax. I've only been here for twenty minutes."

"To watch me?"

He rolled his eyes and stood. "No. This is my reading hour, and you're in my reading space. I'm not giving up my morning routine for some minor inconvenience." He rubbed something off his arm—a minor inconvenience, perhaps. He always wore dark or natural colors. Today, he had on a dark-green shirt and thin black jacket with burgundy on the front. Dark colors to match his sparkling personality.

I threw the blanket off. "Well, I'm not the only mood-killer. You don't have to be so rude about it."

He didn't have time for a retort as the bookcases slid apart and out came Banden, cape flying behind him.

"Good morning!" he greeted with his usual smile. "Orion, so glad you're up. Do you want breakfast before we start the day? I have a butter roll if you want. It's got lingonberry filling."

He handed me a roll in a white cloth. I didn't feel like eating, but my stomach grumbled, and I wasn't sure what the day would bring, so I took a bite of the buttery pastry and followed him as he headed for the bookcases. With a wave of his hand, the bookcases slid apart, revealing a dark tunnel.

"Where are we going?" I asked.

"The training arena, so you can begin your first sorcery lesson," Banden said, starting for the tunnel.

I finished the roll as I followed him through the dark tunnels, Alec falling in step beside me. Torches lit the gravel path, flaring on as we neared them and instantly going out once we passed. The dim lighting cast shadows across Alec's face, and I wasn't sure if it was my imagination, but I thought I caught him side-eyeing me multiple times, like he wanted to say something but was fighting it. It irked me, considering I'd done nothing to him.

"What can you tell me about my grandmother?" I asked Banden's cape. His usual black attire blended in with the tunnel.

"An enigma." His voice echoed. He bent his head to avoid the low ceilings. "She was a puzzle—only wanted certain people to know certain things."

"Anything more specific?"

"Well, I knew her back in my school days. She wasn't very fond of school. A bit of a troublemaker." He chuckled. "Detention started to become her after-school curriculum."

"Sounds like the opposite of Mom," I mumbled, watching my feet.

Mom was a determined woman, ambitious with any project she took on. She'd worked hard to grow her business, and she was in high demand. A genius and one of the smartest people I'd ever known, she created solutions for technology and fixed the most high-tech equipment I couldn't even describe. She was a fixer, brainy, and handy. She used to break things apart, like cameras or computers, so she could learn how to rebuild and improve them. When she wasn't working on her tech business, she was looking at how to improve things, to "reinvent the wheel," but better and more efficiently. Her talents and skills were almost like magic.

"Sometimes things need to fall apart in order to fix them," she had said to me not too long ago when I found her tearing apart my cell phone. It had suddenly stopped working. She had fixed it within an hour.

The tunnel was like a maze and had so many twists and turns I began to wonder how far Banden was going to make me walk. As we rounded a corner, a flash of light hit us. I covered my eyes with my hand, but once we entered what I assumed was the training arena, my eyes widened. Cheers and thunderous booms resonated off the walls as we entered what looked like a massive dining hall without furniture. The ceilings, held up by pillars, were high for an underground room. Random stones were stuck into the walls as if someone had attempted to build a wall and then given up. In the center on the tiles of the shattered marble floor was the silhouette of a fierce blue griffin. In the center of the arena, a swarm of people dressed in dark, skintight clothing surrounded a girl and boy who looked around my age. The hollers and cheers of the spectators collided with thunderous claps of magic volleying between the two teenagers.

"Who are all these people?" I turned to Alec.

"Kick his ass, Rae!" someone yelled from the sidelines, momentarily distracting Alec.

As if the cheer gave her power, the girl fighter, or Rae, flung ice shards at her opponent. Strands of her black layered hair were matted against her shiny neck and forehead as she dodged fiery bullets.

"Look out, Julian!" someone warned. An ice shard flew toward Julian's face, but he ducked, and it exploded against the stone and dirt wall.

"Helping the participants is forbidden. You know the rules!" a woman yelled from across the arena. She wore a black robe with flames embossed at the bottom, and she was scribbling something in a book. A man in navy-blue robes stood next to her, holding a book as well.

"They're evaluating Rae's and Julian's performances," Alec said in my ear, his breath tickling my cheek and catching me off guard. I was so sure he had been ignoring me. His eyes widened. "Incoming!"

I followed his gaze to a giant ice shard headed right for us.

"Duck!" someone yelled.

Everyone around me crouched like they'd been practicing for years. Someone gripped my shoulder to pull me down, and I lifted my hands above my head as a shield. As the shard came for my face, my body filled with adrenaline, like it was high on caffeine and ready to burst. Wavelengths of power surged from my arms to my hands, and a smoky light flashed around my outstretched hands, colliding with the shard and blasting it to pieces before it hit the stone wall and sprinkled over us like confetti.

It was Alec's hand on my shoulder. He removed it, eyes wide. Everyone who'd crouched down now stared at us as they slowly rose to their feet.

"How did you—?" he began to ask but shook his head. "Did you see where Banden went?"

I remained quiet, unsure of the answers to both of his questions. He wasn't the only one who was shocked. Like when I had slammed the door in front of Banden and sent that figure to the concrete, my powers had once again acted on their own accord. Or at least it felt that way. The spectators' eyes were still glued to me. I could hear whispering.

"Follow me," Alec said, starting for the crowd. The stares followed us as I stayed blindly in Alec's shadow.

Banden conversed with a woman in the far corner. She was taller than he was, and like the moon in the night sky, her long white hair and pale skin contrasted with her dark clothing. Her dark, skintight clothing hugged her thin frame, and the long jacket she wore reached to her knees. Her shirt was laced up, and she wore tall boots. I imagined her pulling a long sword as sharp as broken glass from those boots. Her green eyes darted past Banden, latching on to me.

"Orion Candor." The words left her faint-pink lips. She was maybe in her forties. Her electric eyes, fascinated and hungry, never left me, as if I were a new weapon she could use. I couldn't stop staring at her.

"Orion, this is Celeste Silavin, owner of this arena." Banden introduced the intimidating woman.

"At last, we meet, Orion." Her voice was rough and deep, like fire had scorched her throat. A dull, gold, thin chain hung from her neck.

"You know who I am?" I asked.

"I saw Corinne in you the moment you walked in," she said, smiling. I couldn't tell if she was overly friendly or secretly wanted to kill me.

"Celeste is letting us use the arena for your training," Banden explained.

"Come," she said, gesturing toward a mosaic-covered door in the corner. "I'm sure you have plenty of questions."

Banden waved for me to follow, while Alec stayed behind. I followed Celeste and Banden to the colorful glass door in the far corner of the arena. The door opened of its own accord, the royal-blue of the room beyond it the last color I expected to see. I'd expected the walls to be black, the floor garnished with skulls. Nevertheless, the room still threatened violence. Rows of swords and spears were staggered across the walls. A sleek black desk was surrounded by stacks of books, and a candelabra on the desktop illuminated a line of daggers. Maps with red circles and x's were piled on a table in the corner.

"Have a seat," Celeste demanded more than offered. I followed Banden's lead by sitting on one of the stone stools nearby.

Celeste sat in a velvet chair and tossed her white hair over her shoulders. Her sharp eyes zeroed in on me. "Orion, I'm sure this is all very overwhelming for you, so I will get to the point. You're in MISTIC's headquarters, or The Cave. MISTIC stands for Magical

Intervention Society for Tactical Intelligence and Combat. We're a covert spy ring with a mission to take down Cyril Obsidian, or the Obsidian King, as he likes to call himself—Isoria's most feared sorcerer. We gather intelligence on Obsidian to understand his motives and weaknesses. We don't work for King Leo, ruler of Isoria, as he prefers to handle things his way. And his way has certainly failed." She mumbled the latter, briefly breaking eye contact with me.

"We operate in secret to help protect and defend Isoria our way, the efficient way. But, as secretive as we may be, we think Obsidian may know there's an intelligence ring out to destroy him. We're hoping he believes it's a royal organization led by King Leo. Isorians live with eyes at the backs of their heads. Anyone can hand anyone over to Obsidian by kidnapping Isorians and forcing them to join his movement. We're here to stop that and put an end to his terror. Although I started this organization to destroy Obsidian, and that continues to be our primary goal, I plan for MISTIC to be Isoria's first and official intelligence ring. King Leo doesn't know what it takes to run a well-organized spy network, and I hope we can work together one day. So, any questions?"

Yes, many, I wanted to say, but I started with my most burning one. "So, you're telling me there's a king trying to overrule another king?" It was unreal. I felt like I was in a history textbook and they were playing a prank on me. I felt like I had used a time machine and was sent to the 1600s or some fantastical dimension.

Celeste reached into one of the desk's drawers, pulled out a scroll, and flattened it across the table. Buildings, landmarks, and geographical features like mountains, trees, and valleys molded like paper-mâché littered the beige paper. Above each site floated sketched ribbon labels written in a cartographer's handwriting. I counted twenty main towns and cities. Two enormous buildings stole the show: King Leo's palace and the United Royal Imperium of Isoria. Apparently, Isoria was its own country somewhere in the Atlantic Ocean and was about the size of Switzerland. On the far left side of the map, an island significantly smaller than Isoria was shadowed. A strip of land connected it to Isoria, but it was blacked out and titled, "Shadow's Pass." The ribbon above the island read, "Fort Obsidian."

"This map shows changes that occur in Isoria's landscape and what it looks like in real time," Celeste explained. "Judging by your face, you probably noticed Westwin has been destroyed. The village was claimed by Obsidian and his followers, who are known as Pawns. They rose to power in the spring ten years ago. Obsidian raided Westwin, and he and his followers slaughtered men, women, children, and anyone and anything in their way. He and his Pawns marked the area as their territory. It was an especially devastating loss for King Leo because Westwin was Isoria's central trading port. The takeover is known as the Siege of Westwin."

A shiver ran down my spine, and my chest went stiff as Banden's words crept into my thoughts: *There was talk of an uprising that scared her, so she left Isoria.*

"Obsidian was an ex-knight to King Leo," Celeste continued. "As King Leo tells it, Obsidian grew tired of following orders and sought his own power. He persuaded and forced many Isorians to rebel against the king and his laws. Isoria has a running list of problems, so some were easily influenced. No one knows Obsidian's exact intentions, other than he wishes to destroy King Leo.

"King Leo planned an ambush on Obsidian, but Obsidian's forces were waiting at the border of Isoria before the king's troops could reach the island. King Leo underestimated Obsidian's power. His army couldn't cross Shadow's Pass—that passage between Isoria and Fort Obsidian. They say it's haunted and guarded by magi who were transformed into Chosen Shadows, or mutated beings. King Leo's army tried to fly over Shadow's Pass but was electrocuted by the vast shield that protects the fort. It's a kind of magic Isoria has never seen. The loss was detrimental to King Leo's already waning reputation, and he hasn't attacked the island since. As Obsidian hides in his fort, protected from another ambush, his powers have been mysteriously amplified. MISTIC is trying to understand this."

I nodded, trying to absorb the crash course in Isorian politics. I wanted to pinch myself to make sure this conversation was real.

Celeste turned to Banden. "As I understand it, Orion has been denied magic all her life. Therefore, she doesn't have proper training, and you want her to be trained by our certified Masters?"

Banden nodded. "Yes, she needs to be enrolled in a school as soon as possible. Although she is not a MISTIC agent, I thought because of her familial connections, you would allow her to train here. I would oversee her education, but I believe she'd benefit from some of the best teachers in Isoria to help her quickly excel. Also, given the circumstances of her . . . history, she could eventually receive agent training for her own and even the ring's benefit."

She nodded. "She'll train with the Masters."

"Perfect. Thank you, Celeste. I'll speak to them now." Banden got up to leave, and I followed him, ready to bombard him about this MISTIC matter, but we were both stopped.

"Ah, Banden, we have protocols, remember?" Celeste stroked the blade of one of the daggers on the desk. "If you don't mind, I'd like to speak with Orion."

His eyes were as sharp as hers. "What for?"

She smiled tightly. "No need to fret, Banden. I just want to have a conversation."

Tension filled the air. Their eyes were fixed, both refusing to be the first to look away.

"I'd rather stay," he challenged.

She raised an eyebrow. "If you must."

I sighed in relief. Being alone with Celeste would be like being trapped with a python waiting for the strike. It was her perceptive eyes. Not even a fly could escape her. We took our seats again.

She turned to me. "I know you have lots of questions, Orion, but I promise that, in due time, everything will make sense." Her strong hands were folded in front of her, thicker and larger than I expected for someone her size. "For starters, you're well-known here."

Banden stiffened beside me.

"What do you mean?" I asked.

"I'm sure you know your grandmother."

I rolled my eyes. "How could I not?"

She gave another tight smile. "She was a MISTIC agent, a spy sorcerer, if you will. But I see Banden is correct. You don't know anything about her, do you?"

Her face was expressionless, but I caught the shift in her tone. She didn't believe me. Or doubted my ignorance. How many people knew more about me than I knew about myself?

"To make it easy for you, I know nothing about her, my family, or the fact I come from a line of magic. If there's something you want to know, you won't get it from me," I retorted, more cutthroat than I intended.

Her voice softened as much as her throatiness would allow. "My apologies, Orion. I'm straightening out the facts. You see, Corinne was one of the best spies MISTIC has ever had. She wasn't one of the youngest, but she was sharp-witted and clever and never liked following the rules. Or anyone. She took matters into her own hands. A natural risk-taker."

I didn't expect a rebellious person for my grandmother. She was an enigma, but Celeste's description had changed the old-lady image I had of her.

She continued. "Oh yes. She meant well, but she was impulsive, and her 'I-do-what-I-want' attitude presented her with enemies. She had a knack for finding trouble, and trouble seemed to find her. Her recklessness resulted in consequences."

"*Celeste*," Banden warned in a way that sounded like he'd duel her to keep her quiet.

"It's the facts, Banden," she snapped, her eyes on me. "Corinne was a double agent. She pretended to be loyal to the Obsidian King while feeding us information."

My grandmother as a double agent sounded awesome.

"When you're involved in a spy ring, trouble is guaranteed." She smiled and leaned her head as close as her desk would allow. "Concealing intelligence was her specialty. If you know anything, please help us help Isoria."

It didn't sound like a threat, but her tone sent shivers from my head to my toes. It was like she suspected I was hiding something or knew more than she was letting on.

"All right, thank you, Celeste." Banden stood, his voice sharper than the daggers lined across the desk. "She's overwhelmed as it is."

He grabbed my arm, but I shook him off. "What information?"

Her smile remained. "Orion, know that we as an organization are here for you. You are surrounded by people you can trust, and your safety is our concern."

My safety?

"You aren't an agent, so you don't have to abide by all our regulations. However, you must take our oath." She then turned to Banden. "She knows about us, so she must keep us secret."

Banden nodded. "Of course she will."

"I don't doubt it, but she must take the *full* oath."

His face paled, but he kept his voice level. "With all due respect, Celeste, what intelligence would she come by? She—"

"You know the rules, Banden." She silenced him with a look. "It's that or I have to use a memory-erasing elixir on her."

I raised my eyebrows. "Excuse me?"

But Celeste ignored me for once. "I make no exceptions for anyone. Not even Corinne's granddaughter. You understand the climate we're living in. Without law, there is no order." She paused, this time challenging him. "I can't help but question your eagerness to deny her from pledging. I can't help but wonder—do you, and she, have something to hide?"

His eyes hardened. "No, of course not. Forgive me for my persistence, but it's the consequence that seems unnecessary since she isn't a spy."

"Times are dire, Banden. If I'm lenient for anyone, traitors will question our power and be more apt to commit treason, and more will turn as these traitors recruit others, and more turncoats let loose means a fall in our cause and a war lost. You can find other teachers for her if you choose, but her honesty and loyalty will reward her our training and protection. And I know you want that."

Banden gave a slight, rigid nod, not agreeing with his superior but understanding his place.

"Orion," Celeste turned to me. "Every MISTIC agent needs to pledge their allegiance to the organization. It's about loyalty and putting the cause before yourself. Since you won't be pledging as an agent, I'm not asking you to risk your life. In order for you to use our facilities and receive our protection, you must promise that any intelligence you stumble upon, any intellect that could help us take down Cyril Obsidian, will be shared with us. If you choose to conceal intelligence, that is an act of treason against not only this organization but against Isoria and the hundreds of thousands of lives that could be saved. And if you choose concealment, it will result in your termination."

I raised a concerned eyebrow. "As an agent?"

"Of your life."

My eyes widened, and I turned to Banden, who clearly didn't agree with his superior. Why was Celeste so eager for me to share information about someone I didn't even know? For some reason, she seemed to think I posed some threat and that I might come across information about this evil king. Banden believed this group could protect me, but protect me from what?

She thought she was protecting you by keeping you away from this world. She was even hiding from it herself.

Celeste continued. "Orion, if you choose to associate yourself with our organization, you must give me your word. Your word means you understand the importance of our cause and what must be done to anyone who is an accomplice to treason. Don't forget, Corinne was family, so her family is our family. We protect one another. You'll need allies in this world."

Yet they'll erase my memory if I don't agree. I couldn't help but question Celeste's eagerness to talk about Corinne, and Banden's reluctance. Maybe Celeste was the key to the secrets Banden seemed to be hiding. Like Banden had said, what information would I have come across? Also, I wouldn't want to hide information from an intelligence organization. And if there was a sadistic sorcerer terrorizing this country, of course, I'd do what I could to help.

I nodded. "You have my word. I'll take the oath."

She smiled, her eyes gleaming brightly. "Excellent. We will give you a quick tour of The Cave and then gather in the arena to seal the official allyship before your training."

There was a knock on the door, and it swung open without Celeste's invitation.

"Stop, Julian!" A panicked female voice came as a dirty-blond-haired boy entered the room. "She didn't say we could go in!"

"Oh shit, I'm sorry!" the boy said. "I didn't realize you were with someone." I immediately recognized him as the one who had been dueling outside. After him came the girl who had been his opponent. Her faced whitened as Julian turned to her. "Rae, why didn't you stop me?"

Rae glared at him.

"That's quite all right, agents," Celeste said, waving her hand. "Actually, you two could be of much assistance. Do you mind showing Orion around while I get the arena ready?" She then turned to me and smiled. "She's our new initiate."

CHAPTER 5

Sorry about our intrusion," Rae said as we left Celeste's office. "Julian for some reason hallucinated Celeste's invitation, even as I explicitly warned him against barging in."

"Hey, don't embarrass me in front of the cute new girl," Julian said beside her, nudging her with his arm as we stepped into the hallway.

She patted his arm. "You did that all on your own." She then turned to me, pushing her black hair behind her shoulders. She was of beige complexion, and her hooded brown eyes glistened under her winged eyeliner. "You can ignore about 80 percent of what he says. But I'm not saying you're not pretty!" She quickly corrected herself, lifting her hands. "He has no filter. You'll learn soon enough. Anyway, I'm Rae Shimizu."

She shook my hand. I was mesmerized by her stylish studded and hooped ears. Two earrings stood out: the dark-blue crystal studs on both ears and the sterling dragon that hugged her right ear. Its tail pierced the second hole on her lobe, and three blue, triangular gems reflected on its many scales. Even her clothing was trendy— jeans, a baby-doll shirt with a jagged bottom, and a jacket. She had changed out of the black attire she had worn while dueling. She also eyed my attire and was now looking at my feet.

"Any particular reason you wear those shoes?" she asked, probably questioning their wear and other imperfections.

"Maybe you should ignore half the things she says," Julian said, his brown eyes friendly. His messy, long dirty-blond hair was cut at the sides and swept to one side. It was also so dark it almost looked brown, complementing his olive skin. He had changed his clothing too. A brick-red bomber jacket hugged his muscular but lean arms. He offered his hand. A thick leather bracelet with a red, diamond-shaped crystal encircled his wrist. He flashed a confident smile. "Julian Caballero at your service."

"I'm sorry," Rae apologized. "I realize how weird that sounds when you don't know me. Clothing is usually one of the first things I notice about people. My tip for the day is to consider wearing yellow. It would make your dark hair and blue eyes pop."

"Fashion is kinda her thing. You'll learn soon enough," Julian said, mimicking her.

I was both flustered and trying not to laugh at their friendly bickering. It was then I noticed how oddly their clothing complemented each other. She wore cool colors in shades of blue and white, while his were warm red and black hues. It was also strange how they introduced themselves with both their first and last names, but I went with it. "Orion Candor."

The awkward pause that followed was so quick I thought I imagined it.

"Okay, shall we start the tour?" Julian said.

Outside, off the training arena, tunnels with yellow brick walls and stone floors led to more rooms. It fascinated me how Rae and Julian knew every twist and turn as they explained how MISTIC operated. I imagined this was how a mouse felt lost in a maze. There were many rooms, including an archery range, some kind of obstacle course where someone swung between rings that dangled from the ceiling, a wrestling studio, a gym with weights, an archive room, and an area where a group huddled over a table looking like they were planning for an operation. As we moved through the tunnels, I noticed agents who passed by and stared at me. I wanted to believe they were just curious about the newbie, but I remembered what Celeste said about me being known here because of Corinne. Maybe I hadn't imagined the odd look Rae and Julian had given me when I told them my last name. I tried not to think about it by focusing on the tour.

"There are essentially five main roles in MISTIC," Rae explained, "Surveillance handles aerial stuff, like mapping, blueprints, and understanding the scope of landscapes from the inside out; Mission Captains train agents and are, well, the captains of our various missions; Fielders gather intelligence; Decoders decipher codes and puzzles, especially within the Isorian shadow market; and Profilers analyze intelligence and glean insights to help strategize the missions with Captains. Since you're not actually a full-fledged agent, you don't need to worry about any of that stuff. And that's pretty much the tour."

"It's incredible this is all underground," I said. "Thanks for showing me around."

She beamed. "Of course! So, now that we're done with the spy stuff, let's get to the real interesting stuff. Tell us about yourself. What element do you study?"

"Yeah, and what made you decide to join MISTIC?" Julian chimed in.

"Oh." I was caught off guard, not sure whether this was some kind of test or if they were genuinely interested in me. "I'm not enrolled in a school yet. My history is kinda complicated. I'm new to Isoria. That's why I'm training here."

We rounded a corner, almost bumping into someone. But not just anyone. Alec. I was about to greet him, but he didn't even notice me. His eyes narrowed at Julian, who returned the favor with an equally sharp glare and clenched fists. They seemed to be having their own silent feud, as if telepathically sending each other insults. Neither apologized as Alec disappeared down the tunnel. The interaction had happened quickly, but slowly enough I noticed there was more to the story than an accidental bump.

"Anyway," Rae said, moving on from the odd encounter. But Julian stayed silent, like he was still reliving it. "I'm sure Celeste is waiting for you at the arena. Let's get you officially initiated."

"I, Orion Candor, solemnly swear my undying allegiance to and understand my duties in the Magical Intervention Society for Tactical Intelligence and Combat, or MISTIC. I agree not to disclose or withhold any information, intelligence, or methods from MISTIC. I am familiar with the penalties for violation of this oath. I will faithfully protect and defend the realm of Isoria against all enemies."

Celeste's eyes drank me in as I struggled to write my signature under the oath with MISTIC's ceremonial ink and quill in a brown book with the blue griffin on the cover. The book contained every signature of the magi who'd put MISTIC and its cause before their lives. Celeste wore a satisfied smile and was about to leave me in the middle of the arena, but she paused with a hand on my shoulder.

"This world is a game of deception. Be sure you're playing," she warned in a tone that made my skin crawl. "But be careful how. Truth will prevail, and lies will be punished."

I awaited my first sorcery lesson on the blue griffin on the marble floor with Celeste's words underneath it: "Truth will prevail." I didn't like feeling threatened. Whether Celeste meant it that way or not, she'd left a haunting echo in my head, and questions swirled about her vague accusations toward Corinne. Regardless, I had pledged my loyalty.

Celeste had emptied the arena for my privacy. Alec and Banden could watch as they pleased, but Alec never showed, leaving me with Banden and Master Vera, my Earth teacher. She entered the room in dark-green robes matching the green highlights in her curly black hair. Her dark brown skin shimmered with freckles of silver glitter. When I thought of Masters, I pictured wrinkled old men with long gray beards, not the young, beautiful woman sauntering toward me.

"Master Vera. Pleasure." She offered her hand. Her eyelids were glossed with metallic silver and green, accentuating her caramel eyes.

I didn't properly greet her, distracted as I was by a stack of books levitating behind her. "I thought sorcerers studied the elements. How are you doing that?"

"Eager to start, are you?" she said and slowly lowered her hand toward the floor, the books following the motion. "Earth doesn't only mean rocks or dirt. It encompasses foliage, rock, dust, crystals, minerals, and metal. It deals with almost everything solid."

"What about ice? That's technically solid and liquid."

"I said almost everything. Terramancers can move or pick up ice, but only Aquatists can create, transform, and manipulate it. Got that, honey?"

I nodded, and she continued. "These books are your training tools. As sorcerers, we work with only the elements. You can't charm people or objects, like turn paper into a table or make someone fall in love. Unless you're an enchanter, like Banden."

"I thought he was a sorcerer?"

"He's a Bimedeis, meaning he's part sorcerer, part enchanter. They're extremely rare. Enchanters can cast enchantments and charms to something or someone through recitation. A sorcerer's magic is intuitive but requires practice. When performing a spell, you have to feel the element, like so."

She ushered me backward until we were both about ten feet away from the books. "I start with a target and then an intention, or vice versa. For this situation, it's the target. My target is the books, and my intention is to knock them over." She stuck her hands out as if she were telling someone to stop, and pushed them forward. "The final step is the hardest, which is to *feel* your target—the solidity, the matter, the mass. All of this can be accomplished through practice and listening to instinct. Concentrate, but don't overthink it."

Her hands pushed back and forth like waves, sending the books tumbling to the ground. She lifted her right hand, and without looking at the books, crooked her index finger. Pages rustled as the books restacked themselves.

She smiled. "You can't restack unless you study Earth. That's novice level, and you're learning basics. The further you progress with your studies, the more shortcuts you'll learn." With a swish of her right hand, the books toppled again.

"So, let's try it, shall we?" she suggested. She crooked her index finger to restack the tomes and stepped back to give me some space.

I thought of the fire and ice that had flown between Rae and Julian and tried not to sigh.

"Target, intention, feel," she recited.

Staring at the pile, I tried to ignore my audience—Banden, who sat on a chair in the far corner, and Vera, who watched intently. Trying to mimic Vera's movements with my hands, I attempted to "feel" the books. But I didn't feel anything. I frowned.

"Try again," she encouraged.

Target, intention, feel. But my concentration broke when a door quietly shut in the background. I glanced over my shoulder. Alec had come in and now stood next to Banden, arms crossed over his chest.

I stared at the books again, heat rising to my face as I thought of the green eyes now watching me. I took a deep breath and grounded my feet. This time, it felt as if solid matter was pressed against my palms, like I was touching the books—their mass, their solidity. Excited about my success, I moved my hands, feeling the hardness shift, but the books didn't fall. They *flew* across the floor.

"Okay, not bad," Vera commented with spirit and a hint of amusement. "Your first attempt was not enough power. Your second too much. It's all about control."

Concentrate but don't overthink it. Instinct. I tried again, but my instincts were telling me something different. *Target: books. Intention: knock books down. Feel: not the books but something around them.*

A light, cool sensation filled my palms and traveled down my fingertips, as if my flesh and bones were turning into air. Like when

I slammed the door on Banden, the night with the mysterious figure, and even not too long ago during Rae and Julian's duel, the inside of my body bounced like jelly beans. Holding on to this airy sensation, so natural and smooth, I followed Vera's motions. The cool sensation escaped my hands, and the books toppled to the ground, exactly as they had for Vera.

YES! I smiled at my victory but remained cool. I turned to Vera, whose eyes were wide, her mouth a thin line. Banden stood, and Alec uncrossed his arms, lips slightly parted.

"Huh," Vera mused like she was surveying a new plant species. "Interesting."

"What?"

"Do it again," she ordered, restacking the books.

I blinked, taken aback by the sudden edge in her voice. Despite my confusion, I did what she asked, exactly how I had before, feeling the air around the matter, the cool energy in my hands. The stack of books collapsed.

Vera hesitated as if searching for the right word. "Peculiar."

"Did I do something wrong?" I asked.

"Hun, you played with *Air*, not Earth. Impressive for someone who's never studied sorcery or that spell before."

"I . . . is that bad?"

"Let's try again. This time the way I taught you."

I did, despite my confusion. Searching for solidity rather than using the air felt forced and unnatural. Eventually, however, I successfully knocked them over with Earth.

For the next few hours, I trained with my three other teachers. Master Arnav, my Water teacher, was a little older than Vera. He was draped in a navy-blue robe and pushed his glasses up the bridge of his tan nose every time he spoke. He explained Water was obviously water but also ice, frost, snow, and almost everything liquid. He wanted me to spin water in a cauldron, but I felt the solidity of the pot, used to the Earth spell I had cast for Vera, or found myself feeling the air around it.

Master Katja was much older than Vera and Arnav. She wore the black robe with flames at the bottom I had seen her in earlier and had her brunette hair in a tight bun, revealing the entirety of her paper-white, pinched face. She spoke with a thick, unrecognizable accent, her chin held high with every word she uttered. Studying Fire meant learning about fire, laser rays, lava and magma, heat, explosions, and fireworks. She wanted me to feel the heat of a candle flame and slightly increase its size. But my mind saw those flames that horrible night. The excruciating heat and police sirens were tattooed on my senses. My hands shook when the heat crept up my fingertips. With fire, I saw only destruction.

Sensing my hesitation, Katja told me in her thick accent, "Emotions can affect a spell's performance. Fire, although intimidating, represents more than power. You're so focused on preventing injury that you're distracted from the spell. Yes, fire can be a bit stronger than the other elements, but each element has its strengths and weaknesses. Each can be used for good and bad. I see you using the other elements, Miss Candor. Once you accept Fire for what it is and that *you* are the one creating, manipulating, and controlling it, you will be free."

Air, as I suspected, was the easiest for me—and a therapeutic lesson compared to Katja's. Air encompassed wind, oxygen, gas, fog, and lightning. Master Samir had short, peppered hair, olive skin, wore a sky-blue and white robe, and had rings stacked on his fingers. It only took me two tries to blow feathers by casting a gentle wind. My first wind was too strong, but the second was perfect. Samir was astounded by my quick success.

"I must say, Miss Candor, you are doing phenomenally. One of the fastest students I've ever trained." He was soft-spoken and exuded a peaceful aura with a humbleness that made him appear a lot wiser than he let on. "I believe you're fit for Isoria Academy School of Sorcery."

"Isoria Academy?"

He nodded. "Oh yes. It's the most prestigious school a sorcerer can attend."

"Thank you, but I don't understand why."

He took my inquiry as modesty, or at least that's what I assumed since he smiled and turned to Banden, letting him know we were finished.

The hype from the day died down, leaving me exhausted and drained. I was surprised Banden and Alec had stayed for the entire training. Banden was smiling, but, of course, Alec remained expressionless.

Banden patted me on the shoulder. "You did shockingly well. A lot better than I expected."

"Thanks?"

"What I mean is, usually sorcerers who've never practiced spells struggle immensely with first-time training."

I was surprised, considering I thought I had done horribly, especially with Vera. Even the other elements had taken me awhile to cast.

"If you continue at this rate, we can enroll you in an academy sooner than predicted. Speaking of—you do need homework, but it's an easy read. Read chapter 20 in your spell book. Now, Alec will escort you home. Good work today, Orion. I'll see you tonight."

"How long is training going to last?" I asked.

"Depends on you. It can take as short as a month or as long as three."

My eyes widened. "All the spells you learn as a kid can be learned in a month?"

He nodded. "At a young age, a sorcerer's powers are weak. They're not at their full potential, so it takes longer for children to learn. There's also the obvious factors like comprehension and intelligence."

My life would have been easier had I grown up as a normal sorcerer. Because Mom had hidden this world from me, I was now an abnormal teenager *and* sorcerer. Did she know that Banden would help me and that my powers would act up once she left? Since my conversation with Celeste, I suspected there was more to this story than everyone was telling.

CHAPTER 6

I would have rather practiced more with Fire than traveled Isoria alone with Alec Stone, but I itched to see this storybook country. Banden had encouraged me to stay the night again, but I wanted to see if Mom had gotten in touch with me, and it sucked that technology was banned.

The square suede bag Banden had given me for my book jiggled against my thigh as Alec led me to the tunnel I had believed was my escape last night. I expected it to resemble the tunnel from the chamber to The Cave, but this one was more welcoming, as I should have expected from Banden. Dimly lit oil lamps hung from the gray brick walls, and ivy cascaded to the gravel floor. The walk was silent. Usually, I was fine without small talk when I first met people, but not with a sarcastic and cold stranger in a dark tunnel.

We reached a wooden staircase and climbed to the top, stopping in front of a door with a large tree engraved on it. Alec held his hand inches away from the wood, and a cloudy green light pulsed like a firefly beneath his hand. A trail of green followed his hand as he moved it in various directions. Soon the etched tree leaves turned a lime green, and the door swung open.

When we were both safely out of the tunnel, we turned when we heard a rumbling noise behind us. The door sat in the middle of a tree trunk split vertically in half. The two halves slammed together over the door, becoming one, and it was as if the door had never been there. I stared, wide-eyed, while Alec gently grabbed my forearm and pulled me away. I hated how his touch warmed my body and the security I felt when he stayed close to me. But extra security meant an extra threat.

I turned back around to see a sizable brown cottage made of stone and surrounded by a pasture, a small barn nearby. The cottage boasted a tall brick fireplace, a moss-blanketed roof, and leafy vines that webbed the exterior, as if the building had been abandoned and the earth was trying to grow over it.

"Banden has two houses?" I asked as Alec directed us through a black gate.

"You're not living in Isoria," he mumbled, but his tone made it feel more like an accusation.

I was too tired to start a fight, so I took the route of indifference. "His house is beautiful."

"Banden would be a plant if he could. He takes the *earth* in Earth sorcery too literally."

Maybe the funeral attire he wore daily indicated that he was mourning that he couldn't be a plant.

Alec led me through a village that reminded me of Crystal Manor, with its deserted cobbled streets and cottage shops and houses. They were bright and cheery, like Banden, and yet his house was the only dark color in a sea of hues of reds, blues, yellows, and greens. It felt like we were in a small European village somewhere in the Mediterranean, with terracotta roofs and little black balconies overflowing with vibrant flowering vines that hung from elegant railings. We crossed a bridge over a rolling stream, and a water wheel squeaked in the distance.

The night was still, and stars speckled the sky like glitter. The moonlight enhanced the outline of Alec's strong jaw, and his hair swooped upward as if blown by the wind. The crescent moon was reflected in his eyes under his furrowed brows. He looked so mature for his age. Too bad he didn't have a kind personality to go with his striking appearance.

"Where are we?" I asked, shifting my attention back to the colorful houses. I didn't know how anyone could get used to them, but Alec was clearly unaffected.

"Lightloch. Also known as the Rainbow City."

Tall torches lit the cobbled paths as we walked through a park with abandoned market tents. But something caught my attention. A shadowy figure lurked near one of the tents, half hidden behind a sheet hanging from a clothesline. As I looked more closely, the stranger's eye caught mine, and I backed into Alec, my scream sticking in my throat, reluctant as I was to disturb the still night. Alec steadied me, raising an eyebrow at my sudden anxiety.

A rider on a dark horse emerged from the hiding spot. The horse was decked in black tack, while his rider was wrapped, mummy-like, in black cloth with blue and gold streaks. His obsidian eyes watched us through the small slits in his mask.

"Don't bring attention to yourself," Alec whispered harshly, squeezing my arm. "Stop looking at him and keep moving."

The black steed snorted, pawing at the stones, and the rider's dark eyes met mine as I whipped my head around.

"Who is that?" I asked breathlessly, my heart rattling in my rib cage as I fought the urge to look over my shoulder. I could still feel the rider's eyes on us.

"A Royal Scout."

"What does he want?"

His eyes narrowed. "Trouble. Which you'll attract if you don't quit it. The last thing we need is to be thrown into King Leo's prison."

Everything happened in a blink. There was a rough tug on my shirt, and before I knew it, my knees and hands hit the cobbled road, my cheek inches from the cold stone as Alec forced me down. I thought he had attacked me until I saw the crystal shards of glass scattered about in front of us.

"Run!" Alec commanded, pulling me to my feet. He spun around and crossed his forearms in an X. A blanket of dirt materialized and hung like a curtain, shielding us from the cone-shaped rocks exploding before us.

The Royal Scout.

The horse reared up, and when its hooves came down again, the ground beneath our feet shook, turning our legs to Jell-O. The horse raced toward us as the rider squatted with his feet on the saddle. We jumped out of the way, the horse inches from us as it galloped past. The rider flipped through the air and slammed me to the ground, his hands around my neck. His masked face was inches from mine, his eyes hungrily gazing into mine.

I thrashed my arms and legs as the pressure from his hand threatened to snap my neck.

"He will not rest until he has what's rightfully his," the Scout hissed in an inhuman voice. "Give it to me!"

Suddenly, my assailant was off me and rolling onto the cobbled pavement, but I could still feel the choking grip around my neck as I hurriedly got to my feet. Alec was on top of him, pinning him to the ground.

"Stay away from her, Pawn!" Alec held an icicle-shaped rock inches from the skull of the rider, who hissed like the snake he was. "I stand corrected. *Chosen Shadow.*" Alec squeezed the rider's neck and slammed his head against the ground.

Pawn. A follower of the Obsidian King. Chosen Shadow. A mutated being.

"Free the magi. Poison the poison. The king will not rest until he has what's rightfully his."

"And you will rightfully die," Alec snarled as he bashed the rider's forehead with the icicle-shaped rock.

As the tip of the rock penetrated the rider's skull, red-and-black fluid oozed from his forehead and pooled around his head like a leaky pen. He screeched in agony as his body exploded into black dust and disappeared like fog.

Alec marched toward me, grabbing my arm and pulling me forward. "I need to get you home."

I was still shaking. "What the hell just happened?"

Alec kept a furious pace, like we were still being followed, and remained silent.

We crossed through a stone arch with a gold moon in the center. On the other side were two wooden signposts near the dirt path: Promenade Riders, the side we were on, and Flyers, on the right.

"Perfect timing," he said, looking down the dirt road. "We made the last carriage."

The sound of wheels on gravel grew louder as the silhouette of the wheeled conveyance appeared over the hill. The black coach had lanterns dangling from the top like Christmas ornaments and was driven by a coachman in a puffy shirt and vest. It halted in front of us.

Alec gave the coachman our destination, and the man grumbled in return, "Five isos for Avelin."

Alec pulled out a dark-brown pouch, handed a golden yellow bill to the coachman, then opened the door for me.

I crossed my arms. "Not until you explain what just happened!"

"Please, get inside the carriage," he said through gritted teeth.

"No."

He groaned, briefly looking at the sky as if searching for patience. "I'll tell you in a safer place. Will you please stop being so stubborn?"

The coachman looked over to see if we were in yet, and passengers already aboard threw us dirty looks. I relented and climbed into the carriage.

Inside, it smelled of flowers, wood, and sweat. There were eight passengers. A man in the back made room for us, but it wasn't out of politeness. He gave Alec a look before rolling his eyes in my direction as I plopped onto the velvet cushion next to the man. Although his glaring irked me, I kept to myself, afraid he might shoot a fire ball or something at me. I was still shaken.

A woman holding a basket of corn grumbled to the old man next to her. "Didn't know we were gonna ride with a Pawn Sniffer." They both gave Alec the stink-eye.

I wanted to ask him what the woman meant and why everyone in this carriage was staring at him, but he paid her no heed. So, instead, I leaned close and asked, "How is this carriage moving?"

"Enchanter magic," he said quietly. "Every carriage needs an enchanter to control it."

"And what are Flyers?"

"They're for traveling distances, but sometimes the richer folk use them for faster traveling. They're more expensive than Promenade coaches, which only travel by ground. Flyers are also for traveling to areas outside the realm."

"Like where?"

His eyes narrowed. "Has anyone ever told you that you ask a lot of questions?"

"Would you like me to ask you about the rider back there instead?"

I had spoken louder than I meant to. One of the travelers glared at me.

Alec glared at me, but whatever snappy remark he had thought of using died on his lips. "They go to sorcery schools and hidden magic locations around the world. And before you ask, Flyers are controlled by Aermages, but the carriage moves on a combination of enchanter magic and Air sorcery."

I wanted to ask him more about the schools, but the man next to the corn lady crinkled his newspaper, the bold print stealing my attention: "43rd Pawn Abduction! Kidnapping numbers rise since January." He folded the paper before I could read the rest.

It was ten minutes into the ride when the coachman called, "Avelin!"

Alec nudged me, and I followed him out into what looked like a terminal. Our carriage had pulled up behind another in a long line of carriages. People crowded around, waiting for carriages or exiting them. One carriage came hurtling down from the sky, almost bumping into a carriage in the Flyers line. It rocked from side to side as it landed, and the coachman called over his shoulder, "Sorry, folks!"

Alec led me down narrow cobbled paths that bustled like a metropolitan city. Medieval and some colonial-inspired tenements and shops pressed together, ununiform—all different shapes, sizes, and personalities. Alternating between gable and mansard roofs, many of the buildings had cottage-like exteriors made of decorative half-timbering, brick, stone, and stucco. Flags waved proudly from buildings. They were red on the left and blue on the right with a gold vertical stripe down the middle. Over the three colors were three white symbols respectively – a pegasus, a flower, and a griffin. The flower's disc florets were surrounded by long, flowing petals. Narrow streets led to the city's other districts. There were tents like the ones in Lightloch, although here, the merchants tried luring in the passersby. A man playing a lute at the base of a huge, three-tiered fountain and the laughter and chatter of civilians created a vibrant soundtrack.

"I see the stars in your eyes," Alec said, breaking me out of my reverie. I hadn't realized he'd been watching me. "Avelin may be pretty, but it has its dangerous side. Especially the east side. You must watch where you wander."

"That's like every city," I said, dismissively. "It doesn't mean I can't enjoy what I'm looking at."

I almost ran into a horse and rider, but Alec pulled me out of the way. I rolled my eyes at the stupid smirk he flashed me. In addition to the horseback riders, people zoomed by on bicycles but without pedaling, the wheels spinning on their own.

"Horses, bikes, but no cars?" I mused.

"Cars are ineffective," Alec responded. "Isorian horses are much more efficient for traveling the terrain here and are tougher and bred differently than horses in the nonmagus lands. They're natural mudders, climbers, runners, and swimmers. They're warriors."

Besides Isoria's fascinating modes of transportation, the eclectic fashion of the city was captivating. One girl wore jeans with thigh-high lace-up boots and a velvet corset top. There were flowy dresses, asymmetrically cut shirts, hoods, capes, bell sleeves, and lots of button- and lace-up attire. The men wore T-shirts and jackets with militaristic elements and jeans, joggers, boots, and peasant tops. The fashion could pass in the modern world—modern with a medieval flair. It was all so clean and put together.

But the city's enchantment vanished when I noticed more riders wrapped in black clothing with blue-and-gold stripes. Some walked the crowded streets while others hovered in the alleyways. People kept their heads down as they passed.

"Are you ever going to explain what happened back there?" I asked Alec. "Why are there Chosen Shadows everywhere?"

He surprised me by grabbing my hand and pulling me down an alleyway. He stood inches from me in the tight, dark space.

"Those are *not* Chosen Shadows," he said, his voice low. "They're Royal Scouts, King Leo's guards, specifically on the lookout for Pawns and Shadows." He then muttered, "Although they might as well be the same thing."

"But why was that Shadow dressed like a Scout?" I kept my voice as low as his.

"That's one of the methods they use to kidnap people."

My eyes widened. "You think the one in Lightloch was trying to kidnap us? Do they know we're a part of MISTIC?"

"Shh!" He put a finger to his lips, his eyes filling with fear. "Don't say that word so loudly."

"I'm talking as loudly as you are!" I said, although now I wasn't. I lowered my voice again. "What did he mean by giving him something?"

He shook his head. "I don't know. Just . . . be careful."

So much for MISTIC protecting me. Maybe Celeste thought Alec would be enough to do the job.

Alec guided me through the town before turning toward the dark woods. There, the crowd thinned, and lanterns hung on branches to light the forested path, easing my anxiety. But I was still on the lookout, peeking over my shoulder for any signs of a Chosen Shadow camouflaged as a bush or tree. A stone arch with a golden gate beneath it appeared at the end of the path, though not guarding or enclosing any property, as if someone had intended to build a fence but had given up.

Alec rubbed a silver ring with a dark-green crystal on his index finger, and light emanated from the arch. The gate swung open to reveal a swirling pink-and-white scene that reminded me of the Milky Way, the colors twinkling like stars and fairy dust. But the enchanting and inviting galaxy raised the hairs on the back of my neck. Was I about to enter a rabbit hole?

"Here we are," Alec said. "The portal away from New Jersey." He reached his hand toward me. "You'll have to hold on to me. You don't have a Clavis."

"A Clavis?" I asked, ignoring his hand.

"They open portals for sorcerers." He extended his hand farther toward me. "I promise I don't have cooties."

I hesitantly took it. "Am I going to lose you?"

"Only if you let go. It's one step away. I promise." He squeezed my hand. "Ready?"

I closed my eyes, and we walked into the luminous galaxy. But the light disappeared in one second. It was literally a step away. I was surprised Alec didn't laugh.

The portal, hidden on the outskirts of the woods, wasn't far from the pier. It was invisible to nonmagi, transparent to anyone who walked unknowingly through it. In an effort to keep nonmagus away from it, the woods didn't have hiking trails and housed poisonous Isorian plants that harmed only nonmagus skin. Alec didn't let me bike alone. He waved his hand over a boulder near the portal, and it disappeared to reveal a bike. He'd camouflaged the bike as a rock in case he needed to travel through Crystal Manor.

Though Crystal Manor was beautiful during the day, its quietness and deserted streets made it feel eerie at night. The pier looked as if an apocalypse had struck. The rides were gone, there were remnants of fallen tents, and garbage was strewn about on the ground. It had been a festival of autumn but a revelation of lies and secrets for me. I unchained my bike from the tree I had left it leaning next to.

Back in my bedroom, my mind swirled with images and conversations from the night as I looked through the emails on my laptop. I had received a message from Mom saying she had arrived safely in Europe and missed me already. She bragged about her new project, something about computer communications and gibberish I didn't understand. She also warned she was going to have a pretty busy schedule, and so our contact might be limited until she settled in. Her words boiled my blood.

How could my own mother keep me in the dark for so long?

My fingers pounded the keys, furious words streaming across the screen, blaming her for neglecting her daughter as she moved to a new country without knowing who she was and hiring a babysitter she barely knew who knew more about her than she knew about herself.

The malicious words on the screen blurred through my watery eyes. The cursor hovered over the Send button, but I took a deep, shaky breath, highlighted all the words, pressed Delete, and wrote, "How could you not tell me who I am?"

Maybe that's why I had never felt home anywhere. I didn't belong here. But home was still hard to find. Part of me wanted to return to my normal life, to pretend Isoria didn't exist. But I couldn't go back like nothing had happened, to try to blend in when I couldn't. I'd tried so hard to pretend nothing was wrong with me, thinking that if I remained invisible, my abilities would as well. But concealing them had only made them more glaring.

CHAPTER 7

My routine was the same for the next two weeks. Alec continued to babysit me, walking me from my house to The Cave for training. His sarcasm had dimmed, but I had laid off with Twenty Questions and kept our travels silent. It was the same script every day: I'd meet him outside my house, he'd ask if I was ready, I'd ask about his day, he'd reply with one-word answers like "Fine" or "Lovely," then exchange by asking about my trainings since he never stayed for them.

I once made the mistake of asking him to elaborate on "lovely," and that was when his snarkiness was resurrected. "*Lovely*, by definition, means 'grand or swell,' or 'exquisitely beautiful.' I assume you're competent enough to select the correct definition for this context."

"Thank you, Dictionary," I had grumbled, trying not to take it personally.

Banden came to every training session. He would plant himself in his little corner and come up with homework assignments for me based on the lesson. For one of my lessons, I learned that within the different levels of magic, the more in-depth you studied the elements, the more complicated the spells became. And the more you practiced, the stronger your powers became, like working a muscle. You could also cast spells for an extended period since you'd increase your energy and power strength. And certain spells depleted a sorcerer's energy, or stamina, more than others.

"Because my powers are out of control, does that mean my stamina's on steroids?" I had asked Banden one time as we walked through the tunnels.

Alec snorted, surprising me. I never thought I'd get a chuckle from him. Banden's eyebrows furrowed, clearly not understanding my humor. "I don't see how that's possible considering nonmagus drugs don't affect sorcerers the same way they do nonmagi."

"What about alcohol?" I asked, not that it should matter. The closest I'd ever come to drinking alcohol was the occasional sip of Mom's dinner wine.

Another snort from Alec. "I can tell you from experience that it does not affect us any differently."

"And the drinking age is eighteen in Isoria. Should I remind you?" Banden warned, eyeing him. "Bring up this conversation again in two years on August 13."

He smirked. "As you know, Banden, I'm a raging partygoer."

Banden rolled his eyes but smiled. It was weird seeing Alec joke around and to know he had emotions.

I'd see Rae and Julian too. Our conversations had started with a friendly wave and small talk about my training until we'd become more comfortable with one other and I'd learned more about them with every new conversation. I discovered they both attended Isoria Academy, the school Samir recommended for me. Rae was an Aquatist and studied at Aquium, the Water school. Julian was an Incendor, and studied at Ignair, the Fire school.

"How did you get into such a prestigious school?" I had asked them. "I heard it's difficult."

"I'm a legacy," Rae admitted guiltily. "But I still worked hard. You have to show you're up for the challenge. Otherwise, legacies are overlooked."

"And I'm a genius." Julian pointed to his chest. "Kidding. But the headmaster was impressed with my IEPE results."

"How did you choose your element of study?" I asked. It was like selecting a college major, which I didn't even know what I wanted yet. If college was even an option for me anymore.

"Water always interested me, and I come from a line of Aquiums," Rae explained. "And the spells are awesome. I also got Water as my top element on the test. So I guess it's natural to me."

"Mine was a little more stressful than dear Rae's." Julian gave her a look, and she rolled her smoky-eyeshadowed eyes. "I had no idea. In the end, I chose the element that was the least compatible for me, which was Fire. So I study at Ignair."

My eyes widened. "The test can be inaccurate?"

"Yes and no. For some reason, seeing Water as my top element and Fire as my lowest made me want to explore it. And I'm glad I did. It was one of the reasons Headmaster Iceflyn was impressed with me. I wasn't planning on applying for the academy, but he asked me to consider it."

I had also learned Rae wanted to own her own boutique one day in the nonmagus lands. She was a self-taught designer, and her dream was to bring a bit of Isorian flare to nonmagus fashion. I didn't doubt her ability. Every day, she looked like she was going to walk the streets of NYC. She tended to wear dark-blue, light-blue, white, and beige colors. According to her, Aquatists wore those colors, but sometimes she would wear other colors, like black or green, in the name of fashion. Regardless, her edgy and chic style was always on point.

Julian, on the other hand, wasn't sure about his future, but he liked volunteering for MISTIC and shared Celeste's vision of the organization becoming an official spy network for Isoria, working side by side with the king. He explained that his father and his brother, Stefano, both had or currently worked in Isorian law enforcement, so he shared their passion of serving the country in some way.

I didn't know what I had done or how it had happened, but we were . . . friends. Julian's harmless teasing and peppy personality initiated plenty of eye rolls but many smiles. Rae had this girly yet edgy demeanor, like you thought you could steal a purse from her but she'd turn around and stab you with a dagger. I was grateful for them, but something told me Alec didn't feel the same. Whenever he came to pick me up after my training, he kept his distance as I conversed with them. I could swear his scornful looks weren't due to impatience at having to walk me home but rather from indignation at my new friends. Another mystery to feed my curiosity.

On top of the training and navigating my new magical life, the mysteries surrounding Corinne were always on my mind. I couldn't ask Mom about her. I still hadn't heard from her. She either hadn't seen my message or was ignoring it, although she had said she wouldn't be in contact for some time. Banden gave me vague answers whenever I asked him about her, or he would change the subject. It didn't help that the agents would stare at me whenever I was at The Cave. It could very well be that they were checking out the newbie, but my gut told me it had more to do with Corinne's reputation.

The beast in my powers had finally been tamed—hopefully. Exercising them seemed to restrain their erratic behavior, much like a wolf on a leash. My spell performance increased dramatically, and the Masters couldn't conceal their awe. I could cast gusts of wind and knock over lightweight objects or levitate them, which Samir said was advanced. I could create small waves and water ripples, and I perfected mini water tornadoes in cauldrons. Earth was my second-most difficult element, but I could move, lift, and throw small objects. Fire was still a battle. It represented both strength and destruction. Fire had stolen my home and given Obsidian power over Westwin. Regardless of my fears regarding this element, I had graduated from the candle spell, and my recent project was to create small flames on torches. Soon it became muscle memory. Banden had said it could take a month for me to learn the basics, but after the two-week mark, my teachers believed I was ready for the IEPE. They couldn't believe a sorcerer with my lack of experience had excelled so quickly. I had learned the basics in half the time it normally took.

But for some reason, Banden didn't seem to share my Masters' enthusiasm. He seemed either alarmed or incredulous. I was surprised, too, feeling as if I was either not being challenged enough or the Masters were being way too easy on me. But Banden made me feel it was wrong to be successful. Since when was being a quick learner a bad thing?

On that last day of training, Celeste had watched to see if my Masters had been correct about my advanced training. She wore her skintight clothing, ankle-length jacket, and thin chain, and stood with her arms crossed, her shrewd eyes on me. She made me feel small, which made me want to prove myself. And I did.

"Congratulations, Miss Candor. You are ready," Arnav commended.

"Damn, Miss Candor," Vera praised. "You're the quickest learner I've ever taught."

Katja smiled. "Fire will learn to fear you."

"You have a bright future ahead of you, Miss Candor." Samir didn't have to tell me how he felt. The way his eyes lit up and he smiled whenever I successfully passed his lessons was enough.

"Thank you, Master." I beamed.

But his smile fell, and his eyes were darker than usual. "Swans. Beautiful creatures, but they conceal aggression. The swan flaunts its appearance, not its power."

I blinked. "Sir?"

"You are gifted, Orion, so gifted that envious eyes are watching you. We only know what others let us see. Be a swan. Know who's a swan." He gave me a tight smile and a small nod before exiting the arena after Celeste.

CHAPTER 8

Avelin, the capital of Isoria, had its usual bustle, but it wasn't overwhelming as most cities but more like a town fair. It was clean, charming, and not too noisy. Isorians minded their own business, especially when passing the Royal Scouts who were visible in the streets but also hid in the shadows, like private detectives following hunches.

After Rae and Julian found out I had officially graduated from training, they wanted to take me out to celebrate at this supposedly famous café in Avelin. It was located at the corner of a strip mall, its French stone exterior webbed with ivy. A wooden sign with stars around a mug read, "The Enchanted Mug."

The dimly lit oil lamps and candles along the stone walls sedated the atmosphere. A wooden candle chandelier hung from one of the ceiling's many beams. Giant beige paper menus were nailed to the walls behind the front counter. An ancient, giant tree with twisted bark was planted in the center of the café, and glowing blue ornaments hung from glorious green branches that touched the ceiling. Isorians occupied the scattered sofas and tables, drinking or playing games like chess and cards, while a table of four tried levitating their coffee mugs. In the back stood a small wooden stage where a deep-voiced woman strummed a cello and hummed into a pink flower on a vine that acted like a microphone.

We chose a table by the fireplace, and a man in a white button-down shirt and black velvet pants greeted us and handed out menus made of thick hemp paper tied to wooden boards with leather strings.

"Are you guys hungry?" Julian scanned the menu. "I'm starving."

Even if I was, I didn't know what Dragon's Breath Soup, Stevia Sweet Stew, Berry Veggie Sandwich, Mermaid Molten Cake, or Rokesha Volcano Cookie were.

I set the menu down. "I'm okay."

The man in the button-down approached us again. "Can I get you anything?"

"Three RNPs for the table, please," Rae answered for us. "And the house sandwich for him."

She pointed to Julian, who responded, "Aw, you know me so well."

When the waiter left, I turned to Rae. "What did you order for me?"

"A Red Nugget Pick-Me-Up, or RNP. It's basically a chocolate drink with a hint of strawberry and coffee flavors, but it's not too sweet. You'll love it."

"Wait until you try them spiked." Julian winked.

"Two more years for the both of us, then we'll be legal. But they do taste better that way," she agreed.

"I can't wait to eat." Julian leaned back in his chair, his biceps popping as he crossed his arms behind his head.

"You always want to eat." Rae rolled her cat-eyeliner eyes before turning to me. "How've your powers been, Orion? Still giving you trouble?"

With everything going on, the thought hadn't crossed my mind. I had told them of the weird experiences I had with them: exploding before Banden when I first moved in, the mysterious figure, and during their performance evaluation. Julian had smiled and responded, "Nice!" because apparently it was badass.

I shrugged. "Now that I think about it, ever since I started training, they've been manageable. I've impressed my teachers."

She raised an eyebrow. "What do you mean?"

The waiter arrived, levitating three stainless-steel mugs and a plate. With a flick of his wrist, the three mugs slid perfectly in front of us, followed by Julian's meal. It looked like any ordinary sandwich but with questionable condiments. The sweet aroma of chocolate greeted my nose as steam rose from the dark-brown liquid in front of me.

"Trust me, it's amazing," Rae assured, grabbing her mug. "You were saying?"

I took a small sip, the semi-creamy liquid warming my body like a cozy blanket. It was a wonderful blend of fruity and chocolatey, the perfect comfort drink on a chilly night. I traced the star engraved on the metal mug. "Everyone's shocked by how quickly I learned the spells. Although, I'm having some trouble with Fire. But other than that, they're pretty easy."

She almost choked, her eyes going wide. "Pretty easy? And you said you've never had experience with magic before?"

I shrugged. "I've always had my powers, but I've never practiced any spells. It's elementary stuff. It's supposed to be easy."

"No, not really," Julian mumbled through a mouthful of bread. "Yeah, it's easy stuff, but it still takes time."

"I guess I'm a quick learner."

"Maybe," Rae entertained the thought, although she didn't sound convinced. She shrugged.

I found myself observing the café. It was as if I had entered a storybook, though it clashed with customers' modern clothing; their jeans and sweaters could easily pass in the nonmagus lands. It was also funny thinking about the now-useless cell phone in my back pocket. Nonmagi would definitely Instagram this place.

"So, how do people communicate in Isoria if cell phones don't work?" I asked.

Rae answered, "There are several ways, but the most popular is through Reflection Messaging. It's basically video messaging. You think of who you want to contact while touching any reflective entity, like mirrors, water, or windows, and the receiver will be contacted. But only an enchanter can send a message through any reflection anywhere, so sorcerers buy portable mirrors or glass that have already been charmed by an enchanter, like a compact mirror."

She reached into her bag and pulled out a compact mirror with blue resin and blue and silver abalone shell pieces on the cover.

"Interesting. And why's everything here, like, old but modern at the same time? Like a king trying to rule another king is stuff I learned in nonmagus schools."

Julian brushed the crumbs off his hands. "You ask some weird questions, initiate."

"She's still new to all this, Jul. Have some empathy," Rae chided as she tossed her black hair behind her shoulders. It was sleeker than usual today, like a model on a runway. "Don't worry. I was shocked by it too. I don't live in Isoria, unlike Julian. Well, he dorms at Ignair."

"Any opportunity to be as far away from home as possible," Julian mumbled as if he were talking to himself rather than to us.

"I live in Crystal Manor, like you," Rae ignored Julian. "It's a sanction."

"Sanction?" I asked.

"A town or city located in the nonmagus lands but owned by Isoria. It's for magi who want to live among nonmagi. And Sanctors, Isorians who represent and live in sanctions, help you follow the laws of both Isoria and the nonmagus lands. Sanctions are all over the world. They're the only way you can portal to Isoria. But not all sorcerers live in sanctions. I know there are at least seven in Japan. My father lived in one, while my mother lived close to one. What about Italy and Ecuador, Julian?"

Julian shrugged. "Never came up in conversation with my parents."

"Essentially, it's different around the world."

"So, Crystal Manor is full of magi?" I asked.

She tilted her head to the side. "Not *filled* with. I recognize whoever I've seen around Isoria. Another way to tell is if they're wearing their Clavis." She grabbed her earlobes to show me her dark-blue crystal studs, while Julian pulled up his sleeve to reveal the leather bracelet he had worn when I first met him. "Both of our colors represent the school we study at. But there are ten academies around the world."

"Isoria is the way it is because it's the way it is." Julian shrugged. "It just kinda works. King Leo is the only person in Isoria with the ability to take away a sorcerer's or enchanter's magic. The Bellstemour-Confeld royal family has been in power for centuries because of this. But he can only take away someone's magic if they commit a horrible crime or are caught performing illegal spells, as outlined in Isoria's Code of Law."

"There's also the United Royal Imperium, the governing body that works beside King Leo," Rae added. "It ensures Isorians are heard and works with the king to make sure his power isn't abused. However, he has the final say in anything. He also chooses what to focus on since it's impossible to oversee every little thing that happens. The Isorian Royal Court is also located in the Imperium."

I nodded. "Got it. And Cyril Obsidian wants this power?"

"That's what MISTIC's still trying to solve. We theorize he wants complete domination of Isoria and has convinced his followers to believe they're oppressed by King Leo somehow. Whenever someone encounters a Chosen Shadow, they hiss: 'Free the magi. Poison the poison.'"

My eyes widened. That's exactly what the Chosen Shadow who had attacked me in Lightloch screamed.

She continued. "But we still don't know what's motivating him and what his plans are. One intel suggests he plans to expand the electric shield protecting his fort over other Isorian villages and cities, one by one."

"And no one knows how to destroy this shield?" I asked.

Julian shook his head while picking at the crumbs on his plate. "We think it's a combination of Air sorcery and enchanter magic, but it also possesses magic Isorians have never seen. It's indestructible as far as we know. Our intel speculates it was created by an enchanter or Bimedeis who goes by the name of The Maker. They invent and enhance magical items—from magical trinkets to weapons—for Isorians. Apparently, it's all legal, but it's possible The Maker also works for the Isorian shadow market, an underground market Pawns use to deliver high-grade weapons and illicit magical objects to Obsidian's army. The Maker works through referrals only, and no one knows who they are because their identity is always hidden. MISTIC doesn't even know how to contact them. But again, it's all speculation."

No matter how much time I spent in Isoria, everything about this world felt unreal. Yet here I was, in this enchanting café drinking an RNP with two people who were a part of it. And now, so was I.

"Isoria is ruled by fear and motivated by deceit," Rae continued quietly. "Deception is more than survival. It's a method to obtain power. Many walk with knives behind their backs. You never know who's going to hand you over to the enemy or turn you in as the enemy."

"We're tired of being defenseless," Julian half-whispered. "Joining MISTIC was a way to do something about it. No one knows how Obsidian attained his power or what dark or illegal magic he exchanged his soul for. We want to put an end to it. You can't complain about the way things are if you're not willing to make a change."

"What kind of . . . missions do you usually handle?" I asked.

"Since we're still in training, we're given low-risk assignments," Julian answered in the loudest voice he dared. "Such as stalking people." He smirked, tipping his chair back. "Observing people, gathering and reporting intelligence, dead drops, and watching for suspicious activity for Pawn-catching or for smugglers in the shadow market. Things like that."

"Especially the shadow market," Rae chimed in. She pushed Julian's chair forward, and he flew into the table, glowering at Rae as she giggled.

I shifted in my seat, unsure how they'd react to what I was about to ask. With Banden and Celeste being so secretive about my past and Corinne, I was afraid I'd get the silent treatment or some vague answer from them as well.

"So, my grandmother, Corinne, was involved with MISTIC," I said, keeping my tone indifferent. "Do you guys know what missions she took on and what her role in the organization was?"

They hesitated, confirming my suspicion that they knew something I didn't.

"Well, we never met her, but you deserve to know . . ." Rae bit her lower lip, then leaned toward me. "MISTIC, um, they kinda hate her and are thankful she's gone. They think she's a traitor and the reason Obsidian knows about them."

My eyes widened, remembering what Celeste had told me that day in her office. She had hoped Obsidian thought the organization that sought his demise was led by the king.

Julian nodded. "Apparently, trouble started once Corinne joined. We don't know the entire story, but apparently she was a double agent and became one of Obsidian's most trusted allies. She's the reason we know a lot of what we know about Obsidian now, but"—he looked over his shoulder, scanning for eavesdroppers before continuing—"there's a lot of rumors surrounding how Obsidian knows about MISTIC. Some think Corinne was caught, while others think she intentionally told him about us and joined his cause. Either way, Obsidian discovered this, and his game began. They believe she's the catalyst for the increase in Pawn kidnappings, which, coincidentally, have risen since her death. Our intel says that one of Obsidian's motives is to find and destroy us, obviously."

"But how's that possible?" I asked in disbelief. "Why would Banden be friends with a traitor, or Celeste, the ringleader?"

He shrugged. "They think she's innocent, or at least Banden's convinced Celeste she is."

I couldn't see Banden remaining friends with a traitor. He was like that wise, grandfatherly figure who innately knew right from wrong. Although, I didn't *really* know him, and they had been childhood friends. *Was* Corinne the catalyst for this reign of terror?

Everyone was telling me who to trust, but anyone could be planning to feed me to the enemy. And make my friends my enemies.

CHAPTER 9

After our night out at the café, I invited Rae and Julian over. They were intrigued with the place Corinne had called home.

We arrived at an empty house since Banden usually didn't come home until around seven or eight. They didn't seem that impressed as I showed them around. In Julian's words, this house was "Well, kinda lame for Corinne."

"Well, there's one more room I haven't shown you yet," I said, guiding them to the library doors. I pushed them open and turned on the light, presenting the gorgeous, curious room. I hadn't been in the library since I'd moved in.

Julian's eyes widened. "Oh, yeah, this is what I was expecting." He immediately headed to the mural, Rae joining him.

I found myself at Corinne's portrait. The longer I stared at it, the more I felt like I might have known her, or maybe I was seeing Mom in her. Except Corinne looked like she belonged in the 1920s. Her hair was shorter than Mom's, and her high cheekbones and strong chin contrasted with Mom's softer features. Her painted eyes were also much sharper, and the more I stared into them, the more lies I could see. It was even evident in the way her hand rested beneath her necklace and over her heart, like she was swearing to never reveal her secrets.

That's when I noticed how the rest of her fingers were curled as her index finger pointed to the red pendant. It was so subtle, so innocent, I wouldn't have paid attention to the small, faint black lines. They could have been mistaken as shadows, but they blurred together, creating a shape I had seen in this library. A lion.

I grabbed the silver lion figurine from the desk and turned it in my fingers. There was nothing unusual about it.

I searched every inch of the desk, then tried the fireplace. I went bookcase by bookcase, scanning the shelves for books on lions. Finally, I saw something the other shelves didn't have.

A wooden circle pedestal was tightly screwed to one of the shelves, acting as a separator, with four little holes carved in the wood. I aligned the lion's feet with them, and the figurine fell right into place. A clicking sounded, and the pedestal lifted an inch from the shelf. There was a final click, and the bookcase popped out from the wall.

If Rae and Julian had been paying attention to me before, I hadn't noticed until now. They both jumped around, eyeing me and the open bookshelf.

"Um, what just happened?" Rae asked.

"I swear I just touched the fireplace," Julian said, removing his hand from the mantel.

"It's okay. I did it," I said, equally shocked.

They came over to me as I pulled on the bookshelf, opening the door until a small dark room was revealed. From what I could see, there was only a desk and chair. I turned on my cell phone's flashlight and shone it on the dusty desk. It was scattered with sketches and handwritten documents.

"What in the world?" I said, reaching for the documents.

"Definitely Corinne's house," Julian said, looking over my shoulder as I sifted through the delicate papers, searching for meaning within the words and images.

One phrase had obviously haunted the owner of the documents. It was scribbled repeatedly around the sketches of architecture and nature: *At midnight, it will show. One is the final hour. Find it before they do.*

It was written in bold letters on one document, on another in quotes with numerous question marks, and underneath a sketch of a book with the phrase "How does this correlate??"

Within the pile of scribbles and haunting images lay a torn envelope with a letter written in different handwriting.

I hope you find this,

On days like this, I think about my time at Ignair and how it taught me the value of relationships. Rector Yee has seen me in his office more times than I can count the stars in the sky. I will never forget the times of falling asleep in Professor Ryleigh's class, and before he switched schools, Ozzy throwing paper at me to keep me awake. Or those times spent in the Mermaid's Tail Tavern with Zee, using our female charm on the sucker bartenders for free, wasted nights. Never forget sneaking into Ignair's Underground Training Arena completely drunk while playing hide-and-seek out behind the volcanic rocks. Free to do as you please is a privilege, and my freedom got the best of me. It upset me that Ozzy and Zee never understood why I decided to stop goofing off and focus on my studies. No friend should judge success. Done as I was, I tried salvaging what was left, but, sadly, had to leave. Many people come into our lives for good and bad, but there is always reason and lessons to be learned. Everyone learns, and I wonder if I ever will.

Please stop following me. Without trust, there is no love. And I loved by trusting the most mistrusted. I know too many who know too much. Time is a luxury for me. I cannot finish this journey, but you can. Please, I beg you, keep what you find to yourself, including this note. You are your friend. This world's war is built on subterfuge and foul play. Your allies could be enemies, and sometimes those you most trust are ruthless actors. My findings will lead you to the truth. Please follow my words. Without a leader, there are no followers. The first is only what you need after every period. Follow the leader.

—Cori

I read each sentence with a raised brow. Each sentence made less sense, some displaced, grammatically incorrect, or having no relation to the previous one. A small note slipped out behind the letter with handwriting that matched that of the sketched images, a *familiar* handwriting with strikethroughs on each line:

B—

~~She did this. She made everything worse. I'm scared for my daughter's life. This object—I'm sure Corinne destroyed it when she died. Or at least, I'm hoping. The king will not rest till he finds justice. Till he destroys what will destroy him but save us all.~~

"What does all this mean?" Rae asked, but I barely heard her.

"We may be spies in training, but we ain't Decoders," Julian said, sifting through the documents with Rae. "We're both training to be Fielders—you know, the physical stuff."

She did this. She made everything worse. That was my mother's handwriting. B must be Banden. If Corinne was "she," that meant "Cori" had to be Corinne. Celeste was right. Corinne *had* been hiding something.

I'm scared for my daughter's life.

I was in trouble with a world I hadn't known existed.

"I . . . I think Cori is Corinne and the other note was written by my mother," I said, trying to wrap my head around everything.

There were sketches of unicorns dancing around rocks, a circle of books encompassing a lion head with its mouth open wide, a scepter resting over a book, and a pendant with a swirl. *At midnight, it will show. One is the final hour. Find it before they do.*

My mind spun. What object was Mom talking about, and did it have anything to do with Celeste's interrogation about Corinne's secretive life? Why had she crossed out the words in her note to Banden? Were her speculations incorrect, or did she decide not to send the note to him? Did he know about this room? Were these drawings hers or Corinne's?

"Or maybe she figured it out and you should heed her warning." Rae looked up from the documents, her brown eyes sharp. "If she and Banden are hiding something, it's probably for your own good that you don't find out."

"Agree to disagree, Sun-Rae,'" Julian countered. "Seems sketchy."

"Shut up. You know I hate when you call me that." She smacked him on the arm. "We should stay out of this. We don't know what kind of trouble Orion's family got themselves into. It seems like she was in cahoots with King Leo. She said 'the king.' And whatever 'object' she's talking about, she thinks it's destroyed. So it's probably resolved."

"Always the voice of reason."

"Someone has to be."

"No," I whispered, things finally clicking. If Banden was right about Mom being fearful of Isorian politics, he had to be referring to the Siege of Westwin. And according to my friends, Corinne might be the reason Cyril Obsidian, or the Obsidian King, as Celeste had said he liked to call himself, was suspicious of an opposing intelligence ring. And maybe that's why Alec and I were attacked in Lightloch by that Chosen Shadow who had hissed, *He will not rest until he has what's rightfully his. Give it to me!* Did Obsidian think *I* had the object?

I swallowed. "I don't think she means King Leo."

Their heads turned.

"What do you mean?" Rae raised an eyebrow.

"'The king will not rest till he finds justice. Till he destroys what will destroy him but save us all,'" I read aloud. "I think she means the Obsidian King."

Julian whistled. "Well, good job, initiate. Celeste will love this."

"No, we can't!" I exclaimed, suddenly panicked. "Corinne clearly warned us not to share these documents with *anyone*."

"Orion, we all took the oath when we joined MISTIC," Rae said, crossing her arms. "No secret is to be withheld from the organization. We put Isoria and its people before us."

"Truth will prevail," Julian added. "Which also means—"

"Lies will be punished," I finished, repeating Celeste's words. "I know. But everyone is being so secretive with me, so who's to say they would let me in on their discoveries? Even my own mother." I tried to hold in the panic, anger, and frustration. I had to get in contact with her. "And technically, I said I would bring intelligence to MISTIC, not Celeste. You guys are MISTIC."

"Although I admire your ingenuity, Orion, it's still *treason*," Julian reiterated, his smiley tone vanishing.

I inched closer to the documents, ready to grab them in case I needed to run. "Celeste and Banden know something I don't. If they find out I know about this, they'll do anything to keep me away."

"Yeah, because you'll be executed!" Rae waved her hands and stepped toward me. "This is dangerous. If this object can destroy Obsidian, MISTIC *needs* to know."

"We're only assuming things here. We don't really know what these documents mean."

She crossed her arms. "It's a bit strange Corinne's warning your mother not to share these notes with anyone. What 'truth' did she need to conceal? How to destroy Obsidian?"

"And given her reputation with MISTIC and how *she* might be the reason Obsidian found out about an intelligence ring . . ." Julian added.

"Look, you have to admit something strange is going on," I argued. "If Celeste honestly believed Corinne was a traitor, why would she speak so highly of her? Why would Banden? Either something isn't adding up or we're all missing part of the story."

Rae and Julian had a silent conversation with their eyes, and although I was pushing them to withhold this intel from MISTIC, I shared their doubt. If this information was the key to saving the realm, why hadn't Corinne shared it with Celeste in the first place?

You are your friend. What had happened that she had such distrust?

Julian put a finger to his chin. "You know, there *is* talk of a mole within the organization. It might be smart to do our own investigating and confirm this is real intelligence before we start spreading rumors that could potentially help the double agent."

"And if we're caught with these documents, MISTIC will suspect us," Rae countered.

"They won't leave this room," I resolved.

She thought about it before uncrossing her arms. "Fine. But, Orion, you have to make us a deal. Our loyalty isn't to Celeste. It's to the people of Isoria. We promise we won't tell Celeste if you promise to turn these documents in if we confirm they can be used against Obsidian. We understand the risks. You have our word." She raised her hand.

"We promise." Julian mirrored Rae. "Do you?"

I was grateful to Julian for convincing Rae, but if we were caught, I silently promised to leave my friends out of it.

"I promise," I said, hoping they couldn't hear my hesitance.

My eyes then caught something past Rae—the paper with the two unicorns surrounded by rocks. I had seen unicorns somewhere before besides all over Isoria. Looking at the document from a distance gave me a new perspective. I blinked multiple times, making sure I wasn't imagining it.

The rocks seemed to be randomly placed around the unicorns, but they actually fell in an intentional direction. They were scattered and close together, all different sizes that anyone would lose themselves in the details and oversee the hidden shape they formed—a number one. The first step. You needed the first step in any treasure hunt. It was that first step that set the journey in motion. Everything fell into place afterward.

And I *had* seen unicorns before. I ran out of the room to the fireplace, crouching down to examine the different rocks. Two ferocious stone unicorns reared on either side, each wearing thick necklaces. The necklace on the unicorn to my left had an empty oval shape where a pendant should be while the other's oval was jagged, creating a familiar shape.

"Orion, why are you molesting the fireplace?" Julian stepped out of the room with Rae.

She gave him a look. "Make better word choices, Jul. Orion, what's going on?"

I barely heard them. My head whirled as the pieces fell into place. Where had I seen this shape?

"Yikes," Julian interrupted my thoughts. "Don't take this the wrong way, Orion, but this painting is mad creepy,"

The portrait. I wanted to keep Banden out of this, but he had the missing piece.

My eyes darted to the jagged shape hanging from the unicorn's neck. "We need Corinne's Clavis."

CHAPTER 10

My IEPE was scheduled for Saturday morning, but I didn't feel ready. Everyone's praises should have boosted my ego, but I felt discouraged.

That Friday, the day after the library discovery, I had waited for Alec to take me to Banden's. I was sleeping there that night since my test was early the next day. Accepting his sleepover invitation worked in my favor. I needed to retrieve Corinne's necklace. I thought I had understood what Master Samir meant when he'd said, *Be a swan. Know who's a swan.* It wasn't far off from Celeste's warning: *Be sure you're playing.*

I spent the day in that secret room, magnetized to the documents, obsessed with deciphering the notes and solving the puzzle. There was no denying it; this was intelligence. If I was caught concealing these documents from MISTIC, I had agreed to the punishment. I'd never fathomed I would actually possess intel. I emailed Mom again, texted her, even tried calling, but it was useless. She wouldn't admit to any of this, and it was easier for her to ignore me since she was across the globe.

It was evening when I heard a knock on my front door. I opened it to find Alec waiting in his usual spot against the brick.

"Miss me?" His eyebrow arched. My stomach lurched, and I hated myself for it. He shoved his hands into his jean pockets, his chest muscles bulging underneath his maroon T-shirt. His unzipped brown jacket flapped in the chilly wind, and I tried to ignore how the color brought out the green in his eyes.

I rolled my eyes. "It was peaceful, actually."

He smirked before grabbing his bike. My snark never bothered him as much as his bothered me. He always found a way to laugh at my sarcasm, like he didn't take me seriously, which only boiled my blood more.

We traveled in silence. Once we made our way through the portal, our pace slowed. As usual, I watched the Royal Scouts as we made our way through the crowded streets. *She was even hiding from it herself.* So much work and hard training for the IEPE, all to be part of this dangerous world.

"I have a question." I tried keeping my voice level.

Alec rolled his eyes. "Just one?"

I fought the urge to snap back. "What's the test like?"

He smirked. "There's your charming curiosity."

"And what's that supposed to mean?" I couldn't tell if he was intrigued or annoyed. I hated how ambiguous he was.

"It means you drive me crazy," he muttered.

"Like you're the easiest person to be around," I snapped. I could ignore *some* of his rude remarks, but sometimes he was downright obnoxious. Who'd raised him? "I say one word and you default to insulting me. I never know with you."

His head whipped around. "You're Banden's responsibility. I'm only his messenger. Bother him."

I wanted to punch him. He was ruthless. He could be miserable in his life, but he wasn't allowed to use me as an excuse for his misery.

"You know, I've done nothing to you." I jumped in front of him, stopping him in his tracks. "Why are you such a jerk?"

"Don't bother me," he answered like it was the obvious solution. "It's simple."

"With pleasure. And while I'm at it, I'm telling Banden I don't want you escorting me through Isoria anymore. No reason to torture us both."

I distanced myself from him as we crossed the busy streets. But when I wasn't in step with him, he'd glimpse over his shoulder and stop so I could catch up, only for me to zoom past him. If it weren't for the money, I would have taken a Promenade without him.

His heavy sigh was audible over Avelin's cacophony. He quickened his pace to stay even with me, but I kept my eyes forward. When we reached the carriage line, I kept my back to him.

"The IEPE evaluates your strengths and weaknesses for each element," he said, making my head snap up. "You'll run into different scenarios that'll require you to use an element, choices you'll have to make, paths you'll have to choose. It can be as mundane as choosing your favorite season or as grand as stopping a wildfire from destroying a forest. Your actions dictate which obstacles will be presented and how the course will run. All sorcerers have to take it regardless of whether they know what element they want to study. Although the test was created by Isoria Academy, all sorcery schools around the world use it." His voice had softened, but it was still coated with aggravation, like it pained him to answer the question.

I starved my curiosity to feed my grudge. I couldn't let him think he'd gotten away with being rude. "I'm sorry, but I'm not bothering you. What part of 'simple' didn't you understand?"

He scoffed. "You're childish. Why do I even bother?"

"I'm childish? You answering my question after insulting me isn't an apology. Not like I should ever expect one from you."

His jaw tensed, but then the crinkles around his eyes relaxed. He turned away. "You're right. I'm sorry," he mumbled as he directed his words to the back of someone's head in the carriage lines instead of me.

I didn't reply with an "It's okay," because it wasn't. Talking with him was like playing roulette. I never knew when I'd get black or red. One minute I could have a decent conversation with him and the next I had to worry about his mood swings.

But I took the gamble, my curiosity grumbling all the louder. "Which element did you match with?"

He bit his lower lip. I braced myself for black or red. "I chose Earth. In the end, you have a choice."

"I don't know why you can't answer the question. I asked you what you matched with, not what you chose."

"I don't know why you always have to ask so many questions."

I resisted the urge to strangle him. I should have known he wouldn't answer a personal question. Trust didn't find me easily, but he took it to a stubborn "don't get too close" level. But like Celeste's warning, *Be sure you're playing*, maybe he was playing.

"Julian chose the opposite element the IEPE recommended for him," I insisted, refusing to let him have the upper hand in the conversation.

I wasn't surprised when his shoulders squared and his muscles tightened. He and Julian had silently screamed at one another in the tunnel. I reminded myself to ask my friends about that.

"Oh, yes—sweet Julian Caballero. You've spent a lot of time with him and Rae?" he asked but said it as a fact.

I nodded proudly. "So far they've been helpful and I can trust them."

He snorted. "If trust is what you seek, I'd be more careful who you give it to."

"I didn't ask for one of your random bursts of snooty wisdom."

"It's not wisdom, it's a warning, Candor." His eyes darkened, and the sarcasm in his voice loosened. "You'd be smart to walk around with a knife behind your back."

I rolled my eyes, but as we stood in silence waiting for our carriage, I tried to pretend his words didn't stir the pit of my stomach.

The inside of Banden's one-story home couldn't describe him more perfectly. It was the most relaxing home I'd ever been in. Each room was sectioned by archways, tables were stacked with books and loose papers, and a small telescope peered out a window. The ceiling was hung with little rectangle crystals that glowed a pastel green. Of course, he had *many* plants—large ones by the windows and small ones hanging from the ceiling. Shelves with jars and plants lined the walls, and vines webbed them like wallpaper. Alec was right. Banden would be a plant if he could.

I studied a tapestry near Banden's crackling green fireplace. It depicted a clearing deep in the woods, the trees and shrubbery dense. A wooden bridge spanned a stream and led to a set of tall oak stairs at the base of a castle that glowed a pale green through the vines snaking around its turrets. Yellow lights encircled the edifice, reminding me of fireflies.

"Terrona is beautiful," I said to Banden, who was brewing hot cider in the cauldron above the fireplace. I guessed he preferred cauldrons over pots.

"Yes, it is." He briefly looked up. "That's where I studied and where Alec currently studies. Forest Faeries helped build it. But not all academy castles are in the forest. Each one is found in the atmosphere that accompanies its element. Terrona is in the woods, Aquium is near the ocean, Arayis is in the mountains, and Ignair is by a volcano."

My eyes widened. "They put a school near a volcano?"

He waved his hand dismissively. "Yes. Mount Rokesha. But it's been inactive for centuries."

That explained the part in Corinne's letter where she mentioned playing hide-and-seek with her friends in school.

"How will I know which academy to choose?"

He added apples, cinnamon sticks, and unknown herbs to the cauldron. "Research. Usually sorcerers attend the academy closest to their home. In your case, it'd be Libertaria: Sorcery School of the Eastern States of America. But I'm hoping to get you enrolled in Isoria Academy. Corinne studied there, so hopefully that'll give you an edge."

"Corinne went to a prestigious school?" I could see how Mom would; intelligent, ambitious, straight-A student, the complete opposite of me. I was an okay student. I did my work but didn't stress about effort. Now, I wondered if I had never bothered to reach my potential. The "nonsorcerer" me was so focused on staying average. What would happen if I actually *tried* when I enrolled in an academy?

"Your great-grandmother didn't accept less than great for Corinne—whether in academia, work, or life. Corinne chose rebellion to cope with her mother's high demands during her years at Ignair. She even had people call her 'Cori.'"

Cori—the signature at the bottom of the letter in the secret room. My hunch was officially confirmed: Corinne, Mom, Celeste, and Banden were all hiding something from me. *You are your friend.* And apparently from each other.

"For a while, she didn't mingle with the best crowd," he continued. "It wasn't until her eighteenth birthday she decided to go back to 'Corinne' and turn her life around."

"Pshaw, she was even complicated back then." Like my personality to Mom's, her mother was also the opposite. Mom thrived on structure and rules, while Corinne was a free spirit. I wondered where she studied. "Where do enchanters go to school if the academies are for sorcerers?"

Banden focused on the cauldron. "Enchanters have their own education system. They're homeschooled, taught by mentors or teachers. They're also a much smaller race."

"What about Bimedeises? You went to Terrona."

"We do both, but we're extremely rare. I think there's only a handful of Bimedeises in the world."

A door in the hallway slammed, making us both look up. Alec appeared, holding a towel. He must have finished cleaning up the guest room. "I'm taking a shower. Try not to need me."

"I'll refrain from it," Banden responded, stirring his cider, his finger above the liquid. "When you're finished, can you show Orion her room, please?"

Alec saluted before closing the wooden door behind him. Running water sounded.

Alec had dropped me off and rushed to his evening class while Banden did a quick practice with me. I had struggled with the Fire spells and a little bit of Earth, but everything else had gone smoothly.

I sat on the sofa as Banden came up to me, sipping his freshly brewed cider.

"Well, get plenty of sleep and make yourself at home." He smiled. "If you need anything, take what you like. Of course, know what it is. There are some materials for physician purposes only."

"I see Alec takes that offer literally," I said, motioning toward the bathroom. "I know you're his mentor and everything, but I didn't know you guys were that close."

He took another sip, this time avoiding my eyes. "My apologies. I thought you knew. Alec lives here."

"Oh. Is that normal for apprentices?"

He lifted a shoulder. "Sometimes, depending on the type of apprenticeship."

Was he not from Isoria? I tried to refrain from asking too many questions, not wanting Banden to think I was taking an interest in Alec, which was far from the truth.

"I'm guessing he's not close to his parents?" I kept my voice casual.

A sad smile fell upon his face. "They aren't around to take care of him."

"Oh," was all that came out, and the running water stopped.

Banden patted my shoulder. "I'll be in the chamber if you need me. If not, I'll see you in the morning. I have a big order to prepare. Dragonweed Pox. Who knew someone could be so careless?" He chuckled like I knew what he was talking about, then slipped behind the arched door next to the fireplace. I knew it was his Elixir Chamber by the door's personality—purple with gold lines etching the wood grain and a dragon's-head doorknob.

A minute later, the bathroom doorknob jiggled and Alec stepped into the hall. It took every ounce of willpower not to stare at his naked torso. His damp hair was spiked in chaotic directions from running his towel through it, and his loose-fitting pants hung a little too low for comfort. He wasn't jacked, but all that MISTIC training had left his body defined.

"You ready?" he asked while throwing on a shirt.

"Uh, yeah," I said lamely, looking at the floor. I grabbed my bag and followed him down the hallway.

My room was the last door at the end of the hall. It had a single bed with a nightstand, a trunk at the foot of the bed, a small dresser, and one of the walls had a backdrop with an enchanting forest. It wasn't anything special, yet it felt homier than Mom's childhood bedroom.

"So is this okay for you?" he asked.

I walked in and set my bag on the bed. "Couldn't ask for anything better."

His eyes wandered the room. "Maybe a TV. An Xbox might be nice too."

"You have those here?"

He gave me a look, wet strands of hair falling onto his lashes. "I may be a sorcerer, but I don't live under a rock. You know technology doesn't work here."

I rolled my eyes. "If I had to put a label on our friendship, it'd be 'eye roll.'"

"Woah, friendship? I'd pull on the reins there."

I sighed, rummaging through my bag for my pajamas. "Sarcastic as always."

I could feel his eyes on me, so I tried to act like he wasn't there. The atmosphere shifted, filled with a thickening tension I tried to ignore. Paranoia hit me. Did he know about the secret library? Had my friends broken their promise?

"It seems to come out more around you," he said as if he were realizing it for the first time.

Phew. I never considered myself a paranoid person, but Celeste and this world were teaching me that suspicion was a vital Isorian skill. I looked up from my clothes-hunting, eyeing him as he leaned against the doorframe. "And why's that?"

He hesitated, crossing his arms. "I don't know, to be honest."

"If you hate me so much, why don't you ask Banden to get you off babysitting-Orion duty?"

He eyed the bedside lamp. I couldn't tell if the night was playing tricks on me, but he looked almost guilty.

"I never said I hated you." His voice was quiet and dark, like the shadows in the room. He almost sounded offended.

I wanted to laugh. "I don't know. Your sarcasm seems combative to me."

"Maybe. But it doesn't mean I hate you."

He eyed me like he had more to say. He always had more to say. Sometimes the things he said should be left unsaid. I wondered how some people excelled at hiding their true feelings. Mom always said I was too blunt for my own good.

His thumb fidgeted with the ring around his index finger, and I suddenly had a thought. It was the perfect opportunity. I didn't believe for a second that Banden had only kept the necklace as a souvenir of their friendship. Let's see how much Alec "didn't" hate me.

"So, apparently, my grandmother's necklace is a Clavis. Am I ever going to get one?"

He looked up, stunned, like someone who had been caught lost in thought. But he answered, "Banden will help you once you're enrolled in an academy."

"Can I see yours?"

He flashed me a look. "What an intimate request."

I rolled my eyes and plopped down on the bed. "Forget it."

He always held up a stop sign when asked personal questions. At this point, I couldn't be mad at him, just mad at myself for caring or being even remotely curious about his life. But he pushed himself off the doorway and surprised me by sitting beside me on the bed. I could smell the shampoo in his hair as he gently removed the ring around his long, scratched-up fingers—probably MISTIC's work. I ignored the brush of his fingertips as he gently placed the ring in my hand. The metal band had two small engraved crests on either side of a green stone, each with a wolf and two swords crossed like an X.

"Do these symbols mean anything?" I asked.

I wasn't sure if I imagined the flicker of sadness in his eyes, but his voice was unwavering. "They represent the Stone heraldry. Clavises are customizable."

I remembered my conversation with Banden about Alec's family moments ago. It seemed like a sensitive topic, so I didn't push. He noticed my silence.

"What?" he asked.

I shrugged. "I was just thinking I don't know much about you or your family."

He averted his gaze. "Yeah, well. It's better you don't."

I would have kept prying, but the way his face grew rigid and his eyes turned cold, I knew not to interfere. It was also the perfect segue.

"So," I started, trying to sound uninterested as I handed him his ring back, "do you know why Corinne gave her Clavis to Banden?"

"Corinne wanted him to have it for memories. I don't know why else, to be honest." He sounded distant as he fiddled with the ring.

"Are you sure?" I tried to hide my disappointment.

He lifted a brow. "Yes. Why do you want to know?"

"There's a portrait of Corinne in my house. She's wearing the necklace."

"Okay, so . . . ?"

"So," I stalled, searching for an answer. "I think it's weird Banden has it, you know? She is *my* grandmother."

"Since when do you care about sentimentality toward Corinne?"

Shit.

"I don't. I'm curious. It's strange."

He crossed his arms and had that stupid amused glint in his eyes I hated, like he had me figured out. "All right, Candor. What's going on?"

I turned away, feeling my cheeks flush at the combination of him catching me in my lie and the way I always felt when those green eyes stared deeply into mine.

"Exactly what I told you," I insisted.

"Mmm-hmm, okay," he said, standing up. "You can't keep secrets from me—or Banden, for that matter."

My face heated. I had been fighting the urge to keep cool, but I couldn't take the double standards. I respected his family business, but I had to be transparent about mine?

"So, you're allowed to keep things to yourself, but I'm not?" I challenged, standing up with him. "You don't trust anyone."

Although his distrust was valid.

"I'm a spy. I'm wired to doubt everyone." He briefly averted his eyes. "And you know everything you need to know about me."

"You don't need to be a spy to be a skeptic." My voice rose an octave, but I quickly corrected it, not wanting Banden to hear. "And you know everything you need to know about me."

"If it'll put you in danger, we need to know, Orion. You barely found out you're a sorcerer. You still have so much to learn."

"Yes, magic and Isoria are new to me, but 'if trust is what you seek, I'd be more careful who you give it to.' Take your own advice before you preach."

His eyes narrowed. "Know your place, Orion. Remember, we took the same oath. Celeste isn't as forgiving as I am."

I lifted my chin, keeping my voice steady. "Well, it's a good thing I have nothing to hide."

"Well, good thing, then." He crossed his arms, and I caught that glint in his eye again. I couldn't tell if he was threatening me, but I was betting he and Banden wouldn't rat me out if they suspected anything. *Would they?* But I stared back at him, refusing to be the first to break our little battle.

"Well, my door is on the right if you need me." He finally broke the silence. "Banden's on the left." He headed to the door, grabbed the knob, and paused before looking over his shoulder. He had a slight smirk on his face. "Sleep well."

I stared at the closed door and refrained from grabbing a pillow and screaming into it. He was the most ambiguous person I'd ever met. Despite my frustration, my thoughts wondered what his room—a mystery like himself—looked like. Maybe that's why he didn't want to talk about his family, yet he wore his family's crest on his ring. Maybe it was worse than I imagined. Maybe he lived here because he didn't have a real home. Like me.

I pushed aside my running thoughts and prepared for my plan. I set my watch for one in the morning and slid under the covers, hoping sleep would find me. But like bubbles in a boiling cauldron, my nerves unsettled me.

I woke to the same pit in my stomach I had fallen asleep with. My heart had pounded the entire night.

Moonlight spilled through a crack between the curtains. I tiptoed to the door, holding my breath when the floorboards creaked. My pulse drummed in my ears as I slowly turned the knob and stepped into the dimly lit hallway, right between Banden's and Alec's bedrooms. With each step closer to the purple door, I swore my heartbeat could wake the house.

At the door, I peered down the hallway before trying the knob, sighing with relief when the door opened. A staircase spiraled down into the darkness, like a tower leading to its dungeon. Oil lamps cast moving shadows along the stone walls as I crept through the blackness, looking over my shoulder with each step. When I reached the landing, there was another door, which swung right open.

In the dark, I sprinted to the table, wasting no time. I pulled open the top drawer and found the necklace in between a few sheets of paper. I slipped it into my PJ pocket and ran for the spiral staircase, my stomach in knots. My hand was inches from the doorknob when my body slammed into a hard surface, followed by a fierce wind that sent me flying butt first onto the wooden floorboards.

"What the—" I coughed, using my stinging hands to slowly rise to my feet. My glutes ached as I straightened, flinching from the pain. My fingers fumbled for my pockets. The necklace was still in one piece.

An oil lamp in the corner lit up, making me jump.

"Orion." Alec sat on a chair placed conveniently in the corner, one leg propped up and a smile across his face. His eyes still managed to twinkle in the dim lighting as he looked me up and down. "Elephant pajamas? Cute."

I couldn't disguise my shock. "How did you know?"

His smirk grew as he strode toward me. "You thought Banden would leave his chamber unlocked?"

I clutched the necklace in my hand, mentally trying to plan an escape—although I didn't know any spells and there was nowhere to go.

"I can tell when you're up to something. I didn't tell Banden, but it doesn't mean I'll let you off the hook." He leaned against the apothecary table, crossing his arms in triumph. His cockiness irked me *so* much. "Orion, you don't know enough about this world to handle it on your own. So whatever you know, tell me."

"I have Rae and Julian helping me," I said, hoping that would relieve his anxiety.

He rolled his eyes, his head following suit. "Even more reason to tell me. MISTIC Training 101—don't reveal your allies." He hitched an eyebrow, noticing my small attempt to distance myself from him. "All the exits are charmed."

"How are they charmed? I thought sorcerers didn't have that kind of power," I asked, hoping to stall him.

"We don't. But enchanters do." He lifted himself off the table and reached his hand toward me. "The necklace, Orion."

I hid it behind my back, squeezing it in my scraped palms. "No."

He sighed. "Okay, now I'm tired of playing nice." He raised his hand, palms facing me. The temperature between my hands rose but then left as quickly as it came. The necklace jiggled, loosening my grasp despite how tightly I clutched it, and slipped through my fingers. It flew straight into his palm and swung around his index finger, all in one fluid motion.

"How did you—?" I watched the spinning crystal.

He caught the pendant with his hand. "Earth spell. There's a Defense spell to counter that, but it's too easy with you."

Steam could have poured out of my ears. I pounced on him, but he dodged me, hiding the necklace behind his back.

"I don't think you want to do that," he warned. "Tell me what you're up to, or I'm waking Banden up."

"No!" I cried, blocking his path. "Fine. You're right, okay? I don't know what I'm getting myself into. But it has to do with Corinne."

"What does?"

"Only if you promise not to say anything to *anyone*. Please, Alec."

He studied me for a minute, considering. "Fine. Now, what is it?"

I didn't trust him, but I had no choice. I told him about the fireplace, but I left out the secret room. He eyed me like a hawk watching its prey's every move. I couldn't expect anything less from someone in an intelligence ring.

"So you tried to steal the necklace hoping you could accomplish whatever your grandmother wanted," he summarized.

I nodded. "Can you keep this between you and me?"

He put a finger to his chin. "That would make me an accomplice—you know, since we both took an oath and you promised to share any intel about Corinne with Celeste."

"I didn't say those *exact* words. Besides, everything is theory right now."

"Well, now that you've told me, I'm in."

"Of course you are," I grumbled. I had been naïve in believing I had fooled him. Maybe I should take lessons from MISTIC on the element of deceit. "Can I have the necklace now?"

He held it to his side. "Absolutely not. Besides, Banden would notice if it went missing. Let me know when you need it, and I'll bring it to you."

"Fine."

Banden had to take the protection spell down. He had certain ingredients around his chamber that were charmed, and if someone touched a jar, a bell would sound in his room. Alec grabbed one such jar labeled Cloverweed, which was apparently a rare and expensive plant for treating certain illnesses. Sorcerers sought it because it could be used as a recreational drug. In a matter of seconds, Banden had flown down the staircase and slammed the door open, his scepter raised like a wand. He shook his head in confusion and questioned what we were doing. Alec lied, saying I had been freaking out about the test and he was reviewing some techniques with me, and Banden, who was annoyed about being woken, was either too tired to preach or he understood. He disarmed the alarm, and we made our way back to our bedrooms.

Alec made sure I was in my bedroom, eyeing me until I shut my door. I hoped I hadn't made a mistake by trusting him.

CHAPTER 11

The testing center was located on the outskirts of Erudite Square, home to Isoria's prestigious schools, universities, museums, and famous library. We trotted through the town's old cobblestone streets on Banden's horse, Cerus, a muscular, black Friesian, and I tried not to think about my sore butt as I got lost in the ambiance of the village.

I'd stepped into a time of chariot races and togas. Civilians wore medieval-modern garments, out of place in this village. Pillars lined up like soldiers as they supported concrete and stone structures built with symmetrical precision and ancient artistry. Many of them gleamed with streaks of gold and had statues of revered creatures, like birds, horses, and dragons. I read some of the inscriptions—"The Isorian Preparatory School of the Fundamentals," "Athena's Library of Isoria," "The National Isorian Museum of History and Art." The air breathed curiosity and intellect. Apparently, the village's founder, Athena Erudite, had wanted to emulate classical architecture and believed the atmosphere would inspire a thirst for knowledge in Isorians.

My nerves kicked in when we reached the testing center. It was breathtaking, with its massive Colosseum-like circular shape and gold-and-white marble that reflected like a polished blade in the sun. Four sky-high pillars—white, green, red, and blue—traced the walkway leading to the bronze double doors.

Leaving Cerus outside the magnificent building, Banden and I entered a massive hall bustling with sorcerers. The high ceilings, along with large rectangular windows, accentuated the building's lofty status. Near one of the staircases, sorcerers entered and exited three large rectangular bronze boxes with black gates. One of the boxes soared up toward one of the seven floors, unattached to anything.

Banden led me to a man at a desk with a massive ancient sepia map of Isoria behind it. The man handed me paper and directed us to room three of seventy rooms, where my test maker would be waiting for me outside my obstacle course. I hurried to keep up with Banden's long strides toward an archway with a golden number three at the top.

We ended up in a circular stone room, the atmosphere of which differed completely from the hall. Although more sedated, it resembled a castle dungeon. Fire torches laced the walls, and a dark tunnel at the side was closed off by black iron bars. There were only two people with us. A woman sat on one of many wooden boards attached to the walls while a man sat on a stool in what looked like a box office made out of the stone walls and a glass window. He oddly stared at the stone wall, like he was concentrating or figuring out a puzzle.

"He's your test maker." Banden gestured to the man behind the glass. "He determines your results."

"How does he judge your test?" I whispered back.

"Reptilian Vision, a spell that enhances vision. The test makers can see right through the walls and watch you."

Well, that's creepy. "I hope there are laws against using that spell in public."

A rumbling sounded from the tunnel as the gates lifted. A teenage boy sprinted out, his arms and face shining from sweat, like he had run a marathon. He must have just finished his test. He met the woman on the bench, and they conversed in hushed voices. The test maker called them over and handed the boy a rolled-up scroll.

"Orion Candor?" the test maker called.

Banden sat down on a bench as I approached the man.

"Do you have your registration form?" he asked. His brown hair was tied in a bun, and it was hard to look away from his eyes. Behind his glasses were bright-green irises with black slits for pupils. They looked like fake contact lenses.

I handed it to him, and once he'd reviewed it, his reptilian eyes rolled to me. "My name is Xavier. Let me explain the layout of the test."

Like Alec had said, each obstacle tested a certain element, favoring one or two in particular, but could technically be done with any element if I found a way. I would encounter obstacles, and how I handled each one, completed or not, would determine which elements I was most compatible with. The obstacles were charmed and would "disappear" if not completed within five minutes. There were no consequences, only a point reduction for that element. I'd receive my results once I finished.

"You start and end at that tunnel. Good luck," he concluded.

My heart pounded as the gates lifted, inviting me into the unwelcoming tunnel. All those hard days of training finally put into practice. I'd taken many tests, but this one mattered the most.

The darkness that swallowed me as I entered the tunnel intensified the farther down my boots sloshed in thick, wet sand.

But I wasn't alone. Magic was with me. I could feel all the elements in the air, beneath my shoes, and on the walls teasing me, waiting to be played with. But I knew which one was challenging me in the darkness. No light meant I had to find or create my own, but creating fire without a source was a novice Fire spell, and I was a pre-novice. The Masters had advised me to search for resources around each obstacle.

My hands clung to the cold stone walls, guiding me through the winding tunnel. I hoped to find anything other than rock. When the walls curved, my fingers bumped into what felt like metal, then wood. I would have pulled away, but I recognized the mysterious object. A torch. I gripped the wood, but it refused to lift from the hinges.

Shit. I didn't want help on my first task.

I lifted my hands to the torch, feeling heat around it. Katja had taught me heat was enough to start a small flame. I took a deep breath, imagining myself conquering the spell, controlling it, and fighting the negative thoughts of starting a wildfire and trapping myself in a blisteringly hot cave. I tried and tried, and when a flickering flame did finally spark, it burned out. Sweat trickled down my back as I imagined a ticking clock, each lost second proving what an unsuited sorcerer I was.

Breathe. You can do this.

I exhaled deeply, this time focusing on the task instead of my racing thoughts and pounding heart. After a few seconds, warmth tingled at my fingertips. A small yellow flame flickered, this time growing into a fire that illuminated the cave. There was another torch on the other side, but I wasn't confident I could create another flame. Instead, I used what I had and tried to determine the next step. But the tunnel was at a dead end.

I went for the other torch, tripping over my feet, or so I thought. A faint, gray outline was etched into the heavy sand. I swiped my foot over it, and a crevice appeared in the concrete underneath the sand. I banged my foot against the spot. It was hollow.

I cast an Air Blast to remove the thick dirt, revealing a wooden trap door. But my spell blew out the flame that had taken me so long to create, and I was once again faced with darkness. Refusing to waste time lighting the torch, I dropped to my knees and felt along the door, my hands finding a cool, iron handle. I lifted the door to discover yet another dark tunnel—but with only one way down.

My body shook, but I put one foot forward, closed my eyes, and took a leap of faith.

Blackness surrounded me as a scream was ripped from my throat. My stomach caught in my chest, and my legs kicked the air at the unexpected length of the drop. Then, like a light switch, white replaced black, and my eyes popped open to see a lake below me.

I held my breath as the icy water welcomed me, drilling me deep under. My arms and legs thrashed in the murky water, bubbles webbing around me. I reached for the surface, and as my head was about to hit the air, something gripped my ankle and pulled me back under.

A strand of long, dark-green seaweed coiled around my ankle like a snake, squeezing the blood in my foot. I tried yanking free, the oxygen in my burning lungs rapidly decreasing as my arms and legs flailed. I knew Xavier wouldn't leave me here to die, but it was impossible to remain calm as I fought for air. The white air bubbles circulated around me as I desperately tried breaking free.

And it hit me. I had never learned this spell, but it felt right, and, like I was taught, sorcerers relied on instinct. Holding on to the fleeting thought, I flapped my arms, creating hundreds of tiny bubbles. I stuck my hand out toward them, searching for the light, cool air within them. I positioned my hands like I was holding a ball, then spread my arms to a T. My hands shook as they fought against the water's pressure and held on to the air, forcing a bubble to grow. It expanded like a balloon to triple the size of my head. I forced it over my head, then took desperate but grateful gasps of the air inside it.

When I stopped hyperventilating, I reached down to pull the seaweed off but instantly pulled back when it pricked my finger. My eyes searched the murky water, hoping for a clue as to what to do next, but it was me and the pesky seaweed. I had to do a Water spell.

Or maybe I didn't.

I pointed my hand toward the seaweed, and the water particles fought against the wind I tried to summon. My hands shook and vibrated until a small but sharp Air Blast shot toward the seaweed, like Master Samir taught me when we'd practiced knocking over those tin vases. The blast sent me a couple of inches upward from the sand, snapping the seaweed from its root as it uncoiled like ribbon and released me.

My head was greeted by a cool wind as the bubble popped above the surface. Coughing and gasping, I kicked my arms and legs to stay afloat. A small, forested island lay ahead, and, strangely, although it wasn't nighttime, above me stretched a starry sky.

My adrenaline numbed me to the freezing water as I raced for the island. When my feet touched the ground, I collapsed onto the warm grass with soaking clothes, catching my breath and allowing my aching limbs to sink into the cushiony warmth. As I got to my feet, I felt lighter and warmer, like the grass had revitalized me and soaked up all my aches. I ran my hands over my clothes. My hair wasn't dripping, and my skin was dry.

I forced myself to carry on, ignoring the test's magic tricks. In front of the forest on the island was a floating rectangular stone resembling a tabletop. Two objects sat atop it: an old-fashioned brass telescope and a bag of unknown plant seeds. There was an engraving on the stone: *Choose one.*

The polished telescope itched my curiosity the most. I grabbed it, and the stone board with the seeds melted like candle wax, the residual puddle of silver oozing at my feet.

I pointed the telescope toward the ocean, seeing nothing but darkness through the lens. I tried the trees behind me. Nothing but green. I frowned. It was too late to change my choice considering the melted, gooey silver.

Possible uses of telescopes by pirates, sailors, scientists, and Banden . . .

Stargazing.

I pointed the telescope toward the night sky and closed one eye. Through the lenses, I could see stars speckled across the sky like splattered paint. But the sky was starless outside the lens, like being blind before wearing glasses. Among the starry noise, one of the many constellations twinkled the brightest—a man in a robe pointing his index finger to the left. I went left with my lens and was suddenly blinded by a brilliant white light. I jerked away, dropping the telescope as I rubbed my stinging eyes.

After seconds with blotchy vision and praying this stupid test hadn't permanently blinded me, I rapidly blinked as my eyes refocused on my new brown surroundings.

I took one step forward only to jump back from almost falling to my death. A chasm lay between me and another cliff ahead, heat emanating from below. A violent wildfire raged through the chasm, its vibrant orange flames roaring hungrily up toward me. The air was like an oven.

A few feet away rested a long, wide slab of rock. It was thinner than a cutting board but looked sturdy enough to walk on. Any heavier and I wouldn't be able to maneuver it.

I targeted the slab like Master Vera had taught me with the pile of books. But instead of solid particles, I felt a force press against my hands as if I were touching the matter itself, my hands gravitating toward the fluidity and air around it, a more comfortable and concrete sensation. Lightning-shaped cracks cleft the ground and the slab slowly fell. But in the wrong direction. Toward me.

A wind created by my hands rose up to counteract the descent of the slab. The slab seesawed, then tipped back toward me, the invisible weight pressing against my hands. Sweat trickled down my back as the weight increased. My body temperature rose with the heat boiling below.

I grunted and sent a stronger surge of wind. The slab tilted backward, the edge of it landing with a thud on the grass on the other side of the chasm. Triumph flooded through my veins, and I wasted no time jogging across the rock, forcing my eyes forward as the flames licked at me. A cave met me on the other side, a light at the end of it acting as my guide.

This is it.

But I landed in white. White specs fell from a gray sky, yet no snow lay at my feet. The ground was covered in feathers, and so was my hair. Millions of them, falling. It was suffocating, like being trapped inside a pillow, nothing in view but feathers. I had worked with feathers with Master Samir, but these were already flying. *Everywhere.* How was this an obstacle?

Maybe my eyes were playing tricks on me, but some distance away, a fog floated between the falling feathers. I blinked, and the more I did, the larger the fog grew. A circle formed with three lines striking out from it, and a dark shadow appeared below it. No, not a shadow. It morphed into a slender shape, sending shivers through my blood. Someone or something was with me. And it was creeping toward me, slow as a snail, calculating like a lion.

Like the Chicaneries, this figure wore a cloak and black mask with gray slits for eyes and nostrils. My heartbeat pulsed in my throat and ears. No one had mentioned *beings* being obstacles.

"Annulla," a voice echoed.

I stepped backward as the thing strode closer. "No, I'm Orion."

"Annulla swept her."

Whispers, multiple voices I couldn't understand, echoed all around, as if an army surrounded us. The figure outstretched its hand, and a tall, scorching trail of orange and yellow ignited on the ground, burning feathers as it slithered toward me. I jumped out of the way and crashed to the cushioned ground.

These test makers were *mad.* Why were they testing me on something I hadn't been taught?

Another trail of fire raged toward me. I scrambled to the right and onto my feet. I fired a weak Air Blast, which the figure deflected with a swish of its arm, sparks flying from the impact. It trudged toward me and threw a Fire Ball.

I dodged left, the heat of the crackling flames blazing past me, followed by a sharp burning sensation as a flare scorched my knuckles and seared my left sleeve. I cried out as I cradled my hand, smelling the burned fabric. Before they could burn me alive, I bolted into the unknown sea of feathers.

This suffocating storm of fluff seemed endless, and I escaped toward nothing. But darkness loomed ahead. I welcomed it, desperate to be out of the whiteness and away from the fire monster.

When my feet hit rocky ground, I bent over to suck in air until my lungs weren't burning. I had never thought I'd be grateful for a dark cave. A light streamed at the end of the tunnel, and I picked up speed.

CHAPTER 12

I squinted into the harsh light that flooded the tunnel as the black gates lifted. My body and mind were drained. I understood why that boy from earlier had looked like he'd returned from battle. But I didn't get the chance to process what I had endured. The small stone room was now chaotic, crowded with adults and teenagers.

All staring at me.

A man draped in a gold robe stood with Banden near the entrance. When he caught my gaze, he strode toward me, Banden at his heels. Everyone's eyes followed them.

"Miss Candor," the man announced. He was a little younger than Banden, though he had wrinkles around his eyes and lips. He reminded me of a crow with his crooked nose, which was asymmetrical with his pinched face. His grayish-brown hair was jelled to the side. "Headmaster Jufaris Iceflyn of Isoria Academy, School of Sorcery. It's a pleasure." He offered his hand, which I hesitantly accepted.

"I need you and Mr. Locus to follow me," he continued. Without waiting for a response, Iceflyn spun around, and Banden and I followed. Whispers started as we left the room.

"What's going on?" I murmured to Banden.

But he was silent, giving me a quick glance, his eyes pausing near my waist. "What happened to your sleeve?"

I poked at the shriveled, black material. The burns across my knuckles had subsided, but they still stung. "An accident during the test."

His brows furrowed, and he began to say, "That shouldn't—" but paused when Iceflyn stopped us in front of the sepia map behind the entrance desk, which morphed into a visual of an office. He stepped right through it, and we followed, ending up in the biggest office I'd ever seen.

It had two floors. Double spiral staircases led to the second floor lined with bookshelves. On the first floor, a fireplace with a coffee table and sofas stood in one corner, and a glass desk in the center of the room was entangled with black and gold vines. The academy's crest, plated in gold, graced the front. Two golden yellow banners with the colored version of the crest hung next to two mosaic windows that glowed in the autumn sunlight. The top half of each crest was divided into two colors: blue on the left and green on the right. The bottom half of each was red, and a white stripe separated the three colors. The middle had a gold circle with a fierce pegasus hovering over an open book that contained the letters *I* and *A*.

Iceflyn sat behind his desk while Banden and I stood before him. He held a paper in his hands, keeping its contents hidden from my view, and traced a pencil along the messy handwriting. "Miss Candor, I'd like to start by congratulating you for completing your Isorian Element Performance Evaluation."

"Right, thanks," I said.

"You're here because you want to enroll in the academy. It says on your registration form your preferred schools of choice are Isoria

Academy, School of Sorcery and Libertaria, Sorcery School of the Eastern States of America."

I nodded.

"Mr. Locus has informed me about you, Miss Candor. According to him, you only recently discovered your sorcerer identity."

"That's correct."

His brows furrowed. "Your parents or guardians never told you?"

I shook my head. It was weird sharing my personal life with this man. I gave Banden a look, not sure where this conversation was going.

Iceflyn's mouth was a thin line, his eyes rolling between Banden and me.

"I'm sorry, but what does this have to do with anything?" I asked.

Iceflyn dropped the pencil and paper. "As you may or may not know, the IEPE is designed by Isoria Academy in partnership with the Royal Imperium." He sounded impatient, like I should know why I was here. "If anything strange or unusual is noticed during the test, I am reported by the test maker. And it's even of more particular interest to me since you're interested in enrolling in the academy. This is about your IEPE results, Miss Candor. They proved to be extraordinary. So extraordinary they were difficult to determine."

"Difficult to determine?" Bandon cut in. So he was as confused as me.

"Yes. Although Miss Candor ran her course, she found a way to manipulate each obstacle by using Air spells *only*, except for the first task, which confused your test maker. Never has this happened in IEPE history—at least that I'm aware of. When your test maker notified me of what he was seeing, we decided to end Miss Candor's test early by blocking off the next obstacle."

"You ended it *early*?" I asked. That test was draining enough.

"I'm reading your results." He ignored me, indicating to the paper. "Your test results were outstanding, Miss Candor, meaning they don't match the current claims you're making about your family."

Outstanding and extraordinary? I struggled with every obstacle. If anything, I had performed average. But judging by his tone, he didn't believe that.

"So you think I'm lying?" I challenged.

His voice was calm but accusatory. "I'm simply trying to understand."

"What was so outstanding about her results?" Banden asked, a hint of annoyance in his voice. At least he was on my side. "Because she used only Air spells?"

Iceflyn remained cool and collected, making Banden and me look like the crazy ones. "That's part of it, Mr. Locus. But what amazed me was how quickly she was able to perform them."

"With all due respect, sir, I believe that's not rare. A sorcerer's powers are instinctual."

Iceflyn nodded. "You're quite right. We do design each obstacle where any element *can* be used. Although, it doesn't happen as often as you think. Xavier wouldn't have thought anything of it until she cast a Countervail spell."

Banden, who had been as irritated as I was, now tensed. "What do you mean?"

"What's a Countervail spell?" I asked, missing the shock factor.

Iceflyn explained, "Countervail spells are advanced, at least two levels above where a novice should be, impossible for a beginner. It's when one or more element is fighting against or interfering with your element. When you were in the water, you grabbed air from a bubble and expanded it for oxygen. A First Year struggles with one element at a time. You managed to surpass extreme water pressure to find air and increase it *underwater*. After that, *all* the spells cast were above novice Air spells."

Iceflyn was right. I couldn't justify how or why I did those spells. It was instinct, like I had been taught in training. What did he want from me?

I shrugged. "I'm sorry?"

"You shouldn't be unless there's more you'd like to reveal." He folded his hands on his desk, tilting his head to the side like a curious bird.

"I swear, sir. I just . . . did it. It was instinct. I wish I could tell you more, but I don't understand it myself."

"As I've mentioned, during Orion's training, she excelled quickly," Banden added. "Even her teachers were impressed."

Iceflyn's eyes narrowed. No matter what we said, he wouldn't believe us.

"I see," he finally said, spinning the pencil between his long fingers. "Well, aside from these peculiar events, I'd like to personally inform you, Miss Candor, Isoria Academy has accepted your application and invites you to join us for the academic year. Although your talents are enigmatic, they are extraordinary, and the academy only accepts the extraordinary and hardworking. Congratulations."

"Are you serious?" I was thrown by the turn in conversation. I felt like I got accepted into an ivy league without trying. Banden patted me on the shoulder, although I could still see his hesitance toward Iceflyn. "Thank you."

"These are the forms for the academy if you accept the offer," Iceflyn continued. I took them without hesitation, and he smiled. "I'm sorry, Miss Candor, but you must choose your school without the influence of your IEPE results, as we can't rank them accordingly. Take some time to think about it. Although it appears you know what you're doing."

My fate was decided by the first question: "Please circle your school of choice." I stared at the schools listed: Aquium School of Water Sorcery and Practices, Arayis School of Air Sorcery and Practices, Ignair School of Fire Sorcery and Practices, Terrona School of Earth Sorcery and Practices.

"Do you mind if I take a quick break outside?" I said.

Iceflyn nodded. He needed to review the academy's guardian protocol with Banden. A pang curled in my chest. *That should be Mom.*

"Oh, and, Miss Candor?" Iceflyn said. "You don't have to worry about traveling through another map like you did before. You'll be in Isorian Academy Centre, the academy's main information center, so the door will do."

When I opened the wooden door, I found myself in an ornate, two-story hall. I didn't understand where I was, but down the hall in the center of the floor were rows of desks and secretaries. The walls were painted red, blue, white, and green, with regal gold designs etched in the ceilings, cornices, and beams. I leaned against one of the many pillars with golden floral capitals standing over the academy crest tiled on the floor.

I wanted to text Rae and Julian for advice, but technology didn't work here. The test was supposed to make this decision easier. But with everything happening in my life lately, why would have it gone smoothly? Did I want Air because the results were outstanding? Or because I struggled with Fire, did I want to work hard at it? Or maybe I wanted Water or Earth because I was indifferent toward them.

"Ah, yes. The Thinking Column," a voice said, my head snapping up. "Legend has it every sorcerer who comes here thinks."

Alec wore a wide smirk. A bag hung on one shoulder as he held on to the strap. He wore neutral clothing as always—a black distressed jacket and dark jeans—but his mood was irritatingly yet surprisingly cheery.

"What are you doing here?" I asked, peeling myself off the column.

"I finished class and was planning on meeting up with you and Banden at the testing center, but I was told you were with Headmaster Iceflyn. Where's Banden?"

"With Iceflyn."

He raised an eyebrow. "Why?"

I highlighted the last hour, spilling everything like vomit. I was so desperate to talk about it that a sarcastic jerk sufficed. When I mentioned the Countervail spell and my inconclusive test results, he shared the same shocked response as Banden and Iceflyn.

"Well, for one, congratulations on your acceptance. But they stopped your test *early*?" he asked in disbelief. "And you only used Air spells throughout the entire test?"

I nodded. "I used a Fire spell at the beginning, but once I realized I could use Air . . . I don't know why I did, but it felt right."

"There are cases where sorcerers will use one element over the others for most of the test, but they'll still use others and *not* advanced spells." He shook his head. "I know your powers are different, but you're on a whole other level."

A silence fell between us as I got lost in my thoughts again. I found myself watching passersby, some of whom looked curiously at us. Choosing an element felt like a bigger commitment than choosing a college major.

"So, what do you want?" Alec finally asked.

"To be normal," I mumbled. "Everyone says I do these extraordinary things, yet they become concerned."

I leaned back against the column and slid to the floor. Alec hesitated for a moment, his face unreadable. I thought he would leave until he dropped his bag and sat down beside me, throwing his arms around his propped-up knees. I tried ignoring the heat that always seemed to rise throughout my body when he was close.

"My IEPE results weren't the cleanest either," he said, his gaze forward. "Maybe not as complicated as yours. Two elements were tied. Earth and Air."

My eyes widened. "But they're opposites."

The spell book stated that, generally, if a sorcerer was attracted to one element, she or he would most likely have difficulties with or dislike its opposite.

He nodded. "Earth—one, Air—one, Fire—two, Water—three." He rehearsed his rankings, looking at everything but me. "I've always known I wanted to study Earth. Because Air was my weakness, I was determined to understand it in school, prior to the academy. My determination and hard work rewarded me with top results. The academy was impressed with them, along with my academic grades in elementary schools."

Handsome and intelligent.

Having the same rankings for two elements sounded like more pressure. But he'd wanted Earth. Maybe I was so new to all this I hadn't focused on the element that excited me. During training, I'd fixated on my performance, not the element that sparked joy.

"You've been putting way too much pressure on yourself." Alec turned his head toward me. "One of the many things I've noticed about you."

He stood up, and I was grateful for the sudden distance between us, allowing me the chance to catch my breath.

"Oh yeah?" I rose to my feet. "What else have you noticed?" In another world, I'd be charmed he paid attention, but I knew he was just trained to do that.

"You already made your decision," he said, slinging his strap over his shoulder, "long before you took the test, and you're scared it might be the wrong choice."

"Well, that's specific," I mumbled as I watched sorcerers walk by, some not bothering to hide their stares.

He flashed me a smile as he inched away. "You did say our friendship was an eye roll."

I couldn't help but roll my eyes, watching his back as he headed down the hall.

CHAPTER 13

Arayis: School of Air Sorcery and Practices.

It was always Air, whether I was born to it or had the desire within. I always knew. I needed to learn to trust myself, especially in a world where I needed to trust myself the most.

I returned to the headmaster's office to receive my schedule, a map of Arayis, and a list of supplies I needed to purchase. I analyzed the documents. I had four classes this semester: Introduction to the Air Element, History of Air, Introduction to Air Defense Spells, and Creatures of Isoria I. My classes for next semester, which began on February 23, were Understand Your Opposite: How to Deal with Earth, Air Slicers and Boulders, Oxygen and the Air We Breathe, and Fog and Smoke: The Basics. Two were an hour and a half, twice a week, while the other two were each three hours long, once a week. Classes had started on September 23, so I was a month behind, but Iceflyn assured me I'd be able to catch up with my classmates as long as I put in the effort. I also had my nonmagus courses scattered across the week to make up for my high school education.

Osmus Wicbin was my preceptor, and Arturo Evoras was Arayis's rector. Iceflyn explained a preceptor was a professor and adviser. They helped students choose future classes, settle in school, and offered career advice. The rector oversaw Arayis.

I was offered the rest of the week off to shop for supplies, but Banden wanted me to start immediately. I was also anxious to start and didn't want to fall even more behind. When we left the Isorian Academy Centre, Banden dropped a small brown sack of coins and bills in my hands, along with a polished, wooden, palm-sized Isoria Academy crest that said "Student Carriage Pass."

Banden then explained the currency used in Isoria was isos. The iso symbol was a capital "I" with the two lines, and two smaller lines that ran horizontally parallel through the "I." The bills were called iso notes and the coins were called coins, but they equated to cents. Values 1, 2, and 5 coins were bronze while values 10, 20, and 50 coins were silver. The iso notes 1, 5, 10, 50, and 100 were golden yellow. The value was on each coin and note with either a pegasus, flower, or griffin symbol.

I started to protest, but he wouldn't hear it.

"It has already been paid for, and how do you expect to pay for them, Orion? I said I'd help you. That's what family's for."

Family. The word didn't sit right with me. Yes, he'd known my family for a long time, but he still felt like a stranger. I desperately wanted to trust him, but he and MISTIC were withholding something from me. The letter in the secret room had been addressed to Banden, and he continued to be vague when talking about Corinne or avoided her altogether. Did Celeste suspect Corinne had hidden an object, and if she did, why didn't she ask me about it?

We went to Tea and Vintage Books in Avelin to buy my books and stationary. We then went to Realm of Reflections, where I got a compact mirror with a white quartz stone framed in detailed silver filigree with stars for Reflection Messaging. My favorite store was Clacy's Clavises, where I officially got my own Clavis. The shop was a hidden gem in an empty alleyway. Vines concealed a wooden door on the side of a stone building owned by an art shop, The Crafty Quill. Clacy's sold all kinds of jewelry, objects, and accessories I wouldn't have expected to be Clavises, such as scepters, like the one Banden carried, and diadems and brooches. I ended up choosing a necklace like Corinne, but not because of her. Necklaces were practical, easy to wear, and less flashy.

After selecting a simple silver chain and a light-blue stone (Aermages wore light-blue, white, yellow, and silver), I chose a necklace with silver vines that twisted around a light-blue stone like a cage. The shopkeeper, who was an enchanter and a friend of Banden's, had to charm it to open portals. Banden went with him in the back while I stayed behind admiring the quaint shop.

After the shopping spree, we headed for the Elixir Chamber, where we found Alec reading by the fireplace. Banden volunteered Alec to take me home and ride in the Flyers carriage since that was how I'd travel to Arayis on Monday. It was the only way to get to Arayis because the Artus Mountains, where Arayis resided, were too steep to travel by foot or horseback. I'd be taking the academy's personal Flyers coach, and there would be a separate line for it in Avelin.

With his matted hair and tired eyes, Alec looked exhausted but nevertheless agreed to Banden's request. As we stepped outside, several cuts and scratches on his right forearm became visible.

"What happened to you?" I asked.

He rubbed one of the marks running from his wrist to his elbow. "Training, similar to the performance you saw between Rae and Julian. And, well, fighting."

"Like, with your fists?" I gasped.

"Like, with weapons," he mocked.

"Why use weapons when you have magic?"

"Why learn how to throw a punch when you have a gun?" he countered. "You might not always have enough time to prepare for a spell, and a good fighter can take down a sorcerer through distraction or exhaustion. Worst-case scenario, you might also be in a situation where you can't use your magic. What do you do then?"

I shrugged. "Point taken."

Thankfully, we didn't have to wait long for a Flyer. A carriage from the sky headed our way, and the coachman piloting it gently landed before us, an Air spell cast from his hands to the carriage's wheels.

"Why not always take Flyers?" I asked as Alec handed iso notes to the coachman. "Isn't it quicker?"

"Not necessarily. It's also expensive," he answered as I followed him to the back of the carriage. Like everywhere I went with him, he drew looks from those around us. A girl sat down beside me and peered at Alec before turning her attention to her book.

I leaned in close to him. "Why does everyone stare at you?"

He stiffened but answered indifferently, "I don't know what you're talking about."

He couldn't play dumb with me. I hadn't imagined the girl's curious look. Even when Alec had kept me company at the column, heads had turned toward us. I lowered my voice. "Everywhere I go with you, people stare."

"Is someone staring at me now?" he whispered back.

Not one person was looking—not even the girl, who was now intently reading her book. For the sake of the riders who could hear us, I dropped the conversation.

The carriage moved slowly but graduated to a much faster speed than the Promenade rides I had taken. My body shifted to the side, forcing me to lean into Alec. The carriage slanted steeper and steeper, but the passengers weren't fazed in the slightest by the incline. Within seconds, it returned to a horizontal position. Cotton-candy clouds zoomed past the window across from us. Alec remained silent throughout the ride.

My back pressed against the wall as the carriage tilted downward and bumped up and down as the wheels adjusted to the ground. Once the carriage halted, Alec stood to leave first. I was surprised when he offered his hand to help me down from the carriage, for sure thinking he was mad at me about earlier. And he didn't release my hand when we were both safely on the ground, his eyes intently on my wrist. "What did you do to your sleeve?"

The burnt sleeve. I had forgotten about that. Thankfully, my knuckles didn't sting anymore. "Battle wounds from the IEPE. It was some weird obstacle."

He blinked. "What do you mean?"

I shrugged. "Some creep in a cloak kept calling me Annulla and attacked me with fire."

His eyes widened, and it wasn't long before dark shadows formed beneath them. "Follow me," he growled.

Without warning, he tightened his grip and pulled me away from the crowd.

"Like I have a choice! What's your problem?" I tried fighting his grasp, but he was too strong.

He dragged me into an alleyway between a candle shop and bookshop, looking over his shoulder before releasing me. I massaged my wrist, glaring at him.

"What the hell is wrong with you? And why do you keep bringing me into alleyways to talk?"

"What the hell is wrong with *you*?" he barked. "Didn't anyone explain the rules to you?"

I shook my head. "What are you talking about?"

His eyes were fierce, like they could reach out and strangle me. "Orion, a sorcerer leaves the IEPE *unharmed*."

I froze and looked down at my very real blackened sleeve.

"I've never heard someone say they had to duel another sorcerer during an IEPE," he continued, more worried than angry now.

"Well, Iceflyn did say they were impressed with my results. Maybe they increased the difficulty for me?" I suggested, searching for an explanation.

He shook his head. "Don't be daft, Orion. You still wouldn't come out with scars." He pinched my sleeve, waving it in my face.

I yanked him off. "Why are you so worked up about this? This isn't your problem." I crossed my arms, trying to look defiant but hoping to calm my wildly beating heart. It didn't help that he was worried. Or angry. Maybe our relationship was more than an eye roll. I never knew with him.

"Your safety is Banden's concern. Which means it's mine now," he said like I was extra baggage.

"Let it be his concern, then."

"Orion, what if this is tied to your grandmother's necklace?"

I caught the warning in his eyes and briefly hesitated before logic kicked in. I shook my head. "There has to be another explanation. They clearly thought I was someone named Annulla. Besides, who could know? I've only told you, Rae, and Julian about it."

"It doesn't mean someone couldn't have already beaten you to what Corinne was hiding."

My skin crawled. *The Chosen Shadow in Lightloch.* He had been looking for something. Now this lethal Incendor. But who was Annulla? Did Banden and Alec know what Corinne had been hiding, and was their motive really to protect me, or at least, *only* to protect me?

"Alec, do you know something I don't?" I asked.

"I know your grandmother's reputation," he said, darker than the alleyway. "Just pray she didn't leave you her dirty business to clean up after."

Little did he know. She had. Mom knew something about it, and I needed to find out what it was. And it seemed like someone else wanted it too. Whether it was a Pawn or the Obsidian King himself, someone was after me. And they would come after me regardless of if I stayed out of my family troubles or tried to unearth their secrets. Julian had also said MISTIC suspected a mole within the organization. What if they were after Corinne's secrets? And what if they were already a step ahead of me? I shivered but reminded myself of MISTIC's promise to protect me, which now made me skeptical.

Had Celeste known someone was after me all this time?

CHAPTER 14

My first Arayis class—Introduction to the Air Element with Professor Osmus Wicbin, who was also my preceptor—was at three in the afternoon that next day. I had read some pages of the textbook, hoping it would give me an idea of the curriculum. I'd never put that kind of effort into school before, another differentiator from Mom. She had been a straight-A student, an overachiever who'd be a chapter ahead of her classmates.

I had called her earlier, and, to no surprise, my call had gone straight to voicemail. She was purposely avoiding me. Or something had happened to her. My only assurance was Banden was in contact with her—at least I hoped he was. I would help bring her home, which meant sneaking around solving Corinne's riddles while pretending to take Mom's advice: be a normal sorcerer teenager.

I threw my bike in the bushes, activated the portal, and ran for the Flyers' section. A sign with the words, ISORIA ACADEMY FLYERS ONLY, pointed to a separate line and a sleek, dark-brown carriage with a colossal academy crest outlined in gold on both sides. I held up my pass to the coachman like everyone else did and entered a carriage already filled with chatty young sorcerers. I kept to myself among the excited teens, but their energy fueled me. I was going to sorcery school. Although everyone was telling me the dangers of this world, I wanted to be a part of it. This was where I belonged.

After tilting and bumping to the carriage's motions, I was still bouncing as the carriage landed. As I stepped outside, my breath caught in my throat. It would have been an Instagram moment if technology worked here.

A towering white and sky-blue castle was centered in the middle of a chasm between the mountains, like they had split for the castle to exist. Its blocky yet lean architecture was camouflaged within the peaks. One tower stood out of place with a dome on top, a glass golf ball glistening in the afternoon sun. A long stone bridge led to tall steps with glass doors wrapped in gold vines, while four bridges were symmetrically placed around the castle. The Isoria Academy crest was painted on the cobbled pavement and on the white flags cemented into the bridge railings.

Sorcerers crossed the stone bridge as if they weren't in one of the most beautiful places on the planet. There was something freeing about this place. I felt lighter, like I was on top of the world. I wanted to join the students resting on the lawn and on benches surrounding a small fountain enjoying the castle's wonders and fallen autumn leaves. *This* was where I belonged.

Thankfully, the tall steps weren't as steep as they appeared, and the glass doors were as light as air, opening at only a touch. The high ceiling was partly constructed of glass, the sky in the background accentuating the castle's magnificent height. The structure was airy yet grounded, with many large windows and mirrored staircases and a giant statue of a pegasus at the center. Many students wore the modern-medieval trend. I stuck out like a tourist with my jeans and brown sweater in the sea of light-blues, yellows, whites, and silvers.

I pulled out the map Iceflyn had given me. There were five academic buildings: Nova, Bolt Electrica, Gale Wing, Equinox Hall, and the one I was in, the Kyson Artus Centre, which was mostly offices. Arayis had a boutique, an observatory (the dome), a lounge area, a dining hall, and a garden. Across the four bridges were the stables, a training arena, dormitories, and a path that led to Aerbourne Village.

My classroom was in Nova on the third floor. I followed the map until I reached the back of the castle and found a set of doors leading to a courtyard. All the buildings were connected, but I didn't mind walking in the cloudy, warm weather. I went through more glass doors and climbed a marble staircase. The celestial building was decorated with paintings of astrological symbols. Large birthstones topped pedestals that ran up and down the halls, and constellations dotted the ceiling. It was easy to navigate, and I found my classroom next to an opal stone.

The open door led to a full and chatty room that didn't feel like any typical high school classroom. It was cozy, with mosaic windows, wooden beams over its stone walls, and a giant tapestry with a blue-and-purple starry design hanging across the ceiling. I found a seat at the back.

Ten minutes past the class's start time, the door banged. Conversation instantly halted as a man in a light-blue and white robe strolled down the aisle.

"Good evening, class," he announced, dropping his books on a table at the front of the room. He rummaged through his bag for supplies, wasting no time, like he was making up for the lost time.

His disheveled blond hair and scruff made him look mad. "I apologize for my tardiness. I'm Professor Wicbin, if that isn't obvious. As we know, students are coming and going as they're dropping and adding classes, so we're still keeping the lessons light. We're continuing last week's lesson on Air Ropes. For the fresh faces, I'll briefly explain."

Whew. I wasn't the only new student.

He went straight into the Air Rope lecture. He explained how as our powers grew stronger and as we understood every aspect of the spell, we could create larger ropes and catch and pull bigger and heavier objects, as well as cast multiple ropes simultaneously. As he walked up and down the aisle, a girl with long red-orange hair and striking green eyes raised her hand and answered almost every one of his questions. She was called on so many times I learned her name was Valerie.

"Air Ropes, besides for picking up objects, whipping, or even grabbing, can be used as leverage, support, and extra strength," Valerie answered Wicbin's question about the purpose of Air Ropes, smiling as he nodded.

"Very good, Miss Ruelle. Let me demonstrate."

Wicbin tried lifting a heavy metal bar at the front of the classroom. It barely raised from the floor. He then cast a white-blue stream of air that snaked around the bar and grabbed it again, this time lifting it to his waist.

For practice, we had to cast a tiny rope to lift our pencils. After demonstrating the spell with the correct hand motions and energy, he left us to ourselves. I aimed my hand toward the pencil like he had done, waving it with light strokes. My fingers tingled from the airy sensation, but no white-blue streak appeared. I tried, and tried, only able to feel the power but not execute the spell. If I had done so well in training and my IEPE results were so extraordinary, shouldn't I be better at this? I was even more discouraged when my neighbors were successful, especially Valerie, who was the first one to cast the spell.

Feeling the pressure, I took a deep breath.

The tingles started again, my fingers trembling this time. The airy sensation was stronger, pulsing from my fingertips to my wrist, ready to escape. But neither a rope nor gentle wind materialized. Instead, a smoky white blast shot from my hand, and my chair shot backward, my back slamming into the table behind me. My books bounced in the air and banged against the table, the pages flipping aggressively. Multiple bangs reverberated as the entire table crashed to the floor, books and equipment following. My classmates screamed as I shrunk into my seat, wishing I could melt into the floor. I hid my face in my hand to conceal my humiliation.

Hurried footsteps clicked across the marble, and I finally gained the courage to look at Wicbin. He ran to my row, robe flying behind him. "Is everyone all right? What happened?"

Many passed confused glances, but plenty of eyes glared at me. Wicbin spun around, eyeing me curiously. "New face, I see. Your name?"

"Orion Candor," I breathed, feeling my heartbeat in my throat. "Professor, I'm sorry. I didn't mean to—"

He held a hand up. "I asked for a name. Where magic happens, never expect perfection. Don't apologize for having power."

But I have too much.

With a quick swish of his arm, several wavelengths spiraled toward the fallen tables and righted them. He flicked his other arm the same way, and each fallen book neatly piled itself in front of its rightful owner. Everyone stared in awe. But across the room, Valerie was staring at me. No, *glaring*.

"We must remember not to fear power," Wicbin continued, showing me his back as he ambled down the aisle. "When we *understand* our strengths and weaknesses, we learn *we* have control over them, not the other way around. That's why we're all here, isn't it? Plenty of you were defeated when you couldn't cast the spell. I was watching. But it doesn't mean you failed."

Everyone was silent, forgetting I was there, their eyes now glued to Wicbin, although Valerie occasionally looked over her shoulder to throw daggers at me with her eyes. I sank into my seat, resenting Wicbin's speech, unlike my inspired classmates. I controlled nothing. For the rest of the class, I sat in embarrassment, obsessing over my magical mishap.

When Wicbin dismissed us, I quickly packed my belongings, more than eager to leave. I had been so excited to start sorcery school. Now, I couldn't fathom returning. Maybe I should go back into hiding and finish high school. Why couldn't I be a normal sorcerer?

"Miss Candor?" Wicbin stopped me before I escaped. He stood a few feet away with his hands behind his back. "A word, please."

I followed him to the front of the classroom, ready to accept my fate. He neatly stacked the papers sprawled across the table before looking up. "Well, don't look so guilty. You look like you hexed one of your classmates."

"Am I not in trouble?" I asked, confused.

He snorted, startling me. "No. I've seen much worse. Your actions weren't intentional."

"Then, why am I here, Professor?"

"Why, to make sure you're okay."

"Oh," was all I managed, but the curiosity in his bright eyes told me he was waiting for an explanation. I thought carefully before answering, not wanting to share too much. "My magic . . . does that sometimes . . . without my doing or control."

He tilted his head to the side. I continued, his silence intimidating me. "Something like that may happen again."

His lips curved, the brightness in his eyes sparkling. "Only if you let it." He grabbed his stacked papers. "Feel free to visit me during office hours or talk after class if you need to." When I nodded, he smiled. "I'll see you Thursday, Miss Candor. This should be an interesting semester, hmm?"

More interesting than you bargained for.

With the academy as a new addition to my schedule, the next two weeks exhausted me. I had my nonmagus lessons in the morning and academy classes in the afternoon, then I'd meet with Rae and Julian at The Enchanted Mug to do schoolwork all evening. It was exhausting, but I was slowly getting into a rhythm.

I didn't see Alec at all. Banden wanted him to walk me home after every class, especially since these November days were short and dark by the time I was done, but I'd refused, and there were times where he couldn't. I didn't mind commuting alone. Although I'd watch my back as I passed the Royal Scouts, Avelin was densely populated enough that I didn't worry about my safety. While everyone kept their eyes down when walking past the Scouts, I'd stare curiously at their black horses and dark masks.

Mom was unbelievable. She sent another email and even went out of her way to create a new email chain to completely ignore and not respond to the last two I had sent. Again, she went on about her job and how it had been crazy the last several weeks and how she missed me and hoped we could schedule a phone call sometime soon. I was absolutely pissed and wanted nothing to do with her. She was completely evading my questions.

My powers, as I wouldn't expect anything less, continued to ruin my life. In Introduction to Air Defense Spells with Professor Cesar Stroydor, we learned how to create simple Air Shields, and I accidentally made a hole in the floor. Stroydor, a brawny man with a patterned tattoo along his neck—I was sure the rest of it was covered by his robe—was less verbal than Wicbin about my screwups. He'd raise an eyebrow, shake his head, and roll away in his wheelchair to the next student. His classroom matched his warlike temperament, with coats of arms tiled across the walls, along with weapons and busts of famous Isorian war heroes. He apparently taught most of the war classes, which was no surprise.

Valerie was also in my defense class, so I was graced with her evil eye every day. She towered over me, her red hair fiercely contrasting her pale vampire-like skin. With some of the creatures I'd seen in Isoria, who knew if she was a vampire or worse? I didn't want her to know she intimidated me. To make matters worse, in Wicbin's class, I made my Air Rope too long and ended up grabbing my class-mate's chair and pulling him to the floor, making me his permanent enemy. I also whipped someone in the back of the head with one.

Thankfully, my two weekend classes, History of Air with Professor Harrold Filbert and Creatures of Isoria I with Professor Wilbur Soveus, were purely lectures, so I didn't have to put my powers into action. Both classrooms were in Bolt Electrica, a weather-themed building whose walls were painted with clouds and lightning. Professor Filbert was an interesting fellow. His lanky figure was drowned by his long robes, and he wore large circular glasses on top of a beaklike nose. He walked with an awkwardness in his step but spoke proudly and confidently about Isoria's history. I learned about the Sorcerer Enchanter Revolution, a three-year war fought between sorcerers and enchanters over a decade of enchanter oppression, and how sorcerers had used their fear of enchanters to create propaganda about the "evils" of their magic.

Professor Wilbur Soveus, a short man with the body of a bowling ball, mumbled every word he spoke, his voice hard to hear under his squirrel-tail mustache. He explained how magical creatures lived all over the world but were invisible to nonmagus. However, not all magical creatures the nonmagus had passed down in stories existed, as some were purely fictitious or Isorians assumed so since they had never seen them. The creatures in Isoria either originated here or when they came here from other lands, evolved within the Isorian lands, adapting to the environment to create a new breed of species. The creatures we'd be learning about were specific to and bred on Isoria. I sat behind a boy I had sometimes caught spending time with Valerie after classes. I learned his name was Asher. His silver hair was gelled back, reminding me of a slick metal surface. But unlike Valerie, he rarely acknowledged me, and when he did, it was with a neutral gaze, like I was any other classmate. He also sat in front of me with a girl named Estelle, who I knew nothing about except her cattiness and love of gossip.

On Thursday night, I sat with Rae and Julian at The Enchanted Mug, discussing theories about my powers. It was like I had a mysterious disease with no cure. We sat in our usual spot by the fireplace, but the café was louder than usual, distracting me from my homework. Thursday nights were always trivia nights.

"You never used your powers before, so they might not be used to your sudden commands," Rae suggested as she did her homework. Her hair was in a high ponytail, displaying her pierced ears and my favorite dragon earring.

"Like her magic has a mind of its own?" Julian mocked. Although not as trendy as Rae, Julian was still well-groomed in a maroon knitted pullover, black trousers, and his everyday white sneakers. Everyone in Isoria dressed nicely, while I still opted for my comfort-over-style mentality. I couldn't count the times Rae tried giving me style advice. She'd even (lovingly) threatened to burn down my closet if I didn't learn how to dress like a real Isorian Aermage. According to her, I dressed like a tourist.

"Well, it kind of does. What other ideas do you have?" she challenged, crossing her arms.

He shrugged. "She might not be doing the spells correctly, or she's distracted."

"Are you suggesting she's distracted *every time* she does a spell?" She returned his mockery.

"It's all right, guys," I interrupted. They fought like toddlers when they got into one of their arguments. "I will forever be known as the weird magic freak."

"You're not a freak, Orion," Rae defended me "So your powers are a little haywire. You just started school. Give it time."

Time. That was the other answer I'd get.

"*Freak* suits her."

The three of us whipped around at the sudden shadow cast over our table. Valerie. Asher, the boy from my Creatures of Isoria I class, was with her, nervously biting his lip ring.

"Don't you have better things to do than harass people, Valerie?" Rae crossed her arms, eyeing Valerie up and down. Julian leaned back in his chair, clearly entertained. Or, judging by the sparkle in his eyes, he thought Valerie was hot. He was never stingy when giving a pretty girl his attention.

Valerie ignored her, dagger eyes on me. "Those were impressive stunts you pulled in class. You love attention, don't you?"

My insides were fierier than Valerie's stupid red hair, and before I knew it, I was on my feet. "What's your problem? Is it because of the tables? It was an accident."

I was up to her chest, noticing her broad shoulders and toned arms. Aermages wore light or pale colors, but she had broken the trend with her black attire and occasional navy-blue garments. Her lips curved condescendingly, like I was a pest she could rub off her shoe. "Sure it was."

My hands shook. "Maybe I should have taken you down with them."

"I'm getting a table, Val," Asher interrupted, his voice high and friendly. He clearly didn't want trouble.

"You think you're tough now because of your freakish abilities? I'm not fooled. Watch yourself, new girl." She turned her back to follow Asher, but I wasn't finished.

"How about you watch—" I started, but Rae grabbed my shoulder and pushed me down to my chair.

"Sit down before you make a scene," she ordered.

The commotion from trivia night wasn't enough to distract the table beside us, their focus no longer on the trivia host at the flower microphone but on me.

"It's not worth it," Julian agreed. "Too bad she's a bitch. She's hot."

Rae gave him a look. "He's partially right."

"How do you guys know her?" I asked.

She rolled her eyes. "Everyone in our year knows Valerie. She's considered what nonmagus call a 'valedictorian.' For us, it's a magnaintel. Super smart, excels at her studies. But she seems intimidated by you."

I laughed. "By *me?*"

Valerie scored astronomically higher on the intimidation board. She was clearly the brightest sorcerer in our classes. I didn't need more attention.

She shrugged. "You're competition."

"Like we've been taught in training, read between the lines," Julian added.

My friends then went on about MISTIC training, something about embarrassing someone while dueling her. When they mentioned Alec, I remembered I still had to tell them about the new plan with Operation Corinne. This weekend, we were finally going to end her secrets.

"I was so happy to be paired with him," Julian said. "I released all that pent-up anger I have whenever I see him." He punched his palm.

I perked up. This was the first time Julian had verbally expressed his dislike for Alec in front of me.

"He kicked your ass," Rae chided. He glared.

They were definitely going to hate him being added to the plans.

"So, we on for Operation Corinne tomorrow night?" I asked before they started another one of their quarrels.

Rae smiled wildly. "Hell, yeah. But how are you gonna get the necklace?"

I avoided her eyes. "Yeah, so about that . . . Alec's gonna help us."

Her smile faded, and Julian's expression twisted into one of frustration.

"Why does he need to be involved?" he grumbled.

"He's the only one who can get the necklace. He said he wouldn't tell anyone."

"And you believe him?" He crossed his arms, challenging the smallest spec of faith I had in Alec. It was hanging by a thread, and his doubt had me close to cutting it.

But I tried a different tactic. "Why do you guys hate him, anyway? I can't understand where your anger is coming from if I don't know what he did."

Julian turned away and leaned back in his chair. A team hollered when they answered the trivia question correctly, and I pretended to be interested in them, trying to shield my sudden annoyance. I was so afraid of bruising their feelings, yet they didn't trust me, and if they didn't trust me, should I even trust them?

Rae waited for the group to quiet down. "Jul, maybe you should—" she started, but he stopped her.

"Trouble follows him, Orion," he said, his voice low and rough. "He's so caught up about you, but he doesn't even have control over his own life."

I sighed, unwilling to fight against a boulder. Even if they wouldn't tell me, I still needed their help. But I couldn't jeopardize the plan because Julian couldn't be in the same room as Alec. Alec was already willing to put their feud aside for the heist.

"Julian, I understand if it's hard for you, but Alec needs to be a part of this," I said. "I'm not choosing between him and you."

He shook his head. "No, Orion. You can still count on us. Alec and I can be civil." He didn't sound convincing, but I took it like a stray animal searching for scraps—desperate but hopeful.

CHAPTER 15

That Friday evening, Rae and Julian waited with me in the library, reading the notes in the secret room while Alec retrieved the necklace. Like every Friday night, Banden didn't come home until eleven. He worked longer hours than usual so he would have fewer orders to fulfill on the weekend. He didn't question when Rae and Julian came over since they were here often. But Alec never came here to hang out. His involvement in the mission worried me as much as it bothered Rae and Julian. Whatever we needed to do, I prayed we'd be done by the time Banden arrived.

I was leaning over Rae's shoulder when I heard a knock at the front door.

I jumped for the door. "That has to be Alec."

"I'd rather have a run-in with a Chicanery," Julian grumbled.

I gave him a look before heading down the hallway to open the front door. Alec looked up curiously, loose locks falling over his eyes. He was in black jeans and a black sweater, and I tried ignoring the way the color complemented him. We were all in black attire. I'd even traded my combat boots for my black running sneakers, to which Rae's comments were: "Finally, I see you wear shoes other than those boots!" and "This is the most fashionable outfit you've ever worn." They had instructed me to wear only black because it would be easier to hide in the shadows. Common knowledge when it came to engaging in crime or mischief at night, they told me.

Alec held up the red crystal, which still found a way to glisten in the dark, its secrets a light in the shadows.

"Delivery." He tossed it to me.

I fumbled with it, squeezing the pendant harder than intended and leaving an indent in my skin, which only widened his smirk. I ignored it, refusing to give him any satisfaction. "Banden didn't suspect anything?"

"Nope. As long as I get it back by morning," he said and invited himself in.

I started for the hall. "Follow me. They're in the library."

He immediately fell into step with me. "I bet they're excited to see me. The last time I saw them was when I kicked Julian's ass in training." Although he played cool, his smirk wavered.

"Please play nice," I warned as we reached the library doors.

He rolled his eyes, and I took that as agreement.

Rae and Julian were where I had left them, skimming through the documents behind the bookshelf. They looked up as we walked in, and the room went still. Alec stiffened while Rae and Julian fought with the urge to show detestation, but their eyes betrayed them.

Alec squared his shoulders, his arms tightening with his jaw. I thought he would stay as far away from them as the room would allow, but his eyes widened as he slowly made his way to the secret room. And that's when I realized I hadn't told him about it or the documents.

"What's this?" he asked, standing in the doorway.

Noticing my apprehension, Rae jumped up from her chair and stood in front of the wooden table. "It's a hangout. Do you have the necklace?"

"Yup. So what are those documents you're doing such a terrible job at hiding?" He tried reaching over her arm, but Julian stepped in front of him.

"Thanks for the necklace. Your service isn't required anymore." He puffed out his chest and crossed his arms like a bouncer at a VIP club.

Both of their eyes breathed fire into each other.

"Listen, Alec," I said, stepping in between them. "I didn't tell you the full story because I was afraid you'd tell Banden."

His eyes flared. "Orion, secrets mean there are consequences, which means Banden should know."

"Either you're in or you're out," Julian said, turning into the bouncer again, his usually friendly eyes cold and dark. "We're with Orion, and we're not leaving her. If you go to Banden, she'll never trust you or him. It'll be a vicious cycle. Do you want that?"

I knew I could trust my friends. I had been hesitant in the beginning, but this cemented their loyalty.

Alec was inches from Julian, closer than I expected him to get. "Celeste will have us all hanged if anyone finds out."

"Yes, *if* she finds out," Rae countered, joining Julian. "So don't tell her. We've voiced our concerns. We'll tell MISTC if this proves to be viable information. Why involve them when we don't even know what's involved? And most importantly, what if this intel unknowingly harms Orion? What if she's harmed because they give the info to the wrong person, like the mole everyone is talking about?"

"Alec," I said, gently placing a hand on his forearm. "All I'm asking for is time."

I felt him stiffen underneath my touch. His sharp gaze didn't break, uncertainty scribbled across his face as he fought an internal battle. Banden meant the world to Alec, and I especially understood after learning Banden wasn't only a guardian to me but to him.

"Fine," he mumbled, pulling his arm away from me. "But you have to at least tell me what those documents are."

I nodded my gratitude before giving him the rundown of the sketched images and mysterious object Corinne apparently had that Obsidian wanted. His eyes widened at this, but he didn't protest since he had given his word. I then showed him where I believed the necklace was supposed to fit on the fireplace. He ran his hand over the jagged pattern on the unicorn and compared the necklace to the shape.

"I think your hunch is right." He reached for the fireplace, and when I saw what he was about to do, I jumped in front of him.

"Wait, I'll do it." I held out my hand.

This time he moved the necklace out of reach. "I'm not taking that risk."

"Well, you have to." I snatched it from his hand, surprising him. "Who knows what I'm about to get us into?"

And before he could argue, I shoved the stone into the hollow oval. He yanked me out of the way while Rae and Julian jumped back. A faint red light radiated from the pendant, followed by a clicking noise. Pulsing like a heartbeat, the light intensified, and the painted arch began to gleam like sunlight. We shielded our eyes as white rays of light combined with the red pulsing light. In a blink, the blinding lights vanished, the mural untouched. We all stared at each other.

"What just happened?" I asked.

Rae shook her head. "No clue. It doesn't look like anything changed."

"It disappeared quicker than any food on my plate," Julian commented.

Rae smirked. "And that's a record."

We approached it as if something might pop out and attack us. Alec's eyes searched the painting of the books as he slowly reached out and traced his hand along the wall.

"The light was only inside the arch . . ." he thought out loud, his fingers reaching for the painted rocks, then the painted door. But his hand vanished like it had fallen into quicksand. He jerked it back.

"Are you okay?" I jumped to his side.

"No way," he murmured almost trancelike, as if he hadn't heard me. "It's a Peintura Portal."

"A what?"

He turned to me. "A painted portal. You can only travel to the place that is, well, painted. They're illegal in public places. Usually, you can access them freely, but this one must be protected. If I'm right, this must lead to some library."

Library. Images of the drawings flashed through my mind like camera snapshots—the scepter above a book, the lion with its opened mouth, the swirl reflecting in a pendant . . . and those bone-chilling words.

At midnight, it will show. One is the final hour. Find it before they do.

Without a word, I headed to the secret room and searched the papers for the sketches. I put the scepter and lion head side by side since they were the only two that had images of books. Then there was the image of the swirly pendant. But I realized—it wasn't a swirl but streaks of light. The blinding lights. The portal.

First it was the unicorns on the fireplace, then the necklace to activate the portal . . .

"Orion?" Alec made me jump.

I invited my friends in and displayed the sketches of the scepter and lion. "These pictures both have books in them, and this—" I paused, referring to the necklace, my brain working faster than I could speak—"must be Corinne's Clavis. These images are important, but my mom didn't realize that they're steps, steps that could lead us to what Corinne was hiding. We have to figure out the third step!"

Rae grabbed the papers, looking at them from different angles. She took particular interest in the lion head. "I feel like I've seen this before."

"Yeah, me too." Julian joined her, grabbing a corner. "I can't put my finger on it."

"Yeah, literally, because you'd smear the image off," she said, slapping his hand away.

Alec hung back, his eyes swiftly reading through the papers over Rae's shoulder. "That lion head is on one of the newels in Athena's Library," he said. "That's why there's a rectangle around it."

Julian nodded without looking at him, while Rae's eyes widened. "He's right," she said. "So that means the portal must lead to Athena's Library!"

The third step. I was about to join Rae in her excitement when Alec's dark voice threw a dart into our bubble of joy. "Hang on. There are three staircases on the grand floor alone, and two more floors, meaning we have ten newels to tackle."

Julian challenged the idea further. "So we go in broad daylight and search the newels till we find what Corinne hid? How did she get away with that?"

It *was* absurd. Although I never knew Corinne, I knew enough to know that absurdity was her norm. But then I caught it staring right back at me everywhere I looked, unable to escape. The words were scribbled on almost every document—on the unicorns, the lion, the scepter, the pendant, and the letters. I had repeated them in my head but was finally listening to them.

"'At midnight, *it* will show. One is the final hour,'" I repeated, my voice fading, not wanting to believe it. "It has to be done tonight. The object will show for us at midnight and disappear by one in the morning."

Alec's face hardened. "After closing hours, the library is heavily guarded by Royal Knights. Your grandmother is trying to kill us."

I swallowed, trying to push down the brick sitting on my chest. If it was anything like the notes warned, the risk was worth it.

"'The king will not rest till he destroys what will destroy him but save us all. I need to end this before he ends us,'" I recited, silencing anyone's protests. "If this is actual intel, we have to try."

CHAPTER 16

Cinderella had to return to her ordinary life at midnight. I had to change mine.

We had a few hours to kill before entering the portal. At some point, I had fallen asleep from boredom. Alec was reading when I opened my eyes, and he sat cross-legged against the wall. Rae was on her phone as she sat on the desk chair, while Julian lay on the floor like me, throwing a small flame between his hands like a ball.

"You like to read," I said to Alec, remembering the times I'd seen him reading in the Elixir Chamber. I wondered if he spent a lot of time in Athena's Library, which would explain why he'd recognized the newel in the notes.

He had looked surprised by my comment. "I like to learn what people can't teach me," he answered dismissively, shoving the book inside his bag. Even discussing his hobbies was too personal, but at least I'd gotten a response from him. Like progressing with an untamed animal, I took what I could get.

Finally, it was just before midnight. "Everyone has their Elastocoms?" Rae asked, meeting us by the fireplace and revealing the spaghetti-thin band around her wrist.

We all nodded, each of us showing ours in turn. A MISTIC invention, an Elastocom was a means of secret communication.

When you plucked it, it would send a small snap, like a rubber band, to the person with the matching one. Mine was attached to Julian's, while Rae's matched Alec's.

I made the first move, inching toward the mural as my friends followed. A gust of cold wind encompassed me before I slammed into something hard, followed by a tickling sensation on my cheeks.

A human-sized potted plant with dark-green leaves blocked our path. I moved out of its way, giving everyone room to pass. I thought we were in a museum until I saw the thousands of bookcases. The place was like a cathedral, with three floors reaching up to a tree and pond with salmon painted on the ceiling. The stone arches and pillars were wrapped in gold marble, and crystals in the glossy black floor glittered like a starry sky. One staircase led from the first floor to a set of double staircases on the second and to a giant, old-fashioned clock nailed to the wall above the landing. The moon's rays ghosted through the mosaic windows, illuminating the dark building. Rain pattered against the ceiling, followed by the occasional sound of thunder.

"This library is fit for royalty," I whispered, gawking at its artwork.

"It's creepy at night," Julian's voice echoed, and we immediately shushed him.

"Worst spy ever," Rae hissed.

It was then I noticed the plain vanilla wall behind us. No mural. No escape. I prayed Corinne had thought this plan all the way through.

"Remember, we have one hour," I said, glancing at the colossal clock. "There's ten newel posts in total, three floors, five flights of stairs, and four of us."

The sudden sound of footsteps becoming progressively louder echoed to our right.

"A knight! Get behind the plants!" Julian urged us forward.

The portal was located near the hallway leading to the encyclopedia room. We hid behind two tall ficus plants in the corners of the hallway, Alec next to me behind one plant, Rae and Julian pressed against the wall behind the other plant. I peeked through the giant green leaves, watching a shadowy figure pass by. She wore light-blue clothing and had armor over her torso. Her expression, which I expected to be alert, was sleepy, as if her nightly job was quiet and unexciting. When she was well down the hall, we emerged from our hiding spots and huddled in the darkness.

"How many do you think there are?" Rae asked, looking over her shoulder.

Alec gazed upward, his eyes tracking something. "There's at least one per floor."

"How do you know?" Julian challenged, his tone doubtful.

Alec hesitated before speaking, his body tensing as he looked Julian in the eyes. "I just know. Plus, you can see the knights' torches on the floors above."

We all looked up to where flames floated along the railings of the second and third floors, confirming Alec's theory. Julian rolled his eyes.

"We have to split up," I decided. "We should alternate floors. It'll be easier to sneak around."

Julian nodded. "Rae and I will take the first and third floors."

"No, you take the ground and second floors." When he was about to protest, I used the same excuse I had on Alec. "It's my family's business. Alec and I will take the risk of going to the highest floors."

Julian raised an eyebrow. "You know, Orion, *we're* the ones in a spy ring."

"She has me." Alec stepped forward.

Julian's eyes narrowed. "Yes, but *we're* the Fielders."

"In training," Alec bit back.

Julian's back straightened, and I put a hand to his chest to prevent a brawl while shooting daggers at Alec. I didn't care who started the fire but rather who chose not to fuel it.

I held out my Elastocom. "Remember, two snaps means you found the right newel, one means to keep moving."

They all nodded. Once the plan was finalized, Julian led us on tiptoe through a row of bookcases. We held our breath and watched for guards. My heart pounded with each successful step we took. Never did I have to sneak around before. And, of course, as my first time was possibly the key to saving this world from its shadows, it had had major consequences.

At the end of the row, Julian stopped us with his hand. "There are two of them over there," he whispered, pointing to the center of the floor. Two knights quietly conversed, holding lit torches as the moonlight cast a glow over them. Thunder boomed overhead.

"Alec and I will run for the first floor," I whispered to Rae and Julian. "Wait for us to get there before you take on the ground floor."

When the knights disappeared behind a row of bookcases, Alec and I bolted for the staircase. My eyes were glued to the pendulum on the giant clock, the predictor of my fate. We ran up the first flight, then split up on the left and right staircases. I kneeled on the marble floor and constantly looked over my shoulder as I searched for the lion head. Nothing. I crawled to the other newel, my heart racing as I investigated the sculpted designs. Still nothing.

Across from me on the other staircase, Alec shook his head. Two snaps stung my wrist, making me jump. No for Rae and Julian too.

Alec put his hand out, telling me he was coming to me. I looked for knights as he raced down his stairs and came up mine. His footsteps were as light as air, but I could hear him panting as he got closer. He grabbed my arm and led us up the next flight of stairs.

We'd almost reached the top of the third-floor staircase when Alec grabbed my shoulder and pushed me down, my knees and hands banging against the marble steps. I thought he had tripped until I saw a bright flame at the top of the staircase above us. Alec put a hand over his mouth. I did the same, our chests rising and falling as a red light flashed in our direction. But the staircase must have been steep enough, the night's darkness our protector. The flame slowly floated by.

I dropped my head, letting out a long breath. "Dammit," I muttered. "Seriously, what kind of person *is* my grandmother?"

"A puzzle and mystery with a hint of fire," Alec whispered. When he saw the look on my face, he clarified. "Banden's words."

We raced silently up the steps. Luckily, the staircases to each floor were adjacent to one another. I felt two more snaps on my wrist, and my stomach did flips. That meant one of these newels had to be the one. *Third's the charm.*

Adrenaline flooded my veins as I examined the newel, but my high dropped. I double-checked, then triple-checked. Alec frowned at his newel too.

"How's this possible?" I hissed.

Footsteps and heavy breathing echoed behind us, and we jumped to our feet. I turned around, hands ready, only to find Rae and Julian stumbling toward us.

Julian bent over to catch his breath, while Rae rested her hand on his shoulder. "We were almost caught," she said in between breaths. "I think they're suspicious now."

"I distracted a knight by increasing the flames on one of the oil lamps on the walls," Julian explained. "Any luck?"

I shook my head. "No. Are there other staircases?"

Alec gave me a solemn look. "I know this library by heart. This is it."

My stomach dropped, and I had to fight against the panic growing within me. My fears had become reality. We'd read the clues incorrectly. This dangerous mission had been for nothing. And we had no way of escaping.

Alec saw my fallen face and turned to Julian. "Are you sure it wasn't on the ground floor?"

"Yes." He forced a steady voice and squared his shoulders. "We searched them thoroughly."

"Maybe we should double-check to make sure you didn't miss anything," Alec suggested, trying to keep his voice level as well.

Julian's eyes narrowed. "I told you, nothing's there. We were trained by the same people, you know."

I stepped forward, noticing the way their bodies stiffened like soldiers preparing for battle. "Come on, guys, let's find a way out of here."

But I was filtered out as they inched closer to each other.

"Are you sure *you* didn't miss anything?" Julian shot back, his hands curling into fists.

"Of course not," Alec spat, his voice slightly above a whisper. "It's kinda hard believing you since you know about misreading things, you know."

"Stop." Rae stepped between them. "We need to put this energy into finding a way out of here."

"Maybe you're too blind to see the truth when it's right in front of you," Julian snarled, elbowing her out of the way.

Rae and I shushed them, but their voices only escalated with the thunder outside. We might as well be invisible. They pushed us to the side as they went head to head.

Alec laughed maliciously. "You want the truth? What's it like living with a criminal who cheated his way out of jail time?"

Julian smirked. "Coming from the person whose father actually escaped prison. At least mine had the guts to stand the full trial. Cowards make a run for it."

Alec's eyes filled with fire. "Shut up!" he yelled, shoving Julian against the newel as Rae ducked out of the way. Julian pushed back, sending Alec into a bookcase.

Before Rae and I could even attempt crisis control, a rough voice boomed from somewhere. "Someone's here! Guards!"

The boys' eyes widened at the realization of what they've done, the hatred gone, now remorseful.

"Dammit, you guys!" Rae shouted as several knights came trudging up the stairs.

"Split up!" Alec ordered, grabbing my arm and pulling me down an aisle of bookcases.

"Stop! By orders of the king!" a knight called.

We were stopped by a knight who met us at the opposite side of the aisle. His torch burst into flames, then transformed into a gleaming orange-and-yellow blade. Bidentias. I had learned about them in Professor Stroydor's class. A weapon with multiple identities. We turned around, but another knight boxed us in.

"Let's take it easy, okay?" he said. Both knights inched closer, narrowing the gap. "Now, what are you two doing here?"

I was surprised to see Alec smirk, the orange sword reflected in his eyes. "Escaping."

Alec swished his hand, and a pile of books cascaded from the shelves, ruthlessly smacking the knight. Alec pulled me past the chaos, and we bolted down the next aisle. He bumped into me, almost knocking me down. Sparks exploded near his feet from what I thought were Fire Balls until they transformed. Fire Shackles.

Alec shouted beside me, "Don't let them touch you!"

My lungs burned as we ran haphazardly, dodging Fire Shackles and Alec throwing out spells to hold off our chasers. We'd finally reached the staircase, ready to escape, when something caught my eye, making me pause. An ancient book was encased in a glass compartment on top of a marble stand. And there it was, in plain sight. A lion head sculpted in the marble.

Alec was halfway down the staircase, eyes wild. "What are you waiting for? Come on!"

Knights charged for us, blocking my path to the compartment. Without warning, I dodged left, sprinting down an aisle of bookcases with Alec shouting after me.

"Get the girl," I heard a knight growl. "Leave the Terramancer to me."

Footsteps pounded after me, growing louder. *Think, Orion, think!* Books zoomed past my peripheral vision, and I thought of Alec bringing down that knight. *Trust my instincts.* I stuck my hands out to the side like wings. Without aiming, I let my thoughts and intentions consume me, using them to fuel the energy tingling from my feet, a place I'd never felt power before. The energy traveled through my blood like electricity through a wire. A force vibrated around my hands, a tight sensation at my fingertips. I pulled my hands down, feeling the intensity of the power release.

"What the—" the knight started, followed by the sound of crashing books. A cool wind blew into me like opening a door on a windy day, slowing me down and biting my cheeks. It grew more intense, pushing me back and forcing me into an awkward gait, like I was running in water. My eyes widened as what I'd meant to do wasn't what I saw happening.

Three bookcases had fallen in the knight's path, one resting on his leg. He struggled to free himself as the wind nailed him, his grip slipping from the shelf. Hundreds of books swirled in the air, and I ducked before being smacked by one. I looked up to see a sofa hurtling in my direction. I sprung out of its way, the sofa missing me by an inch as I crashed to the floor.

My body fought the windstorm, my hands shielding my face from flying books. I grabbed the necklace in my back pocket and ran for the showcase, but an icy coolness at my ankle knocked me to the marble floor and the necklace was ripped from my grasp, lifted through the air like a hovercraft. I bolted for it, escaping a row of bookcases falling behind me like dominoes. The necklace smacked against a wall and looped around an overturned table leg. I reached for it, but the coldness from before snagged my ankle and dragged me across the floor. My hair flew in my face as I looked over my shoulder. Like a dog on a leash, I had been caught by a Water Rope at the end of which stood a knight.

"Where do you think you're going, girlie?" he hollered over the wind and falling books.

"Let me go!" I kicked my feet, reaching for a fallen bookshelf to hook on to.

"Make this windstorm stop!" He pulled harder, but with the force of the wind, I couldn't grab the bookshelf, and I slammed full force into him, the impact pulling his Water Rope from his grip. I rolled off him, ignoring the pain coursing through my body. He tried reaching for me with his rope, but a shelf toppled over, blocking the spell. I grabbed the necklace, clutching it until I could feel it indenting my skin, and zigzagged through fallen bookcases and flying books.

I reached the glass case and skidded to my knees, the friction of my jeans burning against the marble. My hands rapidly searched the stand for any indentation or opening.

"Come on, come on," I muttered nervously, slapping the necklace all over, the wind hindering my accuracy. I jammed it into random spaces and indentations across the art before pressing it into the lion's open mouth. The stone instantly glowed, and a thin, long rectangular line etched itself into the marble around a small gold knob below the glass case. A drawer. I yanked on the knob, revealing an old brown book.

There was a hum and a bright zap. A human-sized glowing, rippling image of my house's library appeared in midair. A portal. The escape.

But I wasn't leaving my friends behind. Rae and Julian were battling guards on the first floor, and I had no idea where Alec was. I threw the necklace and book through the portal, an electric buzzing like that of a bug zapper swallowing the items.

"There ya are, girl!" yelled a knight

But the knight stopped in his tracks and looked upward, jaw dropping. The glowing Water spell surrounding his hands disappeared as they fell to his side. I turned to see a cloud of black-and-red smoke floating toward the ceiling, pulsing as thunder reverberated from within it. Then, like a genie escaping a lamp, the smoke grew and contorted, morphing into a human shape.

"Orion Candor," a voice hissed from the cloud. The outline of the figure became clearer. It was like looking at a negative image but on smoky clouds. It was a man with a strong square jaw and sharp almond-shaped eyes. He wore a brocade coat.

"Granddaughter of Corinne Candor, daughter of Seraphina Candor."

A shiver traveled down my spine. "Who are you?" I asked, but I wasn't sure if my small voice could be heard over the rumbling thunder.

The smoky man grinned, his wicked lips outlined in red. "Not who but what. I have eyes everywhere. When you think you're safe, I'll remind you I'm one step ahead. You have what I seek. Bring it to me, or the people you love will fall at my feet, especially the ones who have loyalties to me. I can't wait for when we finally meet, Orion—face-to-face, flesh to flesh. For now, let me introduce myself."

A puff of smoke billowed toward me, and I stumbled back. The smoke flew upward, missing me by a hair as it contorted. Black-and-red-insect legs morphed from the small cloud, then pounded to the floor in front of me. The creature had large, sharp pinchers twice the size of my torso and a long, dagger-like tail. It was no longer the cloud that threatened me but an elephant-sized scorpion. It clawed and snapped at the air, a glittering red-and-black smoke trailing behind as it scurried toward me. When it flung its tail at me, I sent a Blast to block it. It continued viciously snapping and clawing at me as I blocked its advances with Blasts.

Not used to expelling this much energy, I felt myself weaken, and I became clumsier with my dodges. Before I could attempt another Blast, a white-blue icicle shot through the air, slicing through the scorpion's torso. The scorpion screeched as another icicle impaled its left pincher, another penetrating its right. It turned around to face its new attacker, but suddenly, the thunderous black-and-red cloud shrunk, taking the scorpion and thunder with it. A red light brighter than the sun forced me to turn away, followed by a flash, and the smoke and scorpion were gone.

Before I could think, something cool gripped my wrists, and my arms were ripped back behind me, tearing at my biceps.

The giant clock chimed, deep and throaty, vibrating the walls, and the portal disappeared, along with Corinne's items.

One is the final hour.

CHAPTER 17

I fought against the Water Shackles, but each movement tightened the grip around my wrists, triggering an icy burn. The windstorm stopped, books raining from the ceiling and crashing into me.

My knight in not-so-shining armor grabbed my arms and lifted me to my feet like a rag doll. "Fight all you want. You're not going anywhere." I could hear the smile in his rough voice, his victory in my failure.

A cold, burning sensation wrapped around my ankles. More Water Shackles, heavy as iron. As the knight shoved me forward, I discovered they constricted with excessive movement. They were made to keep me walking. To stay submissive. Alec, Julian, and Rae were bound by element shackles, too, a knight behind each of them.

They led us out into the chilly night and down the front steps, silver-lined clouds cloaking the moon. I wondered if, during the day, this view of Erudite Square was beautiful. The colossal building, with its enormous white pillars, glistened in the moonlight, and a statue of an owl sat poised atop a stack of books at the end of each stair rail. At the bottom of the steps, a black carriage waited.

Bars guarded the carriage windows. A crest with a chevron pattern was painted on the side, a red, inverted V over the blue background. There was a griffin under the V, and a flower—similar to the one on the Isorian flag—graced the left and right sides. Although, its petals were sharper and shorter. A gold crown was set atop the crest. The royal family's crest.

As the knights ushered us into the carriage, I caught the one behind me whisper to the coachman, "Maximillian Stone's son. The king is gonna be ecstatic."

Once we were seated, three knights entered and cast a spell, wrapping our shackles around the backs of the seats. When they left, the door slammed shut, then disappeared like fog, leaving us no escape. The carriage wheels rolled, escorting us to prison.

It was in the silence that it hit me. I was going to the king. The king. I'd never met royalty of anything. And I was meeting one as a criminal. I envisioned guillotines and lynching. I wanted to tell my friends what I had seen in the library and that even though we were going to prison, we hadn't failed. But I was afraid we would be overheard, so I asked, "What's going to happen to us?"

Rae sighed heavily. "No idea. Depends on how severe the Royal Court determines our case to be. We could be fined, have to repay our debts through community service, or receive jail time."

Truth would prevail, and if the king didn't punish us, Celeste would.

Next to me, Alec turned his head. "We're going to be fine," he assured, his voice strong. But I couldn't tell if he actually believed it or was just reassuring himself.

"Yeah, because you just know things, right?" Julian mumbled.

He smirked. "See, you get it."

"I see you don't get sarcasm."

"Shut up!" Rae snapped. "It's both of your faults we're even in here."

Julian dropped his head. Alec had forced his invite, and I had warned him about keeping the peace with my friends. He must have had the same thought because his face softened, and he avoided my eyes. It was the most remorseful I'd ever seen him, even if he didn't verbally apologize.

I glared at them. "I'm tired of this feud between you two. What happened in there?"

Surprisingly, Alec smirked, and there was something sinister in the way he looked at Julian. "Would you like to do the honors, dear Julian? After all, you two are supposed to be best buds."

I didn't like how he was baiting Julian. Was he trying to see if this would ruin our friendship?

But Julian returned Alec's smirk with one of his own. "With pleasure. Orion, I was going to tell you. Don't let this prick convince you otherwise. My father used to be a knight for King Leo. He was a commander for the KLE, or the Knights of Law Enforcement. He was an excellent horseman, studied war tactics, law. Alec's father, Maximillian Stone, was his second-in-command."

"Can't wait to hear your fairy-tale version of the story," Alec spat.

"Alec, shut it," I snapped, glaring at him before turning back to Julian. "Ignore him. Keep going."

Julian continued, unbothered by Alec's remark. "Mr. Stone was close to receiving the first commander position for the KLE. My father joined two years after Mr. Stone, but he excelled quickly. He and my father became comrades, but once he noticed my father wanted the position, a silent rivalry between them ensued. My father got the position. Mr. Stone got second in command, and he hated my father for it. Max felt cheated and betrayed. My father was civil, knowing Mr. Stone was hurt, but the tension between them never subsided.

"One evening, my father took off from work, and Mr. Stone took his shift. He was stationed in New Castle, one town over from Westwin. My father received a message from a Royal Scout that a KLE knight had spotted smoke in Westwin. He tried contacting Mr. Stone, who was in New Castle. He couldn't reach him, so he saddled his horse and raced to Westwin, only to find the town destroyed.

"Based on evidence and eyewitness reports, the KLE and King Leo came to believe that a high-ranking knight had been involved in Westwin's demise. And the two knights on the scene were my father and Mr. Stone. They were incarcerated and put on a month-long trial to unveil the secret Pawn. And it all pointed to Mr. Stone."

"The evidence wasn't concrete," Alec spoke slowly, as if to keep his composure.

"But concrete enough," Julian shot back. "On the last day of trial, Mr. Stone's cell was found empty. The Royal Court immediately ruled him guilty. No one has seen him since. King Leo stripped away my father's knighthood, but he didn't want to ruin his reputation, so he helped him get the job as mayor of Crystal Manor, a Sanctor."

I blinked. "Your father's the *mayor*?"

He nodded. "Yes, but my father loved being a knight, Orion. It destroyed him. He endured hell because of that son of a bitch, and it took a toll on my family. My parents separated, and my older brother, Stefano, and I went to live with my father in Crystal Manor while my mother fled Isoria, not wanting anything to do with my father."

"Like your family's the only one who suffered." Alec pulled against his shackles, his arm grazing mine.

Julian sat back in his chair, unlike Alec, who strained against his shackles like he was about to break them and punch Julian. Now Julian had the evil smirk. "How would you know? Your parents are gone."

"Julian." Rae interrupted for the first time, her voice curt. But selfishly, I only wanted to know more.

"Why? Alec graciously handed me the mic," Julian baited. "His mother was taken as a prisoner to the Obsidian King's castle. Besides desecrating an entire village and killing innocents, he sent his wife to the most murderous sorcerer in Isoria."

"I'll kill you!" Alec roared, the restraints around his wrists seeming to feed his rage. The veins in his neck bulged, and his eyes were hard.

"Julian, enough!" Rae's voice cut deep, like she felt Alec's wounds, but Julian wanted to drive the knife deeper.

"What? I'm speaking facts," he grumbled. "Well, now you know, Orion."

The dirty stares, the snide remark from the women in the carriage about him being a Pawn Sniffer—Alec had been blamed for what his father did a decade ago.

"Alec," I said softly, but he shook his head.

"Don't." His voice was darker than the night itself. "Like he said—now you know."

I was surprised none of the knights came in to check on us. Maybe they were hoping we would destroy each other.

The carriage finally stopped. The endless forest of black trees disappeared from the window across from me, an open valley in view.

"Where are we?" I asked. "Where does the king live?"

"On the outskirts of Avelin," Rae answered.

A light flashed, and the door reappeared. A knight came in to release the shackles around the chairs but not those around our hands and ankles.

"Let's go. One at a time," the leader called through the door. There was a knight for each of us waiting in a line. But there were only two from Athena's Library—the leader and the one who had been chasing me. The other knights wore a different uniform, which meant they must work in the palace. They had light-gold armor around their chests over royal-blue clothing.

The carriage had crossed a long, stone bridge blocked by two gold gates guarded by knights and two griffin statues. The palace was breathtaking and bigger than Arayis, with its many towers, long rectangular structure, windows outlined in gold, and gold and silver vines entwined around the white exterior. The navy-blue roof blended with the night sky. The leader motioned for his men to follow him up two sets of marble steps to two huge bronze doors.

Guards stood on either side of the doors and opened them with a motion of their hands, revealing a lavish great hall. Gold chandeliers hung from the tall ceiling, and the matte walls were etched with shimmering designs. A grand staircase led to two more staircases above that, and massive French candelabras lit the hall. We walked along a red carpet toward the staircase, but instead of ascending it, we were directed to two brown doors at the right side of the room. They opened to another glorious room with a glossy checkered floor, pillars lining the sides. The royal crest was tiled in the center. Moonlight glowed through a skylight above two thrones that lay ahead, leaving three figures on a dais in the shadows.

As we approached, my eyes adjusted to the dim lighting and focused on the figures—the king and two of his knights. I stood on shaky legs, hoping I wouldn't collapse. King Leo's astute, hawklike eyes studied us curiously, his sharp chin held high. He was draped in a heavy, dark-blue cape, making him appear larger than he was. Underneath, he wore pants, boots, and a black doublet etched in gold, giving him a modern but old-fashioned look. A large crown, the most reflective and glossiest gold I'd ever seen, gleamed atop his blond hair.

"Your Majesty," the knights spoke in unison, bowing their heads and kneeling, then forcing us to our knees.

"Joel, what is it?" King Leo demanded, his voice deep and gritty.

The knight called Joel rose from his knees. "Your Majesty, these teenagers were caught breaking and entering Athena's Library. That girl," he pointed to me, "created a windstorm on the third floor—shelves knocked over, desks and chairs flipped, books everywhere. We think they entered the library through a portal, although we haven't the faintest clue how. It wasn't an Infinity Portal since it didn't exude a blue light."

I released my breath. They hadn't seen me with Corinne's items. The king looked like he was about to ask more about the portal, but Joel continued.

"But that's not all, Your Majesty." His voice suddenly shook. "Obsidian was there. But not in flesh. He communicated through a Cloudcom and somehow sent a scorpion through it, but the cloud must have made it weak because it was killed easily. It was bizarre, since Cloudcoms can only communicate live messages from their senders, not interact with their receivers."

The Obsidian King. My eyes widened, and my friends shot worried glances at each other. The king's face was white as paper as he gripped the arms of his throne.

His eyes landed on Alec and widened. "You," he half-whispered, rising to his feet. He marched down the steps, and the knight behind me stiffened. When the king stood inches from Alec, I could see his clothing was more extravagant up close, with its velvet material and embellished gold patterns. It was like meeting a celebrity. A celebrity who held my life in his hands.

Alec's breath was shallow and uneven, and a darkness equal to the hatred the king appeared to have for him filled his eyes.

"You summoned him," King Leo growled. "I knew you were one of them."

Alec took a heavy breath, then looked directly at the king. "I don't know what you're talking about. I didn't know he was there."

"Liar!" roared the king. He raised his ringed hand and slapped Alec. Alec grunted, then lowered his head and closed his eyes.

Tears welled in my eyes at the deep cut that formed across his cheek.

"I should have exiled you with your good-for-nothing father," the king spat. "To even think I let Mr. Locus give you a chance."

I lunged forward only to be pulled back like a chained dog.

"It was my fault, Your Majesty!" I screamed.

The knight holding me shoved me in the back. "The king didn't address you, girl!"

Alec spat blood at the ground before whipping his head around. "Orion, it's okay." He then turned back to his aggressor with piercing eyes. "The king's so afraid of the monster he's become one himself."

The next blow came harder, sending Alec to the ground as the knight lost his grip. For a split second, I saw Alec's knight's eyes widen in surprise at the sharp blow. Alec cried out, and his knight went to lift him, but King Leo held up his hand. Rae and Julian could curse Alec, but even now, both were horrorstruck, Rae's eyes shiny and Julian's wide. Blood trickled down Alec's cheek as he struggled to his knees.

"A trial with The Court is not needed," King Leo snarled. "I was a fool once, and I won't be made one again. I won't put my people in danger. Gentlemen, take the other three away while I finally end this."

"No, Your Majesty, please!" I tried to break free. Rae and Julian begged for Alec's mercy, too.

This wasn't his fault. None of it was. My friends were here because of *me*.

As the knights were about to take us away, a voice more piercing and panic-stricken than mine echoed off the walls, and the king's raised hand paused with electric sparks dancing around it. The wooden doors slammed open as a girl bolted toward us. "Father, stop!"

"Calista?" King Leo shook his head as if snapping himself out of a spell or dream.

The girl's dark-brown eyes were wild with fear as she looked upon Alec, who had managed to get to his knees during the interruption. He was staring wide-eyed at her. I was as starstruck as he was. She was around our age but had a mature face. A small silver crown perched on top of long, wavy black hair that flowed like a river to her hips. Her light brown skin was flawless except for a small scar on her forehead, which somehow added strength to her delicate frame. And although she was in a rose-pink nightgown, she looked fierce. Her eyes, although fearful, were harsh, like her father's.

"Your Majesty," she said, her voice now level, eyes hard. "I heard the yelling in the hall. I respect your decisions and believe you are a just king, but please reconsider your judgment. The death penalty is extreme without discernable and concrete evidence."

A minute ago, the king was about to take Alec's life. Now, he looked as if he were lost, like he didn't know where he was or had woken from a charm.

"Your Majesty, if I may . . ." The knight behind me spoke, hesitancy evident in his voice. "I was with the girl when the Obsidian King emerged. It appeared as if he wanted something from her but she didn't realize who she spoke with. He conjured a scorpion to attack her. It wasn't until I killed it that the Cloudcom disappeared."

My jailer was my savior.

I swallowed. "Your Majesty, it was my idea to break into the library. Please don't punish them." My voice shook, afraid the wrong words would cost me my life. "But it wasn't for the Obsidian King. I was dumb, thinking it'd be cool to sneak into somewhere I shouldn't. As your knight claims, I didn't know who the Obsidian King was. I'm new to Isoria and just discovered I'm a sorcerer."

King Leo looked between us and his knights, searching for the answer, seemingly unsure of what to do. Calista's eyes pleaded silently.

He sighed, shaking his head as if to seek clarity. "There are fines for breaking and entering. However, given that my knights never mentioned thievery, I'll spare you the consequences—for now. If property is found stolen or destroyed, if there is even a hint of Pawn suspicion associated with any one of you, you will all pay more than the consequences you should be receiving."

We nodded, except for Alec, who refused to meet the king's gaze.

"And as for you, Mr. Caballero," the king addressed Julian, taking a step toward him. Shock and fear played in Julian's eyes. "I'd never expect to see you here, after all I've done for your family. What would your father think, and how do you think this looks for your brother, who's worked tirelessly for his place in the KLE? Don't make me regret giving your family mercy, too."

Julian dropped his gaze. Guilt lined his face, instead of indignation, like Alec showed.

The king continued. "But this doesn't mean you're all off my radar. I'll have eyes on you." *Like the Obsidian King had warned.* King Leo turned to his knights. "Gentlemen, release them and help them find their way out. We're done here." He spun around without a second glance, marching toward one of the doors next to the dais.

The cold, tight bond around my wrists and ankles released, and I let out a sigh of relief, rubbing my wrists as my friends did the same.

The knights ushered us toward the doors. Calista blended in with us, falling into step with Alec, with me behind them. Rae and Julian were divided by two knights at the rear of the group, separating us for more control.

"How are you?" I heard Calista whisper to Alec, her eyes searching his face.

"Don't look at me like that," Alec whispered back, his sharpness making her flinch. He sighed as if to apologize. "I'm fine. How are you?"

"Don't look at *me* like that," she mocked. Her smile faded as her voice darkened, "A lot has happened since you've been gone. He's changed."

"I know."

Since he's been gone?

"Calista!" King Leo interrupted from afar. He gestured with his head toward the door near the thrones.

Thank you, Alec mouthed before she could leave.

CHAPTER 18

The knights led us to an Infinity Portal within the palace. What I'd thought was a gold, oval-shaped picture frame leaning against the wall became a swirling blue-and-white vortex. Outside the royal family, it was a highly illegal portal for any sorcerer or enchanter to possess and was highly sought after in the shadow market. Sorcerers could simply think of where they wanted to go and be taken there, including the nonmagus lands.

I envisioned Corinne's house, and the portal dropped us on the doorstep. We sneaked inside, and I was finally able to share my exciting news—the book and necklace lay on the ground underneath the library mural.

"I can't believe you found it," Julian said after I told my friends about the glass case Alec had explained was a replica of the Isorian Code of Law.

But the book I had thrown through the portal was a journal I was positive belonged to Corinne. A long strap was wrapped multiple times around the simple brown leather cover. Finally, I would solve the ultimate puzzle. But when I unraveled the string, there were unfamiliar symbols written inside—a language none of my friends knew, not even Alec, who knew a lot.

"I don't think this is a legitimate language," Alec said, skimming the weird symbols before leaving us to take a look at it. He had wiped at the blood on his cheeks, only dry streaks remaining.

There were more than strange symbols. There were sketches of people, nature, and parts of a scepter. One of the illustrations in the secret room had been of a scepter flying over a book. The last step. We had solved her puzzle. But now we were at a dead end. What was the importance of this scepter? Banden had one, but it looked nothing like the one in the journal. This one was shorter and appeared to be made of tree bark. A teardrop-shaped crystal nestled at the top with what looked like long, metal leaves hugging the crystal. Underneath the crystal, four gemstones trailed down the bark. At first I thought the string coiled around the bark from top to bottom was a vine, but then I realized it was a thin chain.

Alec was in a rush to leave, his mood even colder and harsher than usual. He would have left, but Julian said, "Wait, there's something odd about the inside of the front cover."

We all huddled around the leatherbound journal, which lay open on the library desk. Dark-brown stitching outlined the sides on the inside of the cover. Julian rubbed his finger over an uneven circle stitched in light-brown thread in the center. There was no circle on the back cover.

"It's probably a design," I suggested. It looked like any ordinary journal despite the indecipherable language within its pages.

Rae shook her head. "When given any kind of intel, question everything and stay curious." She then reached into her jacket pocket, pulled out a gold case, and released a hidden blade. Even her pocketknife had style.

"I hope you don't mind." She gave me a hesitant look as she held the knife over the circle.

I slid the journal closer to her. "Do what you must."

We watched intently as she dug the blade into the leather, cutting inside the circle with surgical precision. She then peeled the flap of leather back like dead skin, revealing a written etching on the hard cover: *May this guide you to what I've protected with my life: reserve respect.*

Julian groaned. "Jeez, can't this woman ever be straight just once? No disrespect, Orion."

I shook my head. "Your words are much kinder than what I'm thinking. But nice work, Julian. You were right."

He winked. "Of course I was."

"So, this journal isn't what Obsidian's after," Rae concluded. "It will guide us to . . . whatever she was protecting."

"Right, but what does 'reserve respect' mean?" I said.

Alec was quiet, hanging back as the rest of us hovered over the journal, his face pinched in concentration. Finally, he spoke, his voice stiffer than it had been before the library debacle. "It's code. She might be telling us what she guarded. I think . . . it might be an anagram. You know, when words can be rearranged to spell out another word or phrase?"

"Well, you're the closest to a Decoder than any of us, so I don't see the harm in trying," Rae said. Julian hadn't looked up from the journal as Alec spoke. "Let's all find as many words as we can. First, rearrange each word separately, and if we see nothing, we can try mixing and rearranging them together."

We followed Rae's order and started to rattle off the words we could find: *reveres, severer, specter . . .*

"Scepter." Rae found it in 'respect.' "The scepter is in the library notes and journal."

"What about 'reverse'?" I said, pointing out the word in *reserve*. "Reverse scepter. Does that ring a bell with anyone?"

"No," Alec said curtly, already heading for the door to leave. "It's late, I need to go. I don't have time for more puzzles."

I grabbed his arm in an attempt to stop him but almost backed away at the look in his eyes. I'd never seen them so full of hatred. The cut near his eyelid and across his cheek didn't help. But my need for answers was greater than my fear.

"Are you all right?" I asked quietly, confused by his sudden desire to leave—although he had been agitated since we'd returned from the palace and looking for an escape all night. I hated to admit it, but I was genuinely worried about him. He was not one to leave after an important discovery. If anything, he was usually as determined as I was to find answers.

For a split second, I thought he would actually tell me. His eyes briefly softened, and I thought I felt his bicep relax. But his tone was cold and sharp. "Hands off, Orion."

My sympathy for him vanished as quickly as the brief moment of vulnerability I thought I saw in him.

"You owe me an explanation about tonight," I said, referring to what had unfolded at the palace. What was his personal connection to the royal family?

He ripped his arm from my grasp and marched out.

Rae and Julian ended up leaving not long after. They decided we needed to do more research and that we would pick up where we left off later. Rae had to prepare for her morning class, which reminded me I had History of Air. Although I'd barely slept, I was wide awake. As I pedaled to the portal, I mentally replayed the midnight heist, worried that Banden or Celeste would find out. I also called Mom's cell, emailed her, and even tried sending a Reflection Message. But the Reflection Message wouldn't go through.

"If you're looking for the journal, I have it. Please come home. I saw him. The Obsidian King." I left a voicemail.

How would I give Obsidian the journal or this scepter he believed I had, even if I wanted to? If he knew I had it, wouldn't he be more specific with his directions? He might have been bluffing. And *how* had he found me in the library?

I brought the journal to class with me. I shouldn't have been walking around Isoria with it, but the cryptic words and images consumed my thoughts. The previous night was glued to my brain, and I obsessed over every moment and conversation. I hid the journal under the table, studying the symbols until Asher, Valerie's sidekick, and Estelle, the gossip queen, sat down in front of me, their laughter breaking my focus.

"Wait, Asher. I saw Alec yesterday," Estelle whispered.

"Really?" Asher pried. "Where?"

Estelle flipped her hair. "Avelin, in Hercules's Herbs with that famous elixir master, Banden Locus."

Suddenly, the journal wasn't as fascinating.

She continued. "I love a man with a heart who knows how to take care of people."

If you consider 'taking care of people' as becoming the unsolicited police of your life, then, yeah, sure, I grudgingly thought to myself.

"Ugh, I know he has a bad reputation," she lowered her voice, "but is it sick of me to think it makes him even *hotter*?"

They giggled. Estelle peeked over her shoulder at me, realizing they shouldn't have gossiped so loudly since it was no secret I'd been seen hanging around with who they were blushing over. I assumed every stare Alec received was one of pure hatred. Now I wondered how many felt the way Asher and Estelle did and what others said when they saw me with him. It had never occurred to me that Alec's reputation could tarnish mine, though it wasn't like mine was stellar anyway. But as much as a pain in the ass as he was, he was my friend, or at least I liked to think of him that way. If someone slighted him, I'd defend him, even if I didn't fully have him figured out.

As usual, Professor Filbert strolled into the classroom with robes too large for his body. Today's lecture was a continuation of last week's, which had been about the history of Aermages and how they'd established the town of Aerbourne. It was located in a valley in the Artus Mountains, not far from Arayis. The higher in the sky, the closer Aermages felt to the Air element. I found the lecture interesting despite it being three hours long. Even so, my eyes kept wandering to the journal in my unzipped bag.

Grateful for a lunch break at the halfway mark, I sat in a corner of Arayis's dining hall for privacy. It was a magnificent room with silver seating, light-blue glossy floors, and window walls that overlooked the courtyard, from which I could see the mountains in the distance. As I flipped through the journal's pages, I munched on Fae's Honey Fig Sandwich, which contained Dragon Figs, imported goat cheese, honey, and lemon. It was impossible to decipher the markings, but looking at it eased my anxiety.

Filbert stopped his lecture fifteen minutes before class was scheduled to end. "All right, class, I'm pausing here to make an announcement. As you know, Isoria Academy's Autumn Duel is in three weeks," he announced in his nasal voice. My classmates erupted in a mixture of groans, sighs, and squeals. "I want to remind you that you can acquire wisdom from history as you learn about the spells and strategies of our ancestors."

My classmates ignored him, having their own discussions about the duel. Estelle rolled her eyes while Asher clapped excitedly. I wanted to ask what the duel was, but I was already a newbie. I sat in the dark, hoping Filbert would explain further or someone else would ask questions.

"I hear Arayis is in second place. We can beat Ignair this year," a boy said to one of the girls near me, and she bragged about how her spells had improved and she felt she could take on anyone. I gave in, reaching over to tap Asher's shoulder. He turned around, one eyebrow raised, but it wasn't in annoyance, rather, questioning who'd bothered him.

"Sorry, what's the Autumn Duel?" I asked.

Estelle snorted, but thankfully, Asher didn't make a big deal out of it and explained, "It's a competition between all four schools held twice every year. Once in the fall and again in the spring. It's a required assessment to analyze how far along the students are in their studies. The academy makes a competition out of it to encourage better academic performance. The school that wins at the end of the year wins the Champion Dueler's Star Award."

My mind raced. How was I supposed to fight my classmates? I couldn't control my powers in the classroom, and I had accidentally set off a windstorm last night. What if I hurt someone? That should be an excuse not to participate.

"Remember to take thorough notes and practice spells on your own time," Filbert advised, interrupting the conversations between his students. "Everything you learn in this class will help you. Dismissed."

CHAPTER 19

Later that day, I met Rae and Julian at Athena's Library. I didn't know where Alec was, and I highly doubted he wanted to see us based on how he had left my house earlier, which was fine by me. I wasn't going to hunt him down and beg him to help me. I hadn't even wanted him involved in the first place.

We searched everywhere in the library that we could think to look about scepters. We even asked the librarian for suggestions. We explored the wars and magical objects sections and even the encyclopedia room, but we couldn't find anything about a reverse scepter. The only information we could find on scepters consisted of general facts about their history and purposes, including the names of scepters that had been used in past wars by famous enchanters and sorcerers. None of the pictures even remotely resembled the sketches in the library and journal.

Julian approached me as I was skimming through a book.

"Hey, I didn't get the chance to apologize for last night," he said with hands in his pockets. His warm brown eyes were sincere. "I'm sorry for getting us all into trouble. I shouldn't have let that asshole get the best of me."

I nodded. "I accept your apology. But yes, please, let's not repeat last night. You both seem to have too much history with the king."

Alec obviously didn't care what King Leo thought of him, but that hadn't been the case for Julian.

He sighed, then looked down at his leather bracelet, rubbing the red diamond-shaped crystal. It was then I noticed the crystal made up the body of a gold Phoenix, its wings spread wide with its head turned left. "Ever since King Leo pardoned my family, they've been doing everything they can to rebuild their reputation. Proving their loyalty, serving him in any way. My father, a dutiful Sanctor, and Stefano, a KLE in training, who my father seems to be vicariously living through," he mumbled, but the annoyance in his tone vanished as quickly as it came. He grinned. "And me, well, I'm serving him, too. Just not in a conventional way."

Julian had originally told me he joined MISTIC so he could have an active role in helping to take down Obsidian. I wondered how true that was, given his complex family troubles.

Still exhausted from last night's heist, my friends and I called it an early night and decided to try our research again in the morning, figuring that some rest would probably do us good.

It was around two in the morning when my phone rang, waking me up from deep sleep. No one ever called me. I searched my bedsheets for my phone and found it tucked underneath my pillow. My eyes widened at the name flashing across the screen, my heart pounding against my rib cage.

"Mom?" I answered, my voice wavering from my feelings of confusion, betrayal, and relief.

"Orion, honey, I'm so sorry," she said, her voice cracking like mine.

I was on the verge of tears. So she *had* seen my messages. "How could you do this to me?"

"I only wanted to protect you."

"How's lying about who I am protecting me? Look at all the pain and trouble you caused me."

"I know. I'm sorry. Please know that everything I did was to keep you safe. I could've handled it better, but please listen to Banden. He'll look after you."

"Yeah, Banden. So you had him do your dirty work, letting me know that sorcery had been kept from me my entire life?" I spat, my body shaking. I didn't care how angry or rude I sounded, though I was cognizant of the volume of my voice, not wanting to wake Banden next door.

"There's so much to explain, but not enough time." She was rushing on, and her voice was muffled, like her mouth was too close to the speaker. Static crunched in my ear.

I pressed the phone harder against my ear. "Not enough time? I know your job's busy and everything, but you can't have a conversation with me about this? We haven't spoken in over a month!"

"I hate doing this, but you don't know how difficult it was to make this call. Orion, please listen to me. Stay out of trouble. Focus on your studies, socialize, and enjoy being a teenager."

I wasn't sure if it was my imagination, but her voice became quieter and more hurried, like she didn't want to be heard on the phone.

"Mom, are you okay?"

"Of course," she replied too quickly.

"Mom, are the notes in the library yours?"

There was a pause.

"Orion, I need you to trust me." Her voice was sharper than broken glass, with an edge I'd never heard from her. "Do *not* follow your grandmother's past. She made a mistake. I'm handling it."

"*Handling* it?" Then it clicked. "You're not in Europe for business. You've been lying this whole time. Where are you? Are you in trouble?"

"Please, for me, Orion. Stay out of it. I'm okay. I'm safe. I was wrong to hide sorcery from you, but please trust me. I'm begging you."

"You're looking for the reverse scepter, aren't you? The object Corinne had and Cyril Obsidian wants."

"Orion, what you found—this journal. Whatever you do, do not show it to anyone. Too many people have turned their backs on our family. Corinne was right for only trusting herself. It's bigger and more consequential than I imagined. Stay strong and please stay out of trouble. I have everything under control. I have to go."

"But, Mom—"

The line went dead.

I slammed my phone against the mattress, tears stinging my eyes. Every day, I'd wondered where she was, hoping she'd walk through the door so I could hug her but also scream at her for leaving me. The weight on my shoulders was suddenly crushing, and she wasn't here to help me through it. She was the one person in the world I trusted, and she had deliberately deceived me.

This world is a game of deception.

Flashes from the past with Mom hiding in her "workshop," as she called it, came to mind. It was in the basement of our old house. Sometimes she had confidential projects, and she'd explain how it was in her contract that she must keep them secret. But now I wondered how much of that was true. She'd lock the door and wouldn't let me come in until she was finished. Now that I thought about it, I didn't even know who her clients were, but I had never been interested—until now. Maybe Mom's deception shouldn't be a surprise. She had been secretive all my life.

"You've always been a curious child, Orion," she had told me one day when I asked why she locked her door. "Sometimes curiosity must remain unquestioned and unanswered. Even *I* need to remember that sometimes."

If Mom thought she could forbid me from helping her, from possibly saving her from the danger she was putting herself in, she didn't know me at all. Or, at least, who I was now. I had been such a reserved and obedient kid that Mom worried it would have a detrimental effect on my social life. But she never had to worry about "teenage stuff," like dating or drugs or youth rebellion. I never had a reason to rebel. The Orion before sorcery was invisible, docile, and avoided trouble to the point of isolation.

But now I was a trouble magnet. Or I was now a part of a troubled world. I was more determined than ever to uncover Corinne's secrets. And besides needing to help Mom, I had another motivation: someone was after me. Obsidian, a Pawn, the mole in MISTIC, or all three—someone believed I had the answers, and they were following me. A sliver of anxiety crept into my thoughts, but I reminded myself that I had pledged my allegiance to this purpose to receive protection . . . unless. Did MISTIC secretly know I'd broken my oath, and were they gathering the evidence to prove my disloyalty? I squashed these thoughts, convinced they would have confronted me by now. I hoped.

This world was a game, and I had to play not to win but to survive.

CHAPTER 20

I didn't see Alec the rest of the week. Whether he was purposely ignoring me or not, I deserved an explanation about his relationship with the royal family. I tried sending Reflection Messages, but he didn't pick up, and I didn't want to raise Banden's suspicions by asking about Alec. He couldn't hide from me forever.

Any free time I had was spent in Athena's Library, sometimes with Rae and Julian, sometimes without. Not only did we research scepters, but we also explored the history of Isoria's languages. I analyzed the journal's symbols as I sifted through books, searching for any language remotely similar to Corinne's. But nothing helped, and we were stymied once again. My friends suggested it might be time to bring the journal to MISTIC, but I convinced them to give me more time. I had another idea.

That next Monday morning, I brought Corinne's journal to Professor Wicbin's class. I carried it to school every day, but today I had a purpose. Wicbin was my preceptor and most favorable teacher so far, and I felt like I could talk to him. Maybe he knew about the linguistic history of Isoria. To avoid showing him the journal, I had copied the first page on a separate piece of paper.

If he could translate it, hopefully there wasn't anything suspicious enough about the entry that he'd start asking questions.

Our lesson that day was about Air Rockets, which were sharper and larger than Air Blasts but required more energy. Wicbin split us up into different groups in front of the classroom, where multiple drum-shaped instruments were lined up. One at a time, each student had to send a rocket toward them. Thankfully, Valerie wasn't teamed up with me, and unsurprisingly, she succeeded on her first try, unlike my classmates. It wasn't an easy exercise. Air Blasts and attempted Rockets, flew around the classroom like deflating balloons, students dodging or ducking out of the way. I expected my powers to go haywire, but to my excitement and relief, they cooperated with me. The drum pounded as I sent a successful Rocket toward it, and my team members' eyes widened at my sudden success.

Wicbin noticed my work and grinned. "Well done, Miss Candor."

I smiled and couldn't help but peek at Valerie, who rolled her eyes. Maybe Rae was right. She was jealous. I wasn't the gloating type like her, yet I couldn't help but give her a smug look. She was the one who'd started this rivalry, and I was learning that I wasn't the type to stand down from a challenge.

When class finally ended, I took my time packing up, waiting for the classroom to empty. As Wicbin assembled his belongings, I was at his desk before he could leave. He wasn't surprised when he whirled around to see me, and he had a smile on his face. "Can I help you, Miss Candor?"

"Professor, I wanted to ask you something—" But I caught my tongue, suddenly second-guessing this. *Too many people have turned their backs on our family.* How many had shared our secrets, and how many had we trusted who didn't keep them? But I was out of options, and even if he translated the symbols, it didn't mean he'd understand what he was reading. "Do you know anything about Isorian languages?"

He chuckled, crossing his arms. "Enough to tell you a whole year's worth. I'm well versed in most Isorian languages. What do you need to know?"

"What are the languages, exactly?"

He leaned back against the wooden table. "Isorian scholars don't know for certain how the realm originated or where our ancestors came from, but they believe the first language to have ever been recorded in Isoria consisted of symbols like hieroglyphics." *Bingo.* "The first written and spoken language is unknown, but the earliest historians have documented French, Italian, and Latin roots, which we refer to as the ancient alphabet. Enchanter spells are spoken in this integrated language. Maybe our ancestors were European or inspired by European culture. Besides the language, Isoria's architecture and design also support this theory. But we've graduated with the evolution of history, eventually utilizing English as the common language, since it's universal." He paused, searching my face. "I'm sorry. I could bore you for centuries. Does any of this help?"

My heart pounded with the jittery excitement in my stomach. "Actually, yes. What do you know about symbols?"

He pursed his lips. "That's a dense topic in itself. Because Isoria houses many different creatures and species, we also have a history of mingling our language with theirs. For example, unicorns and dragons are two of the most intelligent creatures on the island. To harmonize with them, Isorians communicate through symbols. Dragons have their own alphabet, called Draconese and sometimes referred to as Dragian or the Dragon Word. But only Dragon Tamers study it."

"So, sorcerers used only symbols for communicating with creatures?" I asked.

He sighed but not in frustration. "Not exactly. It's believed during war and tragedies, such as the Four Kingdoms War, the Sorcerer Enchanter Revolution, and the Siege of Westwin, that militaries developed their own language to share intelligence. That's where our linguistic history becomes complex, because those symbols have no roots, just pure imagination."

A made-up language. If Corinne's writing was devised for a specific purpose, who was she trying to communicate with? I reached into my bag and pulled out the copy. "I found these symbols. Does this look like a made-up language to you?"

He immediately took it from me, fascinated, studying the paper with such determination I thought he didn't hear me. "Where did you get this?"

"Research," I answered vaguely. "From Athena's Library. Came across it in a book I forgot the name of." *Not a complete lie.*

"I've never seen a language like this," he said, distant. "It's definitely devised."

My face fell. "Oh, okay. But are you sure there isn't a slight possibility it's not?"

"It's possible but unlikely. If you'd like, I could hold on to it and do some research."

If he was correct, I was at a roadblock. But I had to do my own research before accepting one person's word.

I shook my head. "That's nice of you, Professor, but no, thank you. You've helped me a lot." I extended my hand for the paper.

He was either reluctant or hadn't heard me as he continued studying it.

"Oh, of course," he said uncomfortably, like he'd crossed some sort of boundary. "Languages greatly fascinate me. They teach us so much about our history."

I nodded. "Right. Well, thanks again, Professor. I'll see you Thursday."

But he stopped me. "Miss Candor, feel free to update me on your research. If I find anything of use to you, I'll send it your way."

I smiled. Having an extra set of eyes on this would be helpful, and maybe he knew some experts. "That would be great, thank you."

He nodded as I turned to leave. I thought he would leave with me since he had been about to before I stopped him, but he stayed put, watching me. Maybe he didn't want to walk out with me since we already said our goodbyes. As I exited the room, I was so wrapped up in my thoughts I jumped when my name was called.

There he was, leaning against the wall, face tilted as his green eyes focused on me. His leg was propped up against the wall, and with his all-black attire—sweater, pants, and boots—he reminded me of a stray cat, not belonging to anyone but himself. That was Alec Stone for you. When I met him, he'd refused to fully face me, and that was when I'd glimpsed the remnant of pink near his eye and cheek. *He's ashamed of his scar.*

"Ah, so he finally decides to show face," I said coldly.

"Banden wants me to show you something at the chamber." Alec's voice was low, monotonous. He usually came straight to the point but decided to riddle me with wisdom when he felt playful.

I raised an eyebrow, wondering what for and nervous that he had spilled about the journal.

"It's not about . . . that night," he assured.

I could hear the pain in his voice. The king's fury sent a pang to my chest. Alec falling to the floor, whimpering from the blows, and a menacing hatred I'd never seen in a person before. It almost made me afraid of him, wondering what other dark secrets he kept buried.

"Orion," he started, this time fully facing me. I fought the urge to gasp.

His face. A scar traced his skin from the corner of his left eye to his nose. His left eyelid was partially closed, irritated, and swollen.

"I want to apologize for what happened with Julian," he continued. "I was an idiot and almost jeopardized everything."

The scars and bruises made me want to tell him it was okay. But it wasn't. He wouldn't have them if he hadn't lost control with Julian. *Maybe.* What would have happened had the king not forgiven us? But the longer I stared at his busted-up face and apologetic eyes, the more my fences came down.

"I want the truth, Alec. You expect me to trust you, yet you're keeping secrets about knowing the royal family? The king—"

But he stopped me from repeating what we both didn't want to relive. "I'm not keeping it secret, I—" He paused, sighing in frustration. "I'm afraid of what you'll think of me."

I blinked, not expecting such a vulnerable answer. Last night must have shaken him up. "Since when do you care what I think?"

He hesitated, his intense gaze making my cheeks warm. "I don't know," he admitted, confusing me even more. He sighed and started down the hallway. When he noticed I wasn't following, he called over his shoulder, "Are you coming?"

CHAPTER 21

Y ou haven't even seen the best part of your school," Alec said as he led me through two glass doors engraved with gold vines that led to the back of the castle. "Sky Garden is what Arayis is known for."

I gave him a pointed look. "I've been a little preoccupied lately."

We descended the stairs and walked along a gravel path that divided three ways: two paths crossed two bridges over the chasm, while the third led to some hedges. A white wooden sign post with four arrows read Stables, Dormitories, Aerbourne Village, and the path we were following, Sky Garden. The tall hedges lined the path, blocking my vision of what lay ahead, except for the silhouetted mountains in the distance, faded by smoky clouds.

"Next, you're going to tell me you don't know you're near Red Halo Island." When he saw my blank face, he raised an eyebrow. "The dragon island?"

"*Dragon* island? As in big, fiery flying beasts?"

"Well, they're not all like that. Some aren't even fire breathers. Like sea dragons. I thought you at least knew about the island."

"Well, I don't," I mumbled, annoyed by his you-should-know-this attitude. "I'm still learning, you know."

The path ended, revealing a dream. Beyond the marble railing, the mountains parted, unveiling a canyon that ended at the crisp blue ocean, a waterfall pouring into it. Different shades of blue, white, and yellow angelic flowers bloomed on the ground and shrubbery, some floating on the gentle ocean breeze. Stone benches circled a fountain with a winged dragon, its water flowing down like a canopy.

We chose a spot near the railing at the edge of the cliff, high in the mountains toward the sky with a panoramic view of the sea. In the distance was the faint silhouette of an island I assumed was Red Halo. I was surprised this area wasn't as populated as other parts of the garden—probably why Alec had brought me here. As he stared into the crystal waters, the light breeze played with strands of his dark hair.

"The waterfall was created by Aquatists." He broke the silence but spoke only loud enough that I could hear him over the waterfall's rumbling. "A gift from the Aquium originators."

He was stalling. Our faces were inches apart, his eyes briefly looking into mine before he turned away. It probably wasn't the appropriate time to be thinking about his looks, but I couldn't help it. Although his scar seared part of his face and one eye remained semiclosed, he was painfully attractive, and overhearing Asher and Estelle obsess over him seemed to heighten my attraction. But I had to get a grip. It was useless caring for him that way. I couldn't waste my time on someone who guarded his emotions and whose heart was like a fortress. And yet, hadn't some of his layers peeled off around me?

He nervously rubbed his ring before holding it up to me. "This crest is a symbol of the Stone heraldry. Every knight receives a family coat of arms." I remembered the Phoenix on Julian's bracelet and assumed that was his family's symbol. "Before becoming a knight, my father was a shoppe clerk, and my mother was a baker, but the bakery eventually closed, and you can't support a family on a clerk's salary. King Leo, a different kind of man then, learned of my family's financial situation when my father joined the knighthood. When I was four years old, the king invited my family to temporarily live in the palace until we were back on our feet. My mother even worked in the palace kitchen. The king began to enjoy my family's company, and I could tell he'd developed a soft spot for my father. Since I was the only one in the palace who was Calista's age, we became friends over the next two years.

"My father had taken Mr. Caballero's shift that night in New Castle, next to where the tragedy occurred. And with the distraction, the Pawns had managed to break into the palace in an attempt to assassinate King Leo. They weren't successful, but they murdered palace staff and knights and took some as prisoners. My mother . . ." He spoke through gritted teeth, pausing as he turned away. "Calista woke me up in my bedchamber to warn me the palace was under attack. We found my mother shackled by a Pawn. I wanted to save her, but she begged me to hide with Calista. Calista had to drag me away as the Pawn pulled my mother away and led us to one of the palace's many secret passageways to hide until the invasion ended."

He refused to meet my gaze, a pained expression on his face. He swallowed and cleared his throat before continuing. "The trials began, and everyone believed my father had spearheaded the siege on Westwin. On the last day of trial, he escaped his prison cell. I don't know what he was thinking. They wouldn't let me see him the entire trial. He must have thought there wasn't any hope, so he chose to run. The Royal Court immediately voted him guilty."

He dropped his head, shaking it.

No wonder a dark cloud hovered over him. He was in pain, or at least pretended not to be. If the Isorians had sided with Mr. Caballero, then perhaps Mr. Stone had felt that fleeing was the only option.

"After his escape, everyone became paranoid and hateful," he continued, keeping his eyes on the ocean. "They blamed me, believing I had something to do with it. Some even went as far as thinking I'd helped him with the massacre."

I couldn't contain my disgust. "But you were only six!"

"Yeah, well, that's what happens in desperate times." His voice fell flat. "People become desperate."

"I'm sorry," I said, but he brushed me off.

"King Leo's reputation wasn't great at the time. Even now, Isorians don't agree with how he's handling Obsidian and his Pawns. His eldest daughter running away didn't help him. How can a king rule his kingdom if he can't even control his own daughters? Having the son of a criminal living in his palace didn't help his status either."

I gasped. "He had a daughter who ran away?"

He ran a hand through his hair. "Yeah. Calista has, or had, an older sister, Ludovica. No one knows why she left, or, at least, the king has never revealed that information to the public. With everything that has happened, it's no wonder he has the realm on high security and dehumanized punishment." He winced, and I knew he was thinking about his scar.

I thought about the way the Isorians had scurried past the knights in Avelin. The way Alec had feared me causing trouble with the Royal Scout. The way King Leo had immediately assumed Alec was a Pawn. *Those are not Pawns. They're Royal Scouts . . . Although they might as well be the same thing,* Alec had said. Celeste had also insulted the way King Leo was handling Obsidian's rise to power. MISTIC wasn't only created against Obsidian but against King Leo, despite Celeste's dream to partner with him in the future.

"He's paranoid," I realized, studying Alec's scar and looking away before he noticed.

He scoffed. "Any whiff, any small suspicion, and he jumps to deadly conclusions. I don't think he's gotten over how easily his eldest daughter and two most trusted knights slipped away from him."

The feeling that you have no control, that it was your fault people were in danger—I could relate all too well.

"So, what did the king do about you?" I asked.

"He banished me from the palace. I wasn't allowed to visit Calista. Last night was the first night I'd seen her in a decade." His voice faded, like he couldn't believe it happened, that it was a dream. "If it weren't for her, I wouldn't be here today. Many wanted me executed or thrown in prison until death found me. I remember crying on the court floor, confused that I had lost two parents at once. Calista fought the king, saying I shouldn't be blamed for my father's mistakes. She saved me last night. Again."

My heart ached, and I had the urge to wrap my arms around him, but I didn't, not daring to coddle him. "So what happened?"

He smiled, the first positive expression since he'd begun his tale. "Banden happened. I was never gonna have a family again. I was to be sent to Isoria's orphanage in Avelin. No one would want the son of a murderer. But Banden volunteered. He was at the hearing. I didn't know who he was, but he was so willing to help me. So I lived with him and helped him around the chamber. I'd do anything for him, Orion. He's done so much for me—took me in when everyone else saw a monster."

He said it like he believed it. Without thinking, I put my hand on his. He stiffened, eyeing our hands, and I quickly removed mine, embarrassed. I thought he'd keep his distance, but he didn't.

I had a new appreciation for Banden for so selflessly taking Alec in. *Like what he did for me.* But that meant Alec had to run around doing favors, like babysitting me.

"You don't believe that what happened was your fault, do you?" I asked.

He hesitated like he was afraid to answer or was still figuring it out. "There was a point in my life I did. I'd get dirty looks, was bullied at school. Julian and I crossed paths one day. We argued, got into a pretty brutal fight, and have kept our distance since. I got shit from him when I joined MISTIC a few months ago, and he tried convincing everyone to veto my acceptance."

How did Celeste trust someone who could be related to a Pawn? I then remembered that night in the carriage.

"I've been meaning to ask you. What's a Pawn Sniffer?"

He rolled his eyes, and I wondered if he was remembering that night as well. "It's someone with a family member or relative who's a follower of the Obsidian King. All it takes is a whiff or taste of evil to join him. I don't know if either of my parents is still alive," he admitted, focusing on the ocean ahead of us. "I sometimes think my father's still in hiding, living with the shame of being a runaway criminal. And my mom, well, there are rumors that Obsidian enslaves his prisoners or puts them to use for his cause, whatever

202

that means." He swallowed. "I still see her face, the hopelessness in her eyes, the Fire Chains that dragged her away."

I wondered if he believed his father was guilty. He seemed to struggle with the truth. But he had formidable strength, keeping his composure amongst the stares and rumors. Or, at least, that's what I'd seen.

"Be careful with your grandmother's past," he said, and I was surprised by the sincerity in his words, like he wasn't saying it for Banden's sake. "Some people believe she was a spy for Obsidian. Rumors might spread that you're a Sniffer, too, or they'll assume you're one because you're with me. Your mother was right to leave. Corinne was crazy for involving you."

I paused. Corinne *was* crazy. But she hadn't involved me. She involved my mother, which was what I thought.

"I involved myself," I clarified.

He shrugged. "That's what I meant."

I would have believed him. He didn't over explain, which people usually did when they were nervous. He could have said those words and I'd have fallen for it. But emotions got in the way of words. I relied on Alec to conceal his true feelings, holding everything in and wearing his hard exterior like there was nothing but coldness inside him. But I saw something flicker in his eyes, his eyelids briefly widening, faster than a camera shutter but slow enough. He knew what he accidentally did.

"What do you mean Corinne wanted *me* involved?" My voice rose. I lost any sort of compassion I had for him.

He went stiff, his facial muscles hardening, but his eyes softened, and he looked down at his hands.

I shook my head. "I *knew* Banden was keeping something from me. I was hoping I was wrong. And you were in on it. What does Banden know about Corinne's past, and what does it have to do with me?"

This time, he looked up. "I don't know as much as you think I do. Even Banden didn't tell me everything about Corinne."

"You said she was crazy for 'involving me.' Involved with what?" I tried keeping my voice level, aware of the people around us.

Give it to me, the Pawn had said during the attack on us in Lightloch. *You have what I seek,* Obsidian had warned in the library. Was I meant to find this scepter or journal? Was I another piece in Corinne's puzzle? Another pawn, like Mom?

He looked away. "I don't know."

"I don't believe you."

He latched on to my arm, eyes pleading. "You have a right to be upset. It's wrong of him to hide things from you, but you have to understand why he's doing it."

I yanked my arm free. "Alec, you honestly think the best way to protect someone is to lie to them? You even said so yourself that first night in the chamber. And if you agree with him, then why were you so keen on helping me with Corinne's necklace?"

"Are you serious? To look out for you!" He said it like it was obvious, like I should have known that was his intent all along. I almost believed him until he added, "I don't know what Banden would do if something happened to you."

Of course. It was always about Banden or Mom, about how all this might affect *them,* how it would make *them* feel if something happened to me. Everyone wanted to 'protect' me, but 'protecting' me meant lying to me, and it was never about how it actually might be hurting me. The lying only made me want to try harder to discover the truth and unearth what my family had done that had made everyone so fearful and Obsidian's target.

"Yeah?" I said coldly. "And how's all the lying working out for him?"

I turned my back on Alec before he could answer.

He groaned, and called after me, "Orion!"

But I kept my head down as I marched toward the castle, my adrenaline driving me full force. Everyone wanted something from me. MISTIC, Banden, Mom, and now Corinne. Did Banden know my role in all this? He'd promised no more secrets. But here we were. More secrets.

CHAPTER 22

Banden stood in the pasture behind his house, surrounded by three horses as he gave extra attention to a buckskin. His eyes lit up as I approached, and he gave a friendly wave before patting the horse's black muzzle.

"Orion, hello! What do you think of this beauty?" he said, patting the buckskin's neck. "He's yours. Cerus and Alec's horse, Apollo, could use another companion, and you need to learn how to ride. Always traveling via carriage is costly."

All my emotions tangled together in one big web of fury. This man, this stranger Mom had entrusted her life to, was a liar. And yet, so was she. Why was it that everyone who "loved" me lied to me?

"His name is Tirips," he continued. "Isorian horses are stronger and have more endurance than nonmagus land horses. You'll be able to travel far with him. We could buy you an Isorian bicycle, but sometimes horseback is easier. Would you like to meet your new companion?"

"No."

He caught the edge in my voice, his eyebrows raising, eyes widening. "Are you all right?"

"I know you're hiding Corinne from me," I said bluntly. "What did she get me involved with that you don't want me to know?"

If he was nervous, he didn't show it. As if Tirips suspected my hostility, he trotted to the opposite side of the pasture where Cerus and Apollo were.

"Your studies are what's important," he finally answered. "It's all your mother wants from you too."

My hands shook. "That's ironic considering she kept that part secret from me my entire life. Did you know she called to warn me to stay away from Corinne's past? And Alec slipped by telling me Corinne wanted me involved. Mom wanted you to look after me so she could finish Corinne's business, which apparently, is also mine. I know she isn't in Europe."

His face froze, and I wasn't sure if it was because of how much I knew or the fact that Alec had inadvertently revealed his secret. I wasn't one bit sorry for ratting him out. No one had the right to keep my life from me.

He sighed. "Orion, Corinne's not only the secretive, riddle-obsessed person I know you believe her to be. She loved you and your mother very much and asked me to look out for you once you'd move to Crystal Manor."

My eyes widened. "What?"

"As much as I loved Corinne, she kept secrets, even from me," he said, his face tired. "It infuriated me as much it does you. She knew she was going to die. But she died with secrets, one of them being what Obsidian is after. She purposely left her house to you and Seraphina so you would move here. It was her dying wish to have me look after you two. As to why, there wasn't time to explain. Her illness took too much of her energy. She told me you and Seraphina would eventually move to Crystal Manor when you needed me the most. To be closer to you two, I agreed to watch over you while your mother took care of things. Corinne is a dear friend of mine, as is your mother. I'd do anything to help."

"What happened to Corinne?" I asked. Mom had told me she had been sick, but something told me that wasn't the full truth.

He looked away. "She was in hiding somewhere deep in Isoria's largest forest, the Crowned Woods. She had been running from something, or someone. I don't know who or what. She had been shot with a poison arrow and called upon me to heal her—" He paused, taking a deep breath before continuing. "I couldn't. The poison had already circulated through her system. It was impossible to suck out, and her body was already riddled with wounds. There wasn't enough time for her to explain what had happened."

"And she only had time to tell you about me," I finished the story. He nodded, which angered me, not about my grandmother but about that arrow and whoever had shot her. If she had escaped, we'd have answers and my life wouldn't be a mess of lies and enemies I'd never met. *Mom would be here.* "How did she know I would come to Crystal Manor?"

"Because of the risks she took with MISTIC, she knew her past would catch up with her. She had her will written long before she passed. She was always prepared. Everything she did, she did for a reason." He averted his gaze, his voice wavering as if he was trying to convince himself there was logic behind the secrets. "That night in the woods, I had no choice but to leave her. Pawns had been on her trail, and I could hear them coming for her. She begged me to leave her behind. She wanted them to see her dead so they would never search for her again. I tried convincing her otherwise, but she

208

was on her last few breaths, and we both knew I couldn't risk being caught with her. I hid in a nearby tree and watched as they tied her to a horse's back, wanting to leave her for the king," he said through gritted teeth. "Cyril tortures his enemies, alive or dead."

I was sickened, imagining Pawns dishonoring her in the worst way, never imagining such morbidity behind her death. But what had she been running from?

He hesitated, giving me a long stare before saying, "So, I'm doing what I think is right. Seraphina's trying to end all this—for her and, most importantly, for you. To keep your mother safe, you need to be safe. This was what she wanted, Orion."

"But what is she looking for?" I wanted to see if he would mention the scepter. And, quite frankly, I hoped he would have info he could give me since my friends and I still knew nothing.

He shook his head. "I don't know."

"I don't believe you."

He stepped closer. "I'm telling you the truth, Orion. That's why your mother's fearful, as am I. The fire that burned down your home, the figure outside Corinne's house the night you moved in, the figure that came during your test . . . we're not sure what they want."

So Alec had told him about the Incendor during my IEPE. But Banden didn't mention the library incident. Did I at least have some of Alec's loyalty? Or maybe he didn't want Banden to know about his encounter with King Leo. And if Banden didn't know about the scepter, he couldn't know about Corinne's secret room. How much had Mom kept from him? Did she see that, despite his love for Corinne, he was too invested in MISTIC's cause? *Orion, what you found—this journal. Whatever you do, do not show anyone*, she had warned me. Did she mean Banden, too, the man she'd entrusted as my guardian?

"How do you know who started the fire?" I asked.

"A Chosen Shadow broke into your home," he said. "Seraphina killed it before first responders arrived. They disappear like shadows once slain."

It wasn't a freak accident. It had to have been looking for the scepter. At least I had people around me who wanted to keep me safe. Mom had no one. She was the one in real danger. Did Obsidian know where she was?

All these questions pecked at my brain. I wanted to rip my hair out, scream, kick the ground. *She* was the reason I had missed out on magic, why my identity had been hidden. She knew everything and had taken it to her grave. She'd ruined my life and put her daughter and granddaughter's lives in jeopardy.

"Banden, Corinne kept everything—your responsibility, whatever this thing Obsidian wants—secret from me, from you. I appreciate everything you've done for me and my family and how you took me under your wing when you didn't have to." I was grateful for him and tired of the fighting. I wanted to be on his side. This wasn't hurting only him. I could tell him everything right now, but I needed to know he wouldn't go to MISTIC. "Sometimes hiding things does more damage than good, even if we think we have the other's best interests at heart. All I'm asking is for you to trust me."

"Orion," his tone softened yet remained stern. Understanding but rational. "This is why I didn't want to tell you. There's too much ambiguity. There's a reason for all this. I'm choosing to believe that. MISTIC is working on it. Have patience."

My heart dropped to my stomach. He should be on my side. We could end these secrets together. He appeared to be rationalizing Corinne's actions as well, choosing to forgive her. He'd looked past the history of the son of a criminal, trusted an ambiguous friend, and devoted his time to a confused and resilient teenager. He saw the good in everyone, but he used his goodness to mask the truth. Like a crusader, he believed his way was the right way.

"You followed Corinne's orders blindly," I said, angry tears now stinging my eyes, but I refused to let them fall. "Even Mom's. But it doesn't mean I have to. And Corinne didn't tell you to keep all of this hidden from me. You and Mom decided that."

I didn't wait for his answer. I was so frustrated that when I turned around to open the gate, a burst of cool air escaped my hands without my doing and swung the gate open, further infuriating me. Nothing was in my control. Not my powers, not my life.

CHAPTER 23

I might as well have skipped Professor Soveus's class that next day. As the pudgy man had rambled on about nasty creatures called ice hounds in his almost-indiscernible, growly, low voice, my mind grappled with my confrontation with Banden, unable to focus on the lesson.

After class, I spent the rest of the day in the library, furiously practicing spells, trying to distract myself from everything, especially since the Autumn Duel was three weeks away. But my powers were as stressed as I was. I almost broke the desk lamp and knocked books off shelves with erratic Air Bullets. My Air Shields scratched the wooden floor, and my Air Ropes almost made holes in the walls. When I heard the front door open around 7:00 p.m., I locked the library door so Banden would know he wasn't welcome. He also didn't greet me like he usually did, knowing to stay away.

Later that night, Rae invited me to go shopping. It was always a good time for her to shop, even an hour before a store's closing time. Solstice, a clothing boutique in Avelin, was deserted. Rae thought the revelations from my discussion with Professor Wicbin were a great conversation to have over a shopping spree, mostly because she thought we were low profile there.

There were MISTIC agents within King Leo's walls, and Rae and Julian had learned that one told Celeste that three agents had been brought in to see the king, which was of particular interest to her because they had been with Corinne's granddaughter. My friends had almost been interrogated for sneaking into Athena's Library at midnight, but the agent had apparently validated our alibis. Had Celeste told Banden?

"No one at MISTIC knows the agents in King Leo's castle," Rae whispered. The shopkeeper was bent over a wooden counter, sewing fabric without touching the needle. We kept our voices low, but he didn't seem interested in our conversation and constantly ran back and forth to the counter and the back of the store. "Their identities are confidential. Celeste does this to protect them."

"Whoever ratted us out to Celeste also protected us," Julian added, sitting down in a chair in the corner. "Although, since nothing technically happened at the library, they had nothing to prove. MISTIC can only put us on trial if there's evidence. Unlike King Leo . . ."

Rae nodded. "We can't sneak around. We have to stay in the public eye. Celeste definitely has increased her surveillance on us."

"Your safety is more important," I said. "I don't want you two involved anymore. If Celeste is suspicious—"

"If Obsidian is after you, you're the one who needs protection," Julian interrupted, dismissing my concerns.

"Let's decode the journal first," Rae negotiated. "If the contents have anything to do with Obsidian and this scepter, we take it to MISTIC. Deal?"

I nodded, which thankfully was enough for her. She wouldn't be able to hear the hesitancy in my voice. When the time came between choosing their safety over mine and giving up the journal versus handling it on my own, they might never forgive me for the choice I'd make. I hated to deceive them, but it was the only way to find the scepter and keep them safe.

Rae moved on to my wardrobe and insisted on buying me clothes. When I fought her, she used my birthday as an excuse.

"I'm buying you clothes, and there's nothing you can do about it," she asserted, her words final. "You should at least *try* dressing like an Aermage."

I let her skim the racks for me. No matter what I showed her, she ended up choosing something else for me.

"Remind me again why I'm here?" Julian huffed, crossing his arms.

"Moral support and friendship," Rae said. To coerce Julian to come with us, she had convinced him that we were going to a weaponry shop. I'd thought that, too, until I saw the Solstice sign.

"You owe me a trip to Isorian Artillery and Shields," he mumbled, pulling his sweatshirt hood over his eyes.

"I can't believe there's not one book about a reverse scepter," I said, changing topics. I felt like we'd checked every book we could possibly think of, unless we were way off the mark and there was one sitting in the library we'd completely missed. "If Corinne intentionally left a trail of clues, the information has to be accessible somehow."

"Yeah, it is odd," Rae agreed, grabbing a shirt from the rack and holding it up to me. "But I'm sure about one thing. The journal is definitely not Draconese."

I faintly recognized the word, but as she had pronounced it with a thick accent, I almost didn't understand her. Even Wicbin hadn't said it like that. Before I could question her, Julian's eyes widened and he jumped from his chair. He pointed a finger at me. "You made me think of something, initiate. What if the information *is* accessible but not to the public?"

I didn't understand, but Rae caught on. Her eyes went wide too. "I can't believe we didn't think of that. Oh, wait. Yes, I can. Because that room isn't even open to us."

"I can always rely on you to be the buzzkill."

"It's called being realistic."

I shook my head. "What are you guys talking about?"

"There's an archive room in The Cave," Julian explained, talking fast with excitement. "It has a history of all past and current operations. And there's a section on every secret discovered about Isoria— stories that have been lost and erased from the public files. There might be information on this reverse scepter. Maybe it was a part of a past mission, or maybe it's currently active."

"The door is locked," Rae persisted, not sharing his enthusiasm.

"But *I* know how to get in," he said boastfully, puffing out his chest. "I secretly watched every time a captain went inside, and I memorized the passcode. There's a certain pattern you click on the feathers of the two griffins guarding the door. Then you have to kneel before the door like you're honoring it or something. And then it opens."

"Okay, but the archivist practically lives in there to guard it, and only Mission Captains have access to that room."

This time, Rae had Julian stumped. He blew a raspberry. "Yeah. If all the agents were in one place at one time—that's the only way the room would be empty."

We were interrupted by a high-pitched scream, followed by a deeper one, from the streets outside. It wasn't until a woman shouted "Help!" that we were out the door.

I didn't get the chance to process what was happening. All I saw was a Water Tunnel in the shape of straw shooting straight for the torso of a black, mummy-like figure with blue and gold streaks on his clothes in the middle of the street. The Water Tunnel spiraled through the air like a football and landed a couple of feet from a horrified woman and a man lying on the ground. It took me a moment to realize the tunnel had come from Rae. The figure immediately hopped to its feet, and it wasn't until it pounced at me that I realized what was happening. I tried to feel for my energy, to ignite it from my feet to my hands, but I was too slow. It was on top of me, pressing me to the ground.

"The journal," a voice hissed through a slit in the mask the thing wore. "Give it to me. Free the magi. Poison the poison!"

My arms and legs squirmed underneath its grasp, like a bug being smooshed but still alive. Its weight fell toward my face to choke the air out of me, but I managed to free my knee and slam it behind it, loosening its grasp as I coughed and wheezed. I stuck out my hands, but a blaze of fire from Julian streamed past me, followed by sprinkles of ice pebbles from Rae. The figure didn't have a chance to retaliate. A lightning-bright dagger with electric sparks impaled its chest, cracking its bones before it collapsed, and like the Chosen Shadow who had tried killing me on my first night in Isoria, its body disappeared like fog.

When I turned around, a Royal Scout whose gender I couldn't identify, wrapped in blue and gold, sat tall on a horse, a belt of electrified daggers dangling like keys at its waist. Instead of investigating the scene, the Scout took off, its horse ramming into bystanders who'd become interested in the commotion.

Thinking quickly, I ran to where the body had turned to smoke and picked up the sparkling blade. I shoved it into my front pocket and threw my sweater over it to conceal it.

A crowd swarmed around us with gasps and screams. The distraught woman was on her knees, sobbing hysterically over a man contorted like a rag doll in a pool of blood. The hazy eyes behind his glasses stared at the stars. A sickly weight churned in my stomach as my breathing grew shallow—not just because he was dead but because I recognized the man, even without his reptilian eyes. Xavier, my IEPE test maker.

I grabbed Julian's shoulder for stability, and he rubbed the small of my back. Rae covered her mouth, eyes wide.

Horse hooves thundered against the cobbles. A group on horseback trotted toward us, Isorian flags waving proudly as the riders guarded two figures in their midst. King Leo and Princess Calista. Everyone moved out of the royal family's path as King Leo passed the two knights in front of him, followed by Calista, both of them on sleek black horses. In the crowd, I spotted Headmaster Iceflyn in long yellow robes, anxiously watching King Leo and the woman. There were so many people I wondered if Banden and Alec were here.

"What's happened?" the king asked, his voice surprisingly alarmed, not cold and heartless like in the palace with Alec. His horse fidgeted, sensing its rider's discomfort.

"Xavier . . . my boyfriend . . . they killed him!" the woman wailed over his bloodied chest, streaks of red smearing her forearm. It was then I noticed the sparking white dagger skewering Xavier's chest. I almost fainted. The dagger in my pocket seemed to pulse against my skin.

"They?" Calista asked, more levelheaded than her father.

Tears escaped the woman's eyes. "Chosen Shadows or Pawns, Your Highness. It had to be! There was a dark silhouette. Disappeared like his shadow swallowed him. I turned away from Xavier for a second, and there was a dagger in his chest. Those teenagers were faster than your knights. When will this nightmare end? When is the Bellstemour-Confeld family going to fight back? When we're all dead?"

The king's and princess's eyes darted toward us but were drawn away by shouts from the crowd.

"She's right. When's this going to end?"

"Your knights suck!" someone else yelled. "We need more protection!"

"When will you start being our king?"

More yells erupted from the crowd, challenging His Majesty and Her Royal Highness. My friends and I were shoved to the side as the crowd closed in on the riders. The knights aimed their magical swords toward them, sparks of lightning, tongues of flame, icicles, and rock blades at the ready.

There was a tug on my wrist, and I turned around to find a pair of electric eyes locked onto mine. Even though her phantom-white hair was hard to miss, she'd found a way to blend in amongst the hostile mob in her black cloak.

"Follow me, dear," Celeste said, "and get your friends."

CHAPTER 24

It turned out that the main entrance MISTIC agents used to enter The Cave lay under a boulder in the quiet forests of Lightloch. It led to similar underground tunnels like the ones in Banden's chamber, although we went straight through a dirt wall and ended up at the headquarters. A crowd had gathered and stood around the marble griffin on the floor of the arena, their whispering tongues untamable. I stayed in the back with Rae and Julian since we'd arrived later than everyone else.

"Xavier was a brave soldier, faithful agent, and loyal friend," Celeste announced from a small wooden stage, her deep voice reverberating off the walls. "He will be missed, and we salute him for his service and dedication and for putting a cause greater than all of us before himself. Xavier's death will not be in vain, and it must not be taken as a lesson but as a warning."

A warning for *me*. That Chosen Shadow had been looking for the journal. How did he know I had it?

"Cyril Obsidian is fighting a silent war, a war our combat-intelligent and traditional war-hero king has never experienced." She continued. "Cyril is growing stronger, and he wants us to know it, instilling fear so we destroy ourselves and make the work easier for him. But unlike our king, we will fight back. We are prepared, we are smart, we are well equipped, and we are passionate and fierce and strong in what we believe in. We will restore freedom to our world and end this reign of terror."

My mind raced along with the crowd's streaming questions. Xavier's lifeless eyes haunted me, creeping into my every thought, and I suddenly felt claustrophobic. And then it hit me. *If all the agents were in one place at one time—that's the only way the room would be empty*, Julian had said in Solstice.

I turned to Julian, giving him a look, and gestured with my head toward the tunnel. We were not far from it, just needing to squeeze past the back of the throng so we wouldn't be noticed by Celeste. At first, Julian seemed hesitant, but he must have realized this was our only opportunity.

"We'll be back," I whispered to Rae, gesturing toward the tunnel.

She caught on, her eyes wide. "Are you crazy?" she hissed. "This isn't the time to be challenging the Archive's security!"

"Challenges are opportunities in disguise." Julian winked.

I could tell Rae wanted to protest, but she probably figured it was pointless, so she said instead, "Please be careful."

Julian and I moved as quickly as we could without raising suspicion. Thankfully, everyone was so engrossed in Celeste's speech and asking questions that we went unnoticed.

"What does this mean for us?"

"Does Obsidian know about us?"

"Do you think he'll come for all of us?"

"What's the next tactic?"

We waited for Celeste to show us her back as she called on another agent. Then we bolted for the tunnel.

"It's at the very end," Julian kept his voice low as we lightened our footsteps on the stone. The yellow tunnels echoed, and the last thing we needed was for someone to hear us.

I didn't know how long we ran, but it was enough for me to question if we'd ever make it before the crowd dispersed. But I could still hear their voices echoing in the tunnels. Finally, Julian stopped us in front of a wrought-iron and wood door.

"This is it," he said. Two massive iron griffins stood on their hind legs as they reared in the air, the talons of each reaching for the other's. Abstract designs were etched into the wood, and the words "Truth Will Prevail" were engraved in an arch above the creatures.

"If you remember what I said earlier, the feathers need to be punched in a certain order," Julian explained, then hovered his finger over the wings of the griffins to illustrate. "Once you do that, you have to kneel before the door. If you enter the password incorrectly three times, the griffins' heads will bow, lock the door, and set off an alarm. "

I nodded. "Let's do this."

I memorized the pattern. The feathers pressed down like a button as I pushed them. Once I had selected the last one, I knelt before the door, my heart pounding as I waited for it to open. But nothing happened. Even Julian looked puzzled.

"Are you sure that was the right combo?" I asked as the feathers popped back into place.

"I'm positive," he said, but I could see his confidence wavering. "Try again."

I did exactly as I had before, and still, nothing happened.

"We only have one more try," I said, trying not to panic as I kneeled before the door. "We're obviously doing something wrong."

I placed my hand on the stone floor to support myself, and as I did, a faint light glowed underneath my fingertips. I pulled my hand back and was about to jump away when I realized what was happening. There was a purpose to the kneeling.

The once-gray stone was now iridescent, and black, foggy words appeared. *"Truth will prevail.* I stared at the words, my mind automatically responding with *Lies will be punished.* Celeste's words had left an imprint on my brain. I noted there was only one quotation mark, which might mean I had to finish the phrase. I touched the stone again, and the words faded. I traced my finger along the stone, the letters following behind in the same shadowy font: *Lies will be punished."* Writing out those words twisted my stomach, reminding me of the oath I was breaking with this act alone.

The door gently opened, and I jumped to my feet.

"I'll stay out here and watch," Julian said. "Hurry."

I wasted no time. Once I stepped inside, the oil lamps along the limestone walls illuminated, revealing a room with rows of dark-brown wooden bookcases filled with a mixture of books, folders, boxes, and journals. A table stood on the right side of the room, and behind it on the wall was a giant iridescent square similar to the stone I had used to unlock the door.

I went to the square and repeated what I had done to the floor stone but wrote the words "reverse scepter." Like the floor stone, the words appeared and disappeared like fog on a steamy mirror. In their place, one record came up: *Scepter, Annulla; shelf 12, row 3, The Lost File: Annulla's Scepter.*

My eyes widened, and I grabbed my wrist as I remembered the sting of the hooded IEPE Incendor's deathly flames. They had called me Annulla. *Annulla swept her.* No, their words had been muffled. It was Annulla's *scepter.*

I headed for the shelf and searched the row for *The Lost File: Annulla's Scepter.* It was a flimsy brown folder with rings. I opened it to find a giant image of a teardrop crystal, the long, metal leaves that surrounded it unfurled like angel wings. Four gemstones trailed down the long bark with a gold chain twirled around it. It was the scepter from the library documents and Corinne's journal.

On the next page was a paragraph: *Annulla's Scepter, nicknamed the "Undoing" or "Reverse" Scepter, is a mythical scepter believed to undo any ancient, royal, political, or modern spell the average or masterful magi cannot. Each gem represents one of the four elements of sorcery, while the chain represents enchanters. It is thought to be created by Cicero Annulla, a powerful Bimedeis who believed that some of the consequences of magic shouldn't be permanent. There are no verified accounts of those who have seen or owned the scepter, only unverified stories passed down orally, which is why the scepter is believed to be a myth. Cicero is also believed to be fictional and conceived to explain the origins of the scepter.*

I read it until the sentences were ingrained in my mind. What spell did Obsidian want to *undo*? I remembered Mom's handwriting in one of the notes. *Till he destroys what will destroy him but save us all.* I had flashbacks to past conversations: *As Obsidian hides in his fort, protected from another ambush, his powers have grown and been mysteriously amplified,* Celeste had told me in her office. *No one knows how Obsidian obtained his power, what dark or illegal magic he exchanged his soul for,* Rae had said that night at The Enchanted

Mug. Both comments suggested that Obsidian's immense power was artificial.

Till he destroys what will destroy him.

There was a knock on the door.

"Orion, I hear people coming!" Julian's voice was muffled on the other side of the door.

But I couldn't leave yet. The folder had another section marked, "Inactive." I quickly flipped through the old beige papers, which seemed to be of four agent profiles: *Captain Aanya Gupta, Rhenelle Heeler, Zachary Rodriguez,* and *Azor Kilroy.* Each profile had a headshot and general information, and under *Mission Name* read, *Operation Light a.k.a. Annulla's Scepter.* There wasn't much in the descriptions but a sentence or two of the same information that was in the summary paragraph about the scepter.

It was then I noticed a similarity, an *odd* similarity about all the agents. Their *Status* read, *Deceased,* and their *Cause of Death* said, *Unknown, presumed dead by Mission Captain.* And the captain's cause simply read, *Unknown.*

"Orion!" Julian hissed again. He then murmured something in Spanish, and I was positive I heard the words "chica" and "loca."

I scrambled to put the folder back exactly the way I found it, then raced for the door. I grabbed the handle, only to pause when I heard Julian yell, "Hey, Mina Li the Archivist! How you doing?"

"Shit," I breathed, leaving the door open a crack so I could see out. Julian no longer guarded the door but stood in the corner of the tunnel in front of a girl with long black hair. She was dressed in dark jeans and a leather jacket.

"Julian Caballero . . . the Fielder," Mina said, giving him a weird look.

"Look what I learned how to do!" he said, holding out his hands like he was begging for food. There were crackling sounds, almost like mini explosives, and I saw what looked like small fireworks in his hands, smoke and sparks flying above his head. Mina jumped back in alarm, and I took that as my cue. I bolted from the room and sped down the opposite tunnel, stopping halfway to wait for Julian.

There was coughing, and I heard Mina say, "That was really . . ." cough, "something."

"Just really something?" came Julian's voice. "Fireworks are a level-two spell. I taught myself this."

I heard a patting sound. "You're really something, Julian."

From down the tunnel, I saw Mina cross over to the door, and I could tell she was waiting for Julian to leave so she could perform the password. I wasn't sure if he'd said anything to her, but I saw him nod and make his way down the tunnel toward me.

"Quick thinking back there," I said as we moved through the tunnels.

"I think I made Mina more suspicious of me, but you're worth the risk." Julian winked. "Anyway, you found something?"

My mind whirled from my discoveries as I told him everything, repeating what that little paragraph had revealed and what I theorized.

His eyebrows furrowed underneath his dark-blond bangs. "Undo? Like, reverse a spell?"

I nodded. "That's how I read it."

"Then the scepter *must* be real if Obsidian's after it," he said, keeping his voice low as we passed a few agents. "I wonder if he's seen it before and if Corinne had it or she just knew its location."

"Knowing my grandmother, anything is possible."

"And you think he doesn't want to undo or reverse a spell but rather that he's afraid of the power he has being reversed or undone?"

I nodded. "It makes sense. He wants the scepter to *destroy* it, not use it."

Julian's eyes widened at the realization. "Whoa . . .But the question still remains—why did Corinne hide her intel about the scepter from MISTIC?"

"There's something else I saw," I said, my heart pounding faster. "Apparently the agents, including the Mission Captain, that were assigned the scepter mission, Operation Light, are all dead, and the causes are unknown."

His eyebrows furrowed. "That *is* strange, but we don't know the risks those agents took to get that intelligence. Maybe they died on a mission trying to find more information about the scepter."

I swallowed. "Or maybe they knew too much."

The remaining puzzle piece was Corinne's journal, and we wouldn't know until we deciphered it. But one thing was certain: Celeste knew about the scepter, and something told me she knew Corinne was somehow involved with this not-so-mythical object.

Julian and I stopped before the arena, making it seem like we were a part of the dispersing crowd, hoping to find Rae and inform her of my discoveries. I needed to reach Mom again to tell her what happened, to tell her what I'd found and that I knew what she was after. Instinctively, I pulled my phone from my back pocket, forgetting technology didn't work here, and a gold circle flew out with it. It clanged onto the floor in front of my boots.

The coin. I had forgotten about it.

I reached down to pick it up. It was in pretty good condition considering the number of times I'd thrown these jeans in the wash. It wasn't a nonmagus coin, but I'd never seen the symbol on Isorian currency either.

Had it been a Pawn outside Corinne's house that night? Had they hidden in the shadows everywhere I went, watching me, initiating attacks on me, waiting for the perfect moment to strike?

I have eyes everywhere.

"Orion." A voice made me jump and squeeze the metal in my palm. A sharp burning sensation pierced my skin, causing my hand to jerk back and release the coin. I quickly picked it up and shoved it into my pocket before giving Banden my full attention, ignoring the stinging on my palm from the excess pressure on the coin.

I hadn't spoken to him since our argument in the pasture. Anytime he came home, I stayed locked in my room or the library. In the morning, he was up before I was. I'd forgotten about his infamous black pants and cape getup, a contrast to his pale skin. Alec was with him, his eyes holding more weight than Banden's, or maybe I was giving them power. And unlike Alec, Banden was always smiling. Light and dark. Day and night.

"Celeste told me everything. Are you all right?" Banden asked. I could tell he was trying not to let the worry seep through his composure, but his eyes gave him away. If it was even possible, he looked like he'd aged, deep stress lines etched along his forehead and around his tired eyes. Julian caught on to the conversation and slowly backed away from us, and I assumed he was going to search for Rae.

"I'm fine, thanks," I mumbled.

"You're still going to play your little charade, I see." Alec crossed his arms over his chest. He wore a dark-brown jacket I'd never seen, and I tried ignoring how it complemented the hazel streaks in his eyes, a web that could snare someone further into the pool of peridots. A remnant of the wound remained across his cheek and eyelid. But I squashed the sudden softness I felt.

"And you're still an ass, I see," I bit back.

He smirked, his eyes dancing. "You're cute when you're feisty."

"Don't even—"

"Orion, please," Banden interrupted our volley.

"You had no right to lie to me," I said. "My life's already complicated as it is. I don't need you to make it worse."

He took a step closer but kept his distance, trying not to hover. "Orion, I'm sorry for hurting you. You must know that wasn't my intention. Even if you don't forgive me, I'm letting you know I'm here. Please know that is my truth. This is why we need MISTIC. To end Corinne's secrets once and for all. I showed you this world so you could learn how to defend yourself, not fight. Corinne's battles are her own, not yours. She was selfish to pass on her demons and leave us all out of it."

"But like you said, Corinne had everything prepared, everything she did was for a reason."

"Her reasons led to her self-sacrifice, and they are not meant to induce yours." His eyes were fierce, his jaw tense. "Her past is not your present or future."

"Her past has tried to kill me multiple times," I shot back.

"Because I have my hunches that you are provoking it." He took a deep breath, holding in his frustration. "Stay out of it, Orion. When will you see your grandmother is only trying to hurt you?"

He said it almost like she was hurting him as well. Was I the only one who believed in Corinne? Or maybe I didn't want to believe I was choosing to sacrifice my safety and betray those trying to protect me. If Banden wanted to help me, he'd relinquish his secrets. But clearly, his mind was made up. So was mine. Secrecy was the only thing tying us together, yet it was also keeping us apart.

I turned on my heels to find my friends, but a firm pull on my wrist forced me to turn around to those peridot eyes. I was surprised to see them filled with worry.

Alec's grip tightened. "Orion, this is becoming more than some little family secret. Hiding it when it could help save the realm is selfish." His eyes bugged out of his head. Some agents looked our way, and Alec leaned in closer, lowering his voice, still powered with frustration. "Wake up, will you?"

I yanked my arm free as fire stirred inside me, stung he thought so low of me. *Corinne was right for only trusting herself. It's bigger, more consequential than I imagined.*

"Alec, we don't know what's in the journal," I said, praying he wouldn't run to Celeste or Banden. "I told you, once I decode it, I'll share it with MISTIC."

But he wasn't paying attention. His gaze was focused on my hand, his brows scrunched together. "What's that?"

He reached for my hand, but I pulled away. To my surprise, the coin's indentation was still etched into my skin.

"That's your and Banden's fault. I was holding a coin when you scared the crap out of me."

"Let me see the coin," he growled, startling me.

I reached into my pocket and handed it to him. His eyes widened, and the color drained from his face.

"Where did you get this?" he asked, his voice as dark as his eyes.

"The first night I moved in, some guy was hanging around outside my house. I knocked him down with my powers, and he dropped it. What's the big deal?"

"Orion, this scorpion was burned into Xavier's flesh with the words, 'Poison The Poison' underneath it."

Scorpion? I looked more closely at my skin. The pinchers. The sharp horns. The tail. A cloud of fear loomed over me, taking me back to the night in the library. Obsidian's scorpion. And the cloaked Incendor at my test. The fogged circle shape in the feather storm. Lines had poked out of it in a shape similar to the one on the coin. Wouldn't Xavier have stopped the test if he noticed something unusual? But why had Xavier been outside Solstice? And why had that Royal Scout killed Xavier and saved me?

The dots started to connect. That Incendor had definitely *not* been a part of the test. Someone had tried to kill me. And Xavier had let that happen.

Alec sighed, frustrated. "According to intel, this scorpion was seen in Obsidian's castle. We believe it's his official symbol and he's trying to send a message. Corinne made enemies, and they're after you, Orion. This proves it."

"I want all this to end, too, Alec, but we need to be smart about this," I reasoned, trying to keep my voice level as fear crawled up my throat.

"You're being far from smart. I know before Isoria you lived a life of invisibility, but you need to stop acting like you're the hero of this story. You need help."

My jaw dropped. "This isn't about me wanting to be the *hero*. It's so much more than that. How would you feel if you had been lied to your entire life about your identity and people were still keeping secrets from you?"

"Oh, so it's about your obsession with wanting to understand who you are and where you come from when the answer is obvious: from a senseless grandmother who got herself into trouble that caught up to her so she needed someone else to finish the job," he snapped. "You're not the only one with familial ambiguities, Orion. My father might as well have been a stranger, and I don't even know if my mother's alive."

A part of me wanted to be angry, but I felt truth in his words. Was he right? Was I so desperately trying to prove that I was someone? But was it so wrong to want to find purpose in my powers, to want to know there wasn't anything wrong with me and that my powers were meant for so much more than the chaos they brought into my life?

As much as I wanted it, this was bigger than my desire for answers. I hoped I could trust Alec. *Be sure you're playing.* That was the problem with games. Anyone could play, especially in a game where there were no rules.

He sighed. "I understand that desire for closure, believe me, but the only way to receive it is to let go and allow the universe to take care of the rest."

"Alec, this is more than about me seeking closure. This is about possibly saving Isoria, about ending the terror and deception." I would fall to my knees and beg if that's what he wanted. "I just need more time. *Please.*"

There was a moment of hesitation. His irises shifted back and forth as his eyes scrutinized mine. He scoffed. "Fine. Get killed for all I care."

I flinched at his harshness, watching him as he stormed away and disappeared into the tunnel.

Hiding was useless. Obsidian would come for me whether I was alone or surrounded by guards. Did he know I was associated with MISTIC? Xavier had to have been the suspected mole, but were there more within the organization? Or was this the kind of fear Obsidian was purposely trying to implant to turn everyone against each other? *To make his job easier.*

"You should listen to them, you know," a heavy voice said. Celeste appeared out of nowhere, like the sneaky fox she was. I prayed she hadn't heard our conversation. "Owning secrets will not only make you the target but the bull's-eye."

I finally understood why Corinne had put her life on the line and died with what she knew. I was a piece of meat. Everyone wanted a bite of what I had to hide.

She raised an eyebrow. "You don't trust me, do you?"

"I don't know what you mean," I said, keeping my voice even. "I gave my oath, and I meant it."

I was expecting one of her tight smiles, but her eyes were smiling. "You'll want allies, Orion. Even the most powerful, the most infamous, the most feared need to trust if they want protection. You must decide whom you should deceive a little less. Cyril is playing a different kind of warfare, one our history has never seen—a war on intelligence only. He has Pawns and Chosen Shadows who stalk our shadows, who find ways to hurt us." She reached for me and grabbed my hand as if it were a delicate flower, then turned it over to see the mark on my palm.

I pulled away. "I hurt myself."

A smile tugged at the corners of her mouth. "That's exactly what he wants from us."

Her electric eyes glowed as she leaned in, an amused look on her face. "Your midnight quest was an interesting one. It was a little out of character for my three agents, but once I heard of your involvement, I couldn't help but wonder *how* valid all your alibis were."

My heartbeat thudded in my throat as heat rose throughout my body, but I kept my chin high to hide my uneasiness. I had to prove myself.

"I think my friends' and my loyalties are the last thing you should be considering. You may have miscalculated who your real allies are. Here's my intelligence." I reached under my sweater and pulled the dagger from my pocket, tossing it to the floor between us. She didn't flinch as the sparkling blade clanged against the marble, but her eyes fell to it. "I know you recognize this from Xavier's chest. It was used by a Royal Scout to save me. That scout murdered the Chosen Shadow. Xavier was my IEPE test maker, and I was attacked during my test by an Incendor who expelled fog shaped like a scorpion. Wouldn't he have noticed it?"

Her expression was unreadable, but her eyes were calculating.

"I would rethink your heartfelt speech for Xavier," I continued. "Someone who's supposed to be on my side tried to kill me. Like you said, you'll want allies, and I think you need me more than ever, especially to uncover Corinne's secrets."

My outward confidence didn't match how I felt inside. My heart hammered, and my knees weakened as I stared into her sharp eyes. I hoped my rebuttal was enough, but it might have damaged instead of helped my cause.

But her lips curved up. "Well, it took one incident for you to figure out what I've been speculating about the past few months. Well done."

I thought she was about to pull a knife on me as she slowly pulled back her jacket. My eyes widened at the electric white daggers dangling from her waist. I was speechless, my brain unable to formulate an explanation. Luckily, I didn't need to.

She continued. "Yes, Orion. I, along with some MISTIC Captains, had our suspicions about Agent Xavier's deception. Terminations for double agents are executed here at The Cave, but to reveal every single one fosters doubt in our system. To rid of them in secret, well, it protects the cause. Xavier was stalking you tonight, and we have the evidence to prove he's been doing so for quite some time. I can show you the intel if you doubt me."

"But," I started, my voice barely above a whisper. Something wasn't adding up. I had to clear my throat to find my tongue. "Chosen Shadows were there, and the woman said they attacked him."

She shook her head. "They were trying to save him."

The woman must have confused Celeste with a Pawn or Chosen Shadow.

"Well, now it seems like you're keeping secrets from the group," I dared to point out.

Celeste's eyes narrowed sharply enough to carve off the ounce of confidence I felt. "When you pledged your loyalty, I promised your protection. Better for Isorians to believe it was Obsidian than reveal the identity of a covert spy ring."

My eyes were glued to hers as my heart thudded in my chest. My mouth was shut because, for once, I had nothing to say. And quite frankly, I was too scared to speak.

"You took an oath, like you stated," she said, her voice even. "I hate to see good lives lost when it can't be upheld."

She turned on her heel and disappeared into the crowd, her absence louder than her presence. Like a queen on a chessboard, she'd left the next move up to me, a pawn in her game.

CHAPTER 25

Celeste had proven that anyone could be my enemy, even a stranger. Xavier had been the mole, but how many more double agents were there in MISTIC? Celeste had killed Xavier like it was a normal practice to eliminate turncoats. I'd pledged my life to a group I didn't even know. How could I trust any of them when deceit was so rampant?

You must decide who you should deceive a little less.

Celeste was right. I did need help, but not from MISTIC. I chose to trust that hiding the journal was the way to save Isoria, and I wasn't doing it for attention, regardless of what Alec thought.

Since the discovery in the Archive room, my friends and I had hit another roadblock. I had told them about Xavier being a double agent and how it had been Celeste who planned the attack in Avelin. They were shocked at first but agreed that Celeste's line of reasoning made sense.

"If anything, it confirms our suspicions that MISTIC doesn't announce every execution," Julian said. "It's not unheard of to have agents go missing or die under mysterious circumstances."

Rae nodded. "Sounds exactly like what she told you. To protect the cause."

We now knew Obsidian was after the scepter, but it meant nothing without the journal coded. My friends also agreed it was odd that Celeste was hiding the scepter from MISTIC, especially since it could potentially save Isoria. They suggested she could be keeping it secret because of the fear of double agents, but there was too much ambiguity. Like Julian had said, we didn't know what happened to those agents. But Corinne might have.

We agreed to take a break from the journal drama and focus on our studies until after the Autumn Duel. They explained that when an agent became so engrossed in a case, they sometimes missed important clues and needed to step away to see it from a new perspective. I agreed, but I was guilty of looking at the journal every now and then. I didn't feel as safe traveling through Isoria anymore. The woman crying and the menacing scorpion were ingrained in my mind. The engraving eventually faded from my skin, but I could still feel it, a phantom of dominance and fear on my palm. I was within reach of Obsidian, even if he wasn't physically here.

Focus on your studies, socialize, and enjoy being a teenager. I had to take Mom's advice, at least for now.

December rolled around, and the temperature in Isoria and Crystal Manor dropped, with Isoria having two light snowfalls. For the past three weeks, I'd been aggressively studying and practicing spells for the duel, using the preparation as a distraction from the Corinne chaos and my broken relationships with Banden and Alec. I discovered that Arayis had a training arena Aermages could use to practice spells. It was about the size of a high school gymnasium and had white floors made of iridescent tiles and a royal-blue wall with silhouettes of Aermages casting spells. I didn't ignore the fact that the Aermages practicing with me made sure to keep their distance, and I didn't blame them. My powers had been their usual self—successful and quick or unpredictable and destructive. There were times my spells would bounce against the walls and hit Aermages or me, throwing me to the floor or smacking me against the walls, clashing with other spells being cast around the arena, and well, staying in everyone's lane but my own. I started to become immune to the glares and scowls. But I learned I had more control over them when I focused all my energy and attention on the spell at hand, not worrying about the fear or letting my emotions obstruct my goal. But it was easier said than done.

Duel day came with a light snowfall. It was almost ironic that it was known as the Autumn Duel. Julian, Rae, and I trudged through the snow-speckled grass in the thirty-degree weather. Julian wore a puffy black jacket while Rae rocked a long velvet poncho. I wondered how she wasn't freezing. But many of the Isorians we passed wore capes as well. Rae always had to be one with the fashion trend.

The stadium was on the outskirts of Erudite Square. Hundreds of First Years hugged themselves as they trekked through the white blanket but bounced with excitement. In the distance, light snow fell on a circular stone building in the open field, like a monument in a snow globe. Torches hung along its walls, and above the wooden door was the academy's crest with the words "Isoria Academy Dueling Centre" below it. Students piled in, the chatter and excitement from inside growing louder as we reached the door.

"I'm gonna kick your ass, Rae," Julian challenged as we waited in line. "I hope we verse each other."

"What about Orion's ass?" Rae teased.

"Orion doesn't know how to fight."

"Hey, what about those knights in the library?" I defended.

He smirked. "You weren't dueling. You caught them off guard."

He was right. My ass was most likely going to get kicked.

"Don't worry," Rae consoled. "No one is skilled at dueling. Julian and I . . . we've had more practice." She then lowered her voice and turned to him. "We can't show off too much. Remember what happened to Isla last year because the previous headmaster was suspicious?"

"Previous headmaster?" I asked.

"Yeah. This is Iceflyn's first year."

"What happened last year?"

She leaned in. "An agent flagrantly showed off her fighting skills. There are many reasons why a sorcerer can be good at dueling, but with everything happening right now . . ."

I nodded and shivered at the notion of King Leo dragging the girl to the dungeons. *The king's so afraid of the monster he's become one himself.* The realm feared Obsidian, but how just was their king, jumping to conclusions and impulsively charging his subjects with treason?

Two guards at the door asked Rae and Julian for their names and schools. When it was my turn, I did the same, and the guard let me through the doors to the massive arena. It was a dome, and the students sat on ascending wooden benches painted in the four school colors. A circular platform stood at the center. Each school section had a banner with its color and the Isoria Academy crest above it: Terrona and Arayis were on the left. Aquium and Ignair were on the right. My friends had told me there were about eight hundred First Years. All First-Year classes had been canceled, and if a professor taught another grade level, they had gotten a substitute so they could watch the duel.

"This is where we split," Julian said. "Our schools sit next to each other since we're rivals." He pointed between him and Rae.

So I'm rivaled with Terrona.

Rae shook my shoulder. "You'll do great. We'll meet up afterward."

Arayis's section was almost filled. I'd made the right choice wearing the clothes Rae had bought me at Solstice. Everyone was dressed in their school's colors. As I searched for a seat amidst the hues of blues, whites, and yellows, I bumped into someone, making me topple backward.

Valerie's pale lips curved upward. She'd found a way to look more lethal than usual. Her hair was redder, her skin paler, her eyes sharper, like fighting gave her strength. She lived for it. She was always looking for a fight with me. "Too bad we're teammates. You wouldn't last thirty seconds against me, and I'm being nice."

"I wouldn't hold it against you," I mumbled and passed her, too jittery and distracted to snap back. The last thing I wanted was a fight before the fight. She seemed content with my remark, a smile in her eyes as I scurried away.

I found a corner seat and kept to myself. A handful of teachers conversed in the middle of the arena with Headmaster Iceflyn in his gold robes, his gray-brown hair gelled to the side. Professors Wicbin and Stroydor were there, their white robes a contrast to the multicolored group. My eyes surfed the crowds and unwillingly wandered to Terrona's section. But it was impossible to spot Alec in the sea of faces. I was disgusted with myself. *Why should I care? I'm an attention seeker, and he doesn't care if I'm dead.*

A loud, deep bell rumbled throughout the arena, silencing the chatter. Iceflyn had his arms outstretched toward a dinosaur-sized bell swinging under the crest.

240

"Thank you, everyone, for attending Isoria Academy's Autumn Duel. I will carefully outline the rules, along with safety precautions." His voice reverberated off the walls. "Although the duel is an assessment to observe how far you've come in your studies, it's also a friendly competition to encourage you to perform your best. The school with the most points will be rewarded as this year's Champion Dueler's Star. Currently, Ignair takes the lead for winning first place the past two years, with Arayis in second place."

Ignair's section erupted into claps and hollers while my Air classmates rolled their eyes and booed them. Iceflyn waved both hands to quiet them down.

"Each school will have the chance to verse one another. You'll be divided into groups within your school. Because there are so many of you, you'll duel in teams with your designated team color. You have five minutes per round to perform any level one spell you have learned thus far. Using higher-level spells is prohibited, and if disobeyed, you, as an individual will be disqualified from the competition and receive a point reduction for your school. Any intentional act of harm against a classmate will result in your team's disqualification. Accidents do happen, and in that case, you will not be held responsible. Now, listen for your name as we separate you into teams."

Professor Wicbin divided Arayis into colors while Professor Stroydor echoed him, repeating names in case the students weren't paying attention. My name was called with the blue team. I couldn't hear the Earth professor assigning teams. He had a long red beard and hair, which was tied in a bun, and he wore glasses and light-green robes. In spite of myself, my eyes searched the Terrona stands again, and that's when I saw him. He sat on the third bench in a corner, like me, his arms crossed as he watched the ginger-haired professor. His eyes immediately fell upon mine, already knowing where I sat. I averted my gaze, officially banning myself from looking at Terrona.

Iceflyn explained the point system. Defense spells were given ten points, offense received fifteen, and counter twenty. The school with the highest aggregate score won. You only versed one person. Attacking another member would result in your team's disqualification since it was interference.

"We'll start with the Red Teams: Aquium versus Arayis," Iceflyn announced. Howls and hoots erupted with zero seconds of silence, like a sports game. Although I'd never been to one, I imagined it would be something like this.

Arayis's Red Team jumped up from the stands to meet Aquium's in the arena. Rae stood there, tall and confident. Although my school was competing, I was rooting for her. Professor Wicbin and the Aquium professor helped their teams line up in formation.

Once the bell rang, I didn't know where to look. I tried focusing on Rae, but my eyes bounced to every player. Sparkling royal-blue Water spells smacked into glistening white Air spells and disappeared in the air. There were several moments where debris from spells would start toward the audience and vanish, like a shield protected the arena. One sorcerer blasted a Water Laser, and her victim crossed his forearms in an X to cast an Air Shield. Rae, swift and smooth, was obviously the most skilled at defending herself and dodging spells.

It was close, but Aquium's Red Team won by five points. Ignair's and Terrona's Red Teams were next. Many of the spells were new to me, and like a magic show, I waited for the next act. Flames reflected across my classmates' eyes as rocks collided into fire and sparked explosions with sizzling smoke, leaving behind the scent of burning matches. Dirt and pebbles shot through the air, exploding against the invisible arena shield. Overall, Aquium's Red Team won the most points of all four schools.

"Our next group is the Blue Team—Terrona versus Arayis," Iceflyn announced. Both sections hooted as students bounced into the arena and my stomach somersaulted. My only strategy was to mimic what had happened in Athena's Library—wing it.

My stomach dropped as I glanced at the Terrona stands. Alec descended the bleachers with the rest of his team. When we reached the arena, he was already looking at me. His eyes didn't say "destroy" like his teammates. I kept my distance, not wanting to be his direct opponent. But, of course, it wasn't my choice. Our partners had been randomly chosen long before the match. And I happened to be randomized with Alec. I kept my gaze down as the professors placed us across from each other.

The bell rang. Alec took a guarded stance, waiting. An energy tingled the blood in my hands, and a gray-blue light glistened around my fingers as I sent a bottle-sized Air Bullet toward him. He instantly dodged it, simultaneously throwing a small pebble at my hip. He could go easy on me, but not vice versa.

I threw another Bullet, but he avoided it with ease and threw another lame rock.

"Orion," he said, trying to make his voice heard over the cacophony. "I don't want to fight you. At least, not yet."

"Bummer," I responded, this time casting a strong wind at his feet. He stumbled but instantly regained his balance. I expected an immediate rebuttal, but he passed his turn.

"Look, I'm—" he began but stuck his arms out midsentence. Icicle-shaped rocks protruded from the ground, blocking my Air Blast. They disappeared, the floor none the worse for wear. "I'm sorry about everything."

Again, he passed on his turn.

"Alec, this is not the time!" I threw an Air Boulder, but he couldn't dodge it this time. It sent him backward onto his butt. That got him mad. In retaliation, he cast a Dust Blast, smacking me in the torso and forcing me to the ground with him. My throat burned as I coughed from the debris. He was on his feet before I had touched the ground.

"You won't listen to me any other time!" he shouted. We both jumped as a boulder exploded between us, tiny particles raining down and clouds of dust blanketing us. As the dust settled, I caught sight of something over Alec's shoulder, wondering if the dirt was playing tricks on my eyes.

"Are you all right?" he asked, but I wasn't listening. In the distance, Valerie watched me. The look in her eyes was frightening—nothing unusual except for the scene above her.

Valerie shot two Air Boulders—larger than any of the ones I'd ever thrown—in our direction. Hundreds of shiny, electric shards as sharp as cutthroat diamonds bedazzled the boulders, which flew straight at me with blazing speed. And Alec was in their path.

I couldn't understand it. She was on my team. Why would she want to hurt me? But there was no time to make sense of it.

"Alec!" I screamed, my heart catching in my throat as I pointed behind him. But that would do nothing. I panicked, extending both hands and mustering all the power I could inside of me. A rough, cool feeling circulated through my hands, along with something

I'd never experienced. The commotion in the arena—the scream-ing and shouting—went quiet, and I was alone with the two lethal boulders.

It was more than a tickling sensation in my blood. The energy streamed through my veins. A shimmering white light veiled my hands, and a bolt of glowing air escaped them and molded itself around the boulders, creating a pounding explosion. Muffled screams sounded in my ears, and I could make out blurry images of people ducking and running, their voices and movements strobing. Everything bled together like a watercolor painting. A stream of electric light from my hands was aimed for Valerie, propelling her straight toward the invisible shield protecting the arena, breaking the enchantment as it disintegrated like liquid glitter. And then I was on the ground, my hands catching my fall.

My ears were ringing, and the voices around me were still muf-fled as a figure ran toward me. I felt pressure on my shoulders, and I was lifted from the ground like a puppet. The figure's blurry face eventually shifted to a clear, fearful expression. *Alec.*

Then the crowd wasn't fuzzy anymore, and the voices suddenly became clear, and in slow motion, I was back in the arena. The audience was frozen, many of the sorcerers staring in horror at the arena. I followed their gaze, and my heart stopped.

A lifeless body lay on the floor near the Terrona stands. Iceflyn, along with Wicbin, Stroydor, and the other professors rushed over.

Valerie.

"No, no, no!" I tried breaking away from Alec's grasp, a dizzy sensation overwhelming me as Xavier's lifeless eyes clouded my mind.

"Orion, stop," he demanded. Tears welled in my eyes as one of my worst fears played out before me. *She can't be dead.* My knees buckled, and if it hadn't been for Alec's embrace, I would have been on the floor.

The entrance doors slammed open as a group of sorcerers in white uniforms marched into the arena. Iceflyn left them to attend to Valerie and stood in the middle of the group of overwhelmed sorcerers. With a swish of his arm, a bell rang, silencing the spectators. "For your safety and others, please remain seated. Students are forbidden to leave the bleachers when the Healers are in the arena. A professor will oversee each school."

On cue, each professor left Valerie to the sorcerers in white and calmed the restless audience. After making sure each dueler on the floor was safe, Iceflyn directed them to their sections and marched over to me and Alec.

"That goes for you too, Mr. Stone," he ordered.

Alec slowly removed his arms from around me, giving me a look before reluctantly following orders and occasionally looking back.

"Follow me, Miss Candor," Iceflyn demanded, starting toward two doors underneath the bell and crest. I had to jog to keep up.

"Sir, is she going to be okay?" I asked. My head pounded as I watched the Healers carry Valerie away.

He said nothing as he opened the double doors leading to a small room with tiled floors and wooden chairs. "Wait here," he instructed. "Leave this room and you face expulsion. Understood?"

I nodded, wincing at the threat. I was convinced I would be expelled regardless. I pressed my ear against the door and heard Iceflyn's voice roar throughout the arena.

"Attention, everyone. The duel will proceed without Arayis." There was immediate booing and shouting. "Arayis has been disqualified for using two advanced spells—a Level Three spell and one past academy education—and for deliberately injuring another student. The duel will continue with Aquium's and Ignair's Blue Teams."

Even if Iceflyn was being fair, the booing continued after the bell rang, indicating a new round. I shrunk against the door. Mom had always warned me about my combative mouth, whether it was with her or strangers. I'd thought it would be what got me into trouble someday, not me *physically* hurting someone. I'd never thought I was capable of that. I couldn't find a balance. I was either black or white. I wanted to be gray—enough to be noticed, not an eyesore.

I was a threat to everyone. I was a monster. I'd hurt someone. Valerie was a warning. Just when I'd had a shimmer of hope that I could be normal, my powers had jerked back on my leash, reminding me who was in control.

The doors flew open, and I jumped back as Iceflyn strode in.

"Sir, I'm *so* sorry. I promise I never meant to hurt anyone—" I started for an apology, but he raised his hand.

"Miss Candor, I know you didn't mean to hurt Miss Ruelle." His voice was gentler and more relaxed than before, but a sharpness remained. "Explain what happened."

My mind worked faster than my mouth as I blurted, "She was trying to hurt me. I saw her send those boulders toward me."

His eyebrows rose. "I'm sorry, Miss Candor. I thought Valerie was aiming for Mr. Stone. You believe she wanted to jeopardize someone on her own team?"

"I know it sounds crazy, but I saw her face, the look in her eyes." The words raced out of me. "I know it doesn't make sense, but the boulders were headed for me, I'm sure of it. And that spell I did . . ." My voice shook, the image of Valerie's limp body resurfacing.

"I don't know what that was. I panicked and ended up hurting someone."

He studied me like that day in his office, making me doubt my confession. If Iceflyn thought Valerie was trying to hurt Alec, that's what everyone else must have seen. I hoped my classmates would forgive me, although I didn't count on it. My actions hadn't been intentional, but no one knew that. No one knew how you felt—only what they saw.

He sighed. "Miss Candor, I know we discussed your . . . talents during your enrollment."

He hadn't believed me then, and he still didn't. Valerie was the injured one, but she had attacked me with an advanced spell first. No wonder she was a star student.

"Sir, I promise everything I told you is true," I said. "But shouldn't you also question how Valerie was able to conjure a Level Three spell? I thought that was impossible for a Level One sorcerer."

"This case requires more investigation," Iceflyn said. "For now, I think it's best if you escort yourself out. Please wait for me outside the arena. As per protocol, I need to file a report."

After he left, I took a few seconds before braving the eyes of my classmates. Booms and explosions thundered from the current fighting, and I hoped everyone was too distracted to notice me. But as I walked past Terrona's and Arayis's sections, I could feel it—everyone's eyes burning holes into me, or, at least, everyone who was sitting in the first few rows. Whispers circulated, and I heard someone mutter, "Screw you." I picked up the pace, holding back the tears, refusing to cry in front of them.

I was about to take the exit to my freedom when I heard, "Orion!"

Rae sprinted toward me and wrapped her sweaty arms around me in a tight, warm hug. She must still be exhausted from her fight. "Are you okay? Where are you going?"

"I'm leaving. Go back to your section before you get in trouble."

She stepped back, her eyes soft. "Orion, we don't blame you. Julian and I . . . we know it was an accident."

I was relieved they knew I'd never intentionally hurt anyone, especially for a stupid competition. Their opinions mattered most.

"Thank you," I said.

I'd always been afraid of my powers, but as I left the stadium, I'd never been more terrified of them. And of myself.

Chapter 26

I was falling but didn't want to crash. Swimming and trying not to drown. I needed to be alone. To process. To breathe.

Friday night, I rejected Rae and Julian's message to hang out. I was grateful for the weekend but dreaded my Saturday morning and afternoon classes. I was already heavily watched by Royal Scouts whenever I walked the Isorian streets—a warning from King Leo. And now my classmates weren't bothering to hide their stares and whispers.

In Defense class earlier, I had sat in the back and separated my desk from the rest, keeping my eyes on Professor Stroydor and my head down as I took notes, feeling the intensity of my classmates' stares. When we practiced the Bounce Shield, my neighbors made sure to scooch their desks away from me. I didn't blame them. Ever since the duel, I'd been terrified of my powers, and it was affecting my performance. I gave up on the spell in a matter of seconds. Stroydor eyed me as I sank in my chair, defeated. Then he rolled past me like he didn't notice, which I was thankful for. When class ended, I rushed out, a weight released from my shoulders.

Professor Iceflyn hadn't contacted me about Valerie. He told me he'd update me if her condition worsened. I swallowed, pushing down the lump in my throat, as I tried not to think of the unknown.

I had an exam on the origin story of Isoria for my History of Air class tomorrow. History was usually my best subject, but I hadn't had the chance to study, and I knew nothing about it. Professor Filbert refused to teach about the origin story. He felt we should already know the story, and if we didn't, we should find a way because it was elementary material. My only option was Athena's Library.

I kept my sweatshirt hood up, hoping to stay incognito, but news traveled fast. Students recognized me. I tried ignoring their whispers, keeping my eyes on my destination like a horse with blinders. To my blessing, the Ancient History section was empty, giving me a break from curious stares.

After my research at the library, I took a Promenade to Avelin. The Enchanted Mug was surprisingly busy tonight, but studying here was better than at my house or the library. At least, not everyone knew me here. For once, I wished I could pretend to be a normal sorcerer trying to get through her studies, hanging out with her friends, and exploring a new world. I'd settled for not being a normal human, but I couldn't even be a normal sorcerer. The universe wouldn't allow it, sending waves at my ship.

I picked the spot near the fireplace where Julian, Rae, and I usually sat and flipped through the books I had picked out. Each told a different version of the origin story. Some did so in great detail over hundreds of pages, while some were vague. I groaned, overwhelmed, and pushed the books aside.

The café was filled with younger sorcerers tonight, some who were blatantly eyeing me and whispering about me to their friends. How did Alec deal with this? It wouldn't be long before I exploded on someone.

I sipped my RNP. Not far from me was a table of giggling girls. I assumed they were laughing at me until I noticed they were ogling something behind me. I followed their gaze to the front counter and instantly regretted it when I locked eyes with a pair of green ones I'd memorized. Alec picked up a cup to go but when he saw me, he froze like I was the only person in the café. I dropped my gaze, pretending to be extremely interested in the words in front of me.

But I couldn't shake the sight of him. Since the duel, my feelings toward him were a tangled mess. I still saw his worried eyes, felt the way his strong arms had anchored me in a sea of chaos and panic.

"You know, from a distance, I might think you were trying to ignore me."

My head shot up as my heart leaped into my throat. Alec gripped the top of the chair in front of me, trying to play cool, but his wary smile betrayed him.

"And up close, I think I might be right."

"I'm trying to study," I mumbled, dropping my gaze.

"Orion." His voice was surprisingly gentle, unlike his aggressive scraping of the chair across the floorboard. He sat without invitation. "Are you okay?"

"I'm fine," I snapped. Maybe I was still angry. Or maybe I didn't want to show him my weakness.

But my hostility didn't bother him. "I wanted to see you. I was tempted to reach out, but I figured you needed your space."

"Since when do you care about what I need? You never have." *You told me you didn't care if I died.*

He furrowed his eyebrows. "If your needs involve hurting yourself, then you're correct. I don't care about what you think you need."

I looked away. I didn't know what to think of him. He was the most enigmatic person I'd met—close tie to Corinne, whom I'd never met.

"Banden's worried too," he continued. "He says you refuse to see him. I haven't seen him this angsty about anything in a long time."

It was true. When Banden found out about the tragic events of the Autumn Duel, he'd tried to see me, but I'd slammed the door in his face. Even so, he had been insistent, consoling me through Corinne's library door as I hid, assuring me it wasn't my fault. He had to meet with me and Iceflyn as the headmaster reported the incident. It was the first time I had been so close to Banden, and I almost waved the white flag, but I instantly put my armor on when I reminded myself why. I had hospitalized a student, and I was in this mess because of my family's web of secrets and lies. Their secrets had created a monster who couldn't control her power.

"When was the last time you saw him like that?" I asked.

Alec half-smiled. "When he took me in."

The table of girls glanced in our direction. Alec noticed my distraction, looked over his shoulder, and they immediately dropped their gazes. He rolled his eyes, clearly annoyed.

I couldn't help myself. "You know they think you're cute, right?"

"Hmm." He looked over his shoulder again, and a brunette with dark lipstick seduced him with her bright eyes. He turned back to me with a curious look, the corners of his mouth tugging up. "Do you think I'm cute?"

Heat rose to my face, and I hoped I wasn't blushing. To mask it, I countered, "Do you think I'm cute?"

He lifted an eyebrow, an amused glint in his eye. "Dear Orion, are you flirting with me?"

I rolled my eyes. "If that's what makes you happy."

The amusement didn't leave his face, and the atmosphere shifted with a feeling I couldn't label as his eyes locked on mine. But he snorted, thankfully loosening the tension. "I'm always being stared at. Whether it's for my father or out of curiosity . . . or admiration." He smirked, teasing, but then his smile faded. "I can't tell the difference anymore, so I don't pay attention."

"But how can you take it?" I asked.

He took interest in my pencil, using a spell to spin it on his index finger. "I've dealt with it all my life. I'm used to it."

"You shouldn't have to be. It's not fair that people judge you by what they think they know."

At this, he dropped the pencil. "Have people been giving you trouble?"

My shoulders sank. "Everyone blames me. I don't know if it's because of Valerie or because they were disqualified from the competition. Or both." I looked at everything but him. It was weird telling him my problems, especially since all our conversations eventually resulted in sarcasm.

"Orion, none of it was your fault," he said, strangely defensive. "You were protecting yourself. And—" he broke off, and there was a gentle shift in his voice, "you saved me. She would've killed me. So thank you."

"You're welcome," I said, shocked to hear those words coming from his mouth. "Anyway, Iceflyn didn't believe me. He thought Valerie had attacked you since you were on the opposing team. I know it sounds ridiculous, but I saw the way she looked at me. It was terrifying."

He shook his head, and I was about to curse him for not believing me until he surprised me. "You're observant. If that's what you saw, I believe you. The question is, why did she do it, and how? She cast a Level Three spell, which is nearly impossible for a Level One sorcerer."

I hadn't expected him to believe me so easily or to compliment me. Since when did Alec Stone give compliments? Maybe he was trying to warm me up so I would speak to Banden again. Maybe it was the ambiance of the café—the low lighting, the cozy fireplace, and closeness of our warm bodies from the tight seating.

I shrugged. "She hates me for some reason. I suspected it was out of jealousy, but I didn't think she'd actually want to kill me."

For once, he was silent, not sure what to make of it either.

A shiver ran up my spine as words crept into my mind, a reminder from Master Samir that felt like ages ago. *You are gifted, Orion. So gifted that envious eyes are watching.* Was Valerie so envious she wanted to kill me?

I exhaled shakily. "What does this mean for me? Do I have to walk around with a bodyguard for the rest of my life? Why did Corinne do all this?" My voice rose higher than I meant, making Alec jump. I put a tired hand to my creased forehead. "My mom, Banden, you—you were all right. Pursuing the past was a mistake."

He shrugged. "Maybe. But running away isn't any better. We're going to help you, okay?" His voice was firm, promising. "Banden will never let anything happen to you. And . . . neither will I."

His eyes were intense, and he sounded genuine. He shifted in his seat, clearing his throat. "Also, you should know I didn't mean what I said about not caring if something happened to you and that you're doing all this for attention. I was frustrated you were being so careless with your life. That anger came from worry."

I knew he hadn't meant it, but it was still nice to hear. "I accept your apology. Plus, you were partially right. Maybe I wanted to prove that my powers have a purpose, that I'm not normal because they are meant for something great."

He sighed, shaking his head. "There's no such thing as a normal sorcerer. What is 'normal,' anyway? We all have our issues, and we're all dealing with our own shit. Besides, your enemies should cower at you, not the other way around. You broke the Bulwark Shield around the arena for Isoria's sake. It's amazing you don't even realize what you did. Sure, your classmates might hate you now, but they also fear you."

"Because I almost killed someone?" I suggested.

He shook his head. "No, because you partially cast a Morph spell, or, more specifically, an Aermorph spell. It's believed when a sorcerer truly understands an element, he or she can transform their body into that element. So, in your case, you become Air, which is perceived to be one of the strongest elements in the Morph state because Air's the most untouchable. You also don't learn about Morph spells until your last year at academy, and only a Master Graduate can teach them. Our education system has four levels: Elementary; Academy, where we will be Prescholar Graduates; University, which are Scholar Graduates, and the highest level of education, where you study at your element's Pantheon to become a Master Graduate."

"Why is a Morph spell so dangerous?"

"Because it could ultimately destroy you." He leaned across the table. "Imagine turning your flesh—every muscle, every organ, every bone—into *air*. You're telling your powers to attack yourself, letting it become you. One wrong move and you could kill yourself."

I remembered how my hands had been transformed into an electric, glowing light. If what he said was true, how hadn't my hands been chopped off?

"Orion," he said sharply. "Your powers have saved your life, even mine. It's living proof of doing the unthinkable. I've read and seen a lot, but I've never come across something like what you can do." There was admiration, excitement, and wonder in his eyes. He praised me like I was his hero. "Don't let them define you. You define them. Once you accept that, you'll do unimaginable things."

I stared at my hands. I didn't see wonderment or power, only destruction and a curse. Could I ever be comfortable with who I was? But how could I when everyone had already defined me?

He eyed the books sprawled around me and lifted an eyebrow. "You trying to learn the origin story?"

I nodded, and was thankful for the change in conversation. "I have an exam tomorrow."

He hesitated for a minute before slapping his hands on the table and standing up. "I know what you need. Come on. Let's go."

"Go?" I asked, startled by his enthusiasm.

"To educate you." He waved his hand. "Come on, you'll love the museum."

I stayed glued to my seat. "I'm not going to a museum. I have my own educating to do."

"I'm helping you, I promise."

Chapter 27

Alec and I rode Tirips to Erudite Square. I would never cease to be amazed by its scholarly and curious character.

Alec halted Tirips in front of a colossal Doric-styled building that looked like it had been stolen from Greece. The pillars and the lively blue-and-gold marble veining added a fantastical element to the classical architecture. The pediment above was sculpted with scenes of sorcerers and animals, and the words "THE NATIONAL ISORIAN MUSEUM OF HISTORY AND ART" were engraved in the stone. Alec dismounted Tirips and helped me down before tying the horse to a stone railing.

"Sorcerers are taught the origin story when they're young," he explained as I followed him up a set of grand steps to the brown door. "History, languages, the arts—they're all extremely valued. That's why your professor is making a big deal of you knowing the story."

The inside of the building was as magnificent as the exterior. Its gray cobbled floors were scattered with gold stones, and its marble walls were etched in classical designs and hung with paintings. In the center was a tall statue of someone named Comet Valor, whose long beard blended with his heavy robes. He held a scepter in one hand and a scale in the other. Below him on the floor was a golden sun that had short, triangular rays and the words of Comet Valor written in the circle: "It is our divergent and similar features that balance not only us but those around us. A world of complete likeness is dull, but a world with differences is vibrant and revolutionary, one in which we can coexist."

We roamed hallways and galleries that recounted Isoria's history through paintings, statues, jewelry, and artifacts. We ended up in a room devoted to the origin story, although there were fewer art pieces here than in the other rooms given its ancient nature. Alec led me to a narrow spiral staircase that ascended to a second floor.

The walls were painted half black, half blue, and golden cages with glowing white crystals hung at various intervals. Three people—a middle-aged man and a woman with her young son—sat on the floor.

"Good. We're right on time," Alec said.

"Right on time for what?" I asked, eyeing the blank walls and cages. "It's an empty room."

"So you think." He went to a corner and sat on the floor, patting the spot next to him. "Have a seat."

I gave him a questioning look but humored him. I eyeballed the white ceiling. "What are we supposed to be looking at?"

"Patience."

I scowled and wrapped my arms around my knees, feeling ridiculous. But the room wanted to prove Alec right. The crystal lights dimmed like in a movie theater. The marble floor softened and transformed into grass. Flowers bloomed and sprouted from the ground, and the walls faded into trees and a view of mountains. The ceiling was now a starry night sky. I turned to Alec, who was already looking at me, smiling.

My eyes wandered around the new place we had suddenly been transported to. "Where are we?"

"Still in the museum," Alec said, an amused look on his now-shadowy face. "I suggest you don't walk until after the show unless you want to bump into the walls for my entertainment."

I gave him a look, but before I could retort, a woman's voice echoed from nowhere.

"Long ago, before the civilization of Isoria you know today, one of the first Isorians walked the magical lands where creatures and vegetation unknown to the rest of the world resided. No one knows exactly where these people came from, but they possessed the skill of sorcery, able to manipulate and create the elements the earth had to offer—water, air, fire, and earth. This group was known as the Elemental People and would later acquire their modern name, sorcerers. And among this group were five powerful sorcerers." As the disembodied female voice spoke, figures took shape in the form of constellations in the starry sky above and *moved*. "They were gifted with extraordinary elemental powers and possessed great understanding and skill."

One by one, each of the constellation sorcerers cast starry spells.

The voice continued. "Blythe Testrian was attracted to the solidity of earth. She believed the trees, ground, dirt, and rock were the most important to sorcery. Without earth, a solid foundation, we wouldn't be here. Kyson Artus was drawn to the wind and atmosphere. Everything had space, he argued, and air was what kept people and animals alive. 'Without the air we breathed, no one would exist.'

"'With the exception of water creatures!' Anastasia Azzurri argued. She believed water was the most fundamental element.

Without water, life would cease to exist. It was water that made the grass and trees grow and kept us alive. Nothing could live without it. And finally, Bryce Ives believed fire was the most powerful of the elements. Without heat, we couldn't provide proper food and nutrition. Without the sun and its light and warmth, there'd be no vegetation, and the world would be a depressing habitat. He also believed fire was the most destructive."

The live-action constellations manipulated their chosen elements.

"These intelligent sorcerers are known as the Original Four. They're what we classify as Masters. They had a deep understanding of their chosen element and devoted their lives to studying each element, inventing many of the spells we use today. They spread their beliefs and educated sorcerers, but these beliefs segregated the community, creating a division among the Elemental People. Communities formed around the element they believed to be most vital to the earth, and it was treason to integrate with different elements. Riots broke out, and tensions rose as each of the Original Four claimed their own kingdom—Arayis, kingdom of the Aermages; Ignair, kingdom of the Incendors; Aquium, kingdom of the Aquatists, and Terrona, kingdom of the Terramancers. Although these four kingdoms were different, they shared one belief: pure blood."

Which doesn't make sense. You weren't necessarily born with the element you were meant to study.

"But a brave sorcerer named Comet Valor refused to accept such division. He was drawn to all four elements and spent almost thirty years studying them, learning to master each one. While it takes the average sorcerer most of their life to master them, Valor was different and particularly extraordinary.

"Comet preached the earth was comprised of all four elements and that we needed them all to survive. One wasn't better than the other. His beliefs were dangerous in a time of segregation. Some saw reason in his words while others saw treason. He gained a following known as the Cometiers and sparked a movement for elemental equality. Violence broke out, and anyone who dared believe in integration was executed by either king or queen.

"Although Comet practiced peace, he was excellent at warfare and assembled a successful military. But he was battling a demon other than his aggressors—himself. Although he was brilliant and his powers were unlike anything anyone had ever seen, they were his downfall. He couldn't control them. Too many elements meant too much focus. Spells backfired on him, and some of his followers became afraid of his destructiveness. Although he lost many of the battles he started, he still won the war."

What if I win battles and still lose the war? It was tiring, frustrating, and downright hard to control something no one understood. My intentions were to do good, yet I still harmed others.

What if I cause my own destruction?

"He overcame his doubts and fears, learning he must live in harmony with himself before he could do so with anyone else. Isoria faced years of segregation and bloodshed, but Kyson's shocking decision to follow Comet and join the Cometiers changed the course of history. It started a ripple effect with the Original Four, who, one by one, learned to accept their differences. The Incendors were the last to see reason, but Bryce relented because his people's views about elemental equality were dividing them. You can't have a king without subjects. This period of history was known as the Four Kingdoms War.

"After four years of bloodshed, the white flag was unfurled. The Original Four signed a peace treaty known as Peace of the Four Kingdoms and ruled their kingdoms in harmony, as did their descendants and other noble houses, for centuries. But it wasn't until a family in the eighteenth century, the Bellstemours, and specifically Bimedeis Drubin Bellstemour, envisioned the lands as one united country and began a crusade to disrupt the four ruling kingdoms. He radicalized Comet Valor's beliefs, believing that having four kingdoms would only cause future segregation. On top of this, Drubin had the power to take away any sorcerer or enchanter magic—something Isorians had never seen before.

"More blood was shed as a seven-year war broke out among the kingdoms and Drubin. However, fearful of the family's ability to eliminate magic and believing in Drubin's mission, sorcerers eventually succumbed, which led to the fall of the Four Kingdoms. Drubin claimed victory and crowned himself king of Isoria—that name originating from the isorile flower, which had been used to cure a sickness that had plagued the lands for a year. Drubin claimed he was 'saving' the land from the 'sickness of division.' The Four Families at the time were forced to relinquish their thrones to Drubin, and their castles became Isoria Academy: School of Sorcery, to celebrate each element. Blue represented Aquium, green Terrona, white Arayis, and red Ignair. A gold pegasus in flight above the drawing of a book represented aspiring to new heights and was chosen as the school symbol. It wasn't until decades later that Isoria Academy's main headquarters was built in Erudite Square.

"And now, because of brave revolutionaries and Isoria's complex history, the four elements of sorcery coexist in amity today."

Overgeneralized but okay. I remembered learning in Professor Stroydor's class that there had been a period in the sixteenth century where sorcerers had become fearful of Incendors and tried to oppress them like they had with enchanters in the nineteenth century, afraid they secretly had the ability to take away magic like the Bellstemours. Isoria had faced many tragedies and wars before it saw "peace." There was nothing peaceful about the country today.

The stars danced across Alec's shadowed face as the sky slowly disappeared. When he caught me staring, I whispered, "What if I never learn to control them?"

One corner of his mouth lifted. Not in a smirky, egotistical way but in the most empathetic way this boy had ever shown me. "Well, that's ultimately up to you, isn't it?"

One minute I had my powers under my belt, and the next, I was sending a classmate to the hospital. Who knew if Comet ever did learn to control his magic? Although he had won the war and accomplished what he believed in despite his weaknesses.

"You're not your powers, Orion," he continued. "They're just a part of you."

"Then who am I?" I mumbled.

"Whoever you want to be. You have that power."

My powers were always my identity. My powers were the reason for my self-doubt, for my isolation, for the constant negative self-belief. But was I using them as an excuse to act that way, to think that's who I was?

It was miraculous. Alec saw that my broken pieces—or what I saw as broken—weren't the sum of who I was. Pain had made him wiser and stronger than he seemed to believe he was. We both believed a monster lived inside us for things that didn't define us. So why didn't he believe his own words?

"You too," I said. "You're more than what happened to you."

He blinked, and I wished I could read what was behind those expressionless eyes.

Power was a funny thing. Some people reveled in it, while others surrendered to it. The Obsidian King promoted fear with his power, while King Leo couldn't seem to manage his. I related to King Leo.

Succumb or succeed. I had to make the choice. We all did.

CHAPTER 28

My little adventure with Alec at the museum had been a blessing, and I left Professor Filbert's room with a smile. Although I didn't know every question on the origin story exam, I knew I'd passed. So far, I had achieved pretty average grade points, but I was proud of myself given I was a full-time sorcery student also juggling nonmagus work and a murderous family secret.

The sky was dull, and snow speckled the grounds as I made my way through Arayis's courtyard. One crazy person was out here in this gloomy and freezing weather, sitting on one of the benches. He looked up, meeting my gaze, and I realized I knew that crazy person. Professor Wicbin.

"Miss Candor, do you have a minute?" he called as he packed up his belongings.

"Sure, Professor."

He caught up with me, his nose pink and skin lighter than usual in the frosty weather. His white-blond hair didn't help his pale appearance. "Let's go inside. I don't want to keep you in the cold."

We went through the glass doors and found a quiet spot in one of the corridors. Two students, one of them Asher, paused their whispering to look at us. I had changed my seat in our class to avoid sitting near him since he probably hated my guts and was sending me mental insults.

"How have you been since everything?" Wicbin asked softly.

A threat to society. I shrugged. "I'm all right. Still trying to understand what happened."

"Well, I had said our time together would be interesting." He tried lightening the mood, but I couldn't see the humor.

"It's not easy," I admitted. "I don't even understand how I do half the things I do."

He scrunched his eyebrows. "So, the Aermorph spell wasn't intentional?"

Oh, great. If my own professor didn't know that, who knew what my classmates thought?

I shook my head. "Not at all, Professor. I swear. Everyone keeps telling me I did this famous advanced spell, but I have no idea how. I only know how scary it was."

He smiled gently. "We're all frightened by the darkness in us."

I now understood Alec and how easy it was to fall and feel like you were losing yourself. I didn't want to believe I was a monster, but my powers had come from me. And I had used them to hurt someone.

"If you don't mind me asking, have you heard anything about Valerie?" My voice was small, afraid he would say something I didn't want to hear.

"I'm not authorized to release that information, and like the Headmaster said, he'll be in contact with you regarding Miss Ruelle's condition if needed." His eyes narrowed, warning me.

I nodded. That's what Iceflyn had ordered, but I had to see her. I had to know she was okay.

"Miss Candor." His voice relaxed again. "Have you had any luck with your language investigation?"

Without thinking, I was about to share my success, but I held my tongue.

Too many people have turned their backs on our family, Mom had warned. *Corinne was right for only trusting herself.*

I shook my head. "Oh, no. Nothing, unfortunately. I'm pretty sure it's a made-up language, like you said."

"Really? That's quite impressive," he mused, rubbing his chin. "Well, my offer stands. I'd be more than happy to help you with your research."

"Thanks again, Professor, but it isn't necessary," I said, trying to sound as defeated as I could. "I've given up. I'm positive it's junk."

His face was blank. I thought I'd offended him, but he nodded. "Of course."

"See you next week."

I started down the hall, only to be stopped again.

"Orion!" Asher called. I wasn't in the mood for a fight, and I contemplated running back to Wicbin, but Asher caught me before I could escape.

"I didn't mean to pry," he half-whispered like he shouldn't be talking to me, then uncomfortably pulled on his light-blue jacket, "but if you're wondering about Valerie, she's still in the hospital— the Azzuri Infirmary in Azzuri Falls."

"Is she okay?" My heart pounded, afraid to hear the answer. I was shocked he was even sharing this information.

He shrugged. "You should see for yourself."

Whatever that I meant, I was grateful for his help. "Thank you for letting me know."

He nodded, then bit his lower lip ring. "You should also know Valerie's been trained to be the best. It's all she's ever known. Good luck."

Before I could ask why he was telling me all this, he turned and started down the hall. Maybe this was his way of telling me he didn't hate me.

I needed to visit the infirmary. If I was a monster, I could at least be a kind one.

Azzurri Falls was the first Water town established under Anastasia Azzurri's rule, and its hospital was the best in the realm. Rae and Julian had wanted to accompany me, but I wanted to do this alone. After all, I was the one who'd sent Valerie there.

Azzurri Falls was on the southern coast of Isoria and was nothing like Avelin or Lightloch. Falls suited the name. Many of the buildings were pebbled, like fish-tank stones, in dark shades of blue, purple, and green. They stood on the many ports and mini islands over a large body of water, with water cascading into the ocean below.

Along the wooden docks, people in small boats offered rides to passersby. For a reasonable price, one of them took me to the infirmary, sailing me through the crystal waters and aquatic town, the scents of fish and seawater filling the air. In the distance, a foggy silhouette caught my eye—a gray outline among the blue waters, its zigzags revealing it was land. Something like lightning flashed in the fog.

"What's over there?" I asked my helmsman.

"Westwin—or once was," he huffed, his voice dry and grainy.

Fort Obsidian. That flash hadn't been lightning. It was the electric shield—although I couldn't see it at all.

"It looks . . . huge." It hadn't seemed that large on the map Julian had shown me, but it stretched along the horizon as big as Azzurri Falls, which was the largest village I'd ever been to in Isoria.

"It slowly grows, a testament to his growing power. That gray smoke you see is Shadow's Pass." He looked ahead as he steered the boat with a Water spell. "At night, sometimes you can hear the screams—louder than the cries of the sea serpent—of his captives and followers transforming into Chosen Shadows."

How could Pawns be "followers" when they were forced into being mutated creatures? *Unless they weren't forced.* The sea winds grew colder, a shiver tracing my spine.

The Anastasia Azzurri Infirmary was one of the largest buildings in the area and was tucked in the middle of a densely populated port. The square edifice reminded me of a turtle's shell with its light-blue tiles. Inside, the floor was tiled with light-green squares, and the white walls were covered in tranquil paintings of the sea and abstract art fit for mermaids. Potted seaweed planters were scattered around the lobby and down the halls. It was one of the most relaxing hospitals I'd ever been in.

A man and woman sat behind a marble desk the same color as the floor. I approached them, blinking multiple times, making sure I wasn't imagining their goldish-yellow skin and chocolate-brown hair.

I cleared my throat. "Hi, I'm here to visit someone."

"Who's the patient?" Her deep-green eyes stared curiously at me.

"Valerie Ruelle."

"Who's visiting?"

I was distracted by her complexion, her sharp features, and the narrowness of her face, her ageless skin making it impossible to determine how old she was.

"Orion Candor. I'm a friend of hers from school."

"Okay, Miss Candor. She's in room 212. You may take the stairs or the Ascenities to the second floor."

She recited the information like she had a database in her brain. A young girl asked the yellow-skinned man to see a patient, and like the woman, he responded with the room number from memory. Both the woman's and the man's tones were similar. They sounded mechanical, impersonal, computerized. Mnemosyates. I had learned about these creatures in Professor Soveus's class. They had a photographic memory, memorizing all information they saw, like pictures, numbers, and words. They were dull creatures, but at least they saved trees.

I headed for the second floor, thankful it was only one flight of stairs. I still didn't understand how to work the Isorian elevators, or Ascenities.

Healers dressed in white went from one room to the next, one group to the other. I dodged out of the way as a group passed me, not paying attention, their noses stuck in the documents they held. This floor, unlike the first, was chaotic. I tried to keep out of the way as I scanned the hall for room 212. When I finally found it, I paused at the wooden door.

Valerie was going to kill me. She was an Aermage, but she'd find a way to set me on fire. I knocked before I could change my mind.

"Yes?" a voice called.

I opened the door to a small room. A sofa chair sat by the window, and in the middle was a cot with Valerie staring right at me. Her hair was in a ponytail, although unusually loose and messy.

And her dress. It was laughable—loosely fitted and *pink*. She looked like she was dressed for Valentine's Day with her red hair. A bedside table was piled with flowers and cards. Guilt twisted in my chest for coming empty-handed.

"Hey, Valerie," I said awkwardly, closing the door behind me. I struggled with meeting her gaze, so I stared at her arm instead. A moon-and-stars tattoo was painted on her forearm, and, unsurprisingly, they circled a fierce sword.

"Oh, great," she muttered, lifting her book higher to her pale cheeks.

A sterile mint-and-lemon aroma hit my nostrils as I approached her. The room felt homier than the ones in the nonmagus lands. There weren't even any machines hooked up to her.

"So, how are you?" I tried. She looked whiter than her normal pale self. But even in her most vulnerable state, the sharpness never left her eyes. She had been born fierce.

She slammed her book shut, making me jump. "Magical. I swam with dolphins. Sang with the birds. Saw a rainbow."

"Has anyone else visited you?" I persisted despite her obvious disdain.

"My close friends, some professors, the headmaster." She spoke to the window, looking out at the waterfall in the distance. "Accidents happen at these duels. But you don't think they'll happen to you until they do."

I took a step toward her. "Valerie, I'm so sorry. I didn't mean any of this, but may I remind you, you were the one who cast those death boulders?"

She sighed. "My memory's fine, and I'm not experiencing excruciating headaches anymore," she answered, sidestepping my accusation.

"But I randomly fall asleep sometimes, so my Healer wants to keep me in this hellhole until it wears off." She whipped her head around. "I know you didn't mean to send me through the Bulwark Shield. If you've come to seek forgiveness, it's been granted. You can leave now."

I froze, taken aback by her confession. "How do you know I didn't mean to hurt you?"

"Because—" She bit her lower lip, stopping herself, and averted her gaze again.

"Valerie, what's wrong?"

She shook her head. "I'm afraid they're going to keep me in this prison longer." Out of frustration, she grabbed her scalp with her fingers. "I remember everything that happened, but I'm so confused I can't understand it!"

"Understand *what*?" I took steps toward her, inches from her bed now.

She sighed heavily, close to tears, and I was kind of glad—not because I wanted her to hurt but because she was capable of it. Under her thick skin, she could feel. "I *was* aiming those boulders at you, but . . . it was and wasn't me."

I arched an eyebrow. "What do you mean?"

She dropped her hands to her sides. "Even if I had some sort of vendetta against you, I wouldn't jeopardize a competition because of bitter feelings. Everyone knows I'm competitive. I want to win, so I wouldn't intentionally hurt someone on my own team. I don't know how I did that Level Three spell, but I clearly remember casting it. I remember feeling angry and wanting to hurt someone."

Don't you always feel like that? But Asher had revealed something deeper. *Valerie's been trained to be the best. It's all she's ever known.* What had he meant?

She was fighting a battle within herself. How could someone cast a spell and not know they were doing it? I suddenly felt some hope.

"I didn't mean to do that Aermorph spell," I explained. "As you know, sometimes my powers aren't in my control. Maybe you were in a similar situation?" Maybe I'd found someone like me, even if the similarity was, unfortunately, with Valerie.

But she squashed that hope like a bug, shaking her head. "No. I know it sounds crazy, but it wasn't me who cast the spell . . . although it was."

I shrugged. "I don't know, Valerie. I'm the last person who can help you with magic."

She snorted. "Which is a little hard to believe since you broke a powerful defensive shield *and* partially did a Morph spell. When Iceflyn came to see me, he questioned me about the incident to see if I remembered anything. Even Wicbin was trying to understand. I don't think he's ever had a student who did something like that before."

Wow, that almost sounded like a compliment.

She opened her arms wide and yawned, slowly sinking into her pillows. "Shit, I'm . . . sleepy," she slurred, her eyes less alert. "You tell anyone about what I . . . told you . . . I'll drive a sword . . . through your back."

I wouldn't hold it against her. I headed into the hallway and closed the door behind me. Outside her room, the excitement from earlier had died down, but the handful of Healers and visitors standing around were now a blur, fading as I tried to wrap my head around Valerie's revelations.

I was about to turn the corner when in my peripheral I caught a glimpse of someone climbing the staircase to the third floor. It was the only person who could stop my racing thoughts only to speed them up again.

Alec.

CHAPTER 29

I had half a mind to call out to him, but I went with the other half. I crossed the floor and climbed the staircase after him. When I reached the third floor, I thought I had lost him when I caught him climbing toward the fourth floor. Already out of breath, I quickly made my way toward the next flight of stairs, silently praying he wasn't heading to the tenth floor. Instead, he darted for a hallway, but it was blocked by white curtains and a brawny man in front of them. Alec showed him a card hanging around his neck, and the man nodded and let him through. A sign on the curtains read, "Registrants & Healers Only."

The sign should be a sign for me to turn around and keep my curiosity to myself, but I had to see what this boy was up to.

My luck arrived when a girl around my age descended a staircase, sparking an idea. I hid behind the corner. I hadn't regained complete faith in my powers, and although my eyes stalked her, I didn't want to hurt her.

I took a deep breath. *I define my magic, not the other way around.*

As the girl reached the second to last step, I repeatedly apologized to her in my head. Her right foot stepped down, and I aimed my hand toward it. There was a slight magnetic pull around my palm, and a gust of invisible wind jetted toward her, the invisible force yanking her from the final step like her foot was caught on a fishhook. She missed the step, sliding to the floor and crying out. But I couldn't focus on my guilt. The guard saw her fall, and as no one else was around to help, abandoned his station and rushed to her side. Once his back was to me, I bolted from my hiding spot and disappeared through the curtains.

I didn't know what I expected, but it wasn't a hallway that looked exactly like all the other ones with green-tiled floors and white walls, though it was much quieter. Only two sorcerers leaned against the walls, looking up as I passed. Alec was nowhere in sight. He must have gone into one of the rooms. It wasn't my business being here. I should have silenced my curiosity.

I turned to leave, feeling guilty for tripping the girl and intruding on Alec's privacy. But a familiar voice at the end of the hall stopped me. One door was open enough that I could peek inside. The room looked much like Valerie's, although this one was livelier and more colorful. The walls were covered in crayon drawings. Stuffed animals littered a purple-sheeted bed and encircled a little girl with short brown hair and freckles. She was all giggles and smiles.

"I drew a picture of the castle this time, but I made it in shades of blue," the girl said in a high, bubbly voice. She held her paper out to someone. My eyes widened when I saw Alec sitting on a chair beside her.

He took the paper with a smile. "It's beautiful, but the Healer said you've been sketching all day, Kaia. Give your arm a rest."

"I'm fine. Oh, you brought your guitar! Play me something." Kaia grabbed his arm, bouncing up and down on the mattress.

"Nah, it's here to keep me company."

"*Alec.*"

His smile widened—an easy, relaxed smile I'd never seen. "I guess I can play something for you. What do you want me to play?"

He plays the guitar?

"Hmmm . . . an original?" Kaia asked sheepishly.

He sighed. "They're not good—you know that."

"They are! C'mon, Alec. It's just me," she begged, bouncing up and down. "Please, please, pl—"

"All right, all right." Alec threw up his hands in defeat and reached down beside him, revealing a sand-colored guitar. Kaia squealed with excitement. "I'm only playing a small part, though. It's called 'Two Hearts.'"

Soon a pretty melody filled the air. It started soft and slow, and as the song progressed, melancholic emotion poured from behind each note, like someone in mourning who didn't want anyone to know. And the more I listened, the more the lump in my throat grew. It was a mistake coming here.

"Alec, who's that?" Kaia asked, interrupting the song. The young girl's eyes landed on me.

My heart leaped in my throat as I jumped away from the door-frame, shakily starting down the hallway. But I only made it a couple of steps before I was stopped.

"Orion?" Alec's voice echoed. Healers sought the source of the caller, then stared at me with blinking eyes. My cheeks flushed as I reluctantly turned around, ashamed, cowering like a dog with its tail between its legs. His hair, as usual, was messy, wild, and confused, like his eyes, as he met up with me. "What are you doing here?"

I could have shrunk into the floor and melted. I cleared my throat. "I was visiting Valerie."

He shook his head, still trying to process my presence. This was the first time I'd seen him off guard. "Valerie isn't on this floor."

I couldn't look at him, so I stared at his chest. The white card around his neck read, "Volunteer."

I am a terrible person.

"I decided to wander around the infirmary," I responded, but I couldn't hide my hesitation. It hurt to lie, but I couldn't bring myself to tell the truth.

"How did you get in here? This floor is heavily guarded."

"Not as guarded as you think." I bit my lower lip, thinking of the girl I had sacrificed.

He opened his mouth, then closed it, obviously at a loss for words. His silence was, honestly, worse than anger.

"How much did you see?" he finally asked, his voice hoarse. I expected him to yell at me for interrupting such a personal moment. That was the Alec I knew—or thought I knew.

"Enough," I admitted quietly and took a step back. "I'm sorry, it was my mistake for coming here. I'll pretend none of this happened."

He rubbed his temples. "No, Orion. It's okay." I was about to leave without his permission, feeling terrible enough, but he stopped me. "Come to The Enchanted Mug with me."

I blinked. "What?"

"I'm not mad at you." He sounded tired, or maybe desperate. I didn't know this Alec at all. "Come with me. Please."

I saw something I never thought I'd ever see from him, something he was so good at hiding and pretending not to feel. It was the first time I'd ever seen him so lost and disoriented. So vulnerable.

Usually, his last name suited him. His guard always up. Hard. Strong. Like stone.

I had so many questions, but I refrained from asking them. *Sometimes curiosity must remain unquestioned and unanswered.* I remembered Mom's words. I was learning.

"Okay," I agreed.

We were silent from the moment we left the infirmary to the minute we settled in the café. Sitting by the crackling fireplace while drinking an RNP warmed me like a cozy sweater on this cold night and calmed my nerves about the boy sitting across from me. Alec had ordered black coffee made from Isorian coffee beans. He didn't drink it, instead tracing his index finger around and around the mug's rim. I'd never seen him this quiet except when I first met him. Maybe all this time, he hadn't been quiet out of rudeness but consumed by thoughts.

"Alec." I broke the silence. "You don't owe me an explanation. I was the one spying, and I crossed a boundary I shouldn't have."

He finally looked up, his expression unreadable—the Alec I knew. I wished his eyes could speak so they'd tell me what he was thinking.

"You don't know what's on the fourth floor, do you?" he finally spoke.

I shook my head.

"The fourth floor, or 'Forbidden Four,' houses disabled survivors of the massacre. Survivors who don't have a home, a family, or are terminally ill."

My eyes widened. "There are survivors?"

He nodded, shifting in his seat and taking a sip of his coffee. "Kaia falls into all three of those categories. She's eleven, the youngest amongst them all. She lost hearing in one ear and is paralyzed from the waist down from the poison the Pawns released across Westwin. It's a miracle she survived."

I didn't know what to say to make the situation better besides cursing Obsidian. Neither Alec nor I were the monsters. Obsidian was far worse—dark to his soul with a monstrous mind.

Alec sighed, and I was shocked when his lips curved slightly. "She loves to draw, and she's fascinated by music. I sometimes let her play with my guitar. She's strong for someone who's gone through what she has. She doesn't remember her parents."

I couldn't imagine being that young and experiencing such a traumatic event—having your hometown burned to ashes, losing your loved ones. My home had been destroyed in a fire, but I always thanked the heavens Mom and I were okay. But when I thought of her, my mind became paralyzed with fear over not knowing what danger she was in, if she was safe, or how she was feeling. I pushed the thoughts away.

"It was nice. I didn't know you played." I didn't know a lot of things about him.

He shrugged. "It's a hobby."

"So, that's why the floor is blocked off? Because they're the survivors?"

"Well, sort of. Originally, Healers believed the survivors had residue of the poison and were contagious, but it was disproved. Now it's because the lucky ones who still have families wanted a private area since they were visiting the hospital so often. The infirmary is their home, so they separated it."

I eyed the ID around his neck. "And you volunteer."

He nodded. "I try to go as often as I can. I'm there to keep some of the patients company, some more than others—Kaia, for example—bring them food, attend to their needs."

I didn't want to pry further, but I hoped my asking was a harmless question, "Why do you volunteer?"

He averted his gaze, drumming his fingers on his mug. "I don't know. I guess it helps knowing I'm helping them in some way."

He believed he held responsibility for the massacre, that he'd played a part in his father's mistakes. *So much pain caused by one parent.*

"I'm sure they appreciate it," I said. Our hands were inches from each other across the table. I didn't know if he noticed.

He snorted. "There are some patients I'm forbidden to go near because they see my father. I get it. I've been going there for about two years, and there's never a time where it's easy. Easier, but never easy." He stared at the fireplace, the flames reflecting in his eyes. "I can't explain it, but seeing you there, although shocking, was relieving." He nudged his nose with his thumb, uncomfortably shifting in his seat before picking up his mug again.

Relieving. I shrugged, ignoring the flutter in my stomach. "Well, you're welcome for spying on you."

His lips slightly curved, only escalating the fluttery feeling.

"But in all seriousness," I continued, "it's brave what you're doing."

"Yeah, well." He eyed his drink again, the smile I'd created gone. He didn't believe in himself, taking the undeserved blame for something his father might have done. It sucked that something this awful had happened to him. Although we hadn't gotten along in the beginning and he had been guarded and unapproachable at our first encounter, I started to see how it was a mask. Everyone covered pain differently, and sometimes it could disguise itself as someone we weren't.

"You're a good person," I said.

He lifted an eyebrow, and a corner of his mouth tugged up. "Did you just compliment me?"

I wanted to slap his wrist, but I was glad his playfulness was still there. "I'm serious, Alec. I know you feel partly responsible for what happened, but you're not your father. We can't choose where we come from."

He studied me before looking down again. "When we first met, I blamed you for things I shouldn't have. When Banden asked me to keep an eye on you, it interfered with my free time, and with my busy schedule volunteering at the infirmary, and school, and," his voice lowered, "training, I took my frustration out on you. And some people, as you know, are predisposed to think negatively about Corinne. Between the stuff I've heard and watching over you, I compared you to her. I should know better than to judge someone by their family. I'm sorry, Orion," he said wholeheartedly, his eyes honest.

"If only I knew all this was happening, I would've talked to Banden for you."

He shook his head. "If I'm being transparent, I started not to mind it. There was a point where Banden noticed my irritation and relieved me from my babysitting duties, but I found myself volunteering anyway."

My cheeks warmed, but I blamed it on the fireplace, refusing to overthink his words. Although I wondered how many of his warnings about staying safe had come from him rather than Banden.

I responded sarcastically to brush the warm feeling away. "And here I was thinking I was a pain in your ass."

He smirked. "You are. But you are the most pleasant pain in the ass I've ever had."

I grinned, rolling my eyes. His eyes searched my face, and I wished I could hear his thoughts. Sometimes I found myself thinking back to the night at Pier Fest and the feeling of being in his strong embrace—my shield, my defense. The way he looked at me now, so curious and genuine, was a sensation I couldn't put a finger on.

"So . . . what happened with Valerie?" he asked, breaking the spell as if it were a curse.

I sighed. Suddenly he felt so untouchable and unavailable that I knew I could never have him the way I sometimes imagined. It could never happen. He wouldn't let it happen.

I told him, explaining everything Valerie had told me in the infirmary.

"So Valerie wanted to cast the spell, but it wasn't her casting it," Alec summarized, his eyebrow lifted. "I have access to the Healers' files. Part of my job is to organize their medical records. Valerie's record showed she went through strict procedures to monitor her memory and tested perfectly fine. Unless . . ." He shook his head. "No, it wouldn't make sense."

"What?" I pressed.

He took a sip of his coffee. "There are charms that force you to do things against your will, which is against the Isorian Code of Law. But the victim doesn't remember when it happens to them, and no one in the academy is an enchanter, so it's impossible."

Regardless, someone was trying to kill me. And between the Incendor during my IEPE and Valerie, someone was close to it. I looked around. The café was basically empty at this point. I reached into my bag and pulled out Corinne's journal, like anytime I started to worry about my life being in danger. It had been awhile since I'd looked at it. At least I felt somewhat better when I did. I stared at the anagram on the inside cover. The giant hole in the leather was slowly stretching and peeling as the days passed, and I wouldn't have been surprised if the leather completely fell off. Even some of the dark-brown thread bordering the sides were frayed.

I flipped to the end of the journal and caught something on the back cover. Something my friends and I had completely missed. How had we missed it?

I asked Alec if he had a knife. I assumed it was the norm for MISTIC agents to always carry around some kind of blade with them. He raised a curious eyebrow, but reached into his pocket and handed me a green pocketknife.

My heart pounded as I dug the blade into the leather on the inside of the back cover. There wasn't a shape or symbol, like the circle that had been on the front cover. Just the light-brown stitching outlining the sides. The same light-brown color the circle had been stitched in.

I grabbed the leather and peeled it back, revealing the entire inside cover. I gasped at the hidden message. At what we had all missed.

Alec had been watching me the entire time. If he had been talking to me, I didn't hear him until now. "What is it, Candor?"

I stared at the new words at the bottom of the cover. They were words I already knew but hadn't thought much of until now. *Follow the leader. I have it.*

Alec and I raced to my house while I explained the importance of the words. I threw the library door open and activated the secret room as I shuffled the documents for the letter. I lifted it to eye level so Alec could read along.

"'My findings will lead you to the truth. Please follow my words. Without a leader, there are no followers. The first is only what you need after every period. Follow the leader,'" I recited.

And then the first sentence of the paragraph: *Please stop following me.*

"After every period . . . Do you think she means the first word of every sentence?" Alec asked, catching onto my crazy, his eyebrows furrowed.

"Maybe." I grabbed a blank piece of paper and a pencil from my bag, and from each sentence, I took the beginning word and listed all of them on the paper, stopping where Corinne had directed me to. But the words didn't form a sentence.

I read them again carefully. It made sense. The first word was the leader in every sentence, right after every period. *The first is only what you need.* She'd made it difficult by not specifying what "first" was.

I had a thought.

Looking at each first word I had pulled out, I wrote down the first letter: On Rector I Or Never Free It No Done Many Everyone = O R I O N F I N D M E.

Orion find me.

Follow the leader. I have it = *Orion find me. I have it.*

My breathing became shallow. When Banden had relived Corinne's death, he had said Corinne wanted to be left behind *so*

286

they would never search for her again. I have it. "It" had to be the object, and the object was the scepter.

"We need to talk to Banden," I said, shoving the letter in my pocket. "Now."

Traveling the streets of Lightloch with Alec at this late hour was flirting with death. The sky was asleep, and the rainbow town was deserted. Everyone seemed to be doing exactly what Obsidian wanted. Hiding. Living in fear, as if a Chosen Shadow could waylay them at any moment.

But my insides jittered for another reason. Corinne was alive, and she had the scepter. Either Banden was lying to me or Corinne had lied to him.

My pocket vibrated, and I stopped in my tracks. I impatiently pulled my phone out, expecting to see Mom's number on the screen, but it was a blocked number. I was about to ignore it when my heart thudded at the sudden realization.

"Alec," I said, stopping in my tracks. "My phone is ringing."

He shrugged. "Okay, then answer it."

"Alec."

He stood confused, and then his eyes widened. "How?"

I took the call. "Hello?"

There was immediate laughter, the hairs on my arms bristling in response. "Orion, dear. How are you?" The voice was disguised, deep, and throaty.

"Who are you?" I asked, shaken by the concept that this phone call was even happening.

"I suggest you find a quiet place to chat if you haven't. Royal Scouts. Don't want to attract them for such suspicious activity with a nonmagus device."

I led Alec to an alleyway, my heartbeat pounding in my ears. "Can you see me?"

That ugly laugh again. "He has eyes everywhere."

He. This was a Pawn. I looked around, but I didn't know what to look for. Cameras didn't exist in Isoria. But this phone call questioned the impossibilities.

"Who are you? How are you doing this?"

"Orion, Orion." It sounded like a parent scolding their child. "Please do realize you're not the only one with unusual power. I just want to talk—Oh, is Mr. Stone with you? I would love to speak with him too."

"Who is it?" Alec mouthed, his eyebrows furrowed.

I shook my head. "Don't know. They want to talk to you."

I pressed speakerphone, and the voice echoed through the narrow alleyway, "Now that we're all together—Orion, you have what I need. The journal."

"It's useless. It's coded," I insisted, ignoring my wobbly legs.

"And lucky for you, I have the solution."

Alec and I locked eyes.

"How?" Alec sounded like he wanted to reach into the phone and strangle the unknown caller.

"So nice to hear from you, Mr. Stone. Yes, I know someone who can help. She goes by the name of Zee."

My eyes widened as I recalled Corinne's letter. *Zee.* She was supposedly Corinne's friend.

"How do we know this isn't a trap?" I said.

"On the sides of the journal's pages—pull them down and you will see for yourself."

I hesitated, afraid that if I flaunted it, someone would jump down from the terracotta roofs above and snatch it from me. But Alec reached into my bag and pulled it out. He opened the cover and showed me the side of the pages, then bent them down to stretch them out. There, hiding on the sides of the pages, was an image of a sharp letter *Z* with a snake dragon encircling it.

"She will be able to decode it," the caller said, a smile in their voice. "She and Corinne have such a lovely history together. Although, I must warn you, they weren't on the best of terms. After all, Corinne was the reason Zee lost her powers. So you might have to get creative."

"And if we don't?" I countered.

The voice laughed, and then there was the sound of something being winded and a loud slam. Ticking, the speed of a fluttering heartbeat. A clock. "This isn't a negotiation, Orion, but a courtesy call."

"No! Please, no!" A familiar, frantic voice suddenly screamed in my ear, draining the blood from my face.

"Mom!" I cried.

"Ah, yes. Seraphina's been very useful to me. We're speaking because of her. You have until morning to bring me what I ask, Orion, or she suffers a terrible fate."

"I'll do whatever you ask. Where do we find Zee?"

"Thanks for your cooperation." I could hear the smugness. "Zee lives in the heart of the Crowned Woods. You'll find her at the Eye of the Heart with the help of Red Steel, the guardian of the eye. Just call his name. That's all you should need to know."

"And where are we supposed to meet you once we complete the mission?" I asked through gritted teeth. I wanted to find him and do much worse than I had done to Valerie.

"I'll be waiting for you at the end, don't you worry." I could hear the grin in his voice. "Oh, and tell anyone about this and you'll have not one death but a massacre on your hands."

CHAPTER 30

We wasted no time. Alec tacked up Tirips as silently as he could in Banden's barn. He then mounted the animal after me, and I grabbed his waist as he gave Tirips a squeeze, sending him into a canter through the dark, cobbled streets of Lightloch. I took in as much as I could, swallowing the panic while praying this wouldn't be the last time I saw this place.

The Crowned Woods wasn't too far from Lightloch. Alec had translated the caller's riddle to "the center of the forest." He'd heard rumors about there being a mysterious "eye" on the ground in the center of the woodlands, which no one truly knew who it belonged to or what it meant. It had always been one of many of the woods' wonders. But as we'd learned, the caller somehow knew it belonged to Zee.

We rode for some time until we reached a forest of tall, ancient trees, their bark twisted like rope, their branches so long their leaves drooped like a delicate blanket. Alec pulled out a Lux Crystal from his pocket and handed me one as well, illuminating the night. The music of humming insects and the chirping of birds played through the healthy, vibrant green. During the day, I bet this woods looked enchanting, but any forest at night . . .

"Does it have Chicaneries?" I asked.

He turned his head, eyeing me over his shoulder with a funny expression. "Yes, but hopefully we won't have to wander that part of the woods. They live near the caves."

"The caves?" I asked, finding that odd. "Why were they in Crystal Manor that night of the Pier Fest, then?"

He avoided my gaze, looking straight ahead again. "Someone had been trying to send you a message, someone who was after Corinne's secrets long before you were."

I shivered, thinking of the figure who'd stood outside Corinne's house.

Alec continued. "Anyway, our main concerns are the Three-Tailed Tigers, Isorian Black Wolves, and Northern Crowned Bears."

"Ha, ha. Perfect."

He patted my arm reassuringly. "If we don't bother them, they don't bother us."

"As in, if we don't run into them, they won't bother us," I muttered. A shiver trailed down my spine as Alec led Tirips toward the path.

There was an ethereal glow to the forest. Remnants of snow dotted the bright-green vegetation like Dalmatian spots. Glossy leaves on low-hanging branches touched the ground, where bright red and purple mushrooms sprouted from fluffy grass, and flowery bushes shimmered around the ropelike tree trunks. I was in a dream in an enchanted forest where a child might believe unicorns and fairies existed. But it amplified my fears. Sometimes beauty hid deceit, and after being in Isoria, I knew danger crept between the shadows and the light. Even the singsong hums and chirps were distant, like the creatures didn't want to be bothered.

"What horrible crime could Zee have committed that she lost her powers?" I asked. I remembered learning about the code in my History of Air class. Magic had its limits and rules so that a sorcerer or enchanter couldn't abuse their power. If a rule was broken, the Isorian Code of Law stated a spell could be performed by the king to eliminate a sorcerer's or enchanter's magical abilities.

He shrugged. "Zee must've gotten entangled in dangerous situations with dangerous people. Corinne flirted with trouble like she was immortal."

And now we are doing it for her.

"How do you know this forest so well?" I asked.

"I know everything." He grinned. I couldn't understand how he found humor in this situation. Maybe MISTIC had taught him how to keep calm under pressure. "I know some parts. I spend a lot of time here since this is where Terrona is. But it's on the outskirts of the forest, toward the way we came."

"Is that why you're not freaked out right now?" I tried to keep my voice level.

"I'm used to it," he said, distant. I wasn't sure what that meant. Maybe he was referring to MISTIC missions.

"So, besides you having an opinion about everything and occasionally having a book up your nose, what do you do for MISTIC?" I lengthened the conversation, trying to keep my mind off my uneasiness.

"You could've called me smart and saved your breath," he responded, making my eyes roll. "I'm a Profiler, which is a glorified way of saying analyst. I study people, locations, evidence—anything that helps me strategize a game plan with the Mission Captain or determine the next steps of an enemy or mission. Sometimes I'll help with lie and deceit detection." He smirked. "Like busting you for stealing Corinne's necklace."

"So you're constantly reading people," I mused. "No wonder you come across as a standoffish jerk. You don't trust anyone."

"The moment you let your guard down is when your enemies strike." His voice suddenly darkened. "That's what you do, Orion. You learn what motivates people, what their vulnerabilities are. You then use that information to manipulate them to get what you want. That's what spies must do."

I heard Celeste: *You must decide who you should deceive a little less.* At the time, I didn't understand her, but now, hearing the way Alec talked, I realized how lonely his way of thinking must feel.

"But you can't go your entire life treating everyone like they're a suspect," I said. "You'll end up alone."

He looked over his shoulder at me. "In this world, Orion, everyone has a motive. I hate to say it, but look at your mother. And you didn't want your friends involved with this. Part of me doesn't blame you for not trusting me and Banden. Can you honestly say you wholeheartedly trust those you care about? Sometimes those closest to us are the traitors and our loved ones are the ones who hurt us the most."

My instinct was to fight back, but he was right. And he was wrong. If I pushed everyone out, I would always be alone. I had been alone all of my life, and I didn't want to continue like that anymore.

"Well, I'd rather love and trust than not have done so at all," I said.

A silence fell between us. I didn't disagree with him, and I also didn't blame him for such dismal thinking—at least not in the world of Isoria.

"During the day, it's peaceful here." Alec surprised me, breaking the silence. "Sometimes, when I need space, I come here. With all the green and the movements of animals and rustling trees, you sometimes forget the cruel world around you."

I didn't know what to say. *This* Alec was being personable with me.

He noticed my silence and glanced over his shoulder. "What? Nothing to say for once?"

"Weren't you lecturing me about not letting my guard down?" I raised an eyebrow.

He rolled his eyes. "Doesn't mean we can't have a conversation. It's called distraction, Orion, from the dire situation at hand. MISTIC could teach you a thing or two."

"Continue," I prompted, not wanting him to think I'd misread the situation—although he sounded defensive.

"I've been coming here alone since I was twelve. My mother is a Terramancer, but she went to Libertaria. She'd come here to paint, and she'd take me with her. It was so boring. She'd spend at least two hours painting, but it taught me patience, and I started to like it." He spoke tenderly about her. "She's free-spirited, patient, selfless, and passionately loves those dear to her. Nothing like me." His voice suddenly fell flat. "All I ended up with was my father's ability to distrust. He was always distant with me. I never really knew him." He snorted. "Maybe that's why I'm so good at my job."

I was the opposite of Mom except for our stubbornness. When we believed in something, it was impossible to change our minds. That's why we were both risking our lives for each other. She had been so concerned about me staying out of trouble that her life was now in danger. I also noted the way Alec had talked about his mother in the present tense, like he hoped she was alive. Did he actually believe it? With everything I'd learned about him tonight and with what I knew about his father, I knew there was no comparison between the two Stones.

"Well, I think you're more like your mother than you realize," I said.

He smiled wearily, an unnamed emotion flickering in his eyes. "You give me too much credit, Candor."

A branch snapped beside us. I thought it was Tirips, but Alec stiffened. He halted Tirips, listening to the shadows as he held up his Lux. "Let's pick up the pace. If there's anything out here, I don't want to be waiting around for it."

He sent Tirips into a canter, holding his Lux high, like a lighthouse, as we blazed through the trees and shadows. He finally slowed to a walk and halted us in front of an odd formation of trees and bushes.

"This is the center, or at least part of it," he said.

I didn't understand how he knew. There wasn't a landmark in sight. The only difference was the golden-greenish bushes that entwined together, creating a long, tall hedge—and a dead end.

"We could ride around the hedges, but this is basically it," Alec said. "The exact coordinates. I even double-checked the map."

"What's behind them?" I pointed to the bushes.

"Not sure."

He dismounted Tirips, then showed me how to do so. I hopped off, landing a little less gracefully than I wanted.

"Is it safe to leave Tirips alone?" I said as we left the animal next to a tree to investigate the bushes. The branches above us intertwined with one another, creating a roof within the trees.

"Tirips is more of a warhorse than you think. He could fly out of here if he wanted to," Alec responded, a smile in his voice I didn't understand. He studied the branches closely. "Looks like they're guarding something, doesn't it?"

"Weird plants with a mysterious presence. You think this is what we're looking for?"

"Beats me. But I'm not too keen on finding out."

I smirked. "Why? You can't crawl through some bushes?"

"Take a closer look, Miss Sarcasm."

I peeked through the branches, holding my Lux and trying to see what Alec saw, but it was all green, tangled branches. I was going to continue with my joke until I finally caught it. Each thin branch was laced with small but painfully sharp golden thorns deadlier than shark teeth.

I backed away. "I stand corrected."

"They're Golden Horned bushes. Their thorns are infused with snakeberry poison. A lot of people learn the hard way." He smirked. "You're welcome."

"Venomous bushes. We must be in the right place."

He cracked his knuckles as if preparing for battle. "You're lucky you're with a Terramancer, but this won't be easy. I'm not sure how much they're gonna fight."

My eyes widened. "Fight?"

"Stay back." He extended his arm in front of me and put his Lux in his pocket, adjusting it so he could still see in the darkness.

He threw his hands up and scrunched his fingers, then moved them in opposite directions like he was opening two sliding doors. Branches cracked and roots were torn from the ground, the sharp sounds disrupting the quiet of the forest. The bushes pulled apart like they were alive. Then the branches on each side squirmed like snakes, reaching for the other side, trying to pull themselves back together. They screeched, violently whipping in the air like hoses let loose.

"Orion!" Alec shouted through gritted teeth over the noise that was worse than scratching a chalkboard. "Run through! Quick!"

"What about you?" I yelled.

His jaw was tensed and his eyebrows were scrunched together as he fought against the beastly bushes. "I'll find a way. Just go!"

The muscles in his arms tightened, and his veins bulged with the struggle. Knowing I didn't have much time, I ran through the opening, dodging the thorny branches flying wildly about. I ducked as one struck at me like a snake spitting venom. I played limbo and jump rope, running and ducking as they shot around me. One was about to whip me square in the face, but I threw a Blast at it, and it jerked away like a wounded animal. When I was safely on the other side, I yelled against the cacophony to let Alec know I was safe.

With a loud grunt, he thrust his arms into a wide T, and the bushes on either side of him slid apart, their roots ripped from the ground as he expanded the entrance. He made a run for it, dodging the flying branches, but the entrance was closing. A flood of panic overwhelmed me. He wasn't going to make it.

"Alec!" I ran toward him and extended my arm.

He grabbed my hand, and I managed to pull him out at the last second, all but a small gap remaining, the bushes fighting to close. Releasing a cry, Alec was pulled from my grip and slammed to the ground. A spaghetti-thin branch had encircled his ankle and was dragging him to his death. I slid to the ground to grab his arm. He cried in agony, the thorns sinking deeper into his skin and red stains oozing through his sock. I pressed my toes into the dirt, sliding against the rough terrain until they hooked onto a tree root, my body stretched like putty.

"Orion, let go!" Alec cried.

"No!" I shouted, pulling harder. I wasn't a Terramancer. I couldn't help him. But the helplessness in his eyes made me want to try harder. "You are not—dying—because—of a stupid—plant!"

Sharp pains stabbed my abdomen and arms as the branch pulled harder, growing stronger, or I was weakening. But I had a lightning-quick thought. My time was zero.

I unhooked my boot, sending us flying toward the hungry bushes. Holding tightly to Alec with one hand, I thrust the other into the air and let out a scream as a strong, ice-cold wind escaped it. The force bent my hand backward, and I painfully fought to keep it upright. We both screamed as we flew in the opposite direction, and I lost my grip on him. The dirt was at my face as I crashed to the ground. Alec landed a few inches from me on his side, grunting. The bushes sat peacefully, having re-formed themselves into a wall as if nothing had disturbed them.

"Alec?" I breathed. As I crawled toward him, pain pulsed through the wrist I had used to cast the spell. The ground felt weird, lumpy, and dry in some places yet wet and soft in others.

I flashed my Lux toward him. His belly rose and fell, but his eyelids remained shut. Then he coughed harshly, and his eyes finally fluttered open, finding mine. "Well, you showed that stupid plant."

I let out a heavy sigh, my shoulders drooping in relief. He slowly rose to a sitting position, gritting his teeth, and grabbed his right thigh.

"Your ankle." I neglected my own pain as I carefully peeled his sock down. He winced as the fabric pulled away from the open wound. Dozens of dime-sized holes oozed a purple-red liquid.

"Could be worse," he huffed. "I could've been paralyzed."

"It paralyzes you?"

He struggled to speak. Sweat beaded on his forehead and ran down his dirt-smudged cheeks. "Well, the poison does, but it's not permanent. Just need a remedy is all."

I pulled off my jacket and wrapped it around his ankle as tightly as I could. I shivered from the cold, but at least I was wearing a sweater. "How does that feel? Can you stand?"

"It might as well be broken." He winced, trying to sit up straight.

I forced myself to remain calm, taking a few deep breaths. "Okay, we should try getting back, then. But another way around those plants."

"No, just help me up."

I bent down to grab his hand, but a searing pain shot through my wrist.

"Your wrist is swelling." He reached for it, but I pulled away.

"It's okay. It was the spell. My hand was fighting against it for some reason."

"It might've required two hands. You were able to yank me free *and* send us flying," he said as I helped him to his feet, his voice filled with shock and awe. "Say what you want about your powers, Candor, but they saved my life. *Again.* Both of ours."

"Yeah," I said, amazed at them for once. "I guess they did."

He lost his balance, and I caught him, forcing him to put his weight on me as he wrapped his arm around my shoulders. We were in an enclosed, dark area, the trees above encircling us like a pack of wolves. Branches weaved into one another, creating a cave that resembled an upside-down nest. There was no escape. Without a horse and with a limping Alec, the rest of this journey was going to be even longer or impossible.

"Okay, now what?" I asked. "How much farther do we have?"

Alec's head dipped, and I thought he'd fallen unconscious, but his eyes were wide open, staring at the ground.

"Lucky for you, two steps," he said, "and we'll be standing exactly on the Eye of the Heart."

Chapter 31

The dirt, contrastingly hard and mushy, formed the iris and pupil of an eye—the heart of the forest.

In my excitement, I almost let go of Alec. "The Eye of the Heart. We figured it out!"

"Yeah, but now what?" He didn't share my enthusiasm, his voice flat.

"Remember, we have to call for Red Steel, guardian of the eye."

"Well, be my guest," he said, extending his free arm in front of me.

"Red Steel!" I called, not sure what to expect. "Red Steel!"

I felt dumb, afraid I'd misinterpreted the directions, until a pair of piercing red eyes appeared within the shadows a couple of feet away. I almost dropped Alec when a coal-black horse emerged, camouflaged with the night. But it wasn't any regular horse. Its mane and tail were made of fire, flames burned near each hoof, and its black-and-silver eagle wings, wider and longer than its body, fluttered slightly as it stood before us.

Alec whispered in my ear. "Is this poison getting to me, or do you see what I see?"

"What kind of horse is that?" I whispered back, afraid it could hear us.

"I don't know. A fire-mutated one?" Alec said. "It's a pegasus bred by Incendors, that's for sure."

The Fire pegasus didn't move an inch. It stood still like a statue as its fiery hair waved like a flag.

"Alec, what do we do?"

He shrugged. "The only thing I know about horses is you ride them."

It remained perfectly still, like it was waiting for the opportunity to attack—or was it just waiting? It didn't attempt to approach, frozen in place.

"Um . . . Red Steel?" I said tentatively.

The horse's ears perked up. Excitement flowed through me, my confidence growing. "Can you take us to Zee?"

At this, the horse took a couple steps forward. I held my breath, but instead of it continuing toward us, it turned around, facing away now.

"Oh, good going," Alec grumbled. "Now you've offended it."

I shook my head. "Alec, I think it wants us to get on."

His eyes widened. "Are you crazy? Ha, why did I even question that?"

I ignored his remark. "You said so yourself. The only thing you know about horses is you ride them."

"A horse with murderous eyes and flames might be the exception."

I moved us forward. "Come on. What other choice do we have?"

"I clearly don't have any." He pointed to his injured leg. "You could drag me into a wolf den at this point."

Red Steel was taller up close, his withers above my head. I cautiously ran my hand across the flaming mane. No heat. I then ran my fingers through it. Nothing. Like magic.

It took a couple of tries to get Alec up. It didn't help that there wasn't a saddle. I grabbed a chunk of its mane, the flames protruding from my grip like I was casting a spell, and took a giant leap as Alec pulled me up. When we were both on Red Steel's back, the animal walked forward and in circles, leaving a trail of fire wherever he stepped. I wondered if he was sick or dizzy until I understood what he was doing—tracing the eye.

Finally, the majestic beast came to a stop at the center of the iris, and the small fire trail etching the eye suddenly erupted into a roaring wall of fire, growing taller and taller around us.

"What's happening?" I panicked, nothing but flames in view.

"Trusting the fire horse, that's what!" Alec barked.

When I thought it was the end of us, the fire disappeared. The forest was gone, a small, dimly-lit cave with a wooden door now in its place.

"I think this is our stop," my voice echoed.

I hopped off Red Steel, then slowly helped Alec down and positioned his arm across my shoulders. The horse was back to watching us. Alec hobbled beside me as I headed for the door. We gave each other hesitant looks before cautiously pushing it open.

The room reminded me of Banden's Elixir Chamber, only more intimidating and darker. There were piles of paraphernalia everywhere—from books to bottles to furniture—signs that a hoarder lived here. A junk-covered stone table was placed at the center of the room. An unlit fireplace was decorated with cobwebs, and sculpted dragons raced along the cave's walls. At the far left corner of the room stood a ledge behind which lay what appeared to be an endless chasm, leading to who knew where.

"Hello?" My voice echoed. "Anyone here?"

The only response was the sound of dripping water. I thought I heard humming, but maybe my mind was playing tricks on me.

"Maybe she—" Alec paused, his eyes widening, "Orion! Move!"

I spun around to see a monstrous face with a long snout and snarling wide mouth with needle-like teeth inches from us. We leaped out of the way but were too slow, and its slimy, blue, snake-like body coiled around us, squeezing tighter and tighter, constricting my airway. Alec's face grew pale.

"Oh, Angel, what did I tell you?" A voice sounded. My oxygen-starved brain thought it was the sea serpent speaking until a woman stepped out from a corner. "We don't kill our guests. Not until I see them first."

The sea serpent loosened its grip, and Alec and I gasped for air. But it still held us hostage, its beady yellow eyes locked on us as hot air expelled from its long nose. One wrong move and we would be a midnight snack.

"Did you call your pet dragon Angel?" Alec growled, squirming in its grip.

The middle-aged woman smiled. "Why, yes. You've even met Red Steel. He's a lot gentler. But don't underestimate my pets," she spat. "They *all* bite."

The woman's curly black hair reached her hips, and although her skin probably hadn't seen the sun for months, she was darker than I was, making her piercing gold eyes stand out. She wore a brown dress and an excessive number of gold bangles on her wrists and ankles. A gold hoop hung from her right nostril, and her ears were covered in similar hoops. She was also barefoot.

"Are you Zee?" I struggled to speak with Angel's body still squeezing my lungs.

She stepped closer. "I ask the questions." Her voice was croaky, rough. "Who are you?"

"I'm Orion Candor, and this is Alec Stone."

Her eyes widened, and she crossed her arms, her mouth curving into a wicked grin.

"Well, well, well. A bitch's granddaughter and a murderer's son. Why does little ol' Zee have this pleasure?"

"Please, we need your help. Desperately. With a journal."

Her eyebrows furrowed. "A journal? You're wasting my precious time for a journal?"

"Not any journal." I couldn't tell if Angel's grip was growing tighter or if I was panicking more than I already was. "It's Corinne's. It's coded."

Zee's eyes narrowed, and she slowly lifted her right hand.

I said the wrong thing. Coming here was a mistake. I closed my eyes, waiting, and heard her fingers snap. Then Angel's body softened, uncoiling, and Alec and I dropped to our knees as the serpent slithered away, disappearing down the ledge into the chasm. A giant splash echoed throughout the cave, answering my question about what was down there.

"Let me see this journal," she hissed.

I handed it to her, and she snatched it. I helped Alec to his feet as she flipped through the pages.

"Why, yes. I gave her this journal," she confirmed, closing it. "And, yes, it's written in code. A language we created long ago." She threw it at me, her voice becoming sinister as she turned to leave us. "There's your confirmation. Good day."

"You're not going to help us?" Alec said, taking a step forward and bringing me with him.

Her head whipped around, her mop of hair flinging behind her. "Listen, here, boy. I owe Corinne nothing. If suffering had a face, it'd be hers."

Corinne had warned in her letter not to trust anyone. What lengths had she gone to in concealing the truth? Apparently, Zee had paid the price for Corinne's actions.

"You have ten seconds to ride Red Steel out of here," Zee sneered, moving slowly back toward me. "I usually have Angel take care of unwanted guests, but I owe your grandmother one thing after all she's done for me . . . though she cruelly drove a sword through my back, leaving me to bleed. Now, go."

A wave of desperation engulfed me. Leaving wasn't an option. "There must be something you want!"

She cackled, lifting a hand to pick at a dirty nail. "And what do you think a girl who can't control her own powers and a boy with a limp can do for me?"

My eyes widened. "How did you know—"

"I may not have my magic, but that doesn't mean I don't have power. I told you once. Get out or—"

"Anything, Zee. You name it. We'll do it. There has to be something you want," I begged. "Please."

She raised an eyebrow. "Why do you want it decoded so badly?"

If Corinne has the key to destroy Cyril Obsidian, everyone will be after this, I wanted to say.

"I need answers," I said instead. "It's a long story, but I never knew Corinne. It's her fault I can't control my powers, or at least I think it is. She's the reason Isoria and magic were kept secret from me all my life. She's so secretive, Zee. You must know this. I'm not so fond of her myself."

She rolled her eyes. "What a sob story," she mocked, studying me briefly before crossing her arms. "All right, I'll do it. But only if you do something for me first."

I didn't know if it was my story that convinced her, but I accepted it. "And what's that?"

Her mouth curved into a devious smile. "I need you to fetch an item for me."

"And what item may that be?" Alec asked cautiously.

"Have you ever heard of the Amora Rose?"

He stiffened. "The ones that grow in the Garden of Grandrose?" When Zee nodded, his eyes darkened. "Why do you want that?"

"I have many customers I have to send away because I don't have it."

"Customers?"

She raised an eyebrow. "You haven't noticed yet? I'm a maglout. Anyway, it's a desired item and extremely difficult to acquire."

"And illegal," he bit back.

She shrugged. "People do desperate things for love."

I was so lost. "Can someone explain, please?"

Alec gave me a grave expression. "Orion, you're asking to deal with a smuggler of the Isorian shadow market," he spat. "The Amora Rose, also known as the Love Rose, has a hypnotic pollen that forces infatuation on someone. To manipulate someone's emotions or attraction to another is considered torture in the Isorian Code of Law. It's against their will. The rose grows in the Garden of Grandrose, which is guarded by Cecile, a bitter Earth nymph. Only two who are truly in love can come out of the garden alive. Otherwise, you're trapped in there. There's no way out."

I swallowed. "Not as romantic as I thought."

"Not only that, but the Code forbids infatuation elixirs of any kind." He glared at Zee.

"So how are we supposed to get this rose if the garden calls for two lovers?" I asked, ignoring Alec's warning about the rules.

"You can trick Cecile," Zee encouraged. "You have to play the part very well. If she doesn't sense any pretense or a love being taken advantage of, you'll be unstoppable."

Alec wasn't buying it. He lowered his voice. "Orion, I don't know if we can do this."

For some reason, my stomach dropped, and anger stirred inside me. "Look, I know it won't be fun playing my boyfriend, but we have to do this."

He shook his head. "No, Orion—"

Zee cleared her throat. "I don't have time for your bickering. Do we have a deal?"

I studied her carefully. "You promise that if we get this rose, you'll decode the journal?"

She nodded. "I keep my word."

If doing business with a maglout was as terrible as Alec made it out to be, especially one who cursed Corinne's name, could I trust her? Maybe not. But the caller had been insistent about Zee. Maybe she was working with him or her.

"We have a deal." I stuck out my hand.

Zee took it and smiled. "Perfect. Now, you'll need a remedy for his leg and your wrist. The nymph will wonder why you'd allow your lover to walk in a garden injured."

I forgot about the throbbing. My whole body now ached because of Angel. Zee went over to a shelf molded into the cave's walls and grabbed a green bottle. Smiling, she handed it to me. "You two better get working on your acting skills. Your relationship reeks of disagreement."

Red Steel encircled us with another fire wall to bring us above ground. The tree branches that held us in the Eye of the Heart unwound to make a space large enough for Red Steel to fly through and over the trees and murderous bushes.

Once we landed near Tirips, Alec inspected the slimy remedy from Zee. Having worked with many of Banden's healing elixirs, he confirmed it was safe. It removed the paralysis in his foot, but his wounds remained. The swelling around my wrist disappeared.

"I don't like this at all," he said as he led Tirips through the forest. "Especially doing business with a maglout."

"I admit it's a little dangerous, but I think we can do it. We don't hate each other *that* much."

He shook his head. "No, Orion. If we get caught . . ."

"Oh." I understood. I winced at the memory of the king's cruelty. I'd thought it was because he didn't want to play my boyfriend. But there wasn't anything he could do, and he knew it. We were pawns in the caller's game, and now we were playing Zee's.

CHAPTER 32

The Garden of Grandrose lay on the outskirts of Crowned Rock, the Earth town established under Blythe Testrian. Long, rectangular, unending hedges divided the rolling hills, creating a labyrinth of green. The maze appeared much smaller from a distance, but up close, the hedges rose well above our heads, even on horseback. Glittering, glowing pastel flowers wove in between the branches of the trees. They also webbed a white arbor, inviting us into the maze.

"I can see why people are attracted to it," I said, staring at the shimmering flowers. "It looks harmless."

"Roses have thorns, and swans can be aggressive," Alec replied, dismounting Tirips.

Be a swan. Know who's a swan. I wondered if Master Samir knew more about me than he had let on.

I hopped off Tirips. "So it's dangerous because of the . . . nymph, I think you called it?"

"It's not only Cecile. There's a much greater threat, I think." He led Tirips to a nearby tree.

I raised an eyebrow. "Besides death?"

"Relationship demise." I couldn't read his expression, his Lux casting shadows across his face as he tied the reins around the tree bark. His voice was as mysterious as the parts I couldn't see. "Those who are confident about their relationships will hang out in the maze, no problem. But it can also tear them apart. If one person suggests going in and the other doesn't agree, it shows a lack of trust in the relationship."

"Who decided Cecile got to judge relationships?" I said.

"Legend has it that Cecile lived in the Crowned Woods. One day, a group of men went hunting in the woods. Cecile was intrigued by one hunter, thus becoming fascinated with humans. Nymphs aren't allowed to interact with other species. But she disregarded the rule and isolated herself, creating the garden maze as a sanctuary designed to attract humans—specifically the hunter. Cecile welcomed magi and left them alone as long as they respected the area. When Queen Alianora of the Earth Nymphs discovered the garden, she banned Cecile from returning to their society. She cursed Cecile by creating the Amora rosebush, saying humans were incapable of love and loved only for selfish reasons. Cecile didn't believe her.

"One day, the hunter, having heard the tale of a beautiful maiden who resided in the garden, went searching for Cecile. They fell in love, and Cecile got her wish. She thought she'd proved the queen wrong, only to have her heart broken. He was after the Rose, trying to win the affections of another. Once he got it, he never returned. Cecile thus cursed false love, and the garden became open to only pure and true-hearted lovers."

I shivered. "I don't blame her, but to trap people in the garden forever? That's a bit extreme."

Alec gave me a pointed look. "She's a nymph. They're not the most kindhearted creatures. They say love can bring out the worst and best in us, and it brought out pure evil in Cecile."

The flowers looked like they belonged in a wedding bouquet, but one wrong move and they could be a funeral spray. Eyeing the arbor before us, I took a shaky breath.

Alec offered his hand, smiling slyly. "You ready, *love?*"

My cheeks warmed, and for once, I was grateful for the dark. I turned away from him and placed my hand in his warm, strong one. "Ready."

We stayed close as we traveled along the gravel pathway, the only sounds coming from our shallow breathing. Alec faced me, pointing to his lips, which were in a forced, pretentious grin. *Be a swan.*

I mimicked Alec's behavior, forcing my shoulders down and swinging my arms, ignoring my heart beating a mile per minute. We remained silent as we made our way through the twists and turns and dead ends. I didn't know how Cecile could see or hear us, and I was terrified of speaking, afraid I'd say something that would kill us.

Alec put out his arm, forcing me to a halt. I thought he saw something, but he came close to me, his lips less than an inch from my ear.

"Smile, and don't freak out," he whispered, his warm breath tickling my skin, "about what I'm about to do."

I smiled as widely as I could, trying to dismiss my racing thoughts. Was he going to bolt? Call for the nymph? Did he see the rose? He leaned in and pressed his lips to my forehead. My face heated, my pulse pounded in my ears, and my body froze. When he slowly pulled away, I was looking at his lips. We stared at each other, and I had a small urge to pull him in again. My panic was driving me to think strangely.

He leaned in to whisper in my ear again. "I'm sorry." He spoke quietly, breaking my trance. I could see the warning in his eyes. *We're being watched.*

I nodded, unable to formulate words. Thankfully, it was enough. He squeezed my hand, pulling me forward.

This was going to be tougher than I thought. Flirting was not on my list of "know-hows." I was embarrassed to touch him in any other way than holding hands, which already sent my stomach in flips. But I fought with my emotions. I was foolish. *You don't like him, Orion.* I figured I liked the idea of his attention, something I'd never received from a boy before. Alec cared about my safety—as a friend, as Banden's family friend.

Alec stopped, pulling me out of my thoughts. "Which way?"

Two identical golden gates lay ahead of us, one leading left and one right. The delicate, pointed bars twisted to create a rose design with what looked like giant pearls atop the pointed ends. We stood flummoxed.

"Left?" I suggested.

He shrugged and led the way but jumped back when a sudden flash of white light pushed us back, preventing us from entering. We tried the other but faced the same blinding barrier.

"One per gate," a faint female voice sang out. We both spun around, looking for the source.

"You must continue separately," the sweet but eerie disembodied voice whispered.

If this garden was for relationships, why did the nymph want to split us up? Alec gave me a hesitant look. We'd come this far.

"We'll find our way back to each other." He squeezed my hand, and I knew he wasn't saying that for show.

I squeezed back before we parted, and we gave each other one last look before disappearing through the gates.

A cool wind tugged at the ends of my hair as the gate closed behind me. Although the shimmering flowers lit the shadowy path, I confidently held my Lux high, hoping to scare off anything in the shadows.

Something snapped behind me. Like a rabbit, I froze, listening and searching the hedges. Apprehension, waiting for the fear, was a fear itself. It allowed the imagination free rein, and mine was racing. I sped up, but a sudden growl and the snapping of branches stopped me.

I turned around, holding in a scream. A monstrous Earth wolf stood not far away. Large thorns protruded from its green-and-brown fur, and its long, narrow teeth snarled at me as its red eyes ensnared mine. Its paws and sharp claws resembled dinosaur feet. Branches cracked with each slow step it took toward me. I hadn't learned about this creature in Professor Soveus's class, but I knew it was not friendly.

An Air Blast rocketed from my hands. The wolf momentarily shook its head, the distraction giving me a head start. I turned off my Lux and ran into the hedges, panting with each step I took—each step closer to my death. I turned left only to find myself at a dead end. My breath caught in my throat as I spun around and found the wolf blocking my path. It looked like it was smiling now, its thick, branch-like tail waving back and forth.

In a blink, it pounced, and I extended my hands in defense, a wave of energy moving from my elbows to my palms to my fingertips and then surging from my hands and slamming into the wolf, sending it backward. Branches cracked as it fell on its side, but it was immediately on its feet. It barked and hurtled my way, forcing me to the ground. I rolled left before its paw swiped my arm off. I tried to crawl away, but it pounced on my shoulders, the heavy pressure ripping a scream from my throat. Its nose was inches from my head, its hot breath on my neck as it hummed a satisfied purr.

Summoning all my strength, I lifted my forearms against the crushing weight and aimed my hands toward one of its hind legs. A gray-white burst of energy shot out like a harpoon, wrapping itself around its green foot. It was enough of a distraction that the wolf turned to inspect his foot, releasing some pressure on my shoulders. Holding on to my Air Rope, I yanked my arms to the left, screaming as agonizing pain shot from my shoulder to my wrist. The wolf slid on its side and smashed to the ground. I jumped to my feet and sprinted in the opposite direction.

It wasn't long before I heard it coming after me again. In the shadows ahead, a golden gate stood illuminated. Not sure if it was the gate I had entered through, I ran for it anyway, praying it was my deliverance. My eyes held on to the glimmering gold like a lifeline.

I grabbed the metal and squeezed through a small opening, slamming the gate shut as the wolf chomped on the metal bars. The gold bars were flimsy, and I was positive the wolf would tear the gate apart, but it backed away as if it couldn't trespass. Its fiery eyes glared at me one last time before it retreated into the shadows.

Panic crept up my throat, but I swallowed it. I took a moment to collect my breath and my bearings. I had to keep moving and find Alec—although something told me that wolf was only a warning.

I took in my new surroundings. A giant fountain surrounded by four large flowerbeds with red-and-yellow flowers sat in an open area. I approached the fountain, mesmerized by its calming waters, but I reminded myself serenity didn't exist in the Garden of Grandrose. If it did, the worst was about to come.

Glowing lotus flowers floated in the fountain, the water rippling as they gently moved about. In the water, a head of tousled brown hair and a strong square face with furrowed eyebrows appeared. The ripples stopped, and clear green eyes stared into mine. Startled, I looked up only to see I was still alone. I looked back at the clear water, but Alec's visage was gone.

A squeaking sounded, and right on cue, Alec came crashing in through the gate. He looked back as if he was being chased by something, but his facial muscles relaxed when he noticed that whatever had been behind him was gone. His hair was stuck to his sweaty forehead, and he held his right knee. It took a second before he noticed me.

His eyes widened, relief flooding his face. "Orion!" He straightened his back, wincing as he limped over to me.

When I met him halfway, he surprised me by enveloping me in his arms and pressing me against his torso as his body shook. "It wasn't real. I thought I'd lost you." His voice was muffled against my hair. "It wasn't real."

"Lost me?" I asked.

His voice quivered. "I ran into an Enoi. It was like walking through endless fog. My head was spinning . . . I couldn't stop coughing . . . I saw my parents, Banden . . . you."

The hallucination fog. An Enoi made magi trip up like they did when pronouncing its full name, Enoizaniculla—a deadly black fog cast by an enchanter that made magi go mad. Alec had a haunted look in his eyes as he tried to process what he had seen.

"I knew our love would be tested, but I didn't think our survival skills would," I said. "You make the monster Earth wolf that chased me seem like a puppy."

"Are you all right?" He released me, alertness returning to his eyes as if my pain had snapped him back to reality.

"All right enough. What about you?"

He nodded, but I could tell he was still shaken up. "Okay, now I know you're safe." He exhaled, then studied our surroundings. "If I hadn't been threatened by fog, I might call this place peaceful."

He walked over to the fountain. He was analyzing the lotus flowers gliding across the water when I joined him. He looked up, startled, like he hadn't expected me to follow. His gaze then caught something across the garden.

"Over there," he whispered, then led us to a flowerbed with red flowers. As we approached it, I saw what he had seen. Blending in with the red flowers were red roses. They looked like ordinary roses until I kneeled next to him, catching a faint glitter. Outlining each petal was a shimmering, silver lining, like gilding on book pages.

"The silver is what makes it an Amora?" I asked.

He nodded. "They're camouflaged. Clever."

"Why, thank you," a voice purred.

We jumped up to find a figure sitting at the base of the fountain. A young woman with green-tinted skin and a kind face studied us with captivating emerald-green eyes. Her long brown hair was woven with flowers and flowed past her hips. She wore a loose-fitting white dress and flowers as jewelry, except for the gold bow and arrow that hung from her neck on a gold chain. Alec grabbed my hand.

Her brown lips curved up. "Aren't you two adorable." She had a dreamlike glow about her, but her aura emitted a nightmare. She moved toward us with grace and poise.

"I see you found my special roses. Tempting, aren't they?" she purred, circling us, a sweet floral scent trailing behind her.

Alec cleared his throat and wrapped his arm tightly around my waist. "They are. I wanted to give one to my Orion. She loves roses." He smiled. I could tell he was nervous, but it wasn't noticeable.

"Oh, you know me so well," I said, burying my head into his chest. He squeezed me, and I could hear his furiously pounding heart—or was it my own?

The angelic woman stopped her circling and raised a perfectly shaped eyebrow. "Oh, please." Her tone shifted. "I've been watching you since you stepped into my garden. And . . ." Three blue birds came out of nowhere and fluttered above our heads. But they weren't normal birds. They had four eyes, two on each side, like an insect. One landed on her shoulder, and she petted it with her index finger. "I've had some help from my friends. Do you know who I am?"

Alec nodded. "Cecile—the nymph who owns this garden."

Cecile smiled. "Very good." Her lips fell. "But I know you have selfish reasons for wanting the Amora." Cracking sounds erupted, and the birds flapped away. "How awful to manipulate someone's emotions, to manipulate love."

The cracking grew louder. Thick, heavy vines, like octopus tentacles, appeared from every corner, encircling us. I pressed tighter against Alec as the black vines closed us in. *Two menacing plants in one night.* I could tell Alec wanted to fight them, but we were obviously outnumbered, and who knew what kind of power Cecile had.

"Your relationship is a lie." She wept like she'd forgotten we were here. She went to the roses, bent down, and plucked one. A new bud grew in its place as she studied the rose in her hand. "Honestly, what kind of monsters are you? Fooling around with emotions." She violently tossed the rose to the ground and stomped on it. "Love may conquer all, but it also destroys us."

I was pressed so tightly against Alec I could hear each breath. But if he was nervous, he didn't show it. He was staring Cecile down.

"We aren't manipulating anyone," he said, carefully watching the vines.

Her eyes narrowed. "Mmm, then why pay attention to my roses, handsome? One of you is lying, or maybe both. Have lovers at home, but they don't notice either of you? Unrequited love? Word of advice, lovies: quit that love."

"You're wrong," I said, surprised by my voice. "There's no one else. We're here for each other."

Cecile cackled, and the vines inched closer. Alec tightened his arms around me, pressing me into him, although we were already about as close as we could be.

"Honestly, my beauty, I was debating about leaving you two alone. You both put on a lovely show. But—" she lifted a long, slender finger. "You reached for the rose. There are two rules in my garden—one, I leave the lovers with the pure, true hearts alone; and two, no one ever goes near my roses."

The color drained from Alec's face. Zee had failed to tell us that piece. She'd sent us to our deaths.

"Now, my beauties. You two will make lovely decorations on my walls. Yes, such beautiful flowers."

My chest constricted as I thought about what had become of those unfortunate lovers and those who'd gone after her roses.

"Please, let her go." Alec loosened his grip on me. "I'm the one who touched the rose. She did nothing. Take me and let her go."

"Alec—" I panicked, but he shushed me. Still, I fought back. "I'm not leaving you."

"Orion." He gripped my shoulders. "I want to stay. You need to go."

I shoved his hands away. "This is the second time today you've traded your safety for mine. I never assigned you that job."

"So valiant." Cecile spoke, her voice seeming softer. "You're telling me, handsome, that you'd stay here with me if I let your girl go?"

"Yes." No hesitation.

She raised a sculpted eyebrow. "Why?"

"Because." His eyes searched my face. The look he gave me wasn't because he didn't know what to say, rather, it was as if he had so much to say he didn't know where to start. "Although she's a pain in my ass and knows how to push my buttons—"

"Gee, thanks," I managed.

He rolled his eyes. "My point exactly. Let me finish." There was a smirk in his voice. "She's the best person to have ever walked into my life, especially in a time where I needed it most. To have her trapped here would be unfair to the world. She deserves to be happy even though she wouldn't be with me. It'll crush me, but she will be free and hopefully find someone to take care of her more than I could here."

The wind was knocked out of me. Our faces were inches apart, his breath grazing my cheek. I was there at the infirmary again, watching him with his guitar and noticing how relieved he was to see me. I mentally replayed how he'd worried about my safety and would rather join me than let me endanger myself. Underneath his thick skin and veneer of sarcasm was a genuine, sensitive person whose heart was bigger than he let on. He was so much more than he pretended to be, even if he had trouble seeing it. He had been through so much but was still able to find good in others. *In me.*

This is all for show, I reminded myself but regretted thinking it, not sure if Cecile could read minds.

He continued. "Although I was furious with Banden for making me follow you around like a guard dog, I found myself drawn to you. Your bravery inspired me, your loyalty to your beliefs and loved ones is absolutely charming, and although you are one of the most stubborn people I've ever met, I couldn't get you out of my head. And when Banden tasked me with watching over you, I tried to suppress my growing affections for you. And failed. Miserably. Although my sarcasm clearly bothers you, you weren't afraid to fight back. That made me like you more, and I started enjoying our conversations, even if it didn't seem like it. I always thought I could do things alone, that I didn't need anyone else, but after meeting you, I didn't want to be alone anymore."

If this was an act, it was a *really* good act. Maybe he was thinking of someone he once loved. Whatever it meant, I felt ridiculous for my watery eyes, convinced it was from the pollen or this near-death experience. But I embraced it, hoping to give Cecile a good show.

"Alec, I care about you"—I was still struck by his words, overwhelmed by a mixture of affection and fear—"so much that I'm not leaving without you."

And I meant it. I refused to let him become one of Cecile's floral decorations.

He shook his head. "Don't worry about me. I'm used to being on my own. I don't want to drag you down with me, not with everything that's happened in my life."

"You're not dragging me down anywhere, and you don't get to decide who likes you. I like you, burdens and all."

"It wouldn't be fair to you. I can't . . . do this stuff. It scares me. You scare me. This is all new to me."

It felt like the emotions between us had changed. Why was he fighting them? Or was this all a part of the script? That was the danger of acting. You started to believe it. Or just because it was fake, did that mean it couldn't be real?

"Alec, it's new to me too."

He shook his head. "Please don't. It'd be selfish of me to start something. You deserve someone who will share his heart, not someone who can barely find his own."

"It's selfish of you to decide what I deserve!" I was closer to him now, inches from his face. I wanted to shake his shoulders, to scream how ridiculous he was being. "Are you making excuses because you're afraid to be vulnerable for once? To trust someone? How can you not believe someone could care for you? I see more than what everyone else sees, more than what you see."

I'd seen the way he was with Kaia, how much he loved his mother and Banden, and how scarred he was from his father's past. He was capable of love. He had plenty to share. He was afraid to show it.

"Air and Earth, complete opposites," I continued. "But I think we balance each other out."

"Or create weakness," he said, averting his gaze.

There was a groan from Cecile. "Well, what are you waiting for?" She broke the moment. I thought she was asking Alec to hand himself over. "Kiss her."

I froze and caught the side glance he gave me.

"You want to watch us kiss?" I spoke for us, making it sound like a weird request. Which it was.

"Near-death experiences bring loved ones closer together, and you can always tell how much people are in love by the way they kiss," she answered like it was obvious. I wasn't sure I agreed with that logic. "You want to prove it? Show me."

Alec stiffened. I wished I knew what he was thinking. *It's acting*, I tried convincing myself. How could he be hesitating? This was our lives. Unless he'd rather die than kiss me.

Before Cecile noticed our hesitation, I did the bravest thing I'd ever done to a boy. I grabbed Alec's face and pulled him to me, pressing my lips against his a little more aggressively than I intended to. His mouth remained shut, stunned by the contact, but it wasn't long before his lips parted and he was kissing me back.

He was gentle at first, slow, hesitant. He placed two fingers under my chin, bringing my face closer. Heat coursed throughout my body as he dropped his hands to my lower back, gently closing whatever gap remained between us. I wrapped my arms around his neck as his kiss grew harder, more longing. The pent-up pressure and tension, the feelings I'd been suppressing and doubting, poured through my fingers as they ran through his hair and my lips as they moved with his. He pressed me tighter against him, as if he wanted this moment to last forever. I didn't know how long we were like this, but finally his kisses slowed, and his face pulled away. Those green irises, so vibrant in the dark, left me in a trance. But it broke when I noticed what was, or wasn't, behind him.

"Alec," I whispered, finding my breath. "The vines. They're gone."

He blinked like he was waking from a dream. He looked past my shoulder. "And so is Cecile." His voice was dry, and he cleared his throat, removing his hands from my waist. He ran a hand through his hair before slowly turning around.

I reluctantly found myself staring at the flowers on the wall—all different colors, shapes, and sizes. They glistened and glowed, alive to represent death. We needed to get out of here.

"Orion." Alec pointed to a pathway that hadn't been there before.

I joined him. Someone had moved the walls to create a path bordered by tall trees, and in the distance stood Tirips.

"That's not the way we came in," I said, suspicious.

"Cecile can talk to animals," he said. "She must have created a shortcut for us and guided him there."

Cecile had been our only chance to save Mom. But what good would it do to get Alec and I killed too?

"Then let's get the hell out of here," I said.

We sprinted down the pathway, but I couldn't help my anxious thoughts. Maybe we hadn't fooled Cecile and were running toward an illusion, or portal, or the walls would close in on us. But when we successfully made it out, a weight lifted from my shoulders, and the tension in my chest dissipated. Once we were safely to Tirips, the hedges shook as they closed and the exit vanished. She'd let us go.

"Alec, we failed," I whispered, on the verge of tears. We'd failed Zee, which meant we'd failed the caller, which meant we'd failed Mom.

"Get on Tirips. We need to leave," he urged. I was about to snap at him for his lack of humanity when I saw the sharp look he gave me.

He didn't halt Tirips until we were in the woods where the maze was no longer in view. I waited for him to explain. He pulled out the tiny green remedy bottle Zee had given us and handed it to me.

I raised an eyebrow. "Okay?"

He rolled his eyes. "Give it a real look."

I looked at him before lifting the bottle to eye level. It wasn't empty. Inside, through the light from my Lux reflecting against the glass, floated specks of silver. *Pollen.*

"The rose Cecile dropped on the ground," he explained before I asked. "I went over to investigate it after . . ."—the kiss—". . . she left. I used the opening she created as a distraction so I could grab the pollen with a spell. I needed to distract you in case Cecile was sticking around so you wouldn't bring attention to it and she would be focusing on us admiring the exit. Using the ones still in the flowerbed would've been obvious."

"Alec, you're a genius!" I couldn't contain my excitement. It was the pollen of the rose that made the love elixirs.

"I know." He smirked. "You hold on to it. It's your quest."

I tucked it safely into my jeans pocket. When he looked over his shoulder at me, I thought about his lips and how I'd never been held so tightly against someone before. I wondered if he was thinking of it too. He ran his hand through his hair, turning away. But beyond our kiss was something much deeper. He had been willing to give his life for me.

"Thank you for helping me," I said. "I understand the risks you're taking."

"You're welcome. Although it's not like I gave you a choice anyway." He smirked before meeting my gaze, and I was lost in his eyes again. What had happened between us?

I couldn't ignore it. "Alec, about what happened back there—"

"It was all a show, I know," he interrupted, looking away like he couldn't believe I was talking about it. "I won't hold it against you. We good?"

The weight in my chest dropped to my stomach. I thought I had felt the emotion and truth in his words, or maybe he had been so afraid of dying he'd put his fake heart on the line. I had taken everything he'd said to heart and made nothing into something. *Or create weakness*, he had said. I was nothing but a distraction was what he'd meant. I was ashamed of my naivety. Spies lied for a living.

All I ended up getting was my father's ability to distrust, he had said to me.

"Right," I muttered, swallowing the lump in my throat. "We're good."

He gave a slight nod, his mouth a hard line, nothing but business in his eyes. I was the fool.

With my arms wrapped around his waist, bumping in the saddle, my thoughts swirled around the garden, and my heart hurt. I had kissed Alec for our survival, but I'd also wanted to. I didn't know how long I had wanted to, but I knew I did. I hated admitting my feelings for him, but I did now, over and over, as we made our way to Zee's.

Yet, if he wanted to give me a cold heart, I'd be sure mine was frozen.

CHAPTER 33

Zee's eyes stared hungrily at us as we entered her cave. "Were you successful?"

I pulled the green bottle from my pocket. "We weren't able to get the rose. Apparently, being in love isn't enough."

Her eyes narrowed. "So you failed."

"We got the pollen."

Zee flashed a wide, ugly smile, then stuck her hand out toward the bottle.

I pulled it toward my chest. "We had a deal."

"I don't break my promises," she said, grabbing a rolled-up piece of paper from the stone table behind her. "Decoded journal, as promised." She flicked her wrist, letting the paper unravel, but quickly rolled it back up with a slight motion of her hand.

"The symbols are translated," she continued sourly. "I can't decrypt the journal. As you know, I don't have my magic. Decoding it manually would take a lifetime."

Alec, tired and irritated by the trials we'd had to endure, was more than done with her nonsense. His eyes narrowed. "Then what are you suggesting?"

Thankfully, Zee wasn't bothered. "Normally, you'd need an enchanter to perform a translation spell, such as an Apokryptic

Charm. But, lucky for you, I have something better. Angel can translate it. Her breed can decipher any language."

He crossed his arms. "How do we know you'll decode it properly?"

"You don't." She smiled, amused. "Do we have a deal or not?"

I hesitated before handing her the pollen. We had no choice at this point. She took a whiff of its contents and smiled contentedly.

"Smells priceless," she murmured and stuck her hand out. "The journal, so I can translate it."

I was more hesitant to give it to her than the pollen, but she snatched it from my hands and pranced to the ledge where Angel had disappeared earlier. She then started speaking in a slithery, throaty language I couldn't understand but recognized. Draconese.

Within seconds, a deep, hollow roar vibrated the walls, followed by the sound of scales slithering against rock, and a monstrous blue head appeared over the ledge. Zee placed the paper and journal in front of the dragon. Its eyes rolled downward, irises glowing, and a gold light flashed over the paper.

Zee picked up the materials and handed them to me. "Pleasure doing business, children. You'll have to wait a few minutes for Red Steel to return. He's on a little errand for me."

I refused to read the journal while we stood in front of her, so we waited outside the cave door. It was dark, but we could see the pages in the light of the torches along the walls. I flipped through the sketches and words only to discover that there were still a few lines written in another language.

"She didn't translate everything!" I was about to storm back into her cave, but Alec stopped me.

"No, she did," he said, running his finger underneath them. "Those are more codes and puzzles. We'll have to sit with it and code everything page by page."

Sketches of parts of the scepter were drawn on different pages, with riddles and sentences that made us scratch our heads.

"Orion, Corinne has Annulla's Scepter." The way Alec's voice shook told me his heart was pounding alongside mine.

"Yes, but . . ." I said, reading the text and skipping to the last page, where the full scepter was depicted. However, the four gems and chain weren't drawn on the scepter, but rather on different pages throughout the journal. "I think we need to build it—not the scepter but find the pieces that make up the scepter, that make it powerful: the four gems and the chain. I think Corinne hid those pieces and this journal will lead us to them."

How had Corinne discovered this mythical scepter was real? She had sent us on one treasure hunt only to lead us to another. I could only theorize because even though some parts of the journal were written in plain English, other parts were coded, like Alec said.

"That doesn't make any sense," Alec said. "Why would she hide the parts if she has the scepter?"

I shrugged. "Maybe she wasn't the one who hid the gems and chain and someone else did, and she just found out where they were hidden. I don't know, but that's why we need to find her."

"Can I see it for a minute?" Alec said.

I handed him the journal. He skimmed through it before exhaling loudly, then slamming it shut, making me jump. I was as infuriated as he was. He turned to me, a look in his eyes I couldn't decipher. They looked pained, but I didn't know where that pain was coming from.

330

"I'm sorry." His voice was so low I thought I had imagined it.

Something slammed into my back, and I whirled around to see a black cloak. A hand collided with my cheek, followed by the smell of lavender and mint. Alec's hard face and shiny eyes were the last thing I saw before the darkness swallowed me.

CHAPTER 34

There was blackness and throbbing pain. My cheek rested on a hard, cool surface. As I slowly blinked back to consciousness, my vision adjusted to see a stone room bathed in dim light.

I lay on the wooden floor, quietly taking in my surroundings. I was in a dome with stone walls and a wide, circular ceiling constructed of millions of glass shards. Beside me was a towering brass telescope, larger than a dinosaur, pointing toward two closed wooden doors set in the glass ceiling. I had seen this from a distance. I knew where I was.

Arayis's observatory.

My bag. The flap was open, and my books were scattered across the floor, except for the most important one. A couple of feet away from me, a tall figure leaned over a table, his back to me. I heard the sound of pages turning.

"Wake up, dear Orion," the man said distractedly. I had déjà vu to waking up in Banden's Elixir Chamber. And although his voice was familiar, this was not Banden.

I slowly rose to my feet, ignoring the stinging in my cheek and the pounding in my head. Fueled by fear and hatred, a surge of energy pulsed from my wrists to my fingertips, and I shot a white

Air Bullet toward my predator. But he simply turned around and waved a hand to deflect it, sending the spell back toward my face. The bullet forced me to the ground, exacerbating the pain across my cheek. Blood dripped onto my sweater, and I wiped at my cheek, smearing red across my hand. My eyes widened at the man who smiled maliciously at me, his blond hair messy.

"Professor Wicbin?" I half-whispered.

"Oh, Orion." He feigned sympathy. "Did you really think a student could overpower her teacher? I taught you what you know." He turned back to the book in his hands, licking his finger as he flipped a page. The journal. He kept his head down. "I knew you were a liar. Corinne might've been a problem-maker, but you're a problem-solver."

"That's why you wanted to help me decode it," I said, but I didn't understand the correlation between the journal and him. A stranger, stranger than Corinne was to me.

He gently placed it on the table beside him. "I think the observatory is kind of nice, don't you? Private, in a tower, insulated." He smiled a twisted smile. "Lovely Corinne. She had many friends. Oh, yes, but quick to make enemies. She never supported me and my goals. What a terrible friend she was."

"You knew her?"

"Knew her? Why, we were the best of friends, Cori and me. Some might say I didn't hang with the best crowd, but I was the best—the best fun Cori ever had."

The way he said her name, like a predator claiming its prey, sent a shiver down my spine. But his comment rang bells, bringing my mind back to the letter in the secret room. I had read the note so many times I had it memorized: *It upset me that Ozzy and Zee never understood why I decided to stop goofing off and focus on my studies.*

Osmus Wicbin.

"Ozzy," I said aloud.

His grin made my skin crawl. "We were the best of friends. Some might even say our connection ran deeper. But that changed when your beloved guardian came along, helped her out of the rut she was 'supposedly' in. Would've failed out of the academy if it weren't for *him*," he growled. He picked up the journal, flipping through the pages again. According to the note, he had been furious when Corinne became serious about her education.

"Banden watches you like a hawk," he continued as he read the journal. "And if he's not around, then Mr. Stone is with you. Pshaw, and Banden was worried about Cori hanging with the wrong crowd. Speaking of whom, how could I be so rude? Gloating without crediting my partner."

Slow steps thudded against the wood, and I spun toward the staircase leading to the top of the telescope. A figure emerged from the shadows. And then I remembered. Before the world had gone black, I'd fallen with it. And Alec had watched me.

Alec rested his arms against the black railing, his eyes directly on Wicbin. It didn't take a fool to see he was doing everything in his power to avoid my gaze. It was better for him that he wasn't down here. Had I been an experienced Aermage, I would have electrocuted him to ashes.

This world is a game of deception. Be sure you're playing. Everyone was playing, even the ones I trusted most. I'd questioned everyone yet trusted the one person I shouldn't have.

Wicbin pulled my attention away from my betrayer. "I thought I had finally finished you off with that house fire, finally rid of the Candors and their secrets, only to discover you'd escaped to Crystal Manor. And when that useless Air girl failed to kill you in the duel, well, the Obsidian King decided he wanted you alive after all."

The pieces fell into place. "You were behind all of that?" My voice faltered, trying to make sense of everything, until anger shook my bones. "*Valerie?* You possessed her!" He nodded, a malicious grin on his face. But a spell like that was impossible to do, unless— "You're a Bimedeis."

He smirked. "Clever."

"But you were at the duel. How did you do it?"

"Like I have to tell you anything."

"The fire, the figure at the gates, the Chicaneries . . ."

"You're too kind, giving me all the credit." His eyes darted to Alec, his wicked grin widening.

Alec rolled his eyes, but if I wasn't mistaken, his voice wavered. "We don't need to gloat."

"Why? You should be proud of your accomplishments. Orion, if it weren't for Alec, I wouldn't be where I am now. You thought he was protecting you when he was sucking information out of you. The Chicaneries were him, my dear." When he saw my face, he laughed. "Oh, that's not all. Let's not forget your run-in with the Chosen Shadow in Lightloch, or the king himself, in the library."

"That's enough, Osmus," Alec snapped, but Wicbin was unfazed. His smile only widened.

I have eyes everywhere, Obsidian's fog had warned. *Without trust, there is no love. And I loved by trusting the most mistrusted.* Corinne's words stung. I had been trying to avoid getting trapped like her, to be on my guard, to move with caution.

Be a swan. Know who's a swan.

I had failed. Everyone was a swan. Everyone had a motive. Everyone was in it for themselves. And I wasn't the swan but the fish. The bait.

"And, of course, let's not forget the grand finale." Wicbin continued to rejoice, using my misery as fuel. "Zee has loyalty to no one. You prepared your own trap by inviting Alec to your escapade. His plan worked. He's so much brighter than we all thought."

"You mean darker," I spat, glaring at those green eyes that had once got me undone, now only to ignite detestation. "Deception is your expertise. How could you do this? To Isoria? To *Banden*?"

To me.

"Oh, you thought he cared for you." Wicbin feigned sympathy by pouting. "Deceit has no bounds."

As usual, it was impossible to read Alec's face, but his eyes briefly softened at Banden's name before his eyebrows furrowed, the sharpness returning. I couldn't tell if he was brainwashed or forcing himself not to feel. Or maybe I was again giving him the benefit of the doubt, what he didn't deserve.

"Where's my mother?" I asked, afraid of the answer.

"In hiding," Alec said emotionlessly.

"Hush, Alec," Wicbin interrupted, dark eyes shooting his way. "The Maker is our business."

This time, Alec gave him a hard glare.

My eyes widened, the blood pumping through my veins more intensely than it already was. "What did you call her?"

"Nothing," Alec insisted, but he knew I understood.

Mom's mysterious clients—her disappearing for hours, days, and even weeks, for them. Her hiding in her workshop and keeping the specifics about her projects confidential. Dumping me in Crystal Manor without disclosing the details of the job. *It's possible the Maker also works for the Isorian shadow market,* Julian had said. I racked my brain. Even if she was this secret inventor in Isoria, what if it wasn't the worst I was thinking? My world was crumbling under Obsidian's cruel crown, and I was drowning in his deceit, but I still hoped, still prayed, there was an explanation.

"What did you do to her?" I turned on them, fists clenched. "Did Obsidian force her to build the shield?"

"Enough!" Wicbin's voice sliced through the room. "The king is waiting." He took a calculated step toward me. "I know what Cori is hiding. Now, tell me where she hid Annulla's Scepter, or I'll bring you to the king himself."

We were right. About all of it. Before he caught my hesitation, I questioned him. "What are you talking about?"

His eyes were coal black. "I don't have time for games. Tell me where she hid it."

"I know as much as you do," I said truthfully, hoping to stall him as I tried planning an escape. But I was confused. Had Alec not told him that Corinne was alive and she had the scepter? That the answer was finding *her*?

"Orion, I don't want to hurt you." He stalked toward me, hunched over like it was a full moon and he was ready to transform into a beast. He reached inside his black robe and presented a luminous blue blade.

"But why?" I asked, my heart pounding furiously at the sight of the blade. "Why are you fighting on Obsidian's side?"

That's the part I couldn't figure out. Obsidian wanted this scepter that could erase any permanent spell. What did that have to do with his "followers" and his so-called movement?

Wicbin licked his lips, venom in his eyes. "For far too long, magi have been hiding from nonmagi, living by Isoria's ancient laws that outline consequences for magi when using magic to the nonmagus eye. Not only that, but there are consequences to using magic in general, certain spells we are forbidden to practice. We should be living *with* nonmagi, not living in fear of being discovered by them. We were given this magic for a reason. We shouldn't be policed. King Leo shouldn't have the power to determine when to take our magic away. Obsidian has promised us freedom, to walk the world with our magic freely, and to break our chains to Isoria's law. The system must be destroyed to free the magi. We must poison the poison."

MISTIC's theory was correct. He thought magi were oppressed by the Isorian government. And there were plenty of others who shared this ideology, or who were forced to believe it.

I shook my head. "There's a reason the world works the way it does. We're all given free will, but we need order to prevent destruction and chaos. Magi, even nonmagi, hold too much power without law. You'll disrupt the balance."

"You mean restore it." He shook his blade. "Don't you see? Nonmagi can't exploit us because they'll see *we* have the power. They'll hide from us, and we will no longer be afraid of them. Ancient laws and nonmagi will no longer tell magi how to live."

No matter what I said, he wouldn't listen. I couldn't help but wonder if Alec believed this absurd ideology, too. Maybe he would join anything that was against King Leo.

I swallowed. "This scepter you keep referring to, what does it have to do with Obsidian's goal?"

He took a step toward me. "Destroying it will protect his power to carry on with the movement's cause."

Protect his power.

Till he destroys what will destroy him but save us all.

I was right. The scepter would undo Obsidian's magnified power and save Isoria from his reign of terror.

Wicbin smirked. "Maybe, you'll join."

"Never."

He was to me before I could run. My body slammed against the pebbled wall as he pressed his weight against me, the blade inches from my neck.

"I'm tired of your family's games," he hissed so close to my face I could see the individual beads of sweat on his forehead. "Where is the scepter?"

"Please," I panicked. "I don't know what you're talking about."

It was strange to have once thought of him as my favorite professor. His once-genuine eyes were now emotionless, his teeth bared like a wolf's, as his free hand latched on to my wrist.

"It's a simple request," he said, then screamed in my face, "tell me where it is!"

In my peripheral vision, I could see Alec slowly descending the steps. I hoped against hope that this was a trap for Wicbin, that Alec was on my side and would jump the professor. But he left me there, threatened by death.

"Okay, I'll tell you," I said, and his grip loosened for a second, but the blade remained steady. "It's—" And when I had him slightly distracted, I hiked my knee straight toward his groin. The knife fell to his side as his other hand released me, and I slipped past him and sprinted for the door on the opposite side of the telescope. But the doorknob wouldn't budge. Wicbin laughed behind me.

"I told you I hate games," he growled. A white-yellow energy pulsed around his outstretched hands, and a burst of light zigzagged toward me. I fell to the floor, the flash exploding into crystal particles against the door.

He laughed. "Oh, silly me. Watch for the sparks." Another bolt charged toward me. I rolled out of the way, more crystals shattering across the floor.

For the first time in my life, I wished my powers would go crazy so they could hurt him like they did Valerie. No, more than hurt. I was afraid to stand, afraid one move would result in my death. But staying on the floor was also a death sentence.

I jumped to my feet and fired Bullets after him, one after the other, like a gun. He deflected each one, sending them ricocheting all over the observatory. Another bolt of electricity shot toward me, and I summoned a Shield, but the bolt broke through it and slammed me against the door. Wheezing from the impact of the doorknob against my lower back, I tried to stand, but a Blast knocked me to the floor. Wicbin sent another and another, tossing me around like I was nothing more than a raggedy T-shirt as my bones banged against the floorboards.

"And here I thought this would be a fair fight." He laughed. "Where are your special powers now?"

I tried to find the energy inside me, but nothing came. I was useless. This was it. This was how I would die—at the hand of someone I thought I could trust. Like Corinne, I had trusted the most mistrusted. It was one cut after another. One betrayal after another.

Wicbin, Alec, and now, possibly my mother. I wouldn't be surprised if Banden or my friends came through the door and teamed up to watch me die. If I knew where the scepter was, I might have told him. What was the point of fighting anymore? The lying and sneaking around had only brought me to my defeat. *I failed.*

"Goodbye, Orion," he said as an electrostatic light pulsed in his hands. "You were one of my favorite students."

But as I watched the sparks bounce and sizzle in Wicbin's hands, a voice deep within me found its way out the darkness, begging for me to listen. I didn't want to, but it pushed through.

Don't let them define you. You define them.

My powers were erratic and had caused me despair, but they had also saved me and my friends multiple times. Even everyone around me, although fearful, marveled at them. When I was in control, I felt whole, like my powers were part of me, not against me. They didn't want to hurt me. They wanted to work with me. It was about how I managed them and what relationship I chose to have with them.

I could feel them pulsing in my veins, their energy charged and ready, unthreatened by Wicbin's power. Now, I chose to befriend them, to accept them, to accept that I would learn to be comfortable with the unknown. To know was to experience the unknown.

Wicbin hadn't defeated me. I would fight until the end. It was beautiful and dangerous to have power.

Surprisingly, I found myself grinning. "Too bad. You were my favorite teacher."

I inhaled this new acceptance, the energy in my arms and hands singing the tune I was singing. Wavelengths of that energy escaped my hands, and my hair blew wildly in the resulting wind. The spinning windstorm, like that night in the library, now had a target. As it circled the room, most of its energy was expelled toward my predator. Although raw and powerful and not completely within my grasp, my powers were controlled. Controlled chaos. My books circled the room like a carousel, and I saw Alec grip the table Wicbin had originally used to read the journal to stabilize himself against the pounding wind.

Wicbin thrust his hands up, deflecting the gray-blue winds with his own. Wind battled wind. The opposing spells collided, pushing and pulling back and forth. But mine had the edge, inching closer and closer to Wicbin. Veins on his forehead bulged as he screamed and sweat trickled down his face as my power threatened to overtake his. His arms wobbled, and he suddenly let go, flying backward and slamming against the telescope. He slowly rose to his feet, hunched over, a lethal scowl on his face.

Usually, I would have been drained by the exhausting spell. I didn't know if it was adrenaline or a newfound confidence in my abilities, but I was ready and recharged.

There was a loud bang, and a red-and-yellow blaze of light whizzed through the air, flames in the shape of an arrow nailing Wicbin in the thigh. He cried out as the fire melted his clothes, followed by the smell of burning flesh. He bent down as blood trickled down his leg and smoke rose from the wound. I spun around to the doorway.

"That was a warning," Julian growled, waving another Fire Arrow in his fist. He then winked at me. "How you doing, initiate?"

Rae's hands, gloved in ice, were raised as if she were ready for a boxing match. She was in black clothes like Julian, her hair in a high ponytail, her piercings flashing. "Touch her again and it's going through your heart."

342

Wicbin blew the Fire Arrow out with wind. "Fire Arrow. Adorable," he snarled and looked over his shoulder at Alec. "Looks like we'll have three deaths on our hands tonight."

Wicbin threw a bolt toward us. Rae's quick reflexes pushed us out of the way as Julian ducked.

"You talk too much. Maybe that's why your aim sucks!" Julian sneered, sending another arrow toward Wicbin. It pierced his palm, accompanied by the sound of cracking bones. He cried out even louder.

As Wicbin struggled to remove the arrow, I quickly turned to my friends. "How did you guys find me?"

"Uh, your Clavis has a tracking device in it, something Banden secretly implemented when you first got the necklace," Rae answered sheepishly with her eyes trained on Wicbin. "He doesn't stalk you everywhere you go, but he assumed something was wrong when he noticed you weren't home."

"Alec, let's finish them!" Wicbin roared.

Rae and Julian passed confused glances, then looked from Alec to me. Alec stood near the table with his fists clenched at his side, glaring at Julian like he was the Pawn. The look on my face was all they needed to understand what was going on. Alec had betrayed us. Julian had been right about him from the beginning.

But Alec didn't move, loitering near the table, until I realized what he was doing, Corinne's journal placed conveniently at his feet. Julian threw another Fire Arrow only to have Wicbin deflect it and send a yellow current toward Julian's leg, knocking him to the ground. Rae shot a volley of Ice Bullets from her gloved hands, forcing Wicbin to cast a Shield.

A battle of fire, ice, and lightning exploded in the air as I crawled away from the show. Alec was already running for the staircase, the journal tucked underneath his armpit.

Rae and Julian were taking a beating. Although Wicbin stood alone, he was clearly more skilled. My friends were tossed and thrown to the floor like they were simply diversions. But that's what I needed. Julian caught sight of Alec with the journal and gave me a knowing look. They would hold Wicbin off as long as they could.

Alec didn't see it coming when I threw a gust of wind at his back. He collapsed, the journal sliding down the stairs. His wild eyes caught mine as we both grabbed it in a tug-of-war. But he was stronger and yanked it from my sweaty grasp, then bolted up the stairs. On his heel, I sent Air Blasts at him, but he ducked, then cast a Dust Shield over his back like a turtle shell, my spells deflecting toward me.

But Alec had trapped himself. The staircase ended at the top of the telescope lens where spinning gadgets, contraptions, and brass beams suspended by chains dangled from the domed ceiling. He stopped at the top platform, facing me with the journal clutched in his arms.

"Orion, come to join the party?" He smirked, calm for someone who knew he was out of options. Pounding reverberated, and flashes of light from the fight below illuminated the darkness. A yellow flash of lightning shot in our direction, and we ducked as it almost nicked our heads.

"I can't believe it," I said. There was so much to say, so much hurt and anger and betrayal. I swallowed so I could fight back with a frozen heart like his. "What I don't understand is why."

"You heard Osmus."

Osmus.

I shook my head. "I heard his story, not yours."

"There's nothing to tell. The Obsidian King is rising to power. You know what side I'm on. I hope you do." Although his tone was flat, I thought I heard a sadness or tiredness in it, or maybe I was still hoping he was one of us. The explosions below also made it difficult to hear him.

If trust is what you seek, I'd be more careful who you give it to. He had been warning me this entire time. And I was so stupid for ignoring the signs, believing he was this wounded animal who needed healing. He was what he'd tried convincing me he wasn't—a monster. All the ambiguities finally made sense—why the Chicaneries were in the nonmagus lands, how Obsidian knew I was in the library, how the caller knew where we were, why Alec had kept the journal from Banden. He'd even showed up after my IEPE test when I had been attacked by the Incendor. I'd once felt guilty for the mark on his cheek, for him taking the beating for my actions. It was all a game—him not wanting to be like his father, of wanting to be better, of pretending he cared for me, for everyone. I didn't want to cry or scream. I wanted to make him bleed, to hurt him like he'd hurt me. I wanted him to feel pain.

"Oh, I do." My throat was dry. "Like father, like son. Julian was right. King Leo was right. You're a monster."

His body stiffened, and his eyes widened only to narrow again. "I told you not to trust anyone."

He then turned around and jumped for the small ladder attached to one of the wooden platforms hanging from the ceiling. Surprised by his sudden escape, I raced after him but paused before the landing. It was a long way down. The colossal lens below was delicate enough to break.

But I couldn't overthink it. I took a few steps back and screamed as I jumped for the ladder, grabbing the last rung as the platform swung back and forth, the chains that held it clinking loudly. Sweat loosened my grip as I dangled from the rung, trying to kick up my legs to climb. At the top, Alec looked down behind him.

"Shit, Orion, give it up!" he hollered.

I wasn't strong enough and was slipping. But there was a way. A way Wicbin had taught his students when using Air Ropes. My first class at Arayis. *Leverage and strength.*

I released one hand and felt energy hum through my blood. An Air Rope extended from my hand and snaked around the metal bar while still twined around my palm. I did the same with the other hand and heaved myself up each rung, one by one, my Air Ropes supporting me as I did so. When my feet finally reached the rung, I climbed upward and made it to the top of the rickety platform. Alec was trapped on the other side.

I panted. "Give me the journal, Alec."

He smirked. "Your persistence was always charming."

I sent an unexpected Blast toward him, knocking the journal out of his hands and sending it spinning through the air like a baton. We both ran for it, but it flew off the platform and landed on the telescope lens below. We shared a look, both having the same idea, but Alec got to it first. He zipped down the ladder with me right behind him.

But I missed a step, slipping from the bar and toppling over him as we both crashed onto the lens, which was stronger than I expected. We shoved and grabbed and pulled, our bodies tumbling over each other as we fought for the journal. He managed to break free from my grasp, but I sent another Air Blast at the journal, pushing it farther and farther away from him. My plan was working until the journal slid to the edge of the lens. As Alec was about to grab it, I rammed into him like a bull, knocking the wind out of him but also knocking myself off-balance. My fingers desperately clawed at the rim of the telescope, but it was too late.

I thought I heard shouting. Alec's face grew smaller as the ground came at me, everything around me blurring. I wouldn't call it peace I was feeling but an acceptance that I was falling and relief that my friends would continue this journey. At least I had died trying.

Moonlight illuminated the observatory, and I thought I had reached the end without remembering hitting the floor. But there was a sharp tug on my torso. The world around me spun as my brain tried to grasp the reality that I was still alive. A vine had wrapped itself around my torso, and I dangled from a winged horse like a pendant on a chain.

Once I was steady, my eyes widened. *Tirips. With wings.* And Banden astride him, a vine extended from his outstretched hand. Tirips hovered a few feet off the floor, leaving me space to land safely. My head spun from being tossed and turned in the air and from the fact that I was still breathing. The vine uncurled from around my torso, and Banden set Tirips down in front of me, blocking my view of Wicbin. Rae and Julian had stopped fighting, along with Wicbin. Tirips's black eagle wings flapped as Banden hopped off and immediately sent shards of crystal toward Wicbin, piercing his clothes and skin like razor blades.

"When were you guys going to tell me my horse has wings?" I asked, looking at my horse, which was actually not a horse but a pegasus.

"You didn't give me the chance to tell you in the pasture, did you?" Banden whipped his head around, breathless. "Air pegasi have transparent wings. They appear when the animal wants or needs to fly. Please excuse me."

He threw a Dust Blast, slamming Wicbin against the telescope, and was immediately at Wicbin at the speed of light, dust trailing behind him like he had teleported. He pressed Wicbin against the telescope.

Wicbin cackled. "Oh, Banden, old friend. We meet again. How's Cori? Oh, wait. Dead."

Banden grabbed Wicbin's throat and rammed his fist into his torso. "Don't you dare speak of her to me!"

The rage and strain in his eyes, his bared teeth. Banden thought Corinne was dead. She had lied to him. I wished I could tell him to ease his pain, but not in front of Wicbin.

Wicbin choked, but he still had that evil grin he'd been born with.

"You won't win." Wicbin wheezed, shaking. "Whatever that bitch was hiding, it won't be kept secret for long. If you don't join him, the Obsidian King will destroy all of you. I was there when Corinne died. And I can't wait for you to join her."

A yellow light formed around his hand, sending an electric spark to Banden's side, and Banden jumped back like Wicbin was radioactive. Without warning, a bolt of lightning arched above him and landed in his other hand, creating an arch, then a ring, then a web. The deathly web of electricity zapped toward Banden. It was so quick I couldn't process what was happening.

A scream escaped my lips, but one more piercing, deep, and desperate canceled mine out. The electric web disappeared nearly inches from Banden's face as a boulder bedazzled with sharp crystals exploded before Wicbin, rock particles and crystals raining through the air. In the corner lay a blackened figure, electricity sizzling around the burnt and bloody body. Wicbin lay lifeless, sparks winking out around him as the lightning died.

Suddenly, a bright light near the telescope lit the dark room. Alec stood in front of the yellow vortex, journal in hand. He gave Banden one last look before turning his back on us.

He couldn't escape. Not with the journal.

Without a second thought, I ran for him. Alec seemed confused until he processed what I was doing. I could hear my friends and Banden shouting after me. Alec had vanished inside the portal, with me right at his heel.

CHAPTER 35

It was like traveling through any other portal—only one step over—but instead of landing on my feet, the portal was suspended in the air, and my face and body crashed onto a hard, wet surface.

Ocean waves sounded, and strong winds blew all around me. I finally got to my feet and saw that I was completely surrounded by the ocean. I stood on jet-black rock that formed a small path around a massive mountain made of the same black rock, a wall guarding something on the other side. In the distance was a long, thin rock formation that crossed the water, like a bridge to another landmass. And across that bridge was a curtain of black smoke. That's when I realized. That other landmass was Azzurri Falls. And that black pass was Shadow's Pass. I was at Fort Obsidian or, at least, on the outskirts of it.

"Orion?" a familiar voice said.

I turned around, and my knees buckled. Alec was there, as I expected, because I had followed him to this awful place, but the person beside him who had called my name was the person I was afraid I would never see again.

"Mom?" I said, almost afraid to say it, afraid that this was like that night at Pier Fest, another trick, a Chicanery, a deceit. There she was, no cloak or anything. Just Mom in her usual fashion: jeans, a comfortable top, and work boots. Her hair had gotten a little longer since that day we parted at the airport, reaching just past her shoulders. But even though she looked just like when I had left her, she was different. She'd always had a sharp face, like she was in a perpetual state of focus and concentration, thinking about the latest problem she could solve. But the sharpness she wore now seemed different, like for once, she had a problem she didn't know how to solve.

"Orion!" she said again, breaking me from my thoughts, and before I knew it, I was running toward her, forgetting why I had come or even the fact that I was on the realm's most dangerous territory. None of it mattered because Mom was here. I met her embrace, which was warm and real. Tears welled in my eyes, and all the frustration she had caused me in the past few months melted.

"What are you doing here?" she asked, pulling me away from her, her eyes shiny. She was only an inch taller than I was. She then turned to Alec. "This wasn't part of the plan."

Alec, who I had briefly forgotten was here, rolled his eyes. "Of course it wasn't. She followed me through your portal. But I kept my word, didn't I? She's safe and sound. Although, she knows."

"I know you're The Maker, Mom," I said before she could ask, a million questions now bubbling inside me as the shock of her presence slowly wore off. "No more secrets. I need answers."

She sighed, her hands on my shoulders as she looked out into the ocean before her gaze returned to me. Her hair blew into her face, hiding her sad, hazel eyes. "Alec, can you please give me a moment with my daughter?" she said, her voice soft against the crashing waves.

Alec gave her a sharp look but wordlessly turned away.

"Wait, he can't leave," I said, watching the journal in his hand.

"It's okay, he can't enter the fort without a portal," Mom assured me. "Only I can bring us over."

Right, enchanters created and activated portals.

He stayed within view, leaning against the rock while skimming Corinne's journal. My fists clenched. How dare he read my grandmother's journal? Finding trust or hoping someone was good after they'd cut you deeply was like drowning in an endless sea of doubt, trying to reach the surface, to breathe in hope but your lungs kept giving out. Trust had been broken, and hope was unreachable. But vengeance wasn't. Cutting him back was the only way to bleed out the pain. But I took a deep breath. I'd deal with him after Mom.

"We don't have a lot of time. Obsidian will be suspicious if we're gone too long," she said, urgency in her eyes. "I do have a tech business in the nonmagus lands, but it's a guise for the actual work I do in Isoria. I hope you won't hate me after what I'm about to tell you." She sighed before continuing. "I'm hired to enhance or improve magical items, from weapons for individual use to shields to other miscellaneous items. I choose projects that intrigue me and challenge my abilities. 'The Maker' keeps my identity anonymous. I know my clients, but they don't know me. If I ever personally meet with a client, I wear a disguise to keep my identity hidden. I don't control where my creations go or where they end up."

That means they can be traded in the shadow market.

"I understood the risks with my job, but it wasn't until my most recent project that I realized how dangerous it could be. I didn't know what I was getting myself into before it was too late. I got a referral from this mysterious contact to build an ambitious shield that could protect an entire village. I assumed this contact worked for King Leo and was looking for a way to protect his palace since he wanted to keep it secret, given the rumors that someone named Obsidian was planning a revolt against the king. I'd never worked on such a task, and you know me: the bigger the challenge, the greater my determination. For months, I was lost to the project, obsessed with making it work. And I did it."

Her brain was both miraculous and dangerous. Her pride always got the best of her. She had to be the best at everything, and she was a staunch believer that there was a solution to every problem.

"When it was time to implement the shield, I thought my client was going to take me to King Leo, but I was portaled here on the night of the Siege of Westwin. I tried to take back my creation, but I had no choice. Obsidian would have taken the materials to make the shield with or without me. The caveat is the shield needs upkeep every six months by a team of enchanters and sorcerers. I traveled to Isoria from New Jersey to lead and direct the team. But I couldn't take it anymore, knowing I had invented the very thing that has protected Obsidian all this time.

"Corinne's death, although tragic, came at the perfect time. I had Banden take care of you and lie to you about where I was as I offered my undivided attention and services to Obsidian while living here permanently. I also hoped I would learn more about the scepter from him and thought I could finish what Corinne started, but that plan failed, especially when I learned that you were involved. I had discovered the secret room in her library while I was in the process of acquiring the house, which only added to my burden. I knew she had been involved in MISTIC and believed in the powers of Annulla's Scepter. I knew I couldn't keep this world hidden from you forever because of my mistakes, so I distanced myself. I scheduled emails in advance to pretend I was busy with my job. At first, my identity was secret, so Obsidian didn't know we were related, but that was ruined because of him." She gestured to Alec, who still had his nose stuck in Corinne's journal. "So I told Obsidian I broke all ties with you and hadn't communicated with you since I left you at Crystal Manor. I used Alec to stay updated on you as he revealed intelligence to Obsidian."

My heart pounded. *How much has Alec revealed to Obsidian?*

Mom sighed. "Our phone call was so risky, but I had to talk to you. It was one of my greatest inventions. I discovered how to eliminate the magical barrier that bans technology in Isoria. That day you broke your phone, I programmed a Zapstone inside your phone and my phone. It's a rare and insanely illegal crystal where its powder, when inhaled or swallowed, will spark and electrocute someone from the inside, but I discovered it has properties that cancel out the technological magic barrier King Leo has placed on Isoria. It disintegrates after two uses, but I did what I had to do."

"Why didn't you send me a Reflection Message?" I asked.

"Obsidian forbids me from communicating with anyone outside the fort's walls." She held up her wrist where a silver bracelet with molds of two scorpion tails held on to a black gem. "He monitors if I use any type of magical communication. The crystal in our phones cancels out the king's magical barrier while the phone makes a regular call. Wicbin witnessed the phone call. He was always sucking up to Obsidian, so to prevent him from telling Obsidian my secret, I helped him devise a plan that made it look like he'd invented the technology to call you to coerce you to bring Corinne's journal to him. You can't make anonymous calls through Reflection Messaging, so that's why we used the phone. But Alec wanted the credit. He'd been the one waiting for you to find as much information about the journal as you could so he could present it to Obsidian. To eliminate both our problems, we planned to . . . rid of Wicbin together, here, in private, but you appeared instead."

My chest tightened. My mom, capable of murder? Although she had been fighting to survive, so had I. Wicbin would have killed all of us if it weren't for Alec.

She paused, the sadness in her eyes ever growing. "When the time comes, when MISTIC or King Leo decides to wage war, I'll be ready to destroy the shield to leave Obsidian defenseless. You see, Orion, I wasn't protecting you from Isoria. I was protecting you from me. I swear I'm going to make it right. I was wrong for keeping this world from you."

My mind spun. I was furious with her for keeping all this secret from me, but at the same time, I understood why she did it. She felt trapped, knew her mistake, and was trying to get herself out of it. I'd learned that people were definitely not always who they seemed, but you couldn't give up on the ones you loved, and in the end, everyone had a reason for the choices they made. You just had to understand them. I still had so many questions, so many things I wanted to ask her about the shield, the secret room, Annulla's Scepter. But Alec interrupted us.

"Are we done sharing feelings?" he said, approaching us, journal in hand. "We have five minutes to get to the castle before he sends guards after us."

I broke away from Mom. "Alec, you can't give the journal to Obsidian. I can't believe. . . Are you really on his side?"

He scoffed, stepping away. "I'm not the nice guy, Orion, so stop acting like I'm this beaten puppy who needs to be saved."

I took a step toward him. "I'm not trying to save you, Alec, I'm trying to understand you."

I didn't know if it was my imagination, but his eyes seemed to soften for a moment. But his voice was hard as he revealed, "I'm on no one's side, Orion. This is personal, and I'm where I need to be."

Personal? His confession gave me hope, that he wasn't lost to the cause.

"So if you're not against us, we can still work together."

He shook his head. "I have what Obsidian wants, so you can walk away right now, unharmed, and forget your grandmother—forget her secrets. How do you think you've gotten this far? You would've been dead by now if it wasn't for me. I'm the one who convinced Obsidian that instead of killing you, he should use you to solve Corinne's riddles, that if there was anyone who could learn her secrets, it was her granddaughter. I did what I had to do to manipulate you into getting Obsidian what he wanted, what *I* wanted. You're impulsive, outspoken, and you think you're sly, but you wear your emotions in your eyes. It's easy to predict your every move."

That's what you do, Orion. You learn what motivates people, what their vulnerabilities are. You then use that information to manipulate people to get what you want. He had pretended to protect me for Banden's sake when he actually had been trying to stay close to me so he could learn Corinne's secrets. That's why I had been able to so easily convince him not to tell Banden about the journal.

I restrained the anger stirring inside me. I had to convince him to give me the journal.

"You're right," I said. "But you still saved me, and you saved Banden, which makes me think you care, even if just a little. Whatever you're after, we can work together and not have to destroy Isoria in the making. Let me help you."

He rolled his eyes, shaking his head. "You're so naïve, Orion. What about this place is so worth saving? What has it given you but problems and secrets and people who want you dead?"

He was right. But it was true that your darkest hours showed who your true friends were, and I was blessed with the ones I had. When I'd moved to Crystal Manor, I didn't feel at home, and I'd felt just as lost in Isoria. But I had been wrong. It wasn't a *place* I needed to find but people who accepted me for who I was, and most importantly, for me to accept who I was. Home was within and where my friends and family were. I was the one who had hidden from others because I was hiding from myself. I was my own villain. "Yes. My life has been nothing but chaos since discovering where I came from and who I am. But it gave me a home, a place I belong, people I love."

"I'm so moved you found a place of healing," he mocked, his eyes narrowed, "but let me remind you. It destroyed my home, the place I belonged, the ones I loved. It gave me hell and suffering. There's nothing left here for me."

"There are still people here who care for you. What about Banden? Possibly your mom?"

He briefly looked away, and I thought I was finally breaking his walls, but when he looked up, his eyes were hard. "Just let it go. I've made up my mind." He sidestepped me, heading for Mom and signaling he was ready to leave.

And then it clicked. Maybe it was my belief that Alec wasn't acting out of pure evil, that his soul wasn't tarnished, but rather, he was acting out of pain. Maybe some vengeance, too. *You learn what motivates people, what their vulnerabilities are.* The one thing, or *person*, who always softened him, who always seemed to crack his shield just a little, was maybe what had started this in the first place. He'd showed me now. The guilt in his eyes whenever he spoke about her or whenever she was mentioned. *This is personal.*

It was a shot in the dark, a theory, but I had to try.

"This is about your mother, isn't it?" I said, watching him carefully. He paused midwalk, and I knew I had him. "You think she's alive. You want to find her. As you told me, Obsidian doesn't get rid of his prisoners."

I'd never seen Alec so off his guard, eyes wide, body stiff. And I could tell he was angry. Angry I had figured him out. And as much as I wanted to be angry with him, I couldn't, at least, not completely. He wanted to right what he unfairly believed was his wrong, to save the mother he fiercely loved, the one he couldn't save ten years ago.

I continued. "You're right. I may be too outspoken and terrible at hiding my feelings, but your silence is just as loud."

"Congrats. You're a good guesser." He kept his voice level, but I could tell his confidence wavered. "It still doesn't change my mind."

"That's why you're so desperate to access the prison." Mom spoke for the first time. She had been silently taking us in. "You're not the only one who pays attention. Obsidian seems to either trust me or not trust me enough, so I spend a lot of time with him. You've asked if you could have prison duty to 'serve him in other ways.' I thought you were interested in the pay since he compensates his guards well."

Alec's eyes darkened. "Okay, so go tell Obsidian my plan. If anything, he may not believe you, and if he does, he kills me and you lose your contact to Orion while you remain stuck here, *and* you lose your buffer to keep her safe. So far, he's just been threatening her, teasing her. He hasn't unleashed his full power."

I couldn't tell if he was bluffing, if he had that much control over my life. I tried not to show him how much that terrified me. Thankfully, Mom had a rebuttal, "Alec, it may seem like only we need you, but you need Orion too. I know what you're doing. You think by helping Obsidian reach his goal, giving him the thing he desires most, will reward you. But you don't see the way he treats some of his most respected agents. I do. I've seen the way he disposes of them once they've given him what he wants. He uses them like a leech, sucking life out of them until he has no use for them because they *know too much*." She then gave a light snort. "It's only a matter of time before I'm next."

"Don't talk like that," I warned her, refusing to accept it. I'd help her get out of this mess somehow. I turned to Alec. "If you give him everything he wants, how will you know he'll still have use for you?"

For once, Alec was silent. Through his furrowed eyebrows and frown, I could see him trying to work a solution—a tactic, anything to help him carry out his plan. But he was stuck.

"So, I propose a proposition, a way for you to get what you want while also giving me what I want," I said, using his weaknesses against him. "We come up with a lie. Obsidian didn't know about your plan with my mom, and Wicbin isn't here to counter the story. You tell him Wicbin attacked me, died in battle, and that during that battle, the journal disintegrated, but you're positive it hasn't broken my spirit and that I have another hunch on how to find Annulla's Scepter. If you give me the journal, you'll still need intelligence to bring to Obsidian if you want him to trust you. Let him squeeze everything out of you. Let him think he's getting close to using every last drop of you. I won't tell MISTIC you're a double agent, and we'll come up with intel to give to Obsidian to keep him on his toes. We'll find your mother. I promise we will, if you give me the journal."

"You've proven your word means nothing," he said, taking a step closer, those green eyes burning holes through me. "You've played Celeste, but you won't play me."

"Yet you've played me, all of us, including Celeste," I reminded him, masking the pain I pretended wasn't there.

He crossed his arms, his eyes searching mine as he considered the terms. To persuade him, I held out my hand. I pleaded with my eyes, keeping my hand steady. It was all I had to offer.

Finally, he shook my hand. At first softly, as if reconsidering, then squeezing it firmly. "May we play the game against everyone except each other."

I wished I could read his face. I thought I heard a level of sadness in his voice, like maybe he wished it didn't have to be this way. As resentful as I was at his betrayal, my heart still ached for his gentle touch in the Garden of Grandrose, his warm smile with Kaia, and the loving words he'd expressed for both Banden and his mother. I could feel myself still wanting to believe that whatever tie we'd had wasn't completely severed. But now he was stoic as ever, only business in his eyes, and I knew my bruised heart had to catch up to my guarded mind.

He cleared his throat. "We'll need evidence that the journal is destroyed."

With his Earth magic, he ripped the front cover off the journal. I winced at the damage, although that part of the journal was already destroyed from the torn leather. He then held the cover in the air toward the ocean. When it reached the end of the ocean rock, an electric zap set the cover on fire. The electric shield. Alec quickly sent the flaming cover in the air toward me, and I sent a heavy wind toward the flame, strong enough to eliminate the fuel source instead of increasing the flame. The fire winked out, and all that was left was a chalky black cover.

Alec handed me the intact journal while keeping the now-charcoaled cover. As I grabbed the journal, he hesitated, our fingers tugging on it.

"You don't want to make an enemy out of me." His eyes stared into mine, his deep gaze making it impossible to look away. "If you end up crossing me, I promise you'll wish you'd never chased me through the portal."

"Likewise," I said, mimicking his hard tone. "But I think I've proven I'm pretty good at keeping secrets."

He smirked. "That you have."

ACKNOWLEDGMENTS

Wow. I literally can't believe it. I can, but I also can't. I came up with the idea for this book when I was fourteen years old, and it has *finally* been shared with the world (thankfully now, and not when I was fourteen). I published a book, but it would be remiss of me not to mention the incredible people who helped me through the trials and tribulations of the writing process—the cheerleaders who have been there for me and *Secrets of Isoria* since day one.

Thank you, Mom and Dad, for your endless support of my dreams no matter what they are. You taught me to follow my passions and to believe in myself in whatever I wanted to achieve. A special thanks to Mom for being my voluntary publicist by telling every living thing with a heartbeat to read my book. Thank you to my sister, Cassandra, for answering my random (really random) grammar questions and for your overall support. Also, thank you to Penny, my Shih Tzu terrier, for literally just being the bundle of cuteness that you are (and for basically being my emotional support dog).

A big thank-you to my boyfriend, Justin, another cheerleader and personal publicist. Thank you for helping me through my writer's blocks, brainstorming plot ideas, and being my overall sounding board. Thank you for the constant encouragement, even after reading the *many* dreadful earlier drafts of this book. Also, thank you for the amazing professional author headshot.

Thank you to the friends who encouraged me to keep writing, who read the earlier drafts and still thought this story was good, and who supported me and my dream. Thank you for being the best hype women.

And finally, thank you to the team at Eschler Editing for being a part of this journey and helping shape this book to where it is today. Thank you for being patient and so kind in answering my many questions and for walking me through the publishing process.

THANK YOU!

I'm so honored you took the time to read *Secrets of Isoria*. Thank you, truly. If you've enjoyed the adventure with Orion and the rest of the crew, it would be of so much help if you could please leave a review wherever books are sold online—and spread the word!

Visit my website www.cristinamacari.com and connect with me on Instagram and Twitter @cristinamacari for book updates.

About the Author

Cristina Macari grew up in New Jersey and is the proud child of Italian immigrants. She holds a BS in history and double minored in creative writing and international business at the Ramapo College of New Jersey. She has always loved the idea of magic hiding in our modern world and gets lost in creating in-depth worlds filled with adventure and danger. When she is not writing or reading, she can be found spending time in nature, gaming, horseback riding, weightlifting, doing yoga, or playing piano. Visit her at www.cristinamacari.com and @cristinamacari on Twitter and Instagram.

Printed in Great Britain
by Amazon